THE
HYMN
TO
DIONYSUS

THE HYMN TO DIONYSUS

A NOVEL

NATASHA PULLEY

BLOOMSBURY PUBLISHING

NEW YORK · LONDON · OXFORD · NEW DELHI · SYDNEY

BLOOMSBURY PUBLISHING
Bloomsbury Publishing Inc.
1385 Broadway, New York, NY 10018, USA
50 Bedford Square, London, WC1B 3DP, UK
Bloomsbury Publishing Ireland Limited, 29 Earlsfort Terrace, Dublin 2, D02 AY28, IRELAND

BLOOMSBURY, BLOOMSBURY PUBLISHING, and the Diana logo
are trademarks of Bloomsbury Publishing Plc

First published in the United States 2025

ISBN: HB: 978-1-63973-236-4; EBOOK: 978-1-63973-237-1

LIBRARY OF CONGRESS CATALOGING-IN-PUBLICATION DATA IS AVAILABLE

2 4 6 8 10 9 7 5 3 1

Typeset by Westchester Publishing Services
Printed and bound in the U.S.A. by Berryville Graphics Inc., Berryville, Virginia

To find out more about our authors and books visit www.bloomsbury.com and
sign up for our newsletters.

Bloomsbury books may be purchased for business or promotional use. For information
on bulk purchases please contact Macmillan Corporate and Premium Sales Department at
specialmarkets@macmillan.com.

For product safety–related questions contact productsafety@bloomsbury.com.

To everybody who needs a little more Dionysus in their lives

PROLOGUE

Our bards always ask the Muse to find the beginning, but the big joke—I say joke in the loosest possible sense—is that they never then start at the bloody beginning. Find the beginning, Muse, and then they say, well, here we are, seven years into the middle of a big adventure I haven't told you about, there was this witch, right, and this man—and then they sparkle at you like it's clever.

It's not clever. It's irritating.

I am going to start at the beginning, because I'm a knight, and I was taught to report things properly, in a straight line, without faffing around and looking smug that I've remembered the bits I artfully left out to Reveal Unto You later on for narrative effect. I'm not going to sing it to you in poetry, either. Poetry is for things that are made up. I'm just going to tell it.

But I do promise this. One way or another, I will do what the bards always ask the Muse for, after they've done their stupid opening about beginnings.

I'll tell you about rage, and a complicated man.

I

My name is Phaidros. I was born into the Furies, which is the frontline legion of the Theban army. My commander was a joyful trickster called Helios, and his commander was Artemis, the famous lady who won the archery contest every year for ten years at the Oracle Games. I know people from other places say who their parents and grandparents were, but that isn't how Theban legions work. I don't know who my parents were and I didn't even think to wonder about it until I was older. Helios told me different things depending on how he was feeling. Maybe I was the son of a princess; maybe he'd found me on the rubbish heap behind a sacked city; maybe he had been friends with my mother, another knight who had had me with the weird slave nobody liked because he insisted on making his own cheese. He was making a point, not just being annoying. It doesn't matter where a Theban knight is born, or how.

There was a whole pack of us, little knights raised among the tents. It was fantastic. People from other walks of life tell me about growing up in houses, and going to school with tutors who want you to learn about numbers and lying to people—I can't think of anything worse. We ran around a lot, we played in the sea, we helped with polishing armour and making arrows, and our commanders hid honey cakes and toys in among the wreckage after the fighting was over, which was why I always loved big battles. And I met lots of interesting people. When you're five, the best thing in the world is a literally captive audience who has been considerately chained to an oar so they can't escape all the questions you want to ask about what it's like to live in a place made of stone.

The older knights told us that we were from a stone place too—Thebes—but I didn't understand what that was. It was somewhere in the west, the place where the slaves and the grain and the silver flowed back to, but we only ever went as far as a harbour to load it all onto carts before setting out again. It sounded scary. Cities were things you broke and set fire to. It was hard to imagine why anyone would live in one on purpose. It struck me as something between accidental and openly stupid, living in a place stuffed with silver and warehouses and good-looking people who would fetch a lot of gold if you were to sell them to the right sort of gentleman in Egypt.

The first time I met Dionysus was on my first visit to Thebes.

I was four or so when our whole legion finally got leave to come back to Thebes. We'd had lots of shore leave before, but all in different places, usually close to wherever we were raiding—this was a real holiday, and the first time since I'd been born that the knights could come home to see their families. It sounds rough, but five years is a fairly ordinary raiding tour; the world is wide and Poseidon holds grudges. You couldn't expect to come home much sooner.

Everyone was caught between excited and scared. People worried husbands might have got tired and married someone else, or that retired commanders would be angry with them for not sending word, or what presents they should bring for all the children they'd never met. To give you some idea of how big an event this was, I actually have no memories at all of anything before. I used to tell Helios he could have kept me in a box those first years and saved himself a lot of bother; it's a total blank. Thebes outshone everything else.

Don't get me wrong about the clarity with which I say all this. Maybe it was my first real memory, but nobody can clearly narrate anything that happened to them when they were five. The only reason I can do it for you is that for years after we went to Thebes, Helios repeated it to me again and again. It became as established a bedtime story as Death and the Girl, or how Hermes became a god, or Artemis and the arrogant huntsman. He made sure I remembered. He wanted it graven on my soul, so that I would never forget why we couldn't go back.

Helios was in the strange position of having a twin who wasn't also a knight. She lived in Thebes, and we were going to see her. It seemed bizarre to me that they'd been separated like that, but he tipped his head and said some people had to do other things, and so we hurried off the ship to beat the hordes of people making their way towards Thebes too, and rented a horse from a man who didn't want normal iron money, only silver or gold, even though that's forbidden for us, because he traded between cities and there was something complicated to do with something called exchange rates that Helios tried to explain to me, after I saw him produce entirely illegal silver pieces for the man's tiny weighing scales. I didn't understand at the time why he took such pains trying to explain it to someone whose main priority, really, was bouncing; but I do now. If I had mentioned to anyone that he had been carrying silver, he would have been arrested. But I was distracted by a green bird and money was boring.

I got my first sight of Thebes from the brow of the steep hill that tipped the road down towards the Amber Gate.

Thebes is a strange place. It sits in a valley under Harper Mountain and its vales of sacred trees, always somehow in full sun, and I think even a stranger here could guess that it didn't begin in the usual way, with people finding stone for quarries or land to till. It feels different.

Once, there was a warrior from Asia, King Kadmus, who paused here at the springs on his way somewhere else. There was a dragon, and it wouldn't let him take water. After he had killed it, Athena told him to take its teeth and sow them in the earth. People sprang up from them, knights stronger and fleeter than there had ever been, and it's to them we trace back our combat lineages. That's why we're called the Sown. Helios told me the story as we rode down.

So Thebes is a holy city, begun by dragon's teeth sown at the behest of the god of just war. There are grander places—everyone says the whole world is in Memphis, and that there are mighty new kingdoms rising from

3

the dust in Canaan—but there isn't a stranger one. There isn't another place where there are as many temples as chariots, or where the air fizzes with miracles. It's that same prickle that happens if you rub two pieces of amber together and then hold one above the hairs on your arm.

Even being so little, I felt it. Perhaps that was partly because it felt so foreign. I'd grown up ransacking bits and pieces of the Hatti Empire, or even the gold-soaked places along the Nile. I was used to seeing Egyptian gods, and statues of the great Hatti knights in their heavy mail guarding the city gates. I'd never known that there were places like that which belonged to us. I'd never seen *our* gods in marble or bronze. For me, our gods were things you sometimes saw for a snatch in the distance in the heat mirages on the sand, or in the lightning. Wild things.

But there they were. A bronze statue of a gigantic figure on a gigantic horse stood at the gate. The road led beneath the arc of the horse's throat.

"That's Herakles," Helios said. "Do you want to see something fun?"

"What?"

He guided our horse close to Herakles, and very slowly, the giant bronze figure bowed His head to us, a gentle, courteous sort of greeting. I nearly fell out of the saddle.

"He's alive!"

"It's called a marvel," Helios explained. "Inside the statue, there are special devices. They move water, and that moves wheels, and the wheels move the statue. They're very holy, so when we see them, you have to be careful not to touch them, all right? If you break one, you're cursed."

I stared, certain Herakles was about to ride after us. Helios squeezed me, and we rode on through the high gate. Herakles, fortunately, did not.

When he told me the story again later, once we were back at the beaches and the raids, one of my favourite bits was always the marvel Herakles. When you're tucked in bed and cuddled up with your commander and the sentries are tall and strong outside and the perimeter fires are blazing, titan scary things have a way of feeling cosy.

Cities in Achaea usually have two parts. First there's the lower city, which is where most people live. Thebes's lower city seemed to me like a chaos of stone ways that looked like the tiny tunnels inside bones, full of people like I'd never seen before. There were old people all over the place, with grey hair—they hadn't been killed or starved, they looked quite good even, some of them in very fine robes and gold chains. Men and women dressed differently from each other, not all in armour, which seemed risky, and children with no obvious commanders played in the fountains. On the steps of a great temple, a whole flock of priestesses in deep, bright red were playing an intense game of pickup sticks. Nothing was on fire, and nobody was running away from us. Some boys wearing metal collars and dark clothes bowed to us. They were incredibly pale, all foam-coloured, with light hair that didn't look real. I twisted round to see them go, trying to decide if they were normal or some kind of monster.

"They're from the Tin Islands," Helios told me. I must have looked worried. "People are strange there. When they're little, they have white hair, and as they get older, it gets darker."

Sometimes he made things up, but the boys really did have horrible colourless hair, and horrible colourless eyes. "Yuck," I decided.

And then, above it all, is the High City. This is the home of the Palace, and sometimes the grandest temple. In Thebes, the Palace is on a great spar of rock a clear three hundred feet above the town. Helios guided the horse that way, because his sister—and being four, I thought this was a normal thing for a person's sister to be—was the Queen.

The Palace was called the Kadmeia, after King Kadmus who killed the dragon. The halls were cool, pale marble. I hunched against Helios's shoulder as tight as I could. The only marble places I'd been to before were tombs, and I didn't want to walk on the stone. It seemed dead. But it was good to be inside, because it was starting to rain, plinking and shimmering on Helios's armour. He bundled me up in his cloak, and while we waited for his sister, he stood on the steps with me, looking down over the city. He told me what we were seeing: the Temple of Ares, all white. Harper Mountain, in the west. The sacred forest, where only women were allowed to go.

"How come only they can go?"

"To get away from us. Otherwise we'd end up planted in the vegetable patch."

"Why would they plant us?" I said, confused.

He started to laugh, and then he apologised, and said I was completely right, but sometimes people did mistake very troublesome men for vegetables. For months and months after, I made him check me over in the bath for any suspect-looking shoots that might suggest I'd been bad and I was imminently turning into an onion.

I'd never met a *lady* before. All the women I knew were normal women. They wore armour and spent most of their time fixing boats or training; and sometimes I met women who were slaves, who did lots of work. When the Queen came down the steps to find us, I didn't really understand that she was a human. She was so different. She was clean like I'd never seen anyone before. Her clothes were amazing; she had a purple dress, really purple, a colour so expensive I'd have been lucky to steal a purple sock, and it was girdled and pinned with gold, and there was gold in her hair, and on her fingers. I hid against Helios's shoulder, because there was something a lot more forbidding about that purple gown than a knight's armour. I could see it was *for* something a lot less straightforward than armour.

"And this must be your new ward?" she said to Helios. She sounded just like him. "I can't believe they decided you were sensible enough to look after a whole human."

"He's only a tiny human," Helios laughed, scooping her into a hug that crushed me between them. I hated it, because she didn't smell of normal things like armour polish and sweat, but flowers, and something smoky and alien that I realized a lot later was incense. When Helios was telling me the story in the months and years to come, he sometimes lit incense to make me remember that smell. "This is Phaidros. Phaidros, this is Queen Agave."

She bowed to me and I bowed back as well as you can when you're four and holding hard onto someone else's breastplate strap. Helios rubbed my hair, which was what he did instead of saying *well done*.

"Phaidros; are you really?" Phaidros means "bright." "Are you good at puzzles?"

I grew up with that joke. "No, I'm quite stupid actually," I said, because it saved time and humiliation when I didn't know the answer to riddles.

She laughed, and Helios tapped me gently. "I'm quite stupid actually, *my lady*."

"My lady," I repeated, embarrassed.

The bizarrest thing about memories is how, just like things in the real world, they change with perspective. At the time, I remember thinking Helios and the Queen were both unfathomably grown-up and glamorous. But now, looking back, they were children themselves. They must have been about fifteen.

Helios carried me all the way through the Palace's looming halls, out to a garden where there was grass and a great fountain, and he only put me down once there was no more stone. I stayed close to him, not sure about the fountain. The water was moving by itself and I couldn't see how. In it, there was a statue of Poseidon. As I watched, He turned His head.

I tugged Helios's cloak.

"Hello, small knight?"

I pointed. "There's a monster," I said, in the clear way I'd been taught to report dangerous things, like oncoming chariot lines or a cloud of arrows.

"Ah, no. He's a marvel, like Herakles. Come on, let's give Him an offering. He's good, the priests made Him, He's here to watch over—"

I hid under a hedge. Knights take a vow of honesty, but Helios's definition of truth was nearly as snaky as Dionysus's would be later. I was just about old enough to suspect that sometimes he told strategic lies so that he wouldn't have to deal with a small, frightened child in moments when he didn't especially have the time to do that. I'd been convinced until recently that sometimes enemy troops liked to go for a swim face down in the sea so they could say hello to the fish, which they were able to do on account of how foreigners secretly had gills. Having spoken to a lot of foreign slaves in my increasingly good Hatti, though, I was starting to conclude that the gills situation might not quite be what he'd claimed.

He got down on his front to see me. "Honestly. It's not a monster."

"You're full of it, sir."

He hung his head. "That is true. I am."

Behind him, the Queen thought, and then, without worrying about the purple gown or the gold, or looking silly, she climbed into the fountain where the water was knee-deep, sat down on Poseidon's lap, and put her purple veil on Him. I giggled. So did Helios. And then we all played in the fountain, and Poseidon seemed not to mind at all.

Helios gave me a little carved bead to put in the marvel's hand and told me how to say the right prayer, and Poseidon bowed His head courteously, and I was rapt.

It was raining more by then, but it wasn't cold. The summer had been blazing so far even at sea, and it was the kind of rain that comes because the weather is pent up and frustrated after weeks of nothing but searing sky and hot winds. Above the city, the clouds were gathering dark, the dark that would have been dangerous on the sea. If we'd been on the ships, we would have been steering for shore now, and finding a shallow berth where the storm couldn't hurt the hulls. I glanced up at Poseidon, wondering anxiously whether He was annoyed.

Someone came out of the far side of the cloister. I thought at first that they would be coming to tell us to stop being silly and get inside, but they weren't. It was another lady, again in purple, but she was carrying a baby. She sat down with it on a bench a good way from us. Helios and the Queen, who had been having a fight that was she was winning, went quiet. I looked between them, not sure what was happening, and very much wanting to ask if I was allowed to go and play with the baby.

"She's kept it, then," Helios murmured.

I patted the water vaguely, to have something to do with myself. There weren't any fish in it, which seemed like an oversight to me. When I stole a look that way, the baby looked like the best sort of baby. He was big enough not to be too fragile, but little enough to think everything was interesting. I wasn't allowed to just run off, though. The last time I'd done that, I'd gone straight under a chariot, which is what happens to stupid children. There didn't seem to be any chariots around here, but then, I'd thought that before too.

"Well, that's the law, isn't it," the Queen murmured back. "If the father is a god then you can keep it."

"I mean. I tell the kids all kinds of rubbish but I feel like even Phaidros is big enough to see the holes in that one."

"What am I big enough for?" I asked, still trying to see if there was a way I could swing things round to playing with the baby, who was smiling at me now.

Helios was sitting on the fountain rim. With an uncharacteristic fidgetiness, he lifted me out of the water and onto his knees. I had a clear feeling that he wanted to put something solid between himself and the lady with the baby. I had a surge of protectiveness for him. Sometimes he did just worry about things for no reason. Sometimes after big battles he didn't like loud noises, or the campfires, even though it could be freezing out on the beaches.

"That's our sister," he explained quietly. "She says the father of her baby is Zeus."

"Is it?" I asked.

"Probably not."

"Definitely not," the Queen said, a bit flatly. "She's been terrorising the slaves for years."

I looked over at the lady and imagined her jumping out of bushes at unsuspecting men trying to get on with the gardening, and wondered how that linked up to having a baby. Then I wondered why Helios and the Queen were so worried about it. Ladies were scary, but babies weren't.

"Can I go and—"

"No. No, no." Helios hugged me tighter, gone taut. Even though there would be no playing, I was glad to be wanted and useful again.

"Why are you scared of a baby?" I asked.

He was never surprised, but something in his expression cracked now.

The rain was coming down harder. Away in the distance, lightning flickered, and it was a long few seconds before the thunder rolled. Helios flinched. I stroked the back of his hand. He was never very good with thunder, even though he knew it was only Zeus dancing.

The Queen put her arm around both of us.

"Don't worry," she said. "I'll do unto her before she does unto me."

A man had come out too, and he'd gone to sit next to the lady with the baby. He leaned over to say hello to the baby, letting it play with his fingertips. I hated him in the immediate way you hate anyone who's allowed to do a thing you'd really like to but can't. Grown-ups could play with babies whenever they wanted—they could even *make* one if they wanted—but here I was, clamped onto Helios's lap, getting rained on and not allowed to play with the baby even a little bit, and no one even seemed to realize it was unfair.

There were still no chariots, either.

Helios stiffened even more. Usually he only went that way when he was about to shoot someone.

"Is that her husband?" I asked, trying to sound older. Theoretically I knew what husbands were and that somebody might expect me to be one, one day. As far as I understood, it was about keeping quiet and polite and doing as you were told, which seemed all right, because that was the same as being a knight.

"No," the Queen said grimly, "that's *my* husband."

She said it as if it meant a great deal, but I couldn't tell what it was, and neither of them explained. I stayed quiet, feeling mutinous, because it was rich to say I couldn't go and see the baby but then talk in ways I couldn't understand.

"Agave," Helios said, very soft. "Let's go inside. I'm sitting out here in the open in full armour; I'm going to get hit by lightning."

She gave him a strange look then, the look people do when someone has said one thing, but it makes them think of something else completely. But all she said was, "You're right. Let's go."

I had an overpowering feeling that the words they'd said to each other had no relationship to the meaning.

Annoyed with trying to decipher Grown-Up Code, I did one last check for chariots—all clear—and then hurried over to the lady to say hello and I was Phaidros and please could I hold her baby because babies were the best things in the world and I was very trustworthy and I had plenty of experience, honest.

Helios would catch me soon and he'd be angry but at least I would have had a baby-hug by then.

The lady laughed. Even if Helios hadn't said she was their sister, I would have guessed. She looked like him and Agave; they all had the same teeth. "Of course, little knight. You sit here."

"That's a big scar for a tiny boy," the man said, the King, so gently that I considered not hating him any more. "What happened?"

"I was careless around a charioteer," I explained, distracted because the lady had just put the baby in my arms, and he was a brilliant baby. He was nicely heavy, and solid, with curly black hair and amazing blue eyes. He was big enough to sit up by himself, and have proper opinions about things; maybe to walk. "Hello. What's your name?"

He bit my knuckle experimentally, looking up at me all brand-new. I squeezed him as much as I dared to, very aware that I needed to make the most of him before Helios noticed I was gone.

"He doesn't have a name yet. Any thoughts?"

"No, I'm good at tents but I'm rubbish at imagining."

They both laughed. The baby squeaked and patted my hands with both of his. I grinned, in love, and distraught at the same time. The only difficult thing about being a knight is that commanders only ever take on one child at a time. I'd never have brothers or sisters, even though I would have liked that more than anything.

And then Helios saw me and ran across as if the King and the princess and the baby were as dangerous as any chariot.

"Phaidros!" Helios exclaimed. "Zeus above—I'm sorry, Semele. He's never run off before."

"But the baby," I tried.

"A," the baby said supportively. I hugged him closer in case someone tried to take him off me. He closed both hands around the ends of my hair against my shoulder.

"*Move*, knight," Helios said incredulously.

"I don't suppose there's any chance I can steal your baby," I said to the lady. Sometimes people didn't want babies. I was forever finding them in baskets outside the sieged cities. It seemed worth a try.

She smiled. "Afraid not. You'll have to get Helios to make you one."

"Takes ages," I said sadly, and gave him back. As Helios propelled me away, the baby waved.

"Nice to see you too," Semele called after us, so sarcastically that even I understood.

"Why is it not nice to see her?" I asked Helios.

Helios swept me up so he could walk away faster. "I'm sorry I ran away and didn't do as I was told, Helios, it was a moment of madness and I'll never do it ever again because I wouldn't put you through watching me get killed like an idiot?"

"I did *check* for chariots," I said feebly. My arms felt light and empty without the baby.

"Oh, right, so it's fine to get lazy while you're in Thebes, because you definitely won't forget to be sensible again once we're back on a battlefield, because the minds of small boys aren't in any way like wax that just sets around the most recent thing it comes across."

It broke over me that probably I wasn't going to be allowed to see the baby again. There were plenty of things I wanted that I wasn't allowed, usually because they were expensive or dangerous or impractical, and I didn't mind, because none of them were important, but the baby *was* important. I looked back, miserable, and pressed my hands over my eyes. Knights are allowed to cry, but you can't make a sound, in case of Enemies.

"Oh, tiny knight." Helios scooped me up and put our heads together. "I'm sorry. There will be other babies to play with when we go home. You know Achilles, my friend in the other unit? He's volunteered to take a ward. He might even have one by the time we get back. That will be fun, won't it?"

"Yeah," I said, and put my head against his shoulder, full of grief anyway.

"You and babies," he said, poking me until I laughed.

I forgot about the lady and the baby and the Queen's husband, because inside, there was a gigantic dog who didn't mind being ridden. Under the influence of the excellent dog, and of the Queen, who told him funny stories, Helios turned back into his normal cheerful self again, though not so quickly that I stopped wondering what had been the matter before. When he put me to bed—next to him, in a genuine, real bed with legs that took you right off the floor, which was exciting—I tried to ask again.

He wasn't the kind of person who brushed off questions just because you were small, even if the question was a difficult one. "The Palace is a dangerous place," he said eventually. "I always forget how dangerous, when I've been away."

"Dangerous?" I said, puzzled, because the only possibly dangerous thing I'd seen was the dog, but she had got her nose stuck in someone's shoe now and she didn't seem very menacing. "Will people try and kill us in the night?" It happened sometimes. I didn't mind. I was usually allowed to go back to sleep after I'd helped to mop up.

"No; no," he said, rescuing the dog. "You're right, it's not that bad."

I couldn't tell what he thought I was right about.

"I'm not sleepy," I said instead. "Tell the story about Death and the Girl."

He folded back onto the bed and creaked. "It's late . . ."

I tunnelled under the blankets and came up in his lap. "Surprise badger!"

He tipped sideways laughing. "Ah, you make a good point. Fine." He moved a pillow upright against the head of the bed and leaned on it. I curled up in his lap, aware I was behaving like a baby but loving having him all to myself. Usually there were his friends and orders and chores and all the rest.

"Once upon a time, there was a girl called Persephone. She was poor, and her mother was the sort of person who wanted her never to leave home or have any adventures, but she was too clever to stay cooped on a farm always. One day, she met Death on the road. Nobody wants to be friends with Death, so he was always lonely. He was a polite person and he bowed to her, and she bowed to him, which surprised him, because usually people ran away; but he was even more surprised when she said, *Listen, I've got an idea . . .*"

I went to sleep dreaming about going to live in Hades with all the souls, and crossing the river with the Ferryman. But under that, I couldn't shake the sense that the princess with the baby had worried Helios far more than meeting Death on the road.

2

I didn't feel like I'd had much sleep at all when someone woke me up. It was the Queen, holding a lamp. She wasn't trying to wake me, only Helios, but I was tucked up against him, so she couldn't shake him without shaking me as well.

"Helios. I need some help. I don't trust the slaves."

"Oh—what?" he asked, confused from dreaming. "Agave—what's the matter?"

"I need some help," she said again, low and measured. "And I don't trust the slaves."

He stared at her as if she had just confessed to flinging someone off the High City, and then he looked down at me. "I—right. Phaidros, you go back to sleep. I'll . . . I'll be back soon."

"What?" I whispered, horrified. I'd never slept by myself, ever. It wasn't safe. If you slept by yourself, then an Enemy could come and kill you in the night about nobody would be able to fight them off. "No—"

He stroked my hair. "No, come on, you're big enough to be by yourself for an hour. Look, the dog's here, she'll keep you company—"

"No, no, I'm not—"

"Obedience is strength," he said softly.

As always, it put a wall down in my head. I couldn't have not done as I was told after he'd said that even if the room was on fire. Knights obey, and if they don't, they're not real knights, and they don't have honour, and the only thing in the world that's ever really yours is your honour. "Obedience is strength," I whispered back, like you're meant to, even if you're scared; especially if you're scared.

"I love you, tiny knight. I'll be back soon."

So they both vanished into the dark corridor, and I stayed where I was, hunched in a miserable ball and staring at all the unfamiliar shadows in the corners. The unmenacing dog was asleep, and definitely not paying attention to the nighttime noises of the Palace. I could hear someone walking on the stone floor a long way away. It was hard not to wonder if they were an Enemy on their way here to kill me while Helios was away. I pulled the blanket with me and hid under the bed.

It didn't help.

He had been gone for years.

This was dangerous. *Dangerous, dangerous, dangerous*—the word thumped around my head in time with my pulse, which was loud. Sitting alone in a strange place is how you die. That was our main rule at camp. No one ever goes anywhere alone. He shouldn't have left me. It was dangerous. Obedience *is* strength, but strength is no good if you're dead.

I crept out into the corridor.

It wasn't that dark. There were banks of lamps lit here and there, not bright, but enough to see the way by. A slave in plain clothes and a bronze collar was trimming the wicks on some of them, and she gave me a puzzled look as I trailed past. I was afraid she would stop me, but she seemed to decide it was none of her business. I had to look back, disconcerted, because grown-ups never just left you alone if you were about alone at night. There could be Enemies.

Maybe she thought I was big enough to look after myself.

I swallowed. "Um. Excuse me. Have you seen Helios?"

"I think the Queen took him over that way, sir."

That threw me. "I'm not sir, I'm four," I said.

"You're Sown," she said, laughing a bit.

"So—over there," I said, looking the way she had pointed. I wondered how you were ever supposed to find anyone in this place, but she was studying me as if she were reconsidering whether or not to put me somewhere, so I hurried away, not sure what was beyond the corner, and then fell over, because there was a statue of Apollo that looked exactly like a person. I picked myself up, and He moved. I knew what He was, but it was dark and I spooked. I ran, and only slowed down when I realized I could hear Helios's voice.

He was in the courtyard with the Poseidon statue, and he was carrying something heavy-looking rolled up in a rug. He set it down on the ground. He had no lamp, even though the rain and the thunderclouds made the night very dark. I could only just see him. An unhappy cry came from somewhere on the ground, and he bent down and picked up a baby.

"Put it down," the Queen told him. She was, of all the odd things, negotiating with a kite. She was trying to find the angle where the wind would take it out of her hands. I frowned. It was stupid to wake us both up just because she wanted to play with a kite.

He didn't put the baby down. "We can just give him anonymously to the Temple of Artemis. They'll find him a family."

"And what if he grows up looking exactly like us?" she asked. The kite caught and sailed out of her hands. She let the reel unspool and the kite shot right into the air, vanishing into the rain, winking with silver thread. But she didn't hold on to it. She tied it to the rug Helios had moved.

"Then people will say, that's funny, you look a bit like the Queen, and get on with the day, because that's what humans do!"

"Move, come on, before the lightning hits—put it *down*, Helios!"

"Agave, please—"

"We haven't killed him. Zeus will decide."

She took the baby off him and set it down with the rug, even though the rain was heavy now. "I said move." She dragged him away from the fountain. The kite did a mad dance on the wind. I watched them go, horrified, waiting for Helios to go back for the baby, but he didn't. The two of them vanished into the cloister opposite. The baby was crying, probably wet and cold now. The kite writhed way above him. If she had meant for it to distract him, it wasn't working. There was nothing peaceful or nice about it. The wind was wild and the kite was straining. I looked over at the other cloister one last time, then left and right (no chariots), then ran out and scooped him up—the rain was so hard now it soaked me straightaway—and rushed back under cover with him.

He was still crying, but in the reproachful way that was more to let me know that he'd been having a horrible time rather than to say he was still having it. His purple blanket was all wet, so I took it off him and put it over the plinth of a column to dry out, and bundled him up in my blanket instead. It was more boring than his, but it was warm. He sniffed and gave me a *now what* look.

I didn't know. I turned around twice, probably looking stupid, trying to think what to do, and brimming with that nasty sort of panic that can drown you. The Queen had left him outside. If I asked anyone for help, they would just put him back, for whatever grown-up reason she'd done it in the first place.

The kite was making a thrumming noise where the wind pulled at the string, the way bows sound if you leave one on the ground as people are marching outside.

The baby didn't seem so upset any more. In case he was worried about being stolen, I told him he was having an adventure.

Only, people in adventures always knew what to do. You didn't catch Persephone umm-ing and panicking when she met Death. She all but grabbed him by the collar and went, "Aha, you're coming with me."

It was with a horrible, heavy feeling that I realized for the first time I was never going to be like Persephone. I was just Phaidros. I wasn't the right kind of person for this at all. I'd been hiding under the bed not long ago.

Over by the kite and the rolled-up carpet, a slave stopped sharply. I slunk back into the dark, because I could see what he was doing. He was looking for the baby.

"Lady?" he called into the corridor behind him. "Lady! It's gone, the child is—" He ran that way.

I still didn't know what to do.

The air was getting a strange taste to it, sharp and bitter, and out in the courtyard, the kite's dance was madder than ever. But the string was bronze. It wouldn't break.

The baby sniffed, and I realized—a lot later than literally anyone else would have realized, never mind Persephone—that he needed his mother, and I should have been running to find her all along. Mothers can protect babies, even if queens steal them. I'd seen mothers do incredible things when cities fell. They could be stronger than Herakles; it was, Helios said, an ancient kind of magic.

I didn't know where her rooms were, but if I asked someone and I was quick, I could maybe get there before anyone managed to stop me, and then he would have his mother and *not* just a stupid Phaidros—

Lightning hit the kite.

I'd seen lightning strike before. You do, if you live mostly in a tent on a beach surrounded by people wearing a lot of bronze. But not like this.

It zithered down the kite string, delicately, and then there was a flash so blinding I fell over backwards. I felt the ground jump. If a titan had pulled free of its chains underground and punched the bedrock, it would have felt like this. And then there was fire. Everywhere, burning things it shouldn't have been able to burn—the fountain, the flagstones—and heat blasted off it, waving the air so much it looked like we were underwater.

All around me, parts of the cloister roof collapsed, flaming, and like it was alive, the fire vaulted from one roof to another to another, tiles exploding, beams breaking, until half the Palace must have been caught in it, and worse, it was in the wind, spinning, not ordinary fire any more at all but a fire animal, raving and whirring with a noise like I'd never heard before and hoped I would never, ever hear again.

I had seen cities fall and all that came with that, but I'd never seen destruction like this. I couldn't even tell what I was seeing. Later, a lot later, I realized that the liquid hell-glow was the sand in the courtyard vitrifying. Molten glass writhed everywhere, and everywhere there was roiling steam and a weird patter of condensation from where the water in the fountain had vaporised, only to condense again as it hit the colder air above the fires. Where it was still in its bedtime plait over my shoulder, the ends of my hair started to smoke. I had to shove it under my tunic. The baby was holding onto me as hard as he could. He was still all right.

Inside the Palace, people were pouring into the corridors, shouting so much I couldn't hear the words from any one voice, and all at once I was paralysed again. I'd never find his mother now. Helios would be going out of his mind trying to find me, but I couldn't remember the way back. We couldn't stay here, but I didn't know where to go.

But what I knew from sieges was that if something was on fire, whether it was a tent or a citadel, you had to get away from it, and you had to do it fast before everyone else realized and crushed you.

So I ran, at random, away from the fire, into the Palace, weaving through people and hunching over the baby so no one could bump him, on and on, until I was outside again, and then I had to stop, because the fires must have broken the stables, and dozens and dozens of horses were escaping across the vast courtyard, lit up orange in the fireglow, their hooves sparking, some of them streaming embers from their manes.

One of them stopped, right next to us. I shied, because I'd always been taught to be careful of horses. Ours bit anyone they didn't recognise and liked to trample most people they did. But this one put her nose right up to me and snuffed at the baby, very gentle. He seemed not to mind. Then she sat down and gave me an expectant look.

"Um," I said blankly, because I'd never seen a horse do that. I was nearly sure that it was against every Horse principle there was.

The baby stretched out with his whole tiny self for the horse.

He wasn't wrong. Tentatively, I climbed onto her back, and the second I had, she stood up again and shot away, after her family.

It was the most frightening thing I'd ever done, including being run over by a chariot. I had to hold onto the baby with one hand and clamp the other round the horse's mane, scared I was going to hurt her and she was going to bite me, only just staying on her back as her gigantic shoulder blades heaved underneath us. And then even worse, she left level ground and charged down the steep steps to the lower city, and I was jammed up against her neck feeling like I was going to slip off at any second, and behind us, the Palace was a column of furious black smoke.

When the horse stopped, we were outside what looked like a temple. There were priestesses in bright red standing outside, watching the fire, murmuring the way people always do when something enormous has happened but nobody can do anything about it.

Very carefully, I let go of the horse's mane and stroked her neck.

In my arms, the baby cooed like it was him I'd stroked.

I hesitated, then blew in the horse's ear.

The baby squeaked and pushed one tiny fist against his ear.

I wondered what I was supposed to do about a baby who was sometimes a horse.

"Hello," one of the priestesses said to me. "You look like you've had an interesting night."

"I'm . . . I . . ." I trailed off, trying to think what Persephone would say, or at least, a grown-up knight, and whether I should run away. I'd never met a priestess before. I'd seen them, but only when they threw themselves off towers when city walls fell. In their bright robes, they look like shot birds when they fall, but up close, she was big, person-sized, much bigger than me, and what if she wanted *me* to jump off a tower? Helios had always been hazy about why they did that and I was worried it was a sort of inherent instinct that might overtake them at any moment. "I found this baby," I said miserably, "and I don't know where my commander is."

"Ah, well," she said, as if that was normal. She lifted me down. "You've done wonderfully, though, you know. You've come to exactly the right place. This is the Temple of Artemis. It's where lost children come."

"It . . . is?" I said, to her but also half to the horse.

The horse was already walking away, shaking her head as if she was trying to dislodge something annoying in it.

The baby laughed.

"He's merry, isn't he," she said, tickling him. He laughed again, happy now. "You found him, you said?"

"I—yes—I don't know where his mother is."

"It's all right. She'll know to look for him here. Come in and we'll get you nice and clean." She held my hand and led me inside.

The temple was quiet inside, but as I sat there and drank a hot honey drink another friendly priestess made for me, people came in with more children. There were other babies, some girls my age, then a boy of about nine, tearstained and smoke-grey. I gave him the rest of my drink to have while someone went to make him one too. As frightening as it had been for me, at least I was brought up for all this, at least I sort of knew what to do, and I'd had help from a possibly magic baby and a horse. It would have been awful if I hadn't. I showed him the baby and he cheered up before too long. The baby seemed like he was having a good time. I tried to concentrate on that, not on the dark pit opening up in my insides, the one that echoed with voices that said, *What if Helios doesn't know about the Temple of Artemis, what if he doesn't find you, what if you just have to live here now?*

In the middle of the courtyard was a great marvel of Artemis, holding a bow. Sometimes, She moved Her head, looking up at the sky, or down towards the temple doors. It made me feel better. Even the Queen couldn't argue with Artemis.

The second I put him down, the baby crawled off to inspect a flower bed and sat in it, looking triumphant. I hurried over too to make sure he didn't eat anything mad, but he didn't. He gave me a flower.

"Thanks." I stroked his head. "Did you—tell that horse where to come?"

It sounded stupid as soon as I said it, and for his part, the baby was more interested in some lemons.

"Phaidros."

I looked up, not wanting to believe it in case I was mistaken, but Helios was there, kneeling at the edge of the flower bed. He held his arms out and I dived into them, and he hugged me so tight I couldn't breathe and the filigree image of Ares on his breastplate printed right into my cheek so that later I looked like I had a strange Ares tattoo, but it didn't matter.

"How in the world did you know to come to the Temple of Artemis, tiny knight?" he asked me, sort of laughing, and sort of crying. He drew his hands over my face to smooth away the ash, rough from sword hilts and reins, and safe. "The priestess said you just turned up on a horse?"

"It wasn't me, it was the baby, he knew, I think he told the horse . . ."

"A," the baby put in, and gave Helios a flower too.

He took it slowly and brushed the baby's cheek with his knuckle. "Who's this then?"

I took a breath to say, *It's Semele's baby,* I took him out of the court-yard because you shouldn't have left him there, what if he'd caught fire, it would be your fault, and how come you don't recognise the same baby just because he's got a different blanket now, but something stopped me. It was a strange kind of pressure inside my head, the kind I felt if I saw a dust plume moving on the road outside a sieged city, or when the ground juddered from chariot wheels.

With a flash of understanding that strikes me now as completely adult, completely impossible for a child of four to arrive at alone—I think perhaps I wasn't arriving at it alone—I realized that Helios did know, but he *wanted* me to lie.

"I don't know," I said. "I just found him."

"Well. His mother will find him here if she's alive."

And at last I understood that she wasn't. I understood what had been in that rug. "What if she's not? Can we take him to the legion?"

"No. The priestesses will find him a nice new family."

"But why can't we—"

"Knight."

I shut up. I'd disobeyed once tonight already and I didn't have it in me to try again. Even when I was much older, even trying to contemplate it was so gear-grinding that it made me freeze and cry. That didn't stop me seeing when he might have been wrong, but it didn't matter.

He let his breath out slowly. "Right. We have to go, before Agave—before the ships go without us. Time to say goodbye."

"Bye," I said unwillingly to the baby.

But he had found a little fox, and unlike every other fox I'd ever seen, it wasn't trying to bite him. It just sat on him looking interested. He sneezed, and so did the fox.

"Funny," Helios observed, puzzled.

"He's magic," I told him, very quiet, because he wouldn't believe me.

But Helios smoothed his hand over my hair and didn't tell me not to be so stupid. "Maybe," he said, sounding strange.

The baby was distracted because the fox was trying to get into his tunic. It was making him laugh. I was glad. He would be all right; he wouldn't miss us.

All of us jumped when horns sounded. They were battle horns. I twisted around to see past Helios, expecting chariots to be bursting through the temple gates.

Helios, though, was looking up towards the High City, back the way we had come, and his expression had shut down in a way I'd never seen before. I followed his eyeline. Pouring down the steps up there were riders. All in black. Black horses, black armour, black helmet plumes, under a black banner.

"Who are they?" I whispered.

"The Hidden." He sounded—wrong. Like he wasn't seeing people riding, but spirits.

"What's—"

He gripped my shoulders. "Phaidros. They're looking for the baby. I've got to take him away somewhere safe. Knights only ever have one child, I can say he's my new ward if I take him, but not if I have you with me too. You have to stay here. Just for now. The priestesses will look after you. I *will* come back for you. I love you, tiny knight." He kissed my forehead and snatched up the baby, who waved at me, and then they were both gone.

Helios always did what he promised, so I decided there was no point worrying about it, and settled down to play with the fox.

"But *then*," I always said, when he told me the story safe in our tent in the camp, because it was my favourite part, "you came back! Here I am. Surprise Badger!"

He caught me up and hugged me, and turned me round in his lap so I could sit with my back to his chest and we could look at my toys together. He had made me the wonkiest hippo who had ever been made, but I loved it and its name was Rameses. "Yes," he always said against the top of my head, "here you are, tiny knight. And what do we do?"

"We never say anything about the baby," I said faithfully. I stole his helmet, which he had been polishing, and put it on. It was the most beautiful thing in the world. Bronze, with silver filigree, a leather lining, and—this was the best part—a visor that was a mask, removable on tiny hinges. Most other officers had them made to look like Ares, or Athena, or heroes from stories, but Helios was the least showy prince there had ever been. It was just a cast of his own face. He said he didn't want to go into battle pretending to be somebody else. "We never saw him and we don't know what happened to him. Echo, echo, echo," I added, because my voice sounded funny inside the helmet.

"Exactly," he said, and he always sounded tight then, and if I looked back, his eyelashes were a blacker shade of black. I'd never asked him why. The things that upset him had always been a bit odd: thunder and sudden noises. Now, I was content enough to add babies to the list.

3

The next time I met Dionysus was at sea.

It was the year when I went from being one of the stars of the legion to being mud on people's boots.

I fought on the front line beside Helios for the first time when I was nineteen. I'd been chafing for years to do it, because nineteen is elderly to join the line for the first time—almost everyone else I knew had gone at sixteen, but all through my teens I was little for my age, and I didn't grow until late. I'd been worried that I never would, but then up I went, and in one summer I was suddenly taller than Helios.

I don't know how knights do it where you're from, but I'd be willing to bet it's similar to us, because it works.

We build the front three lines, at the very least, out of pairs of sworn knights. To swear your oath to another knight is a kind of marriage vow: it is as binding, and as deep. We do this not just because each partner would die to save the other one, but because each one of us would die in order not to *embarrass* the other. Shame is a big driving force. If I screwed up, it would be Helios who caught it from the older knights.

Theban lines famously do not break, and it's because of that battle order. The Spartans do it the same way, and really, so does anyone else relying on heavy infantry. I don't often make predictions for the future, Dionysus being a walking exercise in how it can all go splat when you least expect it, but even knowing him, I'll say very comfortably that the most effective legions will still run that system in a thousand years.

As I say, nineteen was old and some of the officers had thought I would never make it to the vanguard, but they changed their minds when I brought down a chariot, horses and all. I was strong and fast and vicious, with everything to prove after years of waiting, and I was in love with Helios in exactly the insane, all-consuming way the legion prefers.

Now, when I talk to people who served for other nations, they seem to have the same sense that Theban knights are sort of dangerously mad, and maybe our witches give us drugs to make us unafraid of charging cavalry, and it's hard to explain that when your family is there on the line, not waiting at home, the best, most exciting thing you can be allowed to do is join the shield wall. I'd never been so happy as I was that day on the line with my shield covering Helios's right side, and I don't remember being scared. There was nothing to be scared of, except dishonouring him. The best moments of my whole life were on that line. Under our black banners, with my shield locked against his, as the drums rolled and the legion sang the hymn to Ares, a beautiful battle anthem to bring down the sky, never mind Trojan chariots . . . I'd never been so happy.

It was the first year of the long siege, a gorgeous spring, when the fighting was still fierce and none of us was hopeless yet. For a few months, I was Wonder Phaidros, which had the unfortunate side effect of making me into an arrogant prick.

Then one day, I took it too far.

We were marching that day against cavalry, and we were all happy and fizzy, because that meant that if we were quick, we'd get some horses off the Trojan knights. Horses are worth a fortune in Achaea. Looking back, I can't quite believe that I did what I did just because I wanted a nice horse, but people do stupid things for stupid reasons, and that was mine. Or—well. It wasn't that I wanted a horse. I wanted the honour. I wanted to see Helios light up with pride and hit me over the head for being a suicidal moron, and then to hold onto me too tight like he did when he'd just seen me nearly die. That made me feel immortal.

We don't ever break the line.

But there was an incredible black charger, carrying a woman in silver armour. I'd seen her before, often: none of us knew what her real name was, her Hatti one, but we called her Andromache, which means "fighter of warriors." I thought I could throw her, get the horse, and be back in formation very quickly. That isn't what happened, of course. She was older than me, a seasoned soldier, and she did what any seasoned soldier would. When I broke ranks, she ignored me, trusting her horse to kick me down, and aimed an arrow straight past me, then another—she was so fast that I thought maybe Artemis was with her—and another, and she killed three knights before the people on either side could close the shield wall.

That's how Helios died.

So when we set sail to take our cargo of silver and slaves to Egypt a few weeks later, nobody was talking to me, except sometimes to recommend that I kill myself.

They couldn't kill me, because I was the helmsman, which is a difficult job but one I'd always been good at. I might have been an idiot, but I had a good memory for things I saw, whether that was the stars, or the shape of the shallows, or the wrecking shores. Everyone else who definitely wouldn't crash the ship was dead. Those three arrows from the Trojan general had only been the start of what became a total rout.

"If this ship so much as judders," the captain told me mildly, "I will chain you to an oar with the slaves."

Everyone was waiting for me to screw it up. I was too, because you need to be able to go into a calm kind of trance to handle a ship well, and I couldn't reach it. After seven days at sea, I was shocked that I hadn't wrecked us. We hugged the coast as far as possible, because deep-sea sailing was dangerous and stormy, so it was straightforward enough. Steer away from the shallow bits and all would be well. We put in at night; winter was coming, the seas were turning rough, and I twice saw the wind hurling itself into funnel spirals around a harpy as she raged across the horizon. I felt it tug the keel, though we were twenty miles away. I was dreading the open-sea passage to the Nile.

It was just before we were about to leave the coast and strike out into the deep sea, on a bronze evening when I was looking over the side and thinking that perhaps I should drown myself, when someone saw the boy on the shore.

———————

The boy was beautiful. We thought he must have been the son of a noble lady or a queen, because he was wearing a purple cloak against the sea wind. He would be a worth a fortune, and so we pulled in to the shale beach to take him.

He didn't run away. Perhaps he realized he would never run fast enough and he might as well save himself the bother, but it was still eerie to wade out of the sea ready for a fight, only to find him walking out right to us in the tide line, as though he had long since arranged to meet us there.

I was used to snatching people; but he didn't fight, and so instead it was a strange sort of escort, and it was nearly politely that we took him aboard. There was some debate about where to put him. Usually slaves went down in the hold, but ours was already crowded, and there were some angry men down there who might hurt him just because they could. So we put him by the mast. We put chains on him, which he seemed not to mind. He just settled down, looking intrigued through his eerie blue eyes—people grumbled when they saw, because the Egyptians paid less for blue, it was ugly, but otherwise he was perfect—and we sailed away, the trade wind filling our black sails so well it felt like a gift from Poseidon. Some people thought he must be simple because he was so peaceful. I didn't think so. When someone is that calm in a crisis, either they don't know what's happening, or you don't.

I thought maybe I knew those eyes, and even that cheerful calm.

I tried to say that maybe we were the ones who didn't quite see what was happening, but someone smacked me over the head and told me to shut up. The boy smiled at me, like we both knew the punchline of a joke nobody else had got to yet, and held his hands up to show me the manacles as they fell off.

It was strange, having him aboard. Nobody tried to bother him, even when it became obvious he could get out of his chains. There was a . . . not-thereness about him. People had a way of walking past him like they'd forgotten him, and because he didn't talk, it was easy for them to keep forgetting.

I don't know why it didn't work on me. Maybe it was because he could see I wasn't in anyone's good ledger.

Or maybe he knew me, from all those years ago, and the lightning strike. I still had that spectacular scar over my face from the chariot incident.

Even though he was going to be sold in Memphis, even though it was a stupid idea to latch onto him, I was grateful to have another outcast to sit with. He seemed happy to have me. I brought him food, like I was his host and not his gaoler, so we had all our meals together, and I wrapped him up in my cloak at night; the purple one was long since reassigned. He never spoke, and I wasn't certain he understood me, but he seemed like he was listening when I told him about why everyone was so angry with me, and what I'd done.

"I think I just lost my mind," I said, for what must have been the twelfth time. He was doing amazingly well at not shoving me over the side. I was yanking a comb through my hair. After days at sea, we had stopped to take on fresh water that morning, which meant finally getting a proper wash, but when your hair is down to your waist and you live in a salt wind, things are less straightforward on that front than you might like. I couldn't cut it. The only Theban knights with short hair are slaves who *used* to be Theban knights.

He said nothing, but it was a sympathetic sort of nothing. I realized he was waiting hopefully to see if I might give him the comb. Feeling like a pig not to have offered it to him first, I touched his shoulders to get him to turn away from me, and ran the comb through his hair myself. He let me, and seemed happy at least. I wished I could tell if he was pretending not to be scared.

The comb went through easily, though his hair was much thicker and heavier than mine. The sea seemed not to notice him any more than the crew did. He had stayed luminously clean the whole time. Or maybe he just *seemed* clean because he looked so healthy.

The wind was picking up, so I plaited his hair and tucked it under the edge of his cloak, my cloak, which he was holding wrapped close now.

"Warm enough?" I asked. I was, but I'd been up and down all day. He had been sitting still. He didn't always: sometimes he went below to see the slaves, which usually we would have put a stop to, but since he didn't speak, it was hard to see the harm in it. To my surprise, nobody had tried to kill him, not even the captured Trojan knights bound for the mines. I wasn't sure what he did down there, but whenever it was my turn to take their rations down, everyone seemed much calmer than they usually would have.

He nodded, but he didn't look too warm. I hugged him to make sure and rubbed his arms through the cloak. It's never hot at sea. Even if the land is baking, you need layers on the water. To my shock, he laughed; a tiny laugh, low and smoky, but a laugh all the same, and he tucked himself sideways against my chest, unafraid as a puppy, and it meant everything.

I kept my arms around him and tried hard not think about Helios. If I didn't think about him, he wasn't gone; he was just somewhere else, and it wasn't my fault, and there had been no pyre on the shore, and one day soon he'd turn up and it would all have been a horrible dream.

I felt awkwardly like I was a little boy playing at being a host and he was being obliging and playing at being my guest, in an imaginary house and not a ship heading for the slave markets on the Nile, with all the old eagerness I really did used to have for those games. Hosting a guest is sacred. Our word for that is *xenia*—hospitality, but much more profound, a holy bond enforced by Zeus himself. We were a nation of wandering knights, far flung on raids years from home, and although the world would eventually turn, and there would be such things as inns and way-houses, there weren't then. You asked for xenia at the door of a stranger, because it was that or starve on the road, and it took the most phenomenal leap of trust and courtesy to open that door, see a hulking scarred soldier outside, and say, *Yes, come in.* But that was the custom. People did it. We did. It was inviolate. Trust someone like that, and it lasts beyond your lifetime. Every so often, Helios had let someone stay with us, and they stayed in touch forever. Their children would stay in touch forever, and if I had children, they would too. We were all kin. I'd never done it in my own right, and part of me was twisted up with shame, because this, what I was doing now, felt like a deformed mockery of the real thing. We wouldn't stay in touch. It wasn't sacred. We were going to sell him into a horrible life that would probably be very short indeed.

Unless, said a voice that belonged to Helios, *you make it real. It's real if you decide that it is.*

That would mean fighting for him and helping him escape, when the time came. That would mean being his, automatically and forever, in the way Helios had been mine.

I wanted to promise him that straightaway, but I was old enough to know it would be stupid to do that. Fighting for him would mean leaving my unit. However much they all hated me for now, they were still my unit, and duty is honour, and obedience is strength. They were everything I had left. To leave them behind, and the legion, and everything, for a boy I'd known for a few days—that was insane.

And right.

"It's going to be all right," I said, before I could think myself out of it. "I'll look after you. I promise."

It was such a small thing, but somewhere, behind the world, something went in a great ledger, and something mighty took notice.

What had I done? It was childish and impulsive and stupid was what it was, but—I'd said it now. I was bound for the rest of time. I should have been afraid, because what would happen when I couldn't keep that vow, but I only felt glad. If I *could* keep it, if I could just be knight enough, then . . . I'd have a family again. All at once I was lost in imagining a life away from the unit, wandering to different places for no reason except to see them, watching him pick up interesting pebbles on the shore, maybe fighting freelance when we needed money. Maybe we'd find a way to get him all the way back home, wherever that was, and maybe his mother would be a fine lady, with a beautiful feasting hall by the sea and room for another person, if I was quiet and dutiful. When he grew up to be lord of that place, I'd be there, serving, like knights are meant to do.

Maybe the boy understood, because he squeezed my hands.

Down in the hold, the slaves were singing. I'd thought none of them spoke the same language, because the Empire marshalled all its allies from across the world to defend the holy city; but they were all singing the same words. It was a weird tune, nothing like our hymns, and I had no idea what it meant, but a deep-down instinct knew it was something unholy. Someone shouted at them to shut up, but they didn't.

The boy was smiling.

I was off watch for the first half of the night, so I had time to sleep a bit. I hated that I wasn't having nightmares. The Furies should have been

31

hounding me for every second of every night for all but murdering my only family, but no. I slept fine.

I leaned back against the mast, meaning to shut my eyes, but then I stopped. There was a little shoot growing from a knot in the wood. I frowned at it and pulled, expecting it to come free easily, roots only just lodged into some crack in the grain of the timber, but it didn't. It was growing *out* of the wood, not just anchored to it. There were others too, further up, better established, and with a strange, half-horrified and half-repulsed drop, I realized that the wood of the mast was growing. It had been aired and sanded and varnished years ago, but even so—the shoots were making oak leaves. All the way to the top yard.

When I showed the boy, he winked at me.

"The mast," I tried to say the first mate later, because I thought she was slightly less likely than the captain to chain me up below. "Have you seen?"

I think for her—like all true sailors—the sieges and the raids were just vexing interludes between nice stretches at sea. At sea, it was hard to convince her that there could be anything wrong with the world, and I was nervous trying to do it now.

"What about her?"

"She's—growing?"

I felt stupid saying it, even though it was clearly happening hardly four feet away from us. When things are odd enough, they don't go through your mind like normal things do. I think minds have filters; usually, those filters are useful, because they stop you mistaking dreams or mirages or those weird hunger-hallucinations for anything real. But then, truly strange things that are real get stuck in them, and then you can't look at them properly. Or you can look, but then you look away and your mind says, *No, that can't be right, that's silly, we must be mistaken*—and it keeps doing it, every time.

She glanced over, and I thought she would somehow not see, but she did, and frowned. She pulled at one of the new twigs, just like I had; then she sliced it off with her knife, and then dug in the blade a little, but it was just the grain of the mast underneath.

"This is twenty years old," she said, as if the mast had personally betrayed her. "She can't be growing." Nobody ever said "it" about anything on a ship. Ships are made from oaks, which are dryads, and just because you cut down the tree doesn't mean the dryad goes away.

"I think it's him," I said about the boy, who had been watching, looking like he was having quite a lot of fun.

It made the first mate jump. The boy had been right next to us all this time, but she must not have seen. She looked down at him for a long time, and I could *see* him getting stuck in her strange-things filter, even though he was as solid as me.

It only made me more sure.

"Please, he's doing this. You barely see him, that isn't normal—what if he's Poseidon, or Athena, or . . . ?" I couldn't bring myself to say, *Or maybe even the other one, the worst one.* We have hedging names for gods, because true names have a lot of power; we call Poseidon Earthshaker, and politely, Aphrodite is the Lady, the Furies are the Kindly Ones. What we call Death is ha-eides: the Unseen.

"We need to let him go—"

"He's just a bit simple. He's fine," she said, and went on her way.

I sat down with the boy again. Whatever was happening to the mast, whether it was him or not, he was still the only person I could sit with who wouldn't immediately find an excuse to punch me.

After a while, I had to shift about, because ivy had grown round my knee.

When I looked at him, he twisted his nose, looking guilty, as if growing ivy over people were an annoying habit his parents had been trying to school out of him.

"Can I call you Ivy?" I said tentatively. "It's rude not to call you anything."

He smiled, maybe because he understood, maybe just because I didn't mind the ivy. I wondered if there was a way for me to sneak him off the ship and find him passage back the way we had come. I'd need to try. I'd promised him.

The wind was blowing from the north, sending us fast towards the Nile delta, past the Great Isle. In the morning everyone was in a good mood, because the night watch said we had covered a clear forty miles overnight, which was incredible. I only half heard, groggy after a night full of dreams about a great hunt in a forest. I'd never seen any forest, but I felt like I knew this one down to its last root and ant. I could still taste the greenness in the air.

In the night, ivy had grown over my ribs, the way Helios might have put one arm across me. It felt strangely the same, too, even though the boy had his back to me. I unwound the ivy and pulled a blanket over him better. However he was doing it, I didn't care. All I cared about was that he was warm and, if not happy, then not miserable. If I could just keep him well—then he had a chance. He might not die on the sea passage. If he died, I was going overboard.

Like I did every morning and every night, I looked into my kit bag to touch Helios's helmet and say a silent hello to the mask. I was losing sight of him, despite that mask. The man was so different to the bronze; and different, of course, to when it had been cast. He had been fifteen then, younger than I was now. My reflection in it looked more like him.

As the sun came up over the water, staining it wine red, the light glinted wrongly along the mast.

It was covered in vines. Brilliant green ivy, and grapes, already halfway to ripe even though they hadn't been there yesterday, coiling up along the yards. The posts that held up the rail around the deck were unrecognisable. They had turned back into trees in the night; small, but already full of pine cones.

Somebody must once have replaced a plank in the hull with pear wood, because now, there was a pear tree growing on the prow, roots half covering the painted eye there, and seeming—somehow this was madder than anything else—not to mind the saltwater brushing them.

"How did you not see this happening?" someone asked the night watch steersman, who was staring at it all, as bewildered as the rest of us.

"I don't . . . I thought . . ." He had a strange glassy look, one I recognised now.

The boy with blue eyes was exactly where he always was, at the base of the mast; but it didn't look like a mast any more, just the trunks of the vines, and all around them, there were flowers shoving up through the grain of the deck, and moss. He had picked a bunch of grapes, and he offered me one.

I stared at it, because I remembered Persephone. Eating something means you accept hospitality, and with hospitality, there is a covenant you must keep. There are debts you owe that last generations. So I shook my head and knelt down instead, and he looked at me sidelong like he'd just seen me do something quite clever.

"If you keep doing this, the ship will sink."

He only lifted his eyebrows a little.

Of course it would sink the ship. That was the point.

The whole crew had to go up the rigging with knives to cut back the grass waving there. The rope was turning back into hemp. Then we had to climb higher and cut back the vines that had locked the yards in place. They wouldn't turn. I heard someone murmur that even the rudder wasn't working.

I looked downwind. Ahead of us, there was a cliff. There were a lot of very sharp rocks at the base. The water around us was deep. There would be no swimming to safety, even for the people who could swim. Beside us, there were dolphins. The babies loved playing in the bow wave, because it swept them along. One of the bigger ones turned sideways in the water and looked up at us, clearly wondering what we were doing, being so silly and not getting in the water where things were more fun.

As fast as we worked, though, everything grew back. The vines were wrapped tight around the mast and the yards, and they were ageing in front of us; we weren't cutting through tiny new shoots any more, but bark. At the base, they were more like trees. The boy with blue eyes was set up comfortably in a hollow full of flowers now, handing out grapes whenever anyone went by. Unlike me, everyone else was taking them, though they did look uncertain after a couple of seconds about where the grapes had come from. It wasn't invisibility, though. Some people had very much remembered he was there.

It didn't take long for the first person to say we should throw him over the side.

I dropped down next to him. If I'd had any valour at all, I would have said, *It's all right, you're my guest, and I will die for you here before I let anyone touch you.*

But I didn't. I didn't; even though I knew it was wrong, and even though, in the hazy way you understand time when you're very young, I knew that not doing that was swinging my whole life the wrong way, throwing me off course, forever. I knew, but I couldn't say it. Everyone I knew in the world was on this ship. They hated me, and Helios was gone, but they might forgive me in the end. I had never been by myself, ever. To launch myself into the world alone, for a boy who wasn't really a boy at all, however much I wanted to help him . . .

I'd promised him, but had he even understood? Probably not.

And what was that promise worth, anyway? Nothing. I couldn't help. I'd never been able to help. It was a grief dream.

"Do you understand what they're saying? They want to put you overboard. Can you swim?"

He looked like he might laugh. I had a feeling he understood exactly, and he was very happy for everyone to dig themselves deeper into their hole.

"Get him up," someone told me.

"Don't," I tried.

I should have drawn my sword.

I didn't. Years after that, I jolted awake at night burning with shame for that spectacular failure of duty. "Please."

Pathetic.

The boy was watching me, not smiling any more. Whether he understood our language or not, he understood what I'd done, and what I hadn't.

He put his hands down on the deck, and something . . . happened. There was a huge crash from the hold, and in a furious swarm, the slaves burst onto the deck. They were singing their song, and this time it was a battle howl, and they tore into the nearest sailors like I'd never seen even the greatest warriors fight before. A girl ripped out the captain's throat with her teeth, and where the blood sprayed, poppies burst into life, blooming across the deck. There were no more chains around anyone's wrists or ankles, just vines, and under our boots, the planking of the deck heaved as the dryads woke up, and grew, and grew.

The first mate threw me overboard; I still don't know whether to drown me, or to save me.

All I could see was roiling water, and then I was sinking, too stunned to swim, staring at the keel of the ship, which was a rampage of coral and a sapling ash tree where the rudder should have been. It was a floating island, all chaos and beautiful, and part of me was glad to have seen it even though the cost was dying, but only for a flicker, because when people say you feel a lovely calm when you drown, they're lying to you so you don't feel sad about all your friends who will drown in the years to come.

My head was thumping from crashing into the water at the wrong angle, but I remembered to kick for the surface. The water was rough, though, and I could only breathe in gasps between the waves, the salt burning inside my nose and right in the back of my throat, and with a horrible certainty I realized the land was still too far away, and I was going to drown slowly, bit by bit, instead of fast.

Not far from me at all, the ship smashed on the cliffs. People and timber sprayed into the water. The grape-bound mast blasted down with a white plume.

The waves from it slung me towards the shore, not smoothly—I went tumbling like a ball of seaweed, sometimes getting snatches of sky and air, sometimes seeing people hanging in the deep water. Most sailors can't swim. It doesn't take long to drown.

I got hold of a piece of wreckage, or what should have been wreckage; it was a plank with most of a pear tree growing from it, and when I got my arms over it, a pear fell off and thunked me on the shoulder before it floated off, perfect and golden.

The shore was all vicious rocks. Some were under me now, too far down to stand on, some up ahead, and on one of them—on one of them was the boy, sitting as easy as a siren, watching the wreck. He had seen me.

"Khaire," I choked, because I couldn't think of anything else. It's how we say *hail, rejoice,* and, I suppose indirectly, *please don't kill me.* "I'm sorry we took you. I'm sorry I didn't . . ."

He inclined his head and looked past me. I looked too, struggling against the water.

The bodies were gone; not floating any more, not sinking. There were dolphins instead. They weren't the same as the dolphins before. They were smaller, lighter, and they were playing and spinning with so much joy they must have been celebrating something. Maybe something like being unexpectedly alive and a dolphin after being convinced they were going to drown as humans.

"Who are you?" I asked uselessly. "Who should I sacrifice to?"

He smiled, slowly, and there was something ancient and frightening about that smile. "I'll come back for you one day. I'll tell you then."

It was the first time he had spoken and for a second it wouldn't go through my head, that he could. His voice was too old for the rest of him and it was like nothing I'd ever heard before. When a city burns, the smoke has an orange glow from below, from the fires, but that far above all the chaos, it's beautiful. I loved that moment of a siege: standing on the city wall and watching the embers flit and zither into that ashy light, which was really all the palaces and monuments transformed.

He sounded like that ash-glow looked; like the funeral pyre of kingdoms.

By the time I clawed ashore among the flotsam—by some miracle my kit bag was there, with Helios's helmet still in it—he was gone. I walked for a long time over the rocks, looking for him, because even a god shouldn't wander along a wrecking shore alone, but I couldn't find him. Not then, and not for ten years.

Coming back for me meant revenge, and Hades knew what that would be if the warning shot was a smashed ship; but as the seasons rolled together, and the long siege ground on, and the plague came, I wished he would come, because at least then I'd know he was all right, not alone and betrayed on that godforsaken shore.

I don't know when it started—maybe even as I began to panic on that beach—but after a while, I noticed that whenever my heartbeat was loud, it sounded like *Where are you, where are you, where are you.*

4

In the summer Dionysus came to Thebes, it was so hot that there were mirages in the sky. On a day watch on the city wall, looking out over the plains, you'd see the dust plume. Before many hours had crawled by, you'd see cities in the shapes, and giants, just like you do in dense fog at sea. On a night watch, the heat was no less. The hottest part of the day was immediately after sunset, when the white towers glowed like molten bronze and the dust billowed, and armour heated up so badly that if you poured water on it, it steamed. The city was a crucible.

I had to stop halfway up the long flight of steps to the High City and the garrison. Stop and breathe, and sit down with a water flask, even though I could normally take it all at a half run. If I tried that now, I saw green stars.

When I looked back over the lower city, it was through columns of black smoke rising from the temple altars. I could taste the ash and the incense even up here. Sacrifices: to make it rain. So far, none of the gods were impressed enough to intervene. It had been like this for six weeks, and there was a permanent charnel-house-smoke pall over the city. From any distance, Thebes looks like a crown of towers on its hill—now, the crown was burning.

I swallowed some of my lukewarm water, holding my breath so I wouldn't know how badly it tasted of the leather flask, but even then, I couldn't shut out the smoke. The smell of the smoke was the smell of a city falling.

Then, even though it was so hot I could hardly breathe, I was cold.

I wasn't on the steps up to the High City in Thebes any more.

I was outside the walls of Troy. It was freezing: winter. Even though fighting is thirsty work, I had a scarf tucked into my breastplate, because the wind howled off the sea and pushed its way under every rivet. My arm ached; one of the gatehouse towers had just exploded and a chunk of stone had blasted into my shield. The smoke was everywhere, so thick I couldn't see the knights on either side of me, even though we were still more or less in formation.

"There they go!" someone shouted.

I looked up, through a thinner shroud in the smoke, at the spire of a temple—I'd never known which god the temple of was for, but I'd spent more than a decade hate-admiring those spires and their golden roofs, and wondering how they were built so high. People were jumping from the top: priestesses in green, falling like peacocks that had been shot midair.

I had a surge of exhausted joy and joined in when my unit cheered. The priestesses only jumped from a city's towers when it was certain to fall. Their god must have told them we would win. Thank *fuck*. It had only taken thirteen years.

Our trumpets sounded, and the signal flags went up. Advance.

"Mind out," someone said to me, on the steps to the High City in Thebes, here, now, in the broiling summer and the smoke haze from sacrifices.

Even though I knew exactly what was happening—and this was what drove me so mad—even though I *knew* I wasn't really at Troy at all, I was in Thebes, and I was on my way to the garrison for the night—it was so discombobulating that I couldn't even say sorry for blocking the way up the narrow stairway. I just made an incoherent noise and shuffled to the side, not very certain about standing up, because a big portion of my mind couldn't tell if I was on the steps, or if I was among the wreckage outside the city walls on that frozen winter morning with ice forming across the filigree of my breastplate.

"Ah—are you . . . all right?" the woman said tentatively. She was older than me, scribe-looking; yes, with a crate of clay tablets strapped to her back.

"Yes. Sorry." What was I even saying? Was it words? "I'm—it's—it's just the heat." I sounded like a Persian dandy who needed his own special fainting couch.

She looked relieved she wouldn't have to do anything else, and carried on.

Once she had gone, I smacked the back of my own hand to try to make myself recognise what was now and what wasn't. It wasn't like remembering, those flashes. It didn't feel like sitting on some steps and thinking, *Hm, yes, it was cold that day,* all the while fully knowing where I was now, and when. It felt like it was happening again. *Happening,* as real as the heat and sacrifice smoke and the taste of leather flask.

It did work, sort of. My hand hurt. Now. Right. Good.

I was still shaking. It was making the water in my flask slosh.

You go through life imagining you're a decent soldier of use and honour, and then one day you come home and you're just a lump who obstructs the paths of commuting scribes. How the sodding wheel turns.

"Stop it," I said, in case hearing a voice giving an order would help, even if it was my voice. "Come *on.*" I couldn't be late, not today.

When I did get up—victory!—I felt weak, but not so badly as before. I carried on slowly. One step; one step. Gradually, something like strength came back into my knees, and I stopped feeling like I might collapse. All right. Good; good. I might still be on time.

I had no idea what those bizarre little episodes of uselessness were, and I didn't want to find a witch and enquire. It was humiliating and probably it was just hunger and heat. Our rations were down to two thirds recently, which isn't ideal when you train for four hours a day. Hopefully, the visions would die once the autumn finally came, and it had to come soon. We were almost in Harvest Month now—or what would have been Harvest Month, if there were anything to harvest.

Behind me, the sunset was burning orange through the smoke. It was different to Troy.

It was. The sunsets had been a strange kind of indigo there.

It was fine.

At the top, I had to stop again to wait for a funeral procession to go by. There were no mourners, just hot, dusty priests, with six or seven biers draped in cheap beige cloth. All the shapes underneath were far too thin. That was the most I'd seen at once, so far; things were getting worse. I bowed my head. Slaves always die first when the rations go down. They have half as much as citizens even in the best of times.

Every day, I walked up here betting myself that today was the day the garrison would be sent out to deal with bread riots. It was a miracle nothing had happened yet. Rations kept shrinking, which meant the civil granaries were nearly empty, and in the garrison, we were all restless, the way you always are when you know you'll be fighting soon. And we would be fighting soon: we would have to be. If you can't harvest grain, the only thing left is to steal it.

I was hoping we'd be sent to Athens. Athens is always improved by being on fire.

A great archway led into the square. It was a new monument to the fallen, visible right across the city because it was four storeys tall, and it was carved with images of hundreds of soldiers seething before the walls of Troy. In alcoves stood marvels of people who had served with particular valour. There were seven, one for each of the city's seven gates, every one blessed by a temple and half-deified to join the ranks of the war-saints of Thebes. There was a knight who had led the cavalry charge that finally broke the Trojan infantry; a witch who had stayed with us even during the plague and saved at least a thousand wounded; a noble lady who had killed her son when she found out that he had deserted his unit.

Helios should have been up there. He would have, if I had held the line and he'd got the death he deserved.

I tried not to think about him. If I did, I could feel the space where he'd used to be much too clearly. It was person-sized but it was deep, a chasm all the way down to the halls of the Queen Below and the snicker of the waters of the Acheron. It didn't matter what I tried to fill it with, people or work or distractions. Those things just clacked bleakly on the rocks on the way down and vanished into the dark. So it just followed me around, a sort of shadow that the setting of the sun didn't blur or fade. If I sat still for long enough, it sat down next to me and took up all the air.

I'd stopped trying to fill it. Now I was just waiting for the boy with blue eyes to come back for his revenge, and then that would be that.

I stopped in the shadow of the monument and glanced both ways, checking for Guards. None so far, but they were everywhere in the High City. I pulled my cloak out of my bag and, despite a very urgent need to throw it as far from me as I could, I put it on, clipping its buckles to the ones on the shoulders of my breastplate.

"Knight!" a clear harsh voice called.

Ugh.

I arranged my face into the expression of quietly cheerful courtesy it's advisable to adopt around the Guards.

Among the dull smoky buildings and the dull smoky people, the Guard's cloak was vivid purple. She was walking towards me, slowly, because the Guards never rush.

When I first came back to Thebes and I'd been stopped for Inappropriate Apparel, I'd said, *That's a stupid law, I'm not doing that*; and sometimes, six months later, I woke up pouring sweat in the middle of the night, thinking I was still in the airless little cell with no water. It had only been a two-day detention, but gods almighty it had been hot. I'd been convinced I was going to die, without my sword in my hand and nowhere near a battlefield, like a deserter.

She nodded at my bag.

I handed it over. She looked through. There was nothing in it except the flask, a lamp for when I walked home tomorrow night, a little cask of lamp oil, and my ration tablet.

We have two layers of nobility: the knights, who are serving soldiers, and the Guards, who police the knights. That's necessary, I'll very grudgingly admit, because there are thousands of knights. A knight is a free citizen with full civil rights, a vote, and exemption from the death penalty except for desertion. Birth and blood don't matter for knights, only combat lineage: who your commander is, and who their commander was. The Guards, though, are harvested from the five families closest to the throne. They don't serve in the legions.

"Are you carrying silver or gold?" she said, not sounding nearly as bored or as perfunctory as I would have liked.

(Penalty for carrying silver or gold inside city walls: five years of slavery.)

"No, lady." I kept my eyes on the ground.

"Alcohol?"

(Penalty for a knight becoming inebriated on active service: five years of slavery.)

"No, lady."

"Have you recently sent or you do intend to send your slaves for gold, silver, or alcohol?"

It was tempting to say, *Yes, I've got legions of slaves lined up and a giant shipment from Hattusa waiting at the dock. I'm going to build myself a house out of wine jars and then decorate the whole lot in filigree.*

(Penalty for a false confession: ten years of slavery.)

"No, lady."

She was studying my ration tablet. "You're well provided for," she remarked when she saw the allowances. Her eyes ticked over me. "Unmarried, though. Where's your sense of duty, Sown?"

It was rhetorical. I kept looking at the ground. She couldn't arrest me for being unmarried. I'd paid the fine already this month. It said so on the tablet.

She gave the tablet back. "Well. There you are, Polemarch Heliades of the Fifth Unit," she said, irritatingly enunciating every single syllable so it sounded like one word—*pol-eh-mark-hell-ee-a-dees*—with a wryness that said, *In my day we didn't let dishonourable unmarried idiots become polemarch of a whole unit of knights.* "Duty is honour."

"Duty is honour," I muttered, and thought, *Well, when the bread riots come and someone impales on you a big spike, I shall be far too busy looking meekly at the ground like a good knight to notice.* The Athenians, sod them all, have a stupid joke about exactly this. Our word for pupil, as in eyes, is *parthenos.* But that's also our word for a virgin; Athenian teenagers keep their eyes down, because Athenian men are psychopaths. So some smart-arse noticed that we do that too and started calling us the parthenai, which means "the virgins." You'll hear it every time Theban soldiers meet Athenian soldiers. *Oi oi, watch out lads, the virgins are coming.*

As I say, they're much improved by being on fire.

Feeling as though I were wearing a red flag that said COME AND GET ME, I started across the market square. It would have been easier if I'd been able to hear. I wasn't deaf, yet; I could hear someone close to me. But I couldn't hear general diffuse things, like one set of footsteps coming closer to me among many. I started losing my hearing on the day Troy fell. It was odd: I hadn't been too near any explosions and no one had hit me on the head. But that afternoon while I sat in the throne room, with some very good cakes from the palace kitchen, the world fell quiet, as though Athena had put me in an invisible box.

"Need a labourer, sir?"

I just managed to catch myself before I swung round and punched him in the eye. He must have seen me twitch, because he jolted right back from me, hands up. I held mine up too, well away from my sword. When I looked around, there were a dozen people already, looking ragged and determined. Lots of them had clay signs around their necks that said things like STRONG LABOURER or FLUENT IN EGYPTIAN, mostly in the same handwriting, because it would be only one or two of them who could write.

They were all talking at once, and I could only catch random snatches.

"I know olives, and yews—"

"Someone to teach your children? I speak Egyptian—"

"I can weave!"

"I'm worth ten oxen but you can have me for four!"

"No. I'm sorry," I said, completely unable to tell if I was talking loudly enough. "Good luck."

Some of them followed me across the square anyway.

For me, in the legion, slaves were people who you stole from other places. It had been a strange revelation that those people were in the tiny minority of slaves generally. Most people are born into hereditary service— that would be civil servants like scribes and Palace administrators—or they sell themselves. All these people here now would have been farmers or herders or weavers this time last season, struggling but just about making ends meet. Now there were hardly any crops to grow, and the price of wool was sky-high because it was so hard to keep sheep alive in the drought, and even goats were struggling; nobody could make a living any more. So they offered themselves for sale. Instead of paying a merchant, you paid their family, a kind of advance for future labour— only, much cheaper than it would have been if they'd been able to wait for payment until *after* the work was done.

Some of them followed me right out of the square. They only stopped when I passed under the open gates of the garrison.

"Oh, come on," one of the men said. "You're a Sown knight. You could take all of us and you wouldn't even notice."

I would. I'd been trained to look after myself, and *being* looked after was something between awkward and humiliating, and I hated having even the three slaves I did have. I could sweep my own bloody floor. It was legion discipline. I was scared of letting someone else do it. I'd get lazy and repulsive, and when the boy with blue eyes *did* finally come, he'd take one look at me, decide it would be much funnier not to kill me, and I'd have to live until I was fifty and I died of whatever it is you die of when you're too rich and you have too much wine and bits of you start falling off.

"No, thank you," I said.

He gave me a look with murder in it, the kind I'd only seen on battlefields before. "When the lost prince comes back, I hope he fucking curses you."

I stopped moving, because I hadn't heard anything about the lost prince for years. The memory of the baby and the lightning lived deep down, in bedrock cellars in my mind that I never visited. It had been a long time since I'd been down there and remembered that when the boy with blue eyes came aboard my ship, I'd wondered if maybe they were the same person.

"He did that years ago," I said, and shut the gate.

5

This is a thing that might save you time when you travel. Mostly, cities train their nobility to be speakers, and poets, and sometimes just decoratively useless. But every so often, you come to the gates of a place where the Sown are soldiers down to the last child. It can be easy to admire that, and think how amazing it is that a place can have trained its warriors so very well that the city has never fallen to invasion, and kings and empresses from the furthest corners of the world want either to hire them, or leave them well alone.

Don't admire it. Nobody decides one morning that the best way to educate their children is to send them to the army aged—in peace time, at the very latest—seven, and have them raised by knights. It would be idiotic to do that for no reason. Nobody thinks that's a *good* way to bring up humans, not even me.

Perhaps there are some places that are that way because things are always desperate, the fields never yield, and their entire living has to be raiding—but then I always wonder why they don't just move. There are plenty of empty places in Achaea, never mind the world, and colonies are normal. You're not stealing the land from anyone. There are islands everywhere nobody owns. Move off your barren rock to a nicer rock.

No.

All you need to do is count the slaves.

For every citizen in Thebes, there are twelve slaves, and that ratio was going up every day the rain didn't come. And what happens if twelve in thirteen people decide that they don't like the way things are? Right. You need the free citizens—the Sown—to be terrifying.

The Hidden is a small regiment of a hundred and twenty knights. Young knights who haven't yet fought on the front line, but who need practise. Randomly across any given month, we allocate one night—usually with a decent to bright moon—and we send the Hidden out around the city and the farmland about twenty miles around it in every direction. They have only one instruction. If they see a slave on the road who cannot show a Palace seal and isn't accompanied by a citizen who can, that slave is to be shot.

Tonight was the first ride for my cohort. They were all fifteen and sixteen, all too young to have sworn their vows to their commanders yet, or to fight on the front line, but old enough for combat. I'd taught that age group for years now, with the depressing consequence that they looked younger every year.

The moon was huge and full, and so bright we had shadows in the training yard. Some of the higher-strung horses didn't like it, and kept pawing at the black shapes that followed them around on the sand. I watched the younger knights checking each other's armour with the carefulness of people who didn't do it all the time; it wasn't their own armour. You don't wear your armour, during a ride for the Hidden. It's black, without sigils, so that no one knows exactly who it is behind the helmet. Once they looked ready, I punched the lower hem of their breastplates to make sure they were buckled properly, and nobody's hit them in the chin. No: they were good. If you fell off your horse, the first thing armour did was ride up as much as it could.

"Mount up," I said, and the ranks broke up in a swirl of red cloaks. "We're going on the north road."

One of the stupider boys—I called him Feral Jason, because he was a horrendous little bastard and recently my favourite hobby was his subtle persecution—did a wolf howl, so I pushed him off his horse. He landed with a satisfying clank and a squeak he was going to be embarrassed about later, and then, because his horse was a good one with a faultless sense of whether she was carrying a real knight or a moron who just dressed like one, she pretended not to see him on the ground and trod on him: not with her whole weight, but enough to bang her shoe against his armour. I love warhorses.

"This is your first ride as knights, and not knights in training," I said, loud enough to carry through the courtyard. "I know you're excited. But you *are* knights, not animals. You've heard the Knight's Vow a hundred times down the years, but now it's your turn to swear it. Once you swear, there is no going back. You will be held to it always. Are you ready to give that oath?"

"Sir!"

"Swear your oath, Sown."

Like it always did, it brought down a strange solemnity. It doesn't matter how many times you hear other knights quote the vow at each other; it's different when you say it yourself, before your first ride with the Hidden.

Around the edge of the courtyard, their commanders had come out to see them take the vow, unobtrusive in the shade and making an effort not to look too proud or too upset that their wards were growing up. I saw some of them dash a hand over their eyes, or standing close with their shoulders together, nearly propping each other up, because what this meant was that they'd done it: they'd kept a child alive right into knighthood, sometimes through everything at Troy. Most of them would never have expected to see this.

As always when I took young knights through the vow, I had to think hard about banal things, like my lemon tree that never made any lemons. If I didn't, I would think of my ward, and of the little pair of shoes I'd had to donate to another commander in the plague year at Troy, and the clockwork marvel toy that the bronzesmith had had to melt back down, before it ever managed to be a birthday present.

I vow to serve my city, my Queen, and my comrades before myself. I pray to Athena to give me strength and justice, and I swear never to use one without the other; for strength without justice is savagery, and justice without strength is air. I will henceforth forego profit, untruth, and luxury.

Obedience is strength, austerity is freedom, and duty is honour.

I am not myself: I am my legion. We are the Sown, the children of the dragon; in fire we will come, and in ash we will leave, until we too are ashes.

Before I rode with them myself, the sight of the torches streaming by and the black horses bearing black-armoured knights was mesmerising.

I remember being awed by it when I was small, and I remember wanting to go more than anything, for all Helios kept telling me it was different when you were in it. That had been on a beach somewhere in Hattusa. Here, in Thebes, the ride was so much of a spectacle that on likely nights, people brought their children to the garrison gates to see us go, tucked carefully to the sides of the road and out the way; part of the ritual now was to lean down in the saddle and touch hands with any children who were stretching up.

I don't know if you've met a Theban warhorse, but imagine an irritable machine that's going to plough on to where it wants to go even if there is an Egyptian chariot line in the way, and doesn't especially care if you're still on it when it gets there. A hundred of them thundering down the main road is a thing to see, the torches gleaming on the black helmets and black spearpoints. Each knight wears mail; not because we expect it will do a great deal that bronze breastplates can't, but because of the noise it makes. A hundred sets of moving chain mail sounds like Poseidon rising through the ground.

The city gates closed at sunset. It meant traders couldn't start out on any new journeys. Anyone out was either coming towards Thebes, where you had to pay a tax to enter after sunset, or they weren't meant to be there at all.

In the drought, the only water within a day's walk of the city was Lake Copais; the only road there is called Artemis's Way. It isn't by accident that Artemis is the god of the Hunt.

As they opened the North Gate, the watchmen made the sign of the bull at us. I've never been able to work out if was a way to wish us luck, or to keep us away from *their* households, if the time ever came. The bronze gates, each one three feet thick, swung open soundlessly on hydraulics more ancient than some of our gods, and on the wall, the marvels turned to watch us go, each one holding a torch to light the gate for the night, hazy in the smog of the sacrifice fires. Even by the moonlight, the columns of black smoke were rising clear. I could make out the glows of the altars.

I know there are places in Egypt and the wider world where it's different, but our cities have a wall, and then that's it. The city stops there; the watchmen stop there; and mostly, the law stops there. You ride from lights, and people, and tiny glimpses of potters up late in their workshops, painting beautiful things onto wine jars—across a border into a country that doesn't belong to humans. There's the road, and the dark, and on the back of your neck, a heavy awareness that you need to know exactly how long it takes you to shift your grip on your spear and throw it.

I was always more alert to that when I was with a very young unit. For all they were well-trained and mostly sensible, they were still ducklings in some important ways. Knights start young and they do grow up quickly—you can give command of a whole unit to someone who's seventeen and you'll have a perfectly good result—but there is a limit. Things still spook them. They're still brand-new.

"Are those just beacon lights on the road up there, sir?" one of the younger girls asked me over the noise of the horses' hooves. She sounded fizzy and excited, just like I had when I first did this. I was relieved, because when you have to make a group of children murder some people who've done nothing to them, the best way for them to be is excited.

Excited means they're not afraid, they won't waver over what they have to do, they *won't* lose their grip on their swords. The ones I worried about were the ones who could put themselves too easily in the shoes doing the running.

"No, knight. Those are wagons." The lights ahead started to wink out as the people in the wagons realized what was coming up behind them.

"I think they're going away from us!"

"They are. Do you want to fire the flare for me?"

I'd never seen anyone look so pleased with something so small. "Thank you, sir!"

I gave her the arrow with the oil-soaked rag wrapped around the tip, held her spear in exchange, and took the reins of her horse just to be sure as she threaded the arrow into the bow. "Ready?"

"Yes, sir." She touched the tip into the torch of the boy on her other side and fired into the sky. The arrow drew a line of orange into the dark, up ahead of the riders.

Behind us, there was a bang as a hundred spears thunked into a new grip in a hundred gauntlets, shifted from upright to horizontal. I looked back to see if anyone was slow, but they were doing well tonight. We had drilled it a dozen times a day for weeks. They all locked their elbows into place so that the spear shafts stayed level with the cheek plates of their helmets. Theban spears aren't wood but bronze; they're hollow inside, very light, but the young knights train with solid iron, so that when the time comes, they'll be able to hold the real thing steady indefinitely. Here and there in the torchlight, silver charms and blessed ribbons winked. Some of them had tiny clay tabs bound to them with wire, written by priestesses at the Temple of Athena. They said things like MAY I ALWAYS FLY TRUE and NEVER MISS.

The wagons up ahead of us were clear now. They had pulled to the side of the road, and there were people running away over the dusty, scrubby land that, when I was a child, had been brilliant green fields.

I held up my spear so that the ranks behind me could see, and the first lines of the hymn to Ares lifted up into the dark.

Ares golden-helmed, bronze-clad, shield-bearer, city-saver . . .

The horses were trained to chase anything big that tried to get away from them once they heard the hymn, and the second they saw something to go after, they surged.

6

The little knights were fizzy when we got back to the garrison, and some of the younger ones were reenacting especially gory moments. I scooped a bucket of water from the fountain to wash the blood and the road grit out of my hair while I watched them play. It was just before dawn, which was searing pink onto the horizon.

"Keep it down," I called. I couldn't hear much but they were a garrulous bunch, this year. Secretly I liked that about them. Knights should be good at talking. "People are trying to sleep. Jason, that isn't your lamb, let her go."

They did good work of looking chastised.

"Herakles. Offerings. Like real humans," I added, pointing at the marvel in the middle of our courtyard. The new sun was slinging orange and purple across his bronze shield. "Then you've got an hour before the Bull Ceremony. You need to be in day armour, and *not* asleep."

They didn't put Herakles in our yard because they want us to be like him. They put him there because they don't. Everyone knows the first part of his story, about how strong he was and the labours, and the sodding Athenians like to leave it there, but that isn't the end. The end is that when he goes home to his wife and his three children, he's been too long fighting, and one night, he thinks they're enemy soldiers and kills them all.

If you're sitting there saying, *Oh, no, what a dreadful thing to tell children,* then you can fuck off to Athens and enjoy their puke-inducing happily-ever-after stories where everyone prances joyfully off into the joyful sunset like demented morons. It is not a proper story unless everyone murders each other at the end.

The young knights formed into a more or less orderly queue to leave Herakles some arrowheads, or filigree, or something else small but significant.

"Jason," I said, more to my bucket than to him, "a severed hand is not an offering. Put it in the rubbish ditch or I will shove it so far up your arse it will be able to manipulate you like a repulsive little Jason-puppet."

Some of the others laughed and Feral Jason did as he was told, doing what was actually quite a good impression of a sad sock puppet.

Their commanders were coming out to say hello and to ask how it had all gone. A boy called Amphitrion—he was one of my worries—was such a gentle, happy person that a few weeks ago he had bought a sacrifice lamb but had not been able to face the idea of actually putting her on the altar, so now she was a garrison mascot. His commander had come out with her and she was baaing happily. I was trying not to get too attached to her, because at some point Feral Jason would decide he wanted a lamb dinner, but it wasn't working.

Jason's commander was waiting too; he was a chronically tired-looking man with prematurely grey hair, a few years younger than me, and he was a walking piece of irony, because his name was Polydorus, which means "many-gifted." Everyone called him Polynemesis, which means "repeatedly cursed." I saw his expression turn pained.

"Jason," I said as Jason passed me again—not needing to ask what he was doing or planning because if it was upsetting even his commander, who was surely numb to most of his nonsense now, then it was probably as well not to invite it into permanent memory storage—"what makes you imagine I won't tell everyone your favourite thing is silk trousers from Persia, before I plant a pair in a particularly startling shade of mauve among your gear in the next inspection?"

He stopped walking.

"You wouldn't, sir," he said, not sounding very certain.

"Feel free to risk it, then," I said with not very well-concealed glee, because of the pair of mauve Feral Jason–sized trousers waiting for deployment in the secret cupboard under my desk.

He grumped off back to the rubbish ditch to put back whatever horrifying thing it was he'd salvaged from it to start with. I saw his commander relax, or relax as much as a human can if they're permanently responsible for a Feral Jason.

Polydorus saw me watching and came across. Whatever he wanted to say must have been important, because like everyone else about my age, he tended to avoid me. Maybe he was cursed with Jason, but I was cursed generally.

"You know his history?" he asked. He was a superb archer, and he spoke like he shot: straight to the target, with a tight-strung air that said he was waiting for you to forget what you were doing, nock *your* arrow with the cock feather up, and accidentally shoot at a perfect ninety-degree angle right into his eye. Lately he seemed more like that with me than with other people.

I nodded. "His first commander was Ajax. You rescued him after the herd of dismembered goats incident."

Polydorus nodded slightly. "He doesn't choose to be like this. He's a good boy."

He was younger than me, so he couldn't give me orders, but he was on the edge of it. If I stayed unmarried for much longer, I could expect a lot more of that. I'd not done the decent thing and died for Thebes in battle, and barring that, I hadn't done the next most decent thing and had children to start replacing the fallen. I was just here, taking up rations for no reason.

"He is a good boy," I agreed, "but he does choose, and what he chooses is to be a horrible little sod, because you let him."

He looked like he wanted to say something else, but then he changed his mind and bowed—not deep enough—and went fast after Jason. I wondered how long it would be before junior officers stopped bowing. Probably not long. And then; well, it would be impossible to keep control of this unit. I'd seen it happen before, I'd *been* in one of those units with an ageing unmarried polemarch, seventeen years old and at my peak Dick Phaidros stage. We had hounded him. So had the other officers.

He had walked into the sea one morning.

I thought about him a lot lately.

I wasn't going to get married, though. You can't involuntarily attack anyone who makes you jump and be married at the same time. Either I would kill her accidentally, or she would kill me on purpose. Whatever happened, I'd have to live with it, until the boy from the shore came.

I didn't have time to think long, because a scribe arrived, bowed a good distance from me, and gave me a tablet at arm's length. I had to stretch to take it. She looked like she was trying to stay out of easy punching range.

I soon saw why. The tablet said our rations were being cut again; it listed the new weights of everything. It hadn't been a lot before. Now it was what we would have given slaves a year ago.

What I wanted to do was run into the general's office and demand to know, after an introductory scream of primordial rage, what the fuck the Palace thought it was doing. If you don't feed children properly, they don't grow, and you end up trying to defend your city with knights who are a foot smaller than the Spartans. Which the Palace fucking knew already. That was why we always gave slaves less than citizens: if you've got a whole mass of workers whose lives are always horrible and who will absolutely try to kill you once they're miserable enough, you *want* them to be little. And if things were this bad, why hadn't we been sent raiding? Why was the whole garrison just sitting here while everyone starved?

Instead, I walked fast to catch up with a kitchen slave who was just crossing the shady part of the courtyard with a basket of eggs. They were steaming, so they must just have been hard-boiled. The Palace sits on hot springs, and in the kitchens, they used big troughs to boil hundreds of eggs at a time in the hotter pools. "Pardon me," I said quietly. "But if I were to owe you a debt, Sown knight to a good lady, would you mind pretending to faint and letting everyone steal a few eggs?"

"Can I have a lock of your hair?" she said, worryingly instantly.

I cut off a twist of my hair, tied it in a knot, and gave it to her. "Do I want to know why?"

She laughed. "I'll give it to my husband. He's obsessed with you. If I ever go a week without hearing the story about Phaidros Heliades and Princess Andromache, I'll die happy."

"Right," I creaked, hoping that her husband wasn't a lie-in-wait-in-a-hedge type.

She walked another twenty yards or so and then fainted, amazingly realistically.

There was a charged pause, and then everyone close by snatched a couple of eggs each and melted into the cloisters, and within seconds all the eggs were gone. I made a show of helping her up, wrote on the wax stock tablet and signed it with my seal bead (EGGS STOLEN BY JASON POLY-DORIADES, APOLOGIES, SIGN. POL. PH. HELIADES), and escaped with a stolen egg of my own. Around the cloister, the little knights were bartering excitedly with each other for eggs as if it were a feast day.

For a second it was funny and I felt pleased and then, like always, immediately sad because I had no one to tell except the Nothing that had used to be Helios; and then I realized it was the worst thing I'd ever seen.

I hadn't made my offering to Herakles yet—I'd meant to give him the egg, so that one of the little knights could steal it later—but I stopped beside the marvel and stood there staring at it, wondering what I even thought I was doing.

I'd never prayed to the god from the ship. I didn't know his name, so I didn't know which altar to try, but even if I had, I'd never prayed *for* anything to any god: I made sacrifices in the way I paid taxes. Gods are like queens. You pay what you owe and in return they don't notice you.

But if a bad day was going to be watching the little knights die on a raid in Athens, and a good day was finding an egg, then I didn't want to hide beneath his notice any more.

He had been my guest all those years ago. I should have died defending him. All this, everything after, it was just one long wrong turn. If he would come back—then at least I could give him the revenge he was owed. I could die doing something decent, like I should have on the ship, and maybe he might even feel better for it.

I'd know he was all right.

I crossed the courtyard, past Herakles, through the officers' mess, to the shrine for Apollo just beyond. The shrine was a beautiful place, an altar under an archway all filigreed in silver, and a bell above so the god would hear you. The priest, dressed in indigo like all the Apollo acolytes, was tending the altar fire, feeding it the bones of something small to keep the sacrifice going.

"Sir," I said, not sure how to phrase what I wanted to say. "I'd like to make a sacrifice, but I don't know the name of the god. What do you do, when you don't know?"

Despite the heat and his heavy robes, he didn't look annoyed. I'd always liked priests of Apollo. They were so calm it was catching: you always feel better if you sit with one of them for a while. "Why don't you know, knight?"

"I met him once but he didn't say his name."

"How did you know he was a god?"

I'd never told anyone what had happened. Partly it was because saying it aloud would have made me sound insane and everyone would think I'd drunk seawater, but only partly. The bigger reason was that the memory of the ship turning was all I had of the boy on the shore. It was precious and I couldn't just hand it over to anyone who asked for it.

"He was."

"Well, Apollo will know," the priest said reasonably.

I gave him the egg, and he smiled. He must have been tired of killing animals on the altar. It was sticky work.

"What prayer would you like to make?"

"I can write," I said.

"Of course," he said, and showed me the slips of prayer papyrus and the ink. Tactfully, he drifted away to water the god's holy tree, an ancient olive that must have been old when Herakles was born.

Slowly, and carefully, because papyrus is only for holy things and the ink was worth more than I was, I wrote down the prayer. It wasn't really a prayer.

I hope you come soon. Then I hesitated, because you have to say your name, but it felt strange to write my name on something a god would read. *Phaidros from the ship.*

I waited for the ink to dry, then held the papyrus slip in the fire. The flame caught and the paper burned fast, and the smoke rose up into the sky like a distress signal.

7

The black banners of the House of Kadmus snapped above the parade ground as the garrison formed up into its units. I herded the young ones into their ranks at the front, reminding them to do ordinary things they would have done without thinking if they hadn't been tired already: straighten cloak pins, buckle greaves up properly, tie their hair up again if they'd pulled it loose when they came home earlier. The hot wind rippled our cloaks and zithered dust across the open space in front of us.

The Bull Ceremony was a last resort. To sacrifice one bull is a significant thing—they were from the Queen's own herd, the bulls, and each one was worth more than my house. We were about to sacrifice twelve, to all twelve of the gods, because we still didn't know which one we had offended, and which had made the drought. Anyone who was anything to do with the Kadmeia would witness it—knights, Guards, civil servants—along with a thousand citizens in the public stands. It was a desperate, once in a generation ceremony, one I hoped I'd never see again. If it didn't rain after this, then there was nothing left to do but raid.

Up on the balcony of the Palace's royal apartments stood the Queen, the prince, and some tall people in vivid white who might have been Egyptian, all beneath a beautiful moss-green canopy. I kept my eyes on the ground so I wouldn't stare at the Queen. I could almost remember what Helios looked like, if I watched her for long enough. But knights can't go around staring at the Queen.

In the public stands, people had brought scraps of cloth to dip into the blood of the bulls who would be sacrificed today. It was lucky, although probably not lucky enough. It hadn't rained now for ninety-seven days.

The order came for the serving units to march. We would just be watching; the little knights had taken their oath, but they wouldn't be full members of the garrison until they had been in battle.

Ahead of us, the priestesses from the Temple of Athena were dancing the Bull Dance. I'd heard it was so difficult that it took them ten years to learn. Each step had to be a particular distance, each finger had to stay at a particular angle; it was military precision. It was slow, in time with the drums, but I didn't envy them at all. Even our full-armour drills were probably less wearying. At least you did that fast and then it was over. At least you didn't have to hold your arm at an *exact* forty-five-degree angle above your head for half an hour.

The Hymn to Apollo rolled out across the parade. It's the anthem of Thebes.

Holy archer, lord of marvels
Bless this day and all who call you here.

Drums the size of humans were keeping the rhythm, marching pace. It was beautiful, the sterile and rigid order of it. There's joy in perfect unity.

But a little part of me, the part of me that had loved seeing the hull of the ship turn back into trees even though I'd been drowning when I saw it, thought: *There's something dead about all this. Maybe the drought has gone on so long because the gods don't know we're still alive.*

As I was scanning the young knights and helping with the last few buckles and pins, there was an interested stir and gazes started slipping past my shoulders, and I looked round and went heavily down on one knee, because the prince was right behind me. Kneeling burned, because my greaves had already heated up. Behind me, the rest of the unit did the same with a thunk of armour.

The prince's name was Pentheus. It means "sorrow." The gods like to take away children whose parents brag, so Theban tradition is to give them sad names by way of saying nobody was very happy at all, nothing to see here, smite some other bastard in Athens, thank you. But the name suited the boy. He was slight, with a painfully stiff bearing and too many lines

THE HYMN TO DIONYSUS

on his face for the age he was. He was perhaps eighteen, but it was a glassy, spidery eighteen; some of the youngest girls behind me were broader and stronger.

When he put his hands down to take mine and lever me upright again, they were so fragile I was scared to close my fingers over them. I stared at the hem of his red ceremony robe, floor length, so I wouldn't stare at him. Because knights *have* to look at the floor, Theban hems are often worth looking at. His had a ribbon of glorious Hatti embroidery on it—maybe it was an illustration of a story—and the tiny figures there were wearing armour stitched in gold and silver. It was subtle, but it glinted.

"You're Phaidros Heliades?" he asked, and my skeleton went tight, because usually when someone asks me that, it's because they're checking they're not about to stab an innocent person who happens to look like me.

"Yes, lord."

"You were sworn to my uncle."

I was struggling to hear him over the drums, which I could feel through the ground as much as through the air. "Yes, lord."

He nodded once. He didn't move like someone his age. He went slowly, marvel precise. The weight of the crown was heavy, even though he wasn't wearing it yet. "Would you mind if I stood with you to watch this?"

"Please," I said, wondering what was happening now. Princes don't pay attention to unmarried polemarchs of young regiments.

"The Queen is arranging for me to marry an Egyptian," he said, from nothing.

I tried to fit the ideas together and struggled. I'd never heard of it before. Egyptian ladies do not leave Egypt. If you die away from Egypt, your soul gets lost; when your chance of dying in childbirth is one in five, the odds are unattractive for most people.

"Are you going to Memphis?" I said at last. That was the only possible way for him to be on the same continent as his future wife, even though as far as I knew, there had never been a Theban king in waiting who didn't live in Thebes.

He nodded.

"Why?" I said, because I couldn't imagine an African lady being at all interested in marrying the prince of what, to her, would seem like a shack at the end of the world. There were Egyptian shepherds with more land

and more wealth than Pentheus would inherit even when he was king. There was more money, more influence, more culture at the court of the Pharaoh than there was in all the separate cities of Achaea put together, to the tenth power. The whole earth turns around Memphis.

Ahead of us, the drums rolled on, and the priestesses danced, and the hymn stretched up for the bronze sky, where the sun was rising. I looked up, thinking about my futile little prayer burning on Apollo's altar, and wondered if he'd heard, or cared. God of the sun, and god of the wolf: it was hard to imagine that he would ever pass on messages from a broken knight who had burned his altars at Troy.

"The Queen says it will be to our advantage to have some presence at court in Memphis."

It wouldn't. Nobody would involve him in anything. It would be the same as our queen consulting a swamp person fresh from his mud hut on the Tin Isles. "And . . . what do you say, lord?"

"I say she's getting rid of me so she can start again and get a better heir, hoping I die conveniently of marsh fever en route." He kept his tone entirely neutral, like any young Sown person should do, but it was strained.

"Nile's very clean, probably no joy there."

He smiled, a very tiny smile, but still a smile. He looked up at me properly for the first time. "I don't want to go," he said.

"We all go where we're sent, lord; obedience is strength," I said.

The sun was just lifting over the city wall, drawing a clear bright line across my shield, and everyone else's.

At the far gate, some stable hands were leading out the bulls for the sacrifice, very carefully. Bulls in other countries are sometimes about the height of a person. Not ours. They're aurochs; they are to those smaller bulls what Herakles is to me. Their horns are as long as my arms or more, and standing straight, I would perhaps reach the shoulder of a slighter one. These were white and gold, beautiful things, and allowed to roam mainly wild in the royal fields, bred to be the best sacrifice for the gods they could possibly be. I felt tired, more than before. The animals were so lovely, and all of Thebes had been burning sacrifices for weeks. The smoke from the fires was hazing above the ground right now. Maybe it was blasphemy to think so, but I couldn't imagine that twelve more would make any difference.

The part of me that had used to work overseeing rations in the camp outside Troy said, *At least the sacrifices mean people are getting some food.* The gods want the burnt bones of a sacrifice—people have the meat. The Queen was making this sacrifice not just to appease whichever gods were angry with us, but to feed the crowd and stave off starvation. Twelve bulls go a long way.

Pentheus stared unwavering across the parade ground. "What I want is irrelevant. I know, the Queen says so too. It's noteworthy, though, how she always ends up with what *she* wants."

A significant part of me was annoyed to hear him scratch at his responsibilities even that much, particularly while he was surrounded by knights younger than he was whose duties were far harder than his. "Duty is the price we pay for being rich, free, and well thought of all at the same time," I said, because there was nothing else to say.

"But why does it have to be like that?"

I watched him for a second. "Because people as powerful as you, who go through life thinking they have a god-given right to do whatever they want, do not make good kings."

"I don't think I can do whatever I want, but I've never even been away from Thebes. I can't go to Egypt."

Everyone has a turn of phrase that sends them instantly from nought to homicidal. Helios had hated people who said *apparently*. Although he had been far too restrained to punch anyone over a meeting table, there had been a general who he had called Apparently Megara with the kind of raw loathing most people save for leeches.

My nought-to-homicidal thing was, *I can't {insert possible but inconvenient thing here}.*

"You won't asphyxiate the second you see the Nile," I said. I was impressed with myself that I held back from saying, *Well, when I was your age, a crocodile on the Nile once snatched me off the ship, everyone took the piss for months, and there are still people in the garrison who call me Delicious Phaidros: would you like to see the giant scar and then whinge about being married to a fine lady?*

"Why aren't you married?" he asked abruptly, with a spark of irritation. "You must be thirty now, you're breaking the law."

"I punch people who make me jump," I said, hoping he would make me jump.

"There's no exemption."

"What's happening now?" I asked slowly, aware that some of the young knights around us were listening hard.

"Everyone's so fond of telling me that what anybody wants doesn't matter, but I do feel that many of those people might perhaps need reminding what it is to actually have to do something you fear."

Telling a prince what you think of him is an efficient method of suicide, but on balance, execution was less inglorious than being bullied by an insectile boy with no sense of duty. "Have you considered that perhaps the Queen is sending you away because you're a whiny little prick and nobody likes you?"

He stared at me and I had a sharp sense it was the first time anyone had ever said anything like that to him. "You can't say that."

"Off you fuck," I suggested, and thought, *Well, Phaidros, this is it. Probably just as well, it's embarrassing to have survived this long.*

And no boy with blue eyes was coming. Of course he wasn't. Apollo doesn't pass on messages, and gods don't come when you call, even for revenge. His revenge was going to be to let me drag on and on like this. Watching my knights fight over eggs, listening to someone who would be king whine about the lightest duty, while the rations shrank and shrank.

"You were sworn to my uncle!" Pentheus burst out, voice cracking. Suddenly he seemed very small, and lonely. "I just—I thought . . ." He looked away. He was about to cry. "You could speak to the Queen."

I sighed. It wasn't his fault that he was irritating. Royal heirs are never sent to the legions. It would be idiocy. It was why Helios had served but the Queen hadn't. One in three knights die before they're eighteen. Half never make it past twenty-five. Of course he now imagined that he was having a dreadful time in the Palace surrounded by people who did everything for him. He had no idea what dreadful was. Everyone had worked hard to make sure he didn't.

"I met the Queen once," I said, more softly, "when I was a child. Nothing I say would matter." I paused, because he was still Helios's nephew, and I owed him what I could give, which was the advice Helios had always given me. "What *you* say will matter. Negotiate. Be Persephone. If you see Death coming, say, *Fantastic, you're coming with me, and I'm Queen.*"

He didn't laugh, only tilted his head, letting it move through his gears, expressionless. "I don't think I can," he said. "I don't know how."

I still had a primal urge to slap him and tell him to pull himself together, but that isn't how humans work. The way you make a nervy mess of a boy into a someone useful is: you snatch him up in the corridor and pretend to steal him sometimes; you go and find him if he's quiet and you make sure he gets some cake; you play Surprise Badger; and you let him get away with keeping a sacrifice lamb if he does big eyes at you and promises it will be a wonderfully house-trained lamb by the end of the week.

Nobody was going to do any of those things. He was too important.

"Try," I said. "The worst she can do is shout at you."

He gave me a doubtful look.

"Or drop you down a well," I admitted.

"Pardon me if I don't follow your advice," he said gravely. "Only I get the feeling you'd enjoy seeing her drop me down a—"

There was a roar from the crowd.

People were pointing at the sky.

Something was there, a ball of fire and smoke screaming right at the city. For an irrational second, I thought we were under siege and it was something hurled out of a trebuchet, but there was nothing on the arid plain below us. Smoke tore across the dawn, and when I followed the arc, I could see exactly where it was going to land. Right in front of us.

They must have stopped the drums, they must have, but in my head I could still hear them, only it wasn't the steady march of Apollo's hymn any more. They were racing—running, then sprinting, and then faster and faster, and it wasn't like any hymn any more, and if someone had told me that an army of the gods was riding to war I would have believed it.

The thing in the sky howled down and smashed into the parade ground.

I don't know if you've ever seen a ship wreck: when the mast falls and the hull breaks, the water roars up higher than any palace, and you can see Poseidon raging in it. Whatever blasted into the ground then, it made the earth rise like the water would have, like it was nothing. Right along the lines, knights yelled and pulled their shields up overhead. I wrenched mine above me and Pentheus, dragging him with me onto the ground. In the stands, people dove for cover under the seats. I couldn't see the Palace balcony any more. It was lost in the dust long after the burning earth had fallen down again.

Gradually, the dust clouds started to clear. I stood up and gripped Pentheus's arm while I looked him over, but he seemed all right. So did the little knights. Shields came down and tipped dust and fragments of rock onto the ground. Up ahead of us, the priestesses were standing up too, grey. People in the public stands began to ease out from under the seats. The canopy that had been keeping the sun off them was on fire, shedding burning particles over the wall.

Only about fifty feet from us, there was a crater. It was glowing.

I could see the little knights asking each other things, and trying to ask me, but I couldn't hear. I held my hand out to tell them to stay back for another few seconds. Along with some of the other older knights, I slid my shield back onto my arm and climbed over the rubble to the edge of the scar in the earth. The heat was so strong I could barely face into it.

Glass boiled at the base of the crater. Some patches were still white-hot, some making an unearthly crackling noise as it cooled and splintered and broke straightaway.

Leading from the centre out to the edge, quite close to me, there were shapes pressed into it. It was difficult to see properly through the heat, which hazed and writhed, but they were clear enough all the same.

Footprints.

They were only there for a few seconds. Then the glass cooled; the surface dulled, then cracked; and the prints were lost as shards of it shattered and burst.

The most incredible bubble of hope-dread rose in my chest. I'd prayed to the boy from the shore to come, and what if he really had, what if he was here? I'd die in a few seconds, but that didn't matter. I'd see him again. I might even have time to tell him I was sorry. And then, well, Helios had said he would wait for me in Hades, without crossing the river.

Helios said a lot of things, so I wasn't too sure he'd meant it, but maybe he had. Maybe I was about to see my whole family again in the space of the next minute.

I looked around, desperate for someone else to say, *Gods alive, did you see that, someone* walked *out of that*, or maybe even to see a pair of blue eyes I knew from long ago.

I didn't find either of those, and instead, I almost jumped away from my own bones, because right beside me was one of the aurochs, fully twice my size. Its eyes were starry in the light of the molten glass. As if it were worried it had startled me, it bumped its nose very gently against my chest. My shoulders fitted between its horns.

"Help," I said, very quiet. They weren't tame, the bulls. I was lost in the smoke; nobody could see me. Everyone else was talking and theorising, and I couldn't make out any individual words over that hellish cracking of the glass. The bull snorted. Its breath fogged my breastplate. It was twitchy: it didn't like the noise either.

Someone touched my shoulder.

I turned my head just enough to see a tall figure in a black veil. His hand on me was tattooed dark red to his knuckles, like he had dipped his fingers in blood. He didn't say anything, because it would have spooked the bull, but he didn't need to. I let my breath out. A witch.

As if it wasn't a wild monster which could have ground him into mince, he stroked the bull's head and touched its nose to steer it to the side, away from me. When the wind caught the veil, it outlined the side of his face and I thought he might have been about my age, but that was all I could see of him.

The bull looked pleased with him and bumped his shoulder companionably. I thought he was laughing. As soon as its horns were away from me, I backed away from the edge of the crater, my hand on my sword in case he needed help, but he didn't. He must have called to them somehow, because the other bulls were thumping across to him too, shaking the ground. Around us, other people were phantoms in the smoke and the dust, and to me, there was a kind of background roar-shush that was made of people shouting and talking and wondering. Three bulls; four; ten. They dwarfed the witch, but he still didn't seem afraid, and they were still all behaving like happy lambs, snuffing at him and nudging him, but careful of their horns. As the last two came across, he led them away.

"Did you see that?" Pentheus exclaimed, suddenly right next to me. "He just took them away like it was nothing!" He sounded more impressed by that than the crater.

"There were footprints in the glass," I said, not loudly enough.

I caught a few snatches of the voices around us. People were talking about falling stars and signs from the gods, though nobody seemed to be agreeing about what the sign meant. The Queen's prophet had come down from the royal balcony to stand on the edge of the crater, scrying in the molten glass.

"There were what?"

What was he supposed to do about it even if there were? Start a hunt through the crowd for whoever was—what, on fire? Nobody was.

When they have dealings with people, gods look like people. Gods can even look like specific people. Helios swore he once had an entire conversation with me, even though I'd actually been—unbeknownst to him—on a scouting mission at the time. He hadn't just spoken to someone who sounded like me through the tent wall. I had been in front of him: my armour, my scar, everything. I would have thought he was just winding me up if he hadn't been openly disturbed by it. *Something* had been there.

Someone in this crowd, maybe even someone I knew, wasn't a human being at all. I stared around, not even knowing what I was looking for, except maybe—the bubble of hope was still there but shrinking—for someone who was looking for me.

"Where's the prince?"

A Guard was right next to me, trying to make me hear.

Pentheus was running after the witch, little-boy buoyant to see real magic. Just as he started to fade into the smoke I saw him catch up. He looped his arm through the witch's, and then laughed when the witch took his hand and put it on the forehead of one of the bulls.

We have a word, *deinos*. It means "terrible" and "amazing" at the same time—it's one of those inside-out words that means two things which should be opposites. It's a word for horrifying miracles, and beautiful cataclysms, and gods. There was something deinos about the witch too:

enough that I found myself staring hard at the ground where he had walked, in case his steps were burned into the sand.

They weren't. Of course they weren't.

He did look back, though. I couldn't tell through the veil, but I had an uneasy feeling he was looking straight at me. Just for a moment, he was entirely still, a tall black spectre beside the prince and shaded by the Queen's holy bulls against the pounding heat of the glass and the furnace dawn. Then the wind shifted, and they all disappeared into the smoke.

Nobody came to look for me, and there was no flash of blue eyes.

8

Nothing happened, and nothing happened. The crowds started to move away from the smoke, some carrying shards of glass from the crater in case those would bring luck. Slaves came out to start clearing the rubble from the torn-up flagstones, coughing and ash-stained. The prophets clustered together, consulting about what to do, and what it meant, and whether we should still sacrifice the bulls. Feeling like I was caught in the fall between someone kicking my ankle out and hitting the ground, all I could do was herd together the little knights to count them—all present: even Jason, unfortunately, had failed to vaporise—and start seeing them back to the garrison. The more time went by, the more certain I was that I'd tricked myself into seeing those prints in the glass, and the more I felt like an idiot for hoping. Of course there was no god coming.

In among streams of other knights, we reached the training yards as if it were any other morning. There was an excitable buzz through everyone, but it dimmed gradually as different polemarchs herded their units away to training, and the ordinary rhythm of the morning seemed like it was going to start uninterrupted.

It wasn't until we were in our yard and the little knights were fetching their training shields that I heard it.

Someone was singing.

Everywhere is different. In some places, people will tear someone apart for touching a shrine, or taking a god's name in vain. In others, it happens because they slept with the wrong sort of person, or because they preached the wrong kind of politics from their box in the marketplace. It's always different, and to everyone from outside, the one thing that drives people to murder looks bizarre, but every city in the world has its forbidden thing, and everyone reacts in the same way when they see it. Everyone feels deep-down repulsed, and everyone feels the overpowering need to just make it stop, even if you have to hit someone with a brick.

Ours is blasphemous music. We have twelve songs. One for each of the gods. We have sung them for a thousand years, and we will sing them for a thousand more, to remember those who sang them before us. We don't change them: we keep those songs in the same way other cities keep their temples, without tearing them down and building new ones every second hour. Any other music is unholy. It doesn't come inside the city walls. I'd never heard it in Thebes. Even when I heard it outside Thebes, it made me itchy and angry.

And now, someone was singing.

Sing, sing to the lord of the dance . . .

Sometimes, because I was going deaf, I heard things. A kind priest told me once that the less you can hear of the world, the more you can hear of the gods, but I'm not that special and it was never that. It was my clock-work trying to make shapes it knew from the scraps of information it could hear, and often those shapes were completely wrong. I once heard a marvel of Hermes in the market tell me not to forget the cheese. I went still now, watching the little knights. There was something between shock and aversion etched on their faces, which probably mirrored mine. So it was real.

It was Amphitrion.

He was staring into space. His sister was shaking his shoulder, her gauntlet clinking against his breastplate, but he didn't seem to feel it. I got in front of him and held his shoulders to see into his face. His eyes were miles away.

He still didn't see me. He turned away from me, I thought towards his sister, the leather underplating of his armour creaking, but then he kept turning; halfway round, all the way, and then again, spinning slowly between me and his sister, who was normally so steady she would have taken the sky falling in with perfect knightly equanimity, but she looked scared now.

"Knight," I said, quietly. "You need to stop. Now."
"*Sing, sing to the lord of dance,*
Thunder-wrought and city-razing—"
"Stop. Amphitrion—"
"*—king, king of the holy raging—*"
Jason smacked him experimentally over the head. "Hey. Shut *up*."
Amphitrion didn't notice.

"I'm going to get him away," I said, urgency leaning a boot right into my breastbone. If the Guards heard him, he would be arrested and flogged. "Jason, run over to the Ninth Unit, tell his commander *quietly* that I've taken Amphitrion to Ares. Everyone else, wait here."

Amphitrion let me steer him out through the main courtyard, past the marvel Herakles, and down the long steep stairs towards the lower city, to the white towers of the Temple of Ares. I should have kept one hand on him to make sure he kept going in the right direction, but I couldn't bring myself to touch him that much. I felt like I was escorting someone with plague.

Ares is where knights go to recover from injuries and battle madness; or to die from them. The sanctuary is quiet, the priests are all veterans, and they make sure nobody fragile visits. I had no idea what Amphitrion's song was, but it had to be some kind of madness, because he wasn't suicidal.

I could smell the incense forty paces away, and from somewhere inside, a column of smoke climbed into the baking sky. Amphitrion was still singing. If I let him stand still, he turned and turned, dancing, just slowly, but there was something horrible about the slither of moving mail. Heat blasted off the flagstones and rippled so much it looked as though we were walking through clear water.

I eased him under the archway and into the temple gardens, where a marvel of Ares turned his head to watch us come in. I had to look down, the glare off the bronze too bright. Amphitrion seemed not to notice. He had looped back to the beginning of his song. *Sing, sing to the lord of the dance . . .*

"I need help," I said to the priests coming towards us. "I don't know what happened. We were at the bull sacrifice when the star fell, and now he can't stop singing."

As I said it, I heard how strange it sounded, but the priests only glanced at each other, unsurprised. "Thank you, knight. We'll take him from here. He can go in with the others."

"Others?" I repeated, to make sure I hadn't remember-the-cheese hallucinated.

I hadn't.

There were five others. They were together in a cool underground room that must have been used usually for storage, with only a high thin window to let in the light. Now, though, there were pallet beds set up neat and careful, and a table with a water pitcher, and a priest watching in the corner—and five knights spaced out across the floor, turning in the same slow dance as Amphitrion, and singing.

They were all singing different parts of it, but even I could hear it was the same song.

I looked at the priest who had brought us down.

He shrugged slightly. "They've been coming in for the last hour. The Guards have been in and out, but there have been no convictions. It's obviously madness."

Sing, sing to the lord of the dance,
Lightning-born and madness-bearing,
Bring, bring to him wine and ivy . . .

It echoed in the cool brick cellar, so that it sounded like there were a lot more voices than those five.

"What *is* that?" I asked. I wanted to scratch my skin off. "Where did they get it from?"

"We don't know what it is," he said, too gently, and I made an effort to hold myself still. A knight turning twitchy is not something anyone wants to see, even a priest of Ares. "But these two, and your lad, were on the parade ground when the star fell. If it was a star."

"The star did it," I echoed. Maybe there had been prints in the glass, maybe there *was* a god, just not the one I'd thought.

"Seems so," he said, infuriatingly delicately.

"And the other three, who weren't at the parade?"

"The first two spoke to them just after."

I stared at them. Turning, turning. They started a new verse one after the next in an eerie chain—*sing sing sing sing sing*—and I had a weird sense that it wasn't random. "It's *infectious*?"

"Some kinds of madness are." He took a deeper breath, probably getting ready to say something else vague and unhelpful, so I cut him off.

"So some people saw a star or a god come down, and now they're virulently and identically mad," I said. "Is that what you're saying?"

He looked uncomfortable to have it laid out in a straight line. "If you like."

"Of course I don't fucking like. Can you say what you mean, please?"

"I mean," he said, lowering his voice so much I could barely hear him, "the Queen does *not* take kindly to rumours of gods coming to Thebes."

"Not really the Queen's choice whether they do or not, is it?"

Something like understanding broke across his face. "When did you come back from Troy?"

"Six months ago."

"You don't know, then. Every so often, someone declares himself to be the lost prince, the son of Zeus, and the Queen—well, the Queen makes short work of him," he said. His eyes darted to either side as though he were genuinely worried someone might be listening. "I'd be very careful too, if I were you. People have been killed for repeating rumours. Now come on, I don't want you exposed longer than you have to be."

I meant to go, but then I stopped, because I knew the words.

I couldn't have said how, or where from. But they were there, in my head, like I was remembering something from a long, long time ago— the way you remember things that were drummed into you when you were tiny, and the recollection of who by or why is gone.

Sing, sing to the lord of the dance,
Revel-bright and border-breaking
Ring, ring the bells . . .

I wanted to sing it too. Part of me said: *You'll feel so much better if you sing it.*

It felt exactly like that urge to jump when you're on the edge of a cliff.

The priest got me by the arm and tugged me to the stairs. "I don't want you to take this the wrong way, but given that it does seem to be infectious, I'm going to recommend that you *don't* visit again."

Maybe it was too late. Maybe I had it already, whatever it was. Maybe in an hour I'd start singing.

9

Knights train for four hours a day. It doesn't matter if you're tired and stars or gods are falling out of the sky and someone's gone mad. It's four hours a day, every day, unless you go into battle.

The young knights were learning how to turn as a unit. It's difficult. If you're marching straight, but then the order comes to form a shield wall on the right, everyone has to swing their shield right, not knock out the person next to them, and come to terms with the idea that they aren't where they thought in the battle order. The person who *was* ten ranks back on the right side is now in the middle of the front line. Today, they were practising it again and again, and after ten tries, I jumbled them all up so that nobody was ever in the same position for long.

"Come on, again," I said, as shields clattered and tangled, again.

"Sir, we're just so tired," Jason tried. "And that *thing* in the parade ground . . ."

There was an unhappy agreeing murmur from the others.

I let my shield thunk down. "All right. Tell me what you're worried it was."

"A sign from Apollo," Amphitrion's sister said, sounding dull and strange. "He's angry with us."

"Stars fall sometimes," Jason said, with a good effort at knightly unconcern only slightly ruined by the worried crack in his voice. I was glad see to some things did worry him. "My commander says they're just rocks."

"It was Zeus punishing us," someone else said. "The drought's happening because the lost prince is supposed to be on the throne and it won't break until he is."

"It was an actual god, who came down from Olympus. They can look like people, what if someone in the crowd . . . ?"

Footsteps in the glass. There had been footsteps.

"What if it was him, what if it was the lost prince?"

I put my hands up to say quiet, because they were all talking at once and I couldn't hear anything. Lately I couldn't hear, I'd started to use signs, unconsciously at first, but we were developing a kind of code now. They knew my signs for form up, turn, thank you, put that down, where the fuck is Jason.

I looked between them all once they were quiet. "All right. Lots of ideas. It could be any of those. It could be none of them. All of us: we're much too stupid to know. That's what the royal prophet is for. Until Tiresias tells us what it means, it means nothing. We have our own duty. Which is?"

"To train no matter what," someone mumbled.

"Wrong," I said, "it's to fuck up the fucking Athenians. Which," I added, motioning at the corpse of the dead pomegranate tree at the gate, almost mummified from the drought, "we will shortly have the pleasure of doing."

They laughed, and there was a little cheer.

"Form up."

I picked up my shield again too and tried to take my own advice. It was true: there was no point guessing. It was easier said than done, though, and as I counted them through their steps and walked through the turn with them again, I couldn't stop thinking about those prints in the glass, and the smoke from my prayer going up into the sky.

Because I was expecting the Guards to come and interrogate me about Amphitrion, I kept watching the gates. No Guards materialised, though, and after an hour or so, I realized there were no more people moving between courtyards at all, even though it was about lunch time. Plenty of people came to eat in our yard and watch the knights train; it was a nice way to spend an hour. Nobody was here.

Just as I was wondering what was going on, two Guards closed the courtyard gates and stopped a slave going through.

Then an alarm gong rang, and a clear-voiced herald shouted that the Palace was in lockdown: everyone needed to stay exactly where they were.

Lockdown. What?

Maybe some important slaves had run.

Fuck, *another* Hidden ride in the space of twelve hours, if it was slaves. That was going to be unpleasant.

Wanting them to get some rest now if they did have to ride again soon, I called an end to the drill. The little knights broke ranks gratefully and made for the shade and the fountains. From the next courtyard, someone was shouting: I thought I recognised Amphitrion's commander's voice. He must have wanted to get to Ares. Someone was saying no.

The Guards opened the gate just enough to let a Palace scribe slip through. She was important: she was dressed in blue and silver, and she had that amazing, rounded gleam you can only get if you have enough food *and* you don't have to exercise all day; though there was ash in her hair. We all went quiet as she looked between us. Her eyes settled on me, running over the scar on my face.

"Are you Phaidros Heliades?" she asked.

Odd that a royal scribe had come to ask me about Amphitrion. That was well below her. "Yes."

"The Queen wants to see you."

The little knights all looked at me like kittens who had seen a ball of flax swing by.

"It's all right, I'll be back," I promised. My oath snagged as I said it. "I expect."

Nobody knows who built the Marvel Throne. Maybe King Kadmus himself, a thousand years ago, after he defeated the dragon and planted its teeth. But it is a miracle. Built into it, still gleaming even after a millennium, are two dragons. Beneath it somewhere is a hypocaust. The steam powers up and up, through the mechanism inside the throne, until the dragons breathe it into the throne room, masking everything in a weird haze. They move, too, the dragons, turning their heads, shifting their wings, sometimes retracting or baring their claws like lions do. Thebes is full of sacred machinery, but the throne is the nearest I think anyone in my lifetime and many after will ever be to the artifice of the gods.

I'd never been so close to it. The steam was everywhere, and to my surprise, it was cold—not steam, but vapour, somehow. I tried to see through it, worried I was close to the Queen, and I jumped when just up the steps, one of the great dragons slid its claws inward and folded its wings, as if it had decided I was safe. I had to stare at it, because there's a strange twofold thinking that happens when you're near holy devices. On one level, you know that people made them: there was a human smith, once. But on another, you know that that smith was guided by a god, and what you're seeing, what you're *really* seeing, is an echo of what Hephaestus could make for Zeus—a shadow of something divine.

Then there she was, Queen Agave, coming out of the haze, and all my insides twisted, because she could have been Helios's ghost. For all she could have afforded to clad herself in wonders from Africa, she dressed well but plain, her hair long like a knight's, even though married ladies—even widows—usually had it short. It made her look like a man from behind. I could only look at her in little snatches, so that she wouldn't burn onto my eyes.

"Pentheus spoke to you this morning," she said, without preamble. She sounded exactly like Helios, her voice strong from making herself heard over halls and crowds. Like mine, his had been light, but hers was low. If I'd closed my eyes, she could have been him. It was unearthly. A kind of sorrow-joy came up through the flagstones. "What about?"

"He mentioned his coming marriage, lady," I said from on my knee on the floor.

"Why you?"

"I was sworn to your brother." To either side of the throne, four Guards were watching me hard, the hems of their cloaks vivid purple on the stone floor. The dragons breathed vapour again. For the first time all year, my hands were cold. "The prince asked me if I would talk to you. I said I couldn't, since you don't know me."

She came down from the steps and took my elbows to guide me upright. She did it gently, as if she was worried about being careful of me, not anxious that I should be careful of her. She was much taller than I'd thought: my height. Taller than Helios had been. Of course she was. She had grown up in the plenty of the Palace. He had grown up in sieges. "I know you, knight. You came here once with Helios when you were little. We played in the fountain. You probably don't remember."

"No, I do, lady, I just thought you wouldn't."

She was quiet at first. I thought she would tell me why I was here—I suspected it was because Pentheus had complained about me, and she was about to tell me I needed to apologise to him before I was flogged or sent to be a galley slave. I got ready to say that time was, people had been encouraged to tell princes the truth. I had a distinct recollection of a polemarch years ago calling Helios an ungrateful little fuckwit. Helios had not had anyone flogged or enslaved. Helios had thought it was funny, because Helios was a real knight and not an unpleasant little weasel that just thought it was.

"Come and see where the star fell," she said.

She took me towards the open colonnade. The Guards followed, flinty. As we passed outside, everything had the fever brightness reflections do in a bronze shield, and the air shimmered. Away from that cold vapour from the marvel dragons, the heat rammed us. Ash wavered in streams above the flagstones. From the lower city, the columns of sacrifice smoke rose black and huge. It was what the architecture of Hades must have looked like. Everything smelled of burning bone.

Then we were in the courtyard, *the* courtyard, where we had played in the fountain with Helios, and Semele had been there with the baby and the King. I hadn't realized where it was: my memory of the Palace was a child's, everything all gigantic and inexplicable. It hadn't occurred to me it was even possible to find the same place again.

It was empty now, and overgrown with ivy, which was madly green and bright, in spite of the drought. There was a new shrine there, a marble statue of a woman holding a baby; everything else around it was ruined, the old columns still saw-toothed, the flagstones smashed. To the side of the shrine was a twisted mess of bronze that must once have been the Poseidon fountain.

Although Helios had told me the story a thousand times—or maybe because he had told it to me a thousand times—the wrecked courtyard looked unfamiliar. I couldn't remember the open end of it giving way to the balcony; I couldn't remember being able to see the parade ground from here, and even the colour of the stone seemed wrong.

With an uneasy shift, I wondered how much I really remembered, and how much I just thought I did.

We reached the balcony slowly. The sun was high over the plains now, and the light was that violent kind that hammers off armour and crowns. Anyone looking up from the lower city would probably be able to see us lit up here.

The crater, much bigger than I'd thought, was still steaming, though the glass in it was solid now, cracked in shards that had been forced upward into spikes. Some had formed into weird, person-sized loops. The whole parade ground was full of slaves shovelling up the blasted flagstones, loading them into wheelbarrows, sweeping up the dust, cleaning the public stands and the walls.

"Half the Palace thinks that was the Lost Prince coming down to take his crown," the Queen said. "Which is odd, because you'd think that if you could howl down from Olympus in a ball of fire, you could see your way to climbing up to the royal balcony and shoving me off it."

Ah. Maybe she had found out I was the one who had taken the baby, and then she was going to have me strapped to a table until I explained what I'd done with him. What a rubbish way to die.

Completely stupidly, I found myself scanning the people down by the crater in case one of them looked up and he had blue eyes. He wasn't coming, and this thing, the star, the whatever, wasn't him—it couldn't be or I'd be dead now—but I wanted him to be there all the same.

The more I lost my hearing, the more I could hear my own heart. It was loud now.

Where are you, where are you, where are you.

"I was trying to make you laugh but I'm worried I'm less witty than I think," the Queen reported frankly.

I breathed in deeper. No table with straps then. "I was thinking about how odd it is to hear people saying you're a god's aunt. Do gods have aunts?"

"I suppose they must do. Or perhaps the aunts tend not to survive the process. I'm sure if I could incinerate people at will, then family Harvest dinners would have looked different. Do you have aunts?"

That, I thought, was a real knife-edge joke, given that she *had* incinerated people.

Behind that, I thought: *She doesn't care if you have aunts. She's trying to hear you talk over more than a couple of monosyllables. This is an interview.*

Hm.

Even though the sensible thing would have been to grunt and pretend I'd been hit over the head too often to manage sentences any more, I couldn't. I could almost see Helios, standing here with her. It didn't matter about what she had done to her sister. This was dangerous, but dangerous with Helios's twin was much better than safe with the Nothing, and his old helmet sitting beside my bed, dull on the far side and bright on the nearer where I touched it every night and every morning.

Where are you, where are you, where are you.

Not coming.

"Not blood relatives, lady," I said. "But I had plenty of Helios's legion sisters." I paused. "I don't think I would have dared try to incinerate them. They were terrifying. They'd say, *Oh, Phaidros, how nice to see you, you haven't grown at all, bring Helios honour or we'll behead you behind the curing shed.*"

"Did you? Bring him honour."

I thought about it. "Briefly," I said, and waited to see if that was enough, and if she would decide to ask me whatever it was she had brought me here for, or send me away.

"What did you tell Pentheus to do?" the Queen asked me.

"Negotiate," I said, then glanced down, because I'd put my hands on the stone balcony rail and brushed something alive. Ivy, more ivy—growing up around the bannister, which was crazy, because even up here, everything was parched. I'd called him Ivy. He—no. Fuck's sake. Ivy is just ivy. It grows everywhere and it never dies. "With you, about the marriage."

"You told him to challenge me."

(Penalty for treason: twenty years of slavery.)

"Yes, lady," I said.

She smiled and lifted her eyebrows at the crater. Unlike Pentheus, she let all kinds of things skim over her expression, but I had clear feeling it was because she had such perfect control over her own face she could tell it to do whatever she wanted, whereas all he could do was keep it blank.

"No one can find him," she said.

I lifted my eyes properly for the first time, trying to search her for some sign I'd misheard, but I hadn't.

"You will not repeat that to anyone. Officially, the prince is well and cloistered at the Temple of Athena for a short while. Find him, please."

"Me," I said, confused. She would have people for secret things like this. She didn't need me.

"You. You're his uncle by oath." She lifted her hands, precise and slight and marvel-calibrated. "He went to you. He might come with you willingly when you find him."

Willingly. "You don't think he's been taken?"

"No, or we would have had a ransom demand and a trail of distressed slaves reporting being knocked out by now. I'm sure someone could successfully abduct him from the Palace, but not secretly. And significant timing too, don't you think, just when it's on his mind to escape his marriage and everyone was distracted by a fallen star?"

I did have to agree.

"He's hiding with someone. You will ask your questions quietly. If this spreads through the city, I will execute you." She was looking away from the courtyard now, over the lower city, and towards the Amber Gate and the road to the sea. I wanted to ask if we could go back inside. The heat was punishing; sweat was creeping down my back, sticking my tunic to the inside of my armour. She seemed not to feel it. "The Egyptians are here bringing grain, and in return, they'll take Pentheus. No Pentheus, no grain."

Finally I understood the marriage. It wasn't a real marriage. Pentheus was going to Egypt as a hostage.

"The Pharaoh is willing to disguise it as a marriage to save the dignity of a royal house," she added wryly, and I could imagine very well what the Pharaoh thought about Achaean royal houses. *Queen of what, was it? Oh. Yes. That's a lovely rock, with really excellent huts—temples?—I see, temples. And that's a wonderful . . . hat? Crown. Apologies. Of course.*

She finally turned back for the cloister. "Thank you, Sown. Speak to my chamberlain. She'll gather up Pentheus's slaves. He doesn't particularly have friends."

She stopped then, and looked at me for a long time, her eyes tracking over my armour, which was Helios's armour. It was beautiful; in the sun, the filigree Ares blazed across the chest, and the rubies that dripped from his shield shimmered. On the back, stark and silver against the bronze oxidised to look much darker than the ordinary tone, Persephone would be bright on the throne of the Unseen. It was armour made for a prince only a few breaths too young to be king. I tried to get ready to hear her ask for it back.

"I should have spoken to you before now," she said.

The way she was looking at me was the way Helios had on the evening he had finally agreed to swear his oath to me and let me fight on the front line with him, four whole years after the legion had expected him to do it.

Arranged marriages, which those battlefield unions are, sound like they should be straightforward. Ours never was. Helios was hammered out of old-fashioned chivalry, and he had always hated the age gap. In the old days, he said, commanders were only five years older than their wards, and young knights didn't even enter the army until they were twelve. Then, it made sense for them to swear to each other once the ward was fifteen. It wasn't an equal partnership—it wasn't meant to be, it was meant to control insane teenagers—but it wasn't ludicrously unequal. Ours, he insisted, was. Constant wars and emergencies meant the legion wasn't using the system properly any more. He was ten years older than me and I'd known him since I was tiny. That was sticky, at best. Saying I loved him didn't matter: his position was that I only thought I did, because I'd grown up with everyone around me insisting it was the right way to live. On my nineteenth birthday I'd cracked and snapped that that was patronising. He hid in the officers' mess for a month. At my end, a lot of crying and rebellious drinking with the Athenians ensued.

It wasn't until the Athenians said he must have sustained some kind of penetrating cranial injury and gone mad (what sort of man *wouldn't* tear like a hound after a handsome nineteen-year-old?) that I realized he had a point. You're never on the moral high ground if Athenians are agreeing with you.

So I went home at last and knelt in the cold sand outside his tent, where he was polishing his armour in the extremely silent way he had when he was upset, and said I'd stay off the front line until I found someone my own age to swear to if it meant he would be happy, and then he would be free of me. Listening to the Athenians had made me realize how trapped he probably felt. I wouldn't have wanted to be stuck in an arranged marriage to one of me: I was a mix between Feral Jason and a truffle pig.

When he came out, he had looked at me like he'd been expecting a child and found a man he didn't know.

The Queen might have been him, just then.

"Why?" I asked, trying not to let her hear the lump in my throat. "I'm no one."

"You're family." She smiled Helios's smile. "Go and find your nephew, Heliades."

10

The slaves were all frightened. They also had no idea what was going on. Some of them even said they needed to hurry because they would be late for the prince. I sat them down one by one, separate, and made sure the steward saw them away through another door so they couldn't talk to each other on the way out.

The scribe who monitored Pentheus's spending said nothing unusual had moved from his accounts. That seemed more ominous than a great haul of silver missing from the treasury. If he had been running away, he would surely have made some provision for himself. To just vanish, with nothing; it was possible, but I couldn't see that Pentheus would have known how.

Even though I asked upwards of twenty people, from personal attendants to tutors, none of them could think of anyone he knew well enough to run to. No older man at the garrison, no Sown lady with an estate outside the city walls—everyone laughed at that and said he was too young for women—nothing.

So I sent people out to the lower city brothels to check if there were any new additions. I could well imagine someone snatching a worried-looking boy dressed too nicely: they'd be delighted with the opportunity to ransom him if they thought he was from a Sown family, but if they realized he really was the prince, they could have sold him on to Sparta or Athens. He was definitively not sensible enough to lie about who he was.

In case the Queen was wrong and he had been taken somehow, I sent the Hidden. Not my unit, but Polydorus's, with the blessing of the general, who put it about that we would be doing daytime rides now too, since so many field slaves were risking the full heat of the day as a kind of cover.

"Have we found the witch he spoke to at the ceremony?" I asked finally, watching the black-armoured unit split up outside the city walls, fifteen or so knights each riding down the seven roads out of Thebes. The dust billowed in their wakes. "He could be the last person to have seen him."

"Nobody knows who he is," the Chamberlain said. "I've enquired already." She was chilly, and annoyed, I thought, that the Queen hadn't asked her to do this. She managed to project the suspicion that there was no witch, I'd made him up, witches were never men anyway, I was battle mad and unqualified, and *if* I wouldn't mind too terribly, would I perhaps bugger off to a temple to convalesce or die at my convenience?

"Sir?" someone said, and when I turned around, he pointed to the garrison. I thought he looked nervous. "A witch sent me to find you? He's waiting for you at the garrison."

I smiled at the Chamberlain. "Would you like to come?" I said, with evil in my heart.

"No," she said coolly. "And be polite to him. It will be administratively inconvenient if he turns you into something sticky."

Usually, you wouldn't just know if there was a witch in the barracks. You'd Know. Knights are superstitious and witches are lucky, and so generally, all the little knights would be asking for amethyst charms or well-meant-but-actually-quite-sinister spells to set on whoever they'd fallen in love with lately, and people would be bringing her things, and being uncharacteristically inarticulate because of nerves, and all in all, it would look like the Queen was visiting.

The witch who had saved me from the bulls was sitting alone at our Herakles fountain, unnoticed, in the shade of the dying pomegranate trees. People were walking past him—little knights, kitchen slaves, another polemarch—as if they had no idea he was there. It was like he had magnetised all his matter a certain way and now, to most people, from most angles, he was only fractionally more there than the shadows.

Even doing something ordinary, leaning over the water and holding the fountain edge like anyone else, he looked eerie. Maybe it was the red tattoos that cut off at his knuckles, as if he had dipped his hands in blood and not water, or maybe it was the fineness of that black veil, writhing in the hot wind, which he seemed not to feel; or maybe it was the black snake lying across his knees, watching me.

"Sir?" I said.

He looked back, but he didn't stand or bow. Witches don't bow to anyone. "Hello again." Slight accent, one I couldn't trace properly over two words. "Someone said you were looking for me."

It was odd to be recognised. He could only have seen me for a few seconds by the crater, in all that pouring smoke. "Yes. My name is Phaidros Heliades, I'm a polemarch here. I need to ask you some questions about the prince."

He was very still for a second. I wished witches would wear their veils like desert people did, showing their eyes. If you can see someone's eyes, you can see the whole human. Not witches, though.

"Yes," he said. He had one of those voices I could hear very well, even though he wasn't loud; it was low and strong, all smoke and embers, the kind of voice that could sing, or call over a battlefield. "After what he said, I'm not surprised."

"Would you mind telling me what that was?"

Whatever I'd expected, it wasn't what he said. "He asked me whether there is magic that could make someone forget everything."

I sat down beside him to make certain I was hearing properly. "Is there?"

He hesitated, long enough for me to wonder if I'd accidentally asked about something that was sacred or forbidden. "There is," he said eventually, "but it's brutal. I lied, I told him no."

I wondered if Pentheus had hoped to do something to the Queen. He was exactly the right kind of sulky little spider to resort to something terrible the second he didn't get what he wanted.

"What did he say then?"

"He left. But he might have had a different answer from another witch."

Or been kidnapped and sold to a foreign power. If he had stolen out to speak to an unscrupulous witch who'd recognised him, then he could be halfway to Sparta by now, drugged and chained in the back of a wagon. Maybe the Hidden really did have a chance of finding something.

They would have had a much better chance if the witch had said something an hour ago.

"Why didn't you report it straightaway?"

"You mean because the garrison is so reasonable and helpful, and so unlikely to imprison or murder people who interrupt at the wrong moment?" he asked, unflustered.

"Careful," I said, because I had to, though he was right.

He actually laughed. He had a laugh like a campfire in winter, smoky and welcoming. "You be careful."

I caught myself smiling and stopped, because even if it weren't unseemly for a knight, it was fairly horrible on me personally, given that half my face wasn't the way Apollo had made it.

"Well, thank you," I said, having one of those moments where I could hear, in contrast to his, my own accent. It was Sown, which is different from general Thebes: flatter than the full dialect you'd hear in the markets, because we sailed and we had to be understood everywhere. His was something I still couldn't place. It sounded—*old.* I couldn't trace why I thought that. "And thank you for what you did earlier, sir. I owe you my life." I held my hand out.

He tipped his head slowly, and I had an uncomfortable feeling that I was getting a long stare through the veil.

"Be careful of offering your life to a witch," he said. "You never know what we might do with it."

"It's all right, I'm hardly using it," I promised.

When he took my hand, a static shiver went up my arm. He was cool despite the sun. The tattoos on his fingers looked even stranger next to my skin. I wasn't sure, but I thought he was looking down at the difference too. The way he was holding his head now, the light was coming through the veil on one side, and I could see the shadow of his cheekbone. I looked away: seeing him without permission was a kind of trespassing. I tried to take my hand back, but he caught my wrist and looped something round it. Red string, the same red as his tattoos, with a silver charm on it in the shape of a bee.

"Do not," he said, "take that off."

"Why?" I asked, uneasy.

"So that if you stray, another witch will know who to return you to." He waited for me to look at him again. "No matter how far that might be."

It should have been sinister, but it wasn't. Instead I filled up with a strange of sort relief. What he was saying, really, was that if I vanished, he would look for me. I hadn't expected it to be such a good feeling, but it was, and so good that for a ridiculous second I thought I might cry. Mortified, I got up and bowed and said something about being busy. He stayed where he was, motionless except for the wind coiling ghost shapes in the veil. The wind gusted black sacrifice smoke between us and I half expected him to have vanished by the time it cleared, but he hadn't.

"Look after it, knight," he said after me.

"The charm?"

"Your life. It's mine now."

We didn't find anything: not in the brothels, with any other witches, nor on the road. By the time we had finished the search, the sun was setting. On the steep steps down from the High City to the low, the smoke was so dense that even in the blazing gold of the sunset, it was dark, and half the people going up and down were carrying lamps. The other half clapped when they reached corners, so people coming the other way could hear that someone was there. People were wearing cloth masks. I couldn't tell if that was just because of the smoke, or if it was because news about the madness had already spread beyond Ares.

I was going deaf, but I wasn't blind, and after I'd reached the lower city, I was sure: someone was following me. He wasn't making a particular secret of it. I didn't recognise him, but he was from the Guards—you didn't look that healthy otherwise. He saw me notice him and motioned for me to carry on my way. I didn't, and went back to him.

"Why?" I said, once I was close enough.

"You work for the Queen now," he said. "You can expect some scrutiny. On your way, Sown."

I bowed, and decided to take him on a lovely long walk to the night market for the honey I'd been meaning to buy all week. I was tired, but being able to spite an annoying person is an amazing source of energy.

A lot of traders were opening their shops at night now, because the day was too hot. Apollo Square was starry with their lamps, and full of people and steam from cooking stands. Normal traders weren't allowed to sell sacrifice meat, so I had a feeling that this had something to do with how there were suddenly no stray cats or dogs left in town. People were selling all kinds of things: the last of the olive crop, kittens, wax tablets, bolts of cloth, even ice from the mountain. It was chaotic and strange and sometimes you were chased by an angry goat.

The Nothing that used to be Helios came too. It had a weird alchemy. It didn't make bad things or annoying things any worse; but if I came across something that should have been good, or funny, the Nothing warped it. I didn't feel happy. I felt more lonely than I would have if there had been no good things, because I had no one to tell. The worst thing was festivals. I turned into a properly miserable prick at festivals.

It would have been better to just go home, but I wanted the honey, and I wanted to irritate the Guard. When I glanced back for him, I was pleased to see he was looking much more grumpy than he had earlier.

The honey seller knew me quite well now and asked me how I was while she rolled my ration bead onto a tablet smoothed over with warm wax, so she could use it as an invoice for the Palace, which would reimburse her from my account in equivalent goods. The print from the bead showed my name, as well as the sigil of my combat lineage, which was a tiny image of Persephone leading Hades by the hand, all etched mirrorwise onto the bead, which was about the length of the first joint of my forefinger. I still liked using it: you don't get one until you're eighteen, when you come off your commander's accounts, and it still made me feel important and grown-up, even though I was still half convinced I was only pretending about being grown-up. She put her seal over my tablet too, as a receipt. Behind the trader, in tall vases, were bundles of iron money, each spar as long as a javelin. Not for the first time I felt glad I didn't have to lug those around.

"So no luck yet?" she said.

Ever since I'd come home from Troy, I'd been trying to make the honey cakes Helios had used to hide on battlefields for me. I still couldn't do it. It was bothering me a lot more than it should have, because it wasn't really about the cakes. It was that I couldn't remember what he looked like any more. Taste makes you remember.

"Not yet. Are there different kinds of honey?" I asked. "He was using something . . . richer."

"Plenty of different types. Maybe it was something Hatti, if you were at Troy? I can see what I get from the port?"

"Yes please."

"I will investigate," she said solemnly, handing back my tablet and the new honey in its ceramic jar. Her eyes slipped past me towards the column of lights that was the High City. "Were you up there when the god fell? People are saying that anyone who saw it went mad."

"Six people who were close to it went mad," I said. I hesitated. "Just be careful about saying it's a god."

She laughed. "Of course it was a god! What do we think, lads: the business up in the High City, god or lump of rock?" she said more loudly to the stall-owners around us.

"God," they all chorused.

"See?" she said. "It's the lost prince come to put things right."

"Well. I'll see you soon," I said.

As I walked away, something made me look back. At the stall, the man who had been following me, and another who I hadn't known was with him, ghosted up to the honey seller, said nothing at all, and dragged her away. Everyone saw; studiously, everyone pretended not to have seen.

The way home was lined with people begging. Not the people you usually see begging; there were whole families, not ragged yet. As I passed by, not looking at the clay signs they were wearing, I caught a snatch of a song. A woman was dancing in a strange vacant way by the window, singing to herself. I had an instinctive surge of repulsion to hear that, and hear it inside the city from someone who should have known better, but under that, my real thoughts said: *She isn't choosing to do that.*

Just like you do if someone else yawns, I felt the hollow need to sing along with her opening up in the back of my throat. I clamped my teeth shut, disgusted.

Sing, sing to the lord of the dance . . .

Someone tapped my shoulder, and without any intervention from any part of my mind which might have said, *Hold on, it's probably just a flower seller,* my fist shot out, automatic as a broken marvel.

There was an awful crunch as I broke the man's nose. He screamed and collapsed. I put my hands over my face. People were giving me shocked looks, as if I'd chosen to do it. I wanted to yell that of course I fucking hadn't, any more than you choose to jerk your hand away from something that's burning you. But if it's your fist, it's your fault.

I bent to help him up. "I'm so sorry. Will you let me take you to a—"

"Get away from me!" he snapped, frightened.

I stepped right back from him.

He scrambled up and staggered away from me, and it wasn't until he was gone that I realized he had left something behind. It was a mask. I picked it up, meaning to go after him to give it back, but I'd already lost him in the throngs of people going home for the night. I looked down at the mask, wondering what to do with it. Maybe hand it in to the nearest bar, in case he came back for it. I turned it over in case there was a maker's mark on it, then stopped dead in the middle of the street. There was no maker's mark, but there was writing across the inside.

For Phaidros Heliades,
Regards,
Dionysus

11

Normal Sown households are big. I should have been living with Helios, his wife, and any of their children still too little for the legion; as well as my wife, our children, our wards, and maybe even her commander. Generally, you'd have men and women on separate sides of the house, because of how irritating men can be mistaken for vegetables. Polydorus had all of that. I was just me. So, instead of one of the tall townhouses on Copper Street, the Palace administrators had assigned me a strange place right on the edge of Thebes, halfway up the last hill before the mountain. Home was a house and an olive grove, and one crooked lemon tree that never made any lemons, on that wild land on the doorstep of the forest.

The house wasn't really a house. It was five or six habitable rooms on the edge of a great ruined maze. Nobody knew why it was here, but it was definitely a maze and not just a ruined prison or temple: some ways were dead ends, some curled around and around and then you came out only a few feet of the side of where you'd gone in. Here and there on the less-damaged walls, there were frescos in a style very different to the Theban one, and sudden dips where the land had crumbled and exposed the storeys below ground, of which there were at least three. Stand at the edge of my olive grove, among the roots, and look down: what you'll see is a lichen-eaten staircase, delving towards the sound of water.

I'd never explored it properly. Sometimes, some absconding cows got lost down there and I helped the farmers fish them out, but being down below ground made me feel uneasy before too long. It was cold down there, really cold, even though underground places are usually warm, and sometimes there were carvings on the walls that were so old I wasn't even sure people had made them. Whoever had built it, I couldn't help thinking they—maybe like Daedalus at Knossos—had wanted to trap something inside.

The dark was deep on the little path up to the maze by the time I walked it, which was why I had a lamp. But tonight there were torches burning on the verges, marking the curves of the path in a great string. I frowned over that, because my slaves would have set themselves on fire before they did anything that helpful. Very distantly, I started to hear music; drums, pipes. Maybe people laughing. I thought I was making imaginary patterns from the drone of the cicadas, but the further I went, the more distinct it was. Music. Not our music. Something else. I slowed down. I was so tired; too tired to be angry. I wanted to go home, eat something, burn the disconcerting mask, and collapse. I was deaf enough to sleep through it.

Someone was standing under an olive tree, watching me.

For a split second I thought there was something horrifying wrong with them, but it was a mask, not quite like the one I was still holding but not unlike either. This one was a weeping face.

They were just standing there, staring.

In the dark, I couldn't see any eyes beyond the mask; only that twisted expression moulded into the plaster.

"Hey," I snapped. "What are you doing?"

It was one of those moments that, although you understand, later, how it came to be, and you can see its clockwork and what gear moved what and how, is nonetheless—at the time—that particular type of unnerving that clenches all your insides up into a king rat.

The figure in the mask turned around, away from me I thought; and there was another mask. They had two faces.

The second one was wearing a manic grin.

I'd jolted right back before I understood that the sad mask was on the back of the person's head, and the grinning mask was across their face.

Then whoever it was laughed and ran away, down through the olive grove, straight under the house, into the tunnels.

"No, stop! You can't go down there, you'll get l—"

"Aren't you coming?" a voice floated back. "Dionysus invited you."

The laughter faded off into the labyrinth, where it was lost in the music.

I looked down at the mask in my hand, coming to terms with not sleeping for another hour. If this Dionysus was not only going to find out my name and have some poor bastard seek me out on the street to give me a creepy mask, but send people round to harass me until I turned up to whatever blasphemy was going on further along the maze, then I would turn up, and I would make him eat his fucking mask.

Once I was a little way along the path, towards the westernmost edge of the labyrinth where the music was coming from, I saw more torchlight. Voices rose over the music, laughing. Before long, I saw the people too, people in masks and dressed in bright colours, clacking wine cups together. The air was full of smoke and alcohol. And that unholy music, which sounded like nothing ever sanctioned in Thebes. It was wild, and loud, and disgusting.

I pressed my teeth together. The law about Sown knights and alcohol wasn't arbitrary. You do *not* want a bunch of professionally aggressive lunatics each with an armoury's worth of heavy weaponry to be drunk. We're bad enough sober. Even the smell of it was making me edgy.

Lamps like I'd never seen before glimmered everywhere. Mine were just ceramic things with a well for oil, but these were glass; colourless glass, bright glass, glass with images painted on it, glass faceted like a mosaic. They spilled coloured light in patches across tree boughs and threw it upward to make the leaves of grape vines purple or yellow, and there were grape vines everywhere. And ivy: it was rioting right up the trees, so dense that sometimes the shape of them was lost.

I had to turn around as I walked to take it in. It wasn't just that someone had decided this was a good place for a party. Someone was living here, growing things here, grapes and spices, and hibiscus flowers, and bright plants I couldn't even name. Even the moss that grew across the open ruins of the labyrinth was lush. It was impossible. The water it would all need had dried up months ago.

I brushed the shoulder of someone who looked more sober than other people. When she turned around, she wearing a mask too.

"Who started this?" I asked, and didn't add, *Don't mind me, I'll just stab him and be on my way.*

"What? You don't know Dionysus? Everyone knows Dionysus! He was here a second ago . . ."

"What does he look like?"

"He has a silver mask. You'll see. I heard he's from India."

I moved on, half looking for the man, half just trying to keep my bearings. The whole thing was like a fever dream. I'd walked through the ruins before, but I couldn't tell where I was now. In one of the labyrinth's old fountains, pristinely clean, there was wine trickling through the half-worn-away statues of someone else's gods, foaming where it fell any distance, the edge of the wall just too high for anyone to fall into, and lined with endless cups. Servers in animal masks collected old cups, vanishing into the shadows under the vines, behind where the musicians played. Hundreds of people. The gods knew how this Dionysus prick had organised it all and kept it secret at the same time.

No, well: clearly the masks were invitations, and probably the messengers had told people where to come, and to be quiet about it. Probably most people hadn't punched them in the face before they could say anything. But why me? A senior Sown officer, proverbially square: that was madness. And how did he even know my name?

Those brilliant glass lamps lit the way down into the lower passages of the labyrinth. Lots more people were down there. When I strayed that way, a boy who seemed familiar under the mask caught me and slung his arm around my shoulders, alarmingly taller than anyone has any right to be when you remember them being born.

"Phaidros! You were one of my officers at Troy!"

"Stop touching me," I said. "Where's Dionysus?"

He giggled. I'd never seen a knight drunk before—even when I'd been fighting with Helios and drinking with the Athenians, I'd never got to *giggling* stages of drunkenness—and it was getting harder and harder not find it obscene. "Dionysus! I saw him before . . ." He turned around twice on the spot, and nearly fell over.

"Who is he?"

"I heard he came from Hattusa. I think he's a prince."

Hattusa was not in India. Hattusa was across the sea from us: they had forbidden anyone in their sprawling empire to trade with us for reasons that boiled down to thinking we were grubby and annoying. Troy was on the nearer edge of the Hatti Empire.

But the prince part made sense. There were hundreds of people here, and thousands of drachmas' worth of wine. Then the musicians, and the food going round on trays, the slaves who were clearing away cups and bringing new ones: it must have cost a fortune.

"Where did you see him last?" I demanded.

He executed what he probably thought was a flirty wink. "Why don't we go somewhere quiet and I'll tell you?"

I smiled and felt the old scar stretch. "Why don't I make you eat your own kidney?"

He seemed to sober up quite fast. "Up there." He pointed up to a terrace that overlooked everything; two storeys above the sunken part of the labyrinth, the same level as my house way at the other end. There was a stairway. Lamps lit the way up, two on every stair.

I climbed up slowly, weaving through drunk people and laughing people and someone playing with a happy-looking monkey making its way through half a coconut. The music snaked and coiled around everything. It was vile. The more I saw of it all, the more angry I felt. If I didn't find Dionysus soon, I was going straight back to the High City to report it and send in the night watch.

At the top, you could see down into the labyrinth below.

I'd never known there was an open part, but there was, in stretches and starts. Sometimes it vanished under rocks, but most of it was visible, and if you stood here, you could watch the people inside getting lost and doubling back. And couples in not very hidden away corners, pretending they were hidden away.

There was a man standing alone on the edge, watching. He was dressed in dark colours, all blues and greens. Although it was still hot and everyone else here wore tunics with only one shoulder, he had his arms covered. He was the first person I'd seen here not holding a wine cup. His mask was different too. It was silver, and it didn't distort his face, although worked into that silver, I could make out figures in gold, people and animals and trees, polished so smooth the surface looked like you could have run your hand across and it felt nothing; it was a piece of metalwork to inherit, not to buy, and only then for queens and princes. Everywhere else, people were dancing, but there was a perfect stillness to him, and it was making him half-invisible. People were going by him, not seeing him, even though he was standing under a string of lamps. In all the spinning and colours, they seemed primed only to see moving things. He looked the way lighthouses look on a churning sea.

Part of me said: *You're supposed to avoid lighthouses.*

"Are you Dionysus?" I asked, judging the distance between us with my hand on my sword, and where the right place on the back of his neck was.

He looked over and smiled. He took the mask off, and I saw the red tattoos that stained his fingers to the second joint. The witch. Tonight, his hair lay heavy over his shoulder, black clouded with ashy grey, barely moving in the hot breeze, and wound through with bright ivy that I thought at first was enamelled bronze, but it wasn't.

He had blue eyes; the indigo blue at the hem of the sea, full of stars from the lamps.

"I thought you'd not come," he said, and this time, his voice had pyre smoke in it.

I waited to go up in flames.

I'd never known that you can be overjoyed and terrified at the same time, but you can.

Something in his expression turned urgent, and he caught my arms as I sank onto my knees. I hadn't meant to. All my strength vanished. He knelt down with me too.

I stared at him, uncomprehending, and still not on fire.

"This is very unusual," he said, with something between cheer and rue. "Knights don't usually swoon at the sight of me."

I wanted to say, *Why aren't you killing me?* but it seemed stupid.

He put a cup into my hands; water, not wine. I drank it slowly, watching him, trying to understand what was happening.

"Phaidros?" he asked, not as if he were certain I could hear him.

Maybe it was a joke. Maybe he was pretending to be concerned, and in a few seconds, he would laugh that weird smoky laugh and say, hah, got you, and I'd be a hole in the ground.

He gave me his hands to help me up.

Slowly, I was starting to see that nothing was going to happen, at least not now, this second. Even more slowly, the possibility gleamed that perhaps he wasn't who I thought; he was just a witch with blue eyes and a charcoal voice.

Something like my normal thinking staggered back up to the surface, breathed at last, and suddenly I felt very, very tired. He hadn't come, the boy from the sea. He wasn't listening to prayers. Of course he wasn't. The world wasn't like that.

"I—thought you were someone else," I explained, insufficiently.

His remarkable eyes slipped over me again, all the way down and all the way up. "Well, I . . . hope you never meet him," he said at last.

Up close, he was taller than me, almost a head taller. Now I was looking at him properly, I couldn't tell if he was the boy or not. Ten years ago, that boy had been somewhere between fourteen and eighteen. Men change so much in that time—much more than women do—and maybe it was him, but anyone about the right age with blue eyes would probably have seemed right. Was he even the right age? I couldn't tell. Sail long enough and you become terrible at judging the ages of people on land, who all look uniformly youthful and glowy. Sailors age twice as fast. Maybe Dionysus was twenty-five or maybe he was forty. The grey in his hair didn't make him seem any particular age; it just made him look like he had walked through a fire.

"I heard you're from Hattusa," I said, feeling like I was stuck in the moment about five seconds after waking up. At first, I always forgot Helios was dead and my whole unit was at the bottom of the sea, and it was a lovely weightless feeling, but then I woke up all the way and the Nothing took up the whole room. "Or India."

"Or Memphis," Dionysus agreed, without saying if any of them were right, and looking like he hoped I was going to take him up on it.

Of course he was just a witch. I had just collapsed stupidly in front of a witch who had been kind enough to make a joke instead of demanding to know what in Zeus's name was wrong with me and would I mind taking it elsewhere.

"I came to say," I said, "wherever you're from, I'm sure music like this is normal there, but it's forbidden here. And so is wine. Sown knights can't drink, for . . ." I watched bleakly as the boy who'd spoken to me before got in a tussle with someone else and they both fell in a fountain. "Obvious reasons. You need to stop."

"I understand, but I'm not going to," he said.

I let my head drop. I couldn't hurt him now, or even drag him off so someone else could do it. He had saved my life today, with the bull. I owed him his. And—and. He had just been kind when there was no need. "You're going to end up in a cell. It won't be very nice. They won't let you go just because you're foreign and you didn't know."

"I did know," he said.

I waited to see if he was going to explain. He didn't.

I don't know if this is a good thing or a bad thing about me, but I'm one of those people who could have a tablet marked ABSOLUTELY DO NOT UNDER ANY CIRCUMSTANCES TURN THIS OVER on my desk for years, and never turn it over. It isn't that I'm not curious; it's that I'll put up with the curiosity just to spite whoever thought they had such a flawless understanding of humans that they could force me to do anything. Not explaining his spectacular breach of the law struck me as very *do-not-turn-over* tablet-y. For all I was grateful to him, a deep-down part of me decided I would stand here and die before I asked what he meant.

"Well, good luck," I said, turning away and not even sure that I was going to make it home. Maybe I'd crumple on the roadside in a patch of grass. That would be fantastic. It was still hot. Possibly I would be eaten by wolves, but even that was more attractive than trying to argue with a witch.

"Wait," Dionysus said.

He was studying me, which was uncomfortable, because I spent my whole life around knights who were careful not to do that. I couldn't remember the last time someone had looked at me square for whole seconds at a time. Helios, probably; in bed. It was orders of magnitude too intimate from a stranger. "Dance with me," he said.

"What?" It came out flinty.

He took my hands as if we'd known each other for years. I'd forgotten what it felt like. Just for a second I was twenty again. You think you grow out of things, but it's that the world changes around you, not that you do.

"Come on," he said, with no impatience. "It will help."

I smacked him off me. "Have you lost your mind?"

"Did your commander not teach you to listen to witches?" he said, but gently. When I put my hand on my sword, he just threaded his fingertips through my knuckles and lifted it away. I let him, because he had judged right; I wasn't going to use it. "Please, knight. You're here now."

I didn't decide. I hung suspended over *not* deciding like a dead wasp in honey, and time just moved on around me; and so did he.

Until that moment—I think because he was so still—people hadn't noticed him. But when he danced, everyone saw him, and he could dance like I'd never seen. It wasn't the way that the priestesses danced. It was as far from that as the sea is from a still lake. He didn't have to concentrate, or count, or think in angles and inches. He just danced, and his hair spun and his clothes, which were made of fabrics lighter than I'd known you could weave, coiled and shifted like water, sometimes making half-shapes of their own, sometimes pressing to his shoulders or his spine, and it gave him a charge—I could feel it snapping and sharp in the air, and other people could too. It was pulling them towards him and suddenly everyone close to us was touching him and catching his hands and it was *hungry:* there was something dangerous about it, and with a weird unpleasant spike I had a sudden certainty they would have dragged him down if he had been slower, because it was unthinking rapture. I didn't feel it; maybe it was because I could have had that alluring tablet on my desk for years and never turned it over. I was glad I didn't. It looked horrible, and with a nasty bolt, I wondered if I was going to have to pull people away from him before someone hurt him.

He had a way of melding with the lamplight, and for all he was tall, I kept losing sight of him, and when he came around again, he was usually behind me somehow, but the tide of people always brought him back. Masks flashed by, some strange, some horrible, all different. It was good and it was dangerous as well, and in equal parts I wanted to join everyone else and feel that trance too, and I wanted it to stop.

The music lifted and he lifted me too.

It stopped all my thoughts, because it was frightening. I'd been a child the last time anyone had been strong enough to do that.

But it wasn't bad. It was a comfortable, ghost-story fear; a mask over being entirely safe.

Just for a few seconds, I wasn't a knight who was supposed to work like a marvel. I didn't have duties or children to turn into marvel knights too, or strange songs, or a lost prince; I hadn't outlived everyone worthwhile I'd ever known, I hadn't all but murdered Helios myself. I was just me, without a past or a future, the same as those few glorious seconds after waking up, and just then, there was nothing to me except the lamplight and the music and a stranger's hands round my ribs.

When he set me down, he did it so softly I might have been made of glass. Then he was still, just holding me by the hem of my ribcage, and people seemed to forget about him again. Part of me, shut off from the rest inside a Sown helmet that stayed on even when I wasn't wearing the real thing, could see that this was very, very bad: alcohol and excess are the death of honour, and if I stayed here for even a little longer, I was going to end up doing things knights should never do, because the pull of it was riptide strong, which was appalling—things like this had always seemed dirty and ridiculous to me, I'd never even distantly wanted to be part of them, but I didn't want to leave now. I wanted to get that memoryless feeling back. I wanted to see him dance again.

Dionysus looked down at me for a hanging second, and I thought he wanted to say something, but he didn't have the chance, because an arrow sang between us and then the garrison night watch were shouting for everyone to stand still and shut up.

In a way, it was a relief.

12

I 'd never seen so many people in the cells. Each one was made for five or six prisoners, but the Guards crammed twenty into each one, all of us dusty and sweating from the long slog at sword-point back into Thebes, and covered in a fine layer of ash from the sacrifice smoke that still rose from every temple in the city. When I pushed my hand across my forehead, it felt like cement.

I slumped back against the cell wall. Everyone knows that fortunes turn, but I'd always thought I'd have more warning than this. Enemy soldiers would be camped outside the city for ten years. I'd have time to get used to the idea. I'd never thought I would just come home one evening and an hour later I'd be staring slavery in the eye.

It was all very underwhelming. Still; at least it would be cold in Hades. Someone recognised me.

"Really, Heliades? You'll go to the galleys for this."

I nodded once. There was no point trying to say why I'd been there. Helios had always told me to be like Persephone, always negotiate, but Death is much more open to debate than the Guards.

"So he should. He was there from the start, I can't believe he isn't more drunk," Dionysus said cheerfully.

Maybe he thought it was funny. Witches have a dark sense of humour. I heard about one who turned some sailors into pigs when they were rude to her. Well; actually that is quite funny.

The Guard looked at me again. "You aren't drunk."

"No," I agreed.

"And . . . he's trying to stitch you up." She turned to Dionysus. "He was there to tell you to stop, wasn't he?"

No; he didn't think it was funny. He was helping me. I wondered if it had any chance of working.

"What are you talking about?" Dionysus demanded. He was a wonderful actor. "I never heard a word from him."

"Come out," she told me wearily. "Why didn't you say?"

I watched her, half certain she was joking. This was very irregular behaviour, for a Guard.

"No, you're right, I wouldn't have believed you," she said as if I'd answered.

She cast a wary look at Dionysus. If he had been someone else, I could see she would have punched him, but the red tattoos on his hands stopped her. He could curse her. Perhaps he would anyway. Without even a glimmer of the ordinary, sensible fear normal people have for the Guards, he met her eyes and studied her too, but not in the way she was studying him. He was smiling a little, like he was waiting for other people to understand a joke, and I had an overpowering feeling he had only let himself be sent into the cells to keep the other prisoners company.

She slammed the cell door.

The noise was chaos; people were shouting to be let out, it was just music and some wine, most of them too drunk to see what a stupid idea it was to shout and swear at Guards. The air smelled of hot stone and alcohol and sweat, and it was like trying to breathe through a wet cloth. I moved through it feeling dislocated. I'd been sure I was going to end up in the slave market, and I like to have a solid itinerary: I felt indignant that things weren't going as expected, for all this was much better than I'd expected.

I ghosted after the Guards. The one who had let me out smiled at me and then looked alarmed, and twisted the tips of my hair around her fingertip to show me a stray spark in it. I crushed it out.

"Gods, these sacrifices," she muttered, suddenly a normal person now that she didn't have her duty face on. We were moving through a haze of smoke, even just in the corridor.

I brushed another spark off her purple cloak and she nodded, and when we met each other's eyes, there was one of those strange floating moments where we both realized we would have got on brilliantly if not for the circumstances, because we were the same age, and she seemed like the kind of person who probably had a pet chicken called Cassandra and a cracking sense of humour, and we could have been friends. But Guards and knights aren't meant to be friends.

One of the officers hung the keys up outside the main door, which was solid bronze.

"The law says three days," he said, sounding grimly pleased with himself.

In this heat, everyone would be dead in three days.

I looked at the other Guards, waiting for someone to say something, but no one did.

So I lurked in the corridor till they'd gone to their mess room, then stole the keys and looped straight back around above ground, at the edge of the market square, to the low, thin windows that were designed to let all the heat of the day into the cells, but none of the air. I counted along, then knelt down at the fifth one. It wasn't difficult, and I didn't have to be stealthy. The square was empty except for a few people sleeping rough at the far side so that, probably, they could be here first thing when the attendants of Sown lords and ladies came to the market in the morning.

"Dionysus."

He was close to the window already. I gave him the keys through the bars.

He didn't take them. "No," he said. "They'll know it was you."

I made a not very patient noise at him, because it was boiling and I was so tired now I would have cheerfully murdered someone in exchange for an extra hour's sleep. I caught his hand to put the keys into it. The red tattoos looked black in the moonlight. "Make it look like witching. And hurry up, I'm not sitting here all night arguing with you."

He thought about it. "Will you want to see some magic?" He said it with a joyful sparkle that I'd only ever seen in small children before. *Will you want*, I thought to the side of everything, in the part of me that spoke what felt like a thousand languages. Why did that sound so ancient?

I didn't know what to make of that sparkle in an adult man. It should have looked juvenile, but it didn't. I didn't like it: it was a lie, for a start.

He didn't know me. He wasn't enjoying me, or the cell, or whatever mummery he was about to perform. "No," I said. "But you're going to do whatever the fuck you want anyway."

I still have no idea how he did it. Even though I was watching, I didn't see him pass the key around. He didn't talk to anyone else, he didn't explain what they had to do. Perhaps he already had. Perhaps he knew that I would take the key, but even so.

He started to spin. At the end of each turn, he knocked the manacles together, so they banged. It was an eerie thing to see, one slim figure with tattooed hands, the thin light catching on the chains. Maybe because he was tall, maybe because he looked so stark and so different, he didn't quite seem like a person any more, but a thing who happened to have taken the same shape.

In that small room, I thought the other people would just look confused, or tell him to stop moving, there was no space, but that wasn't what happened. Instead, they began to spin too, and to crack the manacles together. With ten people doing it, rather than one, the noise was loud. I glanced to my left, anxious, because someone would hear, but that was clearly the point. It spread to the next cell; I could just make out people beyond the bars. Turn, *bang*, turn; it was louder with every spin, more people doing it, until I could feel ground under me shaking where the cells extended beneath the square. It was marching pace, but getting faster.

A shout came from inside the Guards' garrison, and I saw lights hurry back towards the prison doors, and then inside the corridor through the barred window. The torchlight hurled monster shadows everywhere, and still, everyone spun.

"Hey! What are you doing?"

All the drunken confusion was gone now. Everyone was silent, except for that ribcage-deep thump of the manacles.

"Get in there," someone else said tightly. "If we have to whip them, we do."

The manacles started to fall. The key must have been going around, it *must* have been, but even I couldn't see it. One pair after the next, the manacles opened and slammed onto the floor, and still they danced.

Somewhere deep in the cells, some people started to sing. Even though it was impossible, even though there was no earthly way everyone here could have known it, it didn't take me much by surprise that it was the mad knights' song.

Sing, sing to the lord of the dance
Thunder-wrought and city-razing
King, king of the holy raging,
Rave and rise again.

The cell door opened, and everyone inside paced out. Then the next cell door, and the next. The Guards looked at each other, and I saw them realize they couldn't do anything unless they wanted to start killing people. The dancers looked like they were sleepwalking, just like Amphitrion had looked. The song was shaking the whole square; it would be waking up people in the lower city. The would-be slaves had come to see, and there was already a little crowd at the edge of the marketplace. I went to the middle of the square so I could see the prison gates.

When the first prisoners came out, there was a ragged cheer. I felt it too, a brilliant lift to see the Guards lose, for once. It couldn't last: the Guards were going to be furious the moment they stopped feeling so confused, and the gods knew what they would do next if they caught anyone they recognised, but just for now, it was fantastic.

Once people were out, the eerie song stopped and they ran and scattered, and then I was straining to try to find Dionysus in among all the deep moon-shadows and the smog of sacrifice smoke, and someone knocked me against the wall, but then he was there and we were running much too fast down the steps to the lower city, and struggling to breathe and coughing, and laughing, because it was so stupid.

At first, it was impossible to talk, because the smoke was too thick. With no lamps, we had to go slowly, and when we hit squares rather than roads, we kept losing each other. There was a brief negotiation in which he suggested we hold hands and I explained that I would rather walk into a furnace and explode, thank you, and so as a compromise, he tied our wrists together.

"Where do you live?" I asked, when we were finally on the path up the mountain. The air wasn't clear exactly, but it wasn't choking any more either.

"Along by you, where we were before. It was empty, so."

Witches could live anywhere they wanted to, as long as nobody else was living there first. Anecdotally I'd heard that some witches didn't take that last part too seriously.

I wished he could have chosen somewhere other than next door. It was a quarter of an hour's walk back even from here and I couldn't very well say, *You go on ahead by yourself in the dark, I'll sleep in this tree so I don't have to talk to you any more.* Now we were safe and I didn't think he was a god who wanted to kill me, I was feeling more and more grumpy about having to waste most of my night on blasphemy and then being wrongfully arrested for blasphemy and breaking the sodding blasphemer out of sodding prison, and ashamed that really, the arrest had only been half wrongful.

"That was fun," he said. He sounded genuinely cheerful, the prick.

I looked for a ravine to shove him into. "No, it wasn't. Do *not* do that again," I told him, pulling off the cloth that bound our wrists together.

"No, I saw you laughing." He paused. "Actually that's the first time I've seen a knight here laugh. You all go around looking like it's worst day of your life; why?"

It was, in fairness to him, not a stupid question.

"Theban manners," I explained. "The best compliment you can pay someone here is to say, you're a marvel; as in a clockwork marvel. It means you function the same no matter what's happening. We don't smile much. It isn't rude, but it's . . . crass."

He was looking interested; not, I realized, in the information, but that I'd told it to him. "You're good at talking to foreigners," he said.

I studied him, and he held my eyes, frank and unembarrassed, and very un-Theban, but still . . . "You aren't a foreigner. You're from here."

He smiled slowly. It was increasingly bizarre to meet a grown man who let all his feelings go straight across his face. When I'd seen it before—on Athenians—it was flamboyant, but he wasn't that at all. Just—honest. "What makes you say that?"

"Achaean," I said, more and more sure the more I heard him speak, "is impossible to learn fluently as an adult. You were born here."

"Or I'm half as clever as you and I made an effort."

I shook my head. There are geniuses, and probably somewhere there was a foreigner who, with twenty years of pig-headed and unreasoning dedication, might learn an Achaean dialect as fluently as he spoke Theban, but the only people who had to learn Achaean from scratch were slaves, and a slave was rarely in a position to learn it well. "Why don't you want people to know?"

"It's part of the Witches' Vow."

"You have a vow?" I asked, intrigued despite everything.

He nodded. The air was finally clear. It smelled of green and pollen and moss, which was wrong, because for months it had smelled of dust. *"I swear no living soul shall know me true. I swear to leave behind my family and my home, never to return."*

"Why?" I asked, because that was much harder than the Knights' Vow.

He gave me an apologetic look. *"I swear never to tell why I swore this vow."*

"That seems deliberately irritating," I said. It came out more hostile than I'd meant it to.

He seemed not to care and answered what I'd meant, rather than the way I'd said it. "Witching doesn't work if you know how it works. If I told you why I can't tell you my real name or where I'm from or the rest, most magic would fail for you."

I glanced up at him, wondering where he had learned to translate from Knight to Civilian, because he was doing it very well.

"The next time you're wounded, the legion witches wouldn't be able to take the pain away." He looked down at me, and even in the starlight I saw his eyes catch on the scar on my face. Like before, he did it for too long. If he had been a knight, I would have pushed his temple to make him stop, but I could see already he would probably take that as a hilarious challenge and lick me. "And that seems shortsighted."

I let that roll around my head for a few paces. "So it doesn't work for witches?"

"No."

"Then what happens if you're hurt?" I said incredulously.

"Tough crackers really," he said with a laugh under his voice, the same one I would have laughed if he had asked me if I thought it was unfair I wouldn't live to see forty.

I didn't mean to, but I looked up at him properly then, because hearing him say that, and say it like he had, made me think that knights and witches were more similar than either of us usually noticed.

The way was so quiet that even I could hear the trees creaking. No one seemed to be coming after us, even now. I wondered if actually, so many people had escaped that the Guards would pretend nothing had happened and never mention it again. It was better than admitting that over a hundred people had escaped, singing a forbidden song.

After a little while, because the road was steep here and we were both tired enough that it was difficult to climb and breathe and talk all at the same time, I said, "Why did you organise that dance? You knew it would end in the cells."

Although his playfulness was still there, a veil of something like regret came down over it. "Witching."

I gave up. I wasn't going to try and wrestle a straight answer out of someone trained to tie answers in knots.

We were already at my side of the maze, by the gate under the lemon tree that never made any lemons. I bowed a little and meant to leave him to what was left of his night, but then stopped, because he was looking at something on the path through the gate, and his shoulders had just tacked back.

"What's that?" he said.

It was a dead fox, in a fluffy heap on the ground just past the gate. It was the big vixen who I'd been feeding since the drought had begun; she'd been glossy and healthy yesterday. I looked fast to either side. There were wolves in the forest, but I'd not known them come onto my land before; they didn't like humans any more than we liked them. But it was so dry. Maybe all the things they usually ate had died. I couldn't think of anything else that could, or would, kill a fox. No tracks, though. I moved the fox, trying to see how it had been killed.

"That's unusual," I said slowly.

"What?"

"Its neck is snapped, but I can't see any bite marks."

Dionysus gazed up the steep dark path that led to his side of the ruin. Not afraid, but speculative. He should have been afraid, though. He was tall, but he was no knight.

"Walk you home?" I ground out, because duty is honour even when your duty is to keep an enraging witch alive after he's landed you in a gaol cell for public debauchery.

The merry glow came back. "No, thank you. I think I'll be better off with the wolves or wandering psychopaths."

I sighed. He had made it sound like a joke, but it wasn't. I was too near to the end of my tether. I had an unwilling spike of gratitude. No one had said it to me so politely before. "It probably isn't psychopaths. It's probably my slaves. This will just be the newest thing in their campaign of hexing me to death. You'll be fine."

He looked interested. "You don't want to sell them to someone who they won't hex, or . . . ?"

"Can't. They," I said, a little bit deliriously, draping the fox over my arm to take it in, because the fur would make some useful things for winter, not that I could imagine being cold ever again, "were a royal gift. Oh, you fought so well at Troy, Phaidros, nicely done, Phaidros, first unit over the wall and everything, here's a present for you: the pedigree triplets from Hades who will spend the next twenty years plotting to fucking kill you, there you go, son, enjoy, and guess who has to live alone with the creepy little fuckers on a drought-stricken mountainside?"

"Well," he said, once again deploying his frankly astonishing skill for taking things as I'd meant them and not how I'd said them—seriously, this time, for all I'd tried to phrase it as a complaining joke, "you're mine now. You're subject to no curses but mine."

I looked down at the silver bee charm on its red string around my wrist, and realized I believed him.

He was maddening and shameless and dangerous, but it had been a strange day and all the strangest parts had happened with him, and it felt like I knew him, even though he wasn't the boy from the sea. "Can I ask your opinion about something?"

He looked surprised that I'd want to hear his opinion about anything, but he waited.

"I'm trying to find someone who's missing. It's urgent. But I'm not allowed to make it known that they need to be found, so searching is difficult. How would a witch do it? Although if you say witching," I added, "I will punch you in the throat."

He gave it some thought. "Call a census," he said.

13

I didn't sleep. It doesn't matter how exhausted you are: if it's hot even at night and the god of sleep doesn't like you anyway—his favourite thing was the just-before-dawn nightmare—you just have to learn to function without. I hadn't really got the trick of it.

"Ugh," I said to the ceiling as the sun prised open the horizon.

The just-before-dawn nightmare had been worse than normal. I got up to get away from bed, which didn't feel like a nice place to rest but a horrible horizontal prison cell, and nudged the shutters open. Just outside my window was the little shrine with my wine and honey offering to the god. I wondered bleakly if the ants having the time of their lives on the cup now were some mechanism of transubstantiation, but I was pretty sure they were just ants. *Sacrifice*, the priests said. *You'll be sleeping wonderfully in no time.* I hoped they were all eaten by ants.

I pushed my hands against my eyes. The dream had been horrible. I'd been hunting in a forest. I was chasing something that might have been a lion, but sometimes, when I caught a flash of it through the trees, it didn't seem like a lion at all but a man, but somehow that didn't matter and I was full of joyful bloodlust anyway, and so was everyone else, and through the trees was a weird, awful song, and drums, and drums.

There was a gasp from further into the olive grove, and three sets of eerie grey eyes met mine through the low branches.

I had three slaves in the way you can have toothache, or a family curse. They were princes from Troy: triplets, about fourteen years old now, and easily the creepiest, most unnerving humans I'd ever met. I'd spent an awful lot of the last six months trying to get them to run away. I'd been leaving gates suggestively open and coming home reliably late from the garrison, and saying things like, *Oh, no, I'll have to be gone all night again.* But no. Here they still were. I'd thought they were afraid at first, but I was coming to the conclusion that in fact they didn't want to escape. That was concerning, because more and more, I was worried that what they *did* want might be something to do with harvesting my organs and sacrificing them to Zeus for a return to their previous good fortune.

"What are you doing?" I said slowly. They never talked to me, so speaking to them was pointless, but I was in the habit of trying anyway.

They stared at me for another second, and without any discussion at all, they all bolted in different directions. I shuddered.

The windows of the house were low, so I could just step out. When I found the place where they'd been standing, I could see why they had paused. There was a dead wolf there. It had been killed just like the fox last night: neck broken, no other wounds. I stood looking at it for a while. There was no way the triplets could have killed a wolf.

Eventually, I picked it up and took it behind the house, to the forest border. Men couldn't cross, because it was sacred and dryads are territorial, but I left the carcass in the roots of an oak tree. Other things would be grateful for it. Trees are people, just slower, and ever since I'd come to the maze, I always had a feeling I was living right on the edge of someone else's city, great and ancient; it was probably a good idea to show it some honour.

From just inside came the snick of a broken twig. I looked up, very still. I couldn't hear anything else, but there was a pressure along the back of my skull that said something was watching me, something big, and it was very, very close. Nothing was moving. The forest looked dead: the trees were parched, there were no birds or rabbits, and even the insects had died. Slowly, and I couldn't tell how, because I wouldn't have heard it even from someone leaning right over my shoulder, I started to feel sure that something was breathing.

Probably someone who had run away from slavery last night, after the rations were cut.

The Hidden couldn't ride into the woods, or rather, more than half of us couldn't and the other half didn't like it. If you could make it as far as the forest, you were safe, provided you were able to negotiate with the dryads.

Or it was something else.

I stepped back gradually, two paces, five, then walked fast back to the house, just in time to see the delivery cart from the Palace coming along the road. Usually it was the driver and his assistant, but today, it came with four guards, all in armour despite the warm morning. Frowning, I went down through the olive grove to meet them.

"Morning," the driver called, sounding relieved. "Sorry about the parade, but we keep getting attacked on the road."

He wasn't joking. One of the guards had blood on his face.

I helped them bring everything inside, then sat them all down at the table to bring them some water and some food, because this was my fault. If I'd lived in Thebes, this wouldn't have happened. The driver had been coming every week since I'd been given the house—supplies are how knights are paid—and this was the first time I'd heard of any trouble. They all looked disproportionately grateful to be sitting down.

As they always did, the triplets emerged to help, terrifyingly, silently efficient as always. They understood that I couldn't sell them, I knew they did, because I'd told them that in five languages; which left me bewildered about why they did anything in the house at all. They knew I wouldn't hurt them; maybe someone at the Palace had put the fear of Ares into them, but if that was the case, it had lasted a long time now. I didn't think so. More unnerving mysteries.

"It's escaped slaves," the driver explained, after they'd all told me what had happened. Some men had jumped them from some bushes on a narrow stretch of the mountain path, only three or four, but enough to be scary. "Their rations have gone down so much it's nearly nothing. Well. Field slaves, anyway," he said, watching the triplets, who were healthy and round. "People are running away all over the place. You'll have a fuck of a time keeping up with it, sir, even with the Hidden."

"Running where?" I asked. The next nearest city was Athens, ninety miles away, or Sparta, over a hundred.

He shrugged. "Into the forest? Towards Lake Copais? Dunno if there's still water in it, but . . ." He trailed off and looked worried, and I realized he had been going to say, *that's what I'd do*. He must have thought about it. All civil servants are slaves, from royal ministers and scribes right down to the stable boys and the delivery drivers. His rations were being cut badly too.

I pushed some apples towards him. "Come on, you're spurning my hospitality here. I haven't got the madness, or the fucking plague. Take some things for the road, all of you."

They all laughed but nobody took anything except a few olives.

"Are you sure?" the guard who had been washing his face said. "Your rations are half of what they were a few months ago, sir."

"And I still have most of what I had a few months ago. It's just me here, and the boys. I haven't got a secret legion of ravenous wives locked in the maze."

"Even so," he said, looking excruciated.

"This is a lot of dentistry you're doing on the gift horse," I said.

The driver's little assistant burst out laughing. She was just getting her new teeth, and they were still too big for her.

The guard grinned too. "You're a true knight, sir."

Finally, they all helped themselves properly.

"You should come back with us," the driver said to me. "We can take you round to the garrison. The way it's looking . . . even in broad daylight, I wouldn't like to think of anyone on the road alone. Even a knight," he said over me when I took a breath to say I'd be fine.

Nothing happened on the road, but when we reached the High City on the zigzagging, laborious way for carts and horses, the main square was much more crowded than it had been yesterday. A huge slave market had appeared, hundreds of people selling themselves, clay signs around their necks, sometimes whole families. A tiny little girl with a ribbon in her hair had a sign that said I CAN POUR WINE!

A garrison unit was out, making sure there was a way through for traffic, and so were Palace stewards—they were buying fleets of people at a time, paying relatives with invoice tablets. The preference was always for women, in the Palace: nobody wanted a big angry man who might lose it one morning and stab someone, but it meant the men were struggling, the prices lower than what I'd normally expect to pay even for one very unwell ox. I tried to keep my eyes front, not looking at faces, not reading the lips of people yelling at me that I could afford fifty of them, and not saying that I couldn't afford to *feed* fifty, even with a knight's allowances. The noise was so much that I couldn't hear anything particular inside it, just the roar of bartering and crying and sudden, explosive rows, the ones that always happen when it's too hot and nobody's had enough to eat. And everywhere, over and through it all, the endless smoke of the sacrifice altars.

Getting in through the garrison gates wasn't any relief. The Knights' Court was heaving too, a mixture of units all going to and fro, bringing horses, asking things of harassed-looking clerks bringing armour. Black armour. Before I could find anyone to ask what the fuck was happening, someone caught my arm and yelped when I smacked them off.

"Gods, man, you're too quick for your own good," the general told me.

"Sir—I'm so sorry—"

"No, no, I'm the same, just not quite so—alacritous," he said, shaking his head. I felt terrible. He was the same age as Helios, and so small he only reached my shoulder, maybe just over five feet tall. He had been a general for about ten years: he was one of those courteous, brittle-seeming people who nobody ever wants to upset, the same way everyone is at the mercy of wise kittens. Of course he used it brutally. "Heliades, I'm glad I caught you—can you explain why I'm signing you off to Palace service and giving your unit to Polydorus just as a hundred and forty slaves have run from the Temple of the Mother's estates and I have to call the first all-units Hidden run in ten years?"

"*A hundred and forty!*"

"It's the rations," he said, balancing a tablet on his arm while he peered at a half-peeled pomegranate. It looked off, the rubies going brown. "This tastes . . . distantly of naphtha." As if he hadn't interrupted himself, he went on, "For field slaves they've gone down to almost nothing."

Field slaves become field slaves because they're rapists and murderers, so the conditions for them were pretty shocking even in good times, but it was still a crazy number. Usually the only people who risked running were career criminals with something to run to and a fast ship waiting.

"Yes, and so I have this transfer order for you because . . . ?"

"I'm sorry, sir, the Chamberlain called me in yesterday. It's . . ." I lunged after the first true but boring word I could think of. "Administrative rubbish I inherited from Helios."

"Hm. Make sure the Queen doesn't expect you to inherit *too* much from Helios," the general said with a seriousness I didn't understand. "Duty is honour, but there was a reason he was Helios Polytropos." Polytropos, "many-turning"; it means tricky fucker. I'd forgotten the nickname. Remembering was like a little punch in the stomach and just for a flash, there Helios was, laughing, playing the three-cup game with me. *Round and round she goes, where she stops nobody knows.* I'd never been able to find the ball under the right cup even when I was much older. "You can't be straight down the line and survive the court. Either find a way out, or develop . . ." The general mimed spirals.

"It—is not a permanent thing," I said, not sure what he was saying.

"I should hope not. Those feral little fuckers are going to eat Polydorus alive in forty-eight hours." He lifted the seal bead from its cord round my neck and rolled it along his tablet, which made me stoop forward. He was wise-kittening me. "Well. Good luck, and do hurry the fuck back, would you please." He made the bull sign and waved me away.

I had to wait at the Chamberlain's office for nearly an hour before there was space for the Queen to see me. Helios had always said that most of life in royal service is just about waiting uselessly, but I'd thought he was doing that thing noblemen always do, which was complaining pointedly about glamorous connections so everyone would know they weren't starry-eyed about it. He was right, though. I sat on the steps of one of the pretty inner courtyards, watching a little flock of parakeets. They were perched on a marvel and sometimes it moved, and they'd be startled and fly away, but someone had put grain in its hands, and so they always came back. After a while, I scooped up some grain to see if they'd come to see me too. They did, all soft and green and interested. I laughed and then stopped, because the Nothing was there next to me. I shut my eyes, wishing I could just fucking enjoy something instead of moping around like some twat in a poem.

A Guard appeared, the same one I'd spoken to in the cells yesterday. We stared at each other and then we both pretended not to know each other.

"The Queen will see you."

In the throne room, the Queen was talking to a very tall Egyptian man. I hung back, wary. He must have been with the trade delegation. He was wearing gold around his wrists, and there was gold filigree on his belt, and his broad neck piece was so heavy with turquoise it was forcing him to stand with his shoulders back, as if he were waiting to start a drill. I thought she would ignore me until he was gone, but she tipped her head to invite me over. I went, thinking that it was her way of telling the Egyptian man to move on because now she had other business, but I was wrong.

"Prince Apophis, this is Phaidros Heliades. He was sworn to my brother," she told him in exquisite Egyptian.

I wanted to ask why she was introducing an Egyptian prince to an inconsequential knight, and the man looked like he wanted to ask that too, but he seemed willing to give me the benefit of the doubt.

"Sworn, what does that mean?" he asked.

Egyptians are annoying for the following reasons.

One, they think they're the best educated people in the world, so they ignore most things told to them by people who are not Egyptians, on the reasoning that you must be a moron who lives in a pigsty.

Two, they lisp. It's their bread. There's a lot of sand in Egypt and therefore a lot of sand in their bread, and so the better they eat, the more worn down their teeth tend to be. Noblemen train themselves to speak like that even if their teeth are perfect, because to them it sounds wealthy. To the rest of the world, it sounds like they're all trying to impersonate a five-year-old girl, and it is therefore difficult to not hit them with a rock.

"Married," I said.

"To her . . . brother?" He said it like he thought I must have got the Egyptian word wrong. As though all long-distance shipping doesn't happen in Egyptian; as though you could know how to say "I know it's fourteen per cent port tax but call it twelve between friends and I won't show you your own spleen," but not "married."

"Yes," I said gradually, starting to suspect he might have been so clois- tered as to be inept at life beyond Memphis.

The Queen, I couldn't help noticing, looked suspiciously like a person who was just settling down to watch an especially bloody wrestling match.

"Can I ask what the function of a marriage is, if not . . . children?" he asked, still sounding certain that I'd got the word wrong.

I'd forgotten how much translation you really needed, talking to Egyp- tians; even if you could speak fluent Egyptian. I took a deep breath. I hadn't had enough sleep for this. Maybe I could still find a rock. "To hold the front lines of heavy infantry units in combat."

"Ah—I'm afraid I don't quite understand."

"The line doesn't break," I said, "if no one wants to run away. There's nothing to run to if your family is on the line."

He laughed. "How unique." He thought I was joking. He'd said it in the tone of *piss off*.

"Unique for who?"

"Humans?"

I nearly asked how many humans he had met. Probably it was only about eight. Probably seven of them were slaves, one was his wife, and probably he didn't like any of them because humans are grubby and annoying. Probably his favourite person was a pet hippopotamus called Moses. It seemed better not to take him up on it. Once people are rich enough, they lose their grip on the rest of the world. "If you say so."

"I do," he said, more firmly than he'd said anything else. "In fact, what you're talking about would be *quite* forbidden in Memphis."

I thought he was joking, then realized he was smiling because he thought *I* was joking. "Seems militarily counterproductive?"

He lifted his eyebrows. "Egypt commands the finest fighting force in the world."

I waited. Egyptian humour is a bit different to Achaean humour. "I can't tell if you're joking."

"It's true!" he said indignantly.

He wasn't laughing. But he couldn't really think so. "A hundred and fifty years ago it was, but you were fucking abysmal at Troy. We used to send our youngest units to fight your infantry for practise. We thought your soldiers must all be slaves or something. It might be time to consider a system that doesn't encourage them to scatter if someone sneezes at them."

"I've offended you."

"No?" I said, confused.

"Oh." He looked confused too. "Er . . . indeed." A pause. "Indeed," he said again.

I hoped he was having some kind of serendipitous haemorrhage and I wouldn't have to explain anything else.

"He isn't being rude, he's being Theban," the Queen explained, looking unpromisingly happy about the whole thing. I couldn't tell if I was the victim here or if Apophis was, or what either one of us had done to deserve the other. "Our knights vow to tell the truth."

"Oh, goodness. Do you, indeed? That sounds—awful. Um. Indeed," he said again, which he seemed to say when other people would say "I'm sorry, I'm not sure what's happening any more," and went away.

I watched him go. "Did you introduce us to annoy him?" I asked. Maybe if he was completely at sea then he wouldn't be so strict with his grain, or something.

The Queen smiled, a controlled marvel-smile, but still a smile. "No, to see what you would say." She didn't explain any more, though I had an odd feeling I'd passed some kind of test. She was studying me. "What are you here to report?"

"I came to say we need to search the whole city without raising too many questions. I think the best way to do that is to call a census."

"A census," the Queen repeated.

I cringed inside, because it felt wrong to take the credit for Dionysus's idea; but I couldn't say, *Actually I was discussing state secrets with a passing witch after we were both arrested.* "Is it possible, lady?"

She breathed in deep, in the give-me-strength way Helios had used to do when someone told him to get the siege ladders. "This city has an administrative engine which frequently brings me to my knees. I'm certain it can be persuaded to bear the weight of a census."

She was walking now, leading me towards the old ruined courtyard again, in the shade of the colonnade. Even there, the air was straight from a blast furnace. The red cloak was killing me. Like always now, a pall of sacrifice smoke veiled everything in grey; even buildings close to us looked hazy, and further away, the spires of the Temple of Zeus were ghostly. It was putting grey in my hair where it lay in its tail over my shoulder; the Queen's too.

"I've told Apophis that Pentheus is spending some time sequestered at a sanctuary," she said. "But he won't believe that if it goes on for longer than a week."

"If we send out heralds today to announce a stay-at-home order, we should be able to carry it out tomorrow or the day after."

"Will people obey it or do we need to deploy the garrison?"

"I think they will," I said. "If we conduct the census in the middle of the day, everyone will be at home anyway. The markets are only opening at night now . . ."

An amazing bird landed just next to me. It was gigantic and pink, and it looked nearly as interested to have found a Phaidros as I was to have found a bird.

"Awk," it told me.

"I'll send them out," the Queen said, her eyes going over the bird too. "And I want you to—sorry, how is anyone meant to concentrate when there's a gigantic pink bird? Where did he come from? *What* is he?"

"I don't know," I said, in love with it already. "I've seen them before in the west, but never here. They live in water, out around the islands, and by Pylos."

Looking pleased with itself, the bird did an excited shuffle to the fountain and sat down in it, studying the fish.

"It's going to eat my pedigree fish, isn't it," the Queen sighed.

"But now you've got a fun bird," I offered.

"I suppose."

"Pedigree *fish*," I echoed, hearing it properly.

She gave me a severe stare. "Are you making fun of my fish, Sown?"

"Y . . . es," I decided, because a holy vow of honesty doesn't go away just because the Queen might have you sewn into a bag of snakes and hurled off a cliff for being irritating.

She laughed, and the bird made an oinking noise that set us both off even more. Some of the slaves had come out to see what we could possibly be talking about, and now, there were appreciative murmurs and theories about where it might have come from, and whether it could be an omen. I could see it might be, but of what seemed a bit mysterious. Eagles I understood, but enormous pink joke-birds were less easy to interpret.

The Queen, though, was frowning over the heat-waving city, and the great plumes of dust rising from the western road. "What is that?"

The dust off the road wasn't just the hot wind, but scuffed up by what must have been hundreds of people. I could see the sun glinting on the harnesses of oxen, and children sitting dreary on the back of big wagons, married women riding donkeys. Even from so far away, it was clear something was wrong. Merchant trains were normally alive when they moved, with people coming out well ahead to announce them and advertise, and usually the wagons were bright colours. This didn't look like that.

The bird. It must have come with them on the back of a wagon. Birds were forever hiding in the shrouds of ships or in packed-up tents. One night watch, some people had gone up the mast to let down the sails, and down on the deck, I'd got a rain of confused puffins.

"A city's fallen," I said, very quietly, so no one else would hear. I studied the bird again. The last time I'd seen one, we had been resupplying at a thriving dockside, and merchants had been selling fans made of those incredible pink feathers. "It's Pylos," I added.

"Pylos can't have fallen, there are forty thousand people there."

"Suboptimal," I agreed, because she wasn't really arguing with me.

She didn't let her face move at all. To anyone watching, we might still have been talking about the strange bird. "Find out what happened."

Close to us, a couple of the Guards whose duty that kind of thing must usually have been looked puzzled. I was too. She had mechanisms in place for this, people with clearly demarcated duties—she didn't need to use some half-deaf polemarch she'd scooped out of the garrison for her reconnaissance reports. If she noticed, she pretended not to. I had an odd feeling that I was being interviewed again, but I was already looking for Pentheus: it wasn't about that.

"Yes, lady."

"Heliades," she said, before I could go. "Count them. Grain is coming from Egypt—but not that much."

14

There were easily a thousand people approaching the walls. The crowd was becoming denser, because the watchmen had already closed the gates. There was a dull kind of protest, but everyone seemed to expect it; no doubt the same thing had happened at every place they'd tried before this. The train of carts and wagons and trudging people snaked right back along the westward road, disappearing into the heat haze. Thousands more.

"Where have they come from?" I asked one of the watchmen as she let me through the tiny side gate.

"I can't understand them. Somewhere further than Sparta, it must be."

The second I was outside, I was surrounded by people shouting.

"You have to let us in—"

"We need water—"

"—died on the road—"

It was the way they spoke in the west, sharp and jagged like the rocks along the shores out there. I wouldn't have understood if I hadn't sailed.

"Wait! Wait. Where have you come from, what's happened?"

Everyone yelled at once.

I'd been right.

Pylos, the great city that controlled all the western harbours, had fallen seven days ago.

At first I thought people were telling me it was legions from Egypt or Hattusa taking revenge for what we had done at Troy, stealing as much as they could in recompense for all the Kind Sea shipping taxes they had lost. But that wasn't what they were saying at all.

"No, you don't understand. No one *came*. It was just people. Normal people, in the city," an older man told me as I sifted through people near the gate, trying to find anyone who could understand me. He looked bewildered.

"Normal people in the city," I repeated. It wasn't another language, it was all Achaean, but in just the same way that different cities are wildly different to each other here—I have more in common with Egyptian officers than I do with the aristocracy of Athens—the words we use are different too, and sometimes, so is the grammar. People from the west sounded odd and abbreviated to me, and I knew from years resupplying in their harbours that to them, the way we spoke around Thebes sounded ancient.

"Yes, normal people!"

Someone who might have been his daughter lifted her hands a little in a way that said, it's all right, he's never very specific. "People went mad. Ordinary people. In the end they just burned the Palace down." She blinked once. "I think I did."

There was a prickly silence, and some of the people around us who had been listening too took a sudden interest in their bootlaces and the straps of their packs. I had a feeling that if I asked around, no one would know anyone who did anything at the Palace; but that if I searched the wagons, there would be a lot of newly redistributed grain and gold.

"Mad," I said, with a spider-feeling on the back of my neck. "Mad how?"

"It's over now," the woman said quickly.

At the side gate there was a stir, and between shoulders and wagons, I saw a swift-moving phalanx of figures in black, veiled despite the heat, hands tattooed black-red. People drew back to let them through, and soon voices called out, sometimes with words I didn't know, but it was obvious what they were saying: yes, here, I need a witch. Without meaning to, I looked for someone taller. Yes: he was talking to a family in a wagon, carrying a medicine satchel. I drew my teeth over my lower lip, not liking that he was out here. Nobody could see him properly through the veil at least, but someone as tall and fine-turned as Dionysus would fetch a fortune at a slave market even in Athens, never mind if anyone managed to get him as far as Egypt. All these people were desperate, and it didn't matter if they'd all been scribes and accountants and horse-trainers a week ago. When a city falls, there's an alchemy that turns office clerks into hyenas. He was a clever witch, for sure, but no witching can stop someone punching you in the face and loading you into the back of a wagon.

Which, of course, he would fucking deserve, after almost getting me and a hundred others killed last night in the Guards' cells.

The old man looked wretched. "You have to tell your queen to let us in. We heard Thebes still has supplies, and law, and . . ."

I wanted to say, *Look at the ground: we don't have food.* There were wisps of old grass, blasted to straw. Even just standing in the full sun was giving me a headache. It felt like my blood was evaporating and my veins were trying to pump rust.

"I have to do a headcount and report to the Palace," I said. I had to speak carefully, trying to choose words we had in common. "You'll be told what will happen as soon as we can." I looked around again, more and more worried by new things I was noticing. Very thin children sitting too quiet in the wagons. Young people grey with dust. I couldn't see any water. "If you go around the north side of the city, there are springs."

I shouldn't really have said that, but they would have found out soon anyway. Thousands of people could occupy the springs and stop water going into Thebes if they wanted to force us to open the gates. I waved at a watchman on the wall and then spoke to him through the little side gate when he came down.

"Run to the garrison, tell General Alexandra that a lot of people are about to go to the springs."

"Shouldn't we put a stop to that, sir?" he asked. He was one of those officious middle-aged men who always mistook his own worst fears for good solid common sense. "What if—"

"That's up to the general," I said, cutting under him, but friendly. It wasn't unreasonable to be frightened. "But unless we want a lot of bodies outside the wall, then we'll just supervise."

Then, going slowly under the pounding sun, I started to walk up the road, counting, and wondering exactly what the lady had meant when she said people went mad, and whether I would be able to convince anyone to tell me.

I walked for a mile across the cracked plain, but I didn't find the end of the caravan. I would have gone further, but it was then that I realized I wouldn't make it back if I did. It was too hot. The buckle on my kilt kept burning me whenever I brushed it, and even though it was thick, I had to put my cloak on properly. Where it didn't cover me, my wrists and my hands soon looked like I'd plunged them into scalding water. I would have kept going despite those things, though, if I hadn't started to see the bodies on the wayside. A man collapsed right in front of me. I caught him and lifted him onto the back of a wagon, and tried to tell the people nearby to veer north, to the springs, but they couldn't understand what I was saying.

By then, my count was at three thousand, with no end in sight. It had been stupid to come out with no water. It was such a sailor thing to do: it had just never occurred to me that the heat would be this bad, because at the sea it never was. Angry with myself, I turned back, but then slowed down.

Even with water, it would have been slow going, and dangerous. The headache was getting worse now. Human bodies can endure a lot more than their owners usually think, but I knew the limits of mine and I was about half an hour from collapsing.

Pentheus was inexperienced, but he wasn't stupid. If he had tried to leave the city, the heat would have forced him to turn back very quickly. These people had made the journey because they had to, with the protection of covered wagons. One boy, perhaps with a stolen horse which would also need water, would get barely five miles from Thebes. If he had been taken, with a wagon and supplies, the Hidden would have caught up.

He was still in the city. He had to be.

The hot wind was stripping the topsoil off the ground. Only it wasn't soil any more; it was dust, and snakes of it streamed everywhere, shushing through wagon wheels and the manes of the donkeys and horses. So much of it was moving that where wagons paused at the roadside, drifts of dust heaped up so quickly that people had to excavate the wheels. Because I was sweating, it was sticking to me, and to everyone else; we were all grey with it.

It happened across perhaps two or three minutes.

It got hotter. Noticeably, frighteningly hotter. The air went from ordinarily baked to the way it feels inside a sauna before you pour the water over the stones, almost too hot to breathe. I saw people on the road notice too, slow down, reach for water.

I would have trudged on oblivious if someone hadn't tugged my cloak and pointed behind us.

Horizon to horizon like a brown cliff, so tall it was already shading the sun, was a dust storm. I'd only ever seen them in Egypt. Achaea might be a barren rocky mess, but dust storms—all I could do was stare at it, even when I realized it was moving so fast that I wouldn't get back to the city walls. It had shapes in it, galloping ahead. They looked like the gods were riding into Thebes.

A family beside me were pulling luggage out of a covered wagon so they could get inside it, so I helped, looking around at the same time for the witches. Everywhere, horses were spooking. The ones that weren't tied to anything were panicking and running, and even the oxen, usually as willing to stir as rocks, were lowing and swinging their horns, dragging little carts with them as they thumped away from the dust and the new heat. Two carts crashed into each other and smashed.

The heat was so bad it felt dangerous to breathe. My lungs were cooking. All my thoughts were turning to sludge. We had about the length of time it takes to saddle a horse before nobody would really be able to think any more. Some people would faint. Some would have seizures. In Egypt, we had lost chunks of regiments that way.

I couldn't see Dionysus and assumed he had gone already, until I saw him by a cart marked in blue with the sigils of the Temple of the Mother. Someone was trapped under it. He wasn't strong enough to lift it.

I didn't know what the Witches' Vow was, but I had a terrible feeling it would have things to say about abandoning a patient, even if it did mean you died trying to help.

If you had asked me an hour ago, I would have grumbled that he was a sacrilegious criminal and if he wanted to die then he could do it, thank you; but you're a different person when you have time to think about things.

I ran across and shoved cart upright—both of us together was only just enough—and then the man trapped underneath was scrambling out and running away, and not thanking Dionysus at all.

"Phaidros," Dionysus said, sounding more grateful to see me than anyone ever had.

"Come on," I said, pulling him. "We need to get inside. This heat—"

The dust blasted through us and instantly he was invisible, but I was still holding onto him. Even though it was only a few yards away, the wagon vanished, and it took three tries to find it.

The people already crowded inside were good about squeezing us in, though I was very soon sure it wasn't in the general spirit of xenia. It wasn't normal for witches to take off the veil in public, but Dionysus had to, to breathe, and when it was off, I saw at least four pairs of eyes flick over him, assessing how tall he was, how magnetic he was with his hair tied up high and cindered with grey; how straightforward it would be to just take him and sell him somewhere. I stared back at them, hoping that they were all exhausted enough and starving enough not to want to bother—and acutely aware that I wasn't as strong as I should have been. I'd been losing weight like everyone else. But, the scar across my face did still make me look like I'd tear someone's throat out with my teeth. The eyes skittered away. I nudged Dionysus and gave him my knife.

"Oh, don't be silly," he whispered. It was either deranged optimism, or the cosmically stupid certainty that most very tall men have, which is that nothing is dangerous, neither for them nor for anyone else.

I looked at him hard, not wanting to have to spell out for him what slavery would be like for someone who looked like him. "If I have to come and rescue you from the King of Persia's zoo before anyone has a chance to try and make you breed with another giraffe," I whispered back, very fast so that any of the Pylos people who heard me would struggle to follow in Theban dialect, "you will never live it down. I will follow you around, reminding you about it, even if I have to ride after you as you gallop free across the fucking savannah."

He looked at me as if I'd just said something incredibly kind, and took the knife.

I relaxed a tiny bit, which I regretted, because at least when I'd been thinking about giraffes, I hadn't been thinking about the heat.

The heat. It was like sitting by a furnace, but the quality was different, because with a furnace you can step away, and you can feel a border of cooler air on one side of you, but not this. This was going to kill us all if it went on for long.

"Is there any water?" a little boy asked.

"There's wine," a man said, and gave him a sip from a flask before nodding at him to offer it to me.

I shook my head, wondering what the fuck kind of life they'd had in Pylos, that they had fled the city with wine rather than water. Maybe these boxes were filled with cake and silk trousers.

"No, take it," the man said, more insistently than seemed rational.

"I can't. I'm Sown, we don't drink."

There was sudden, intense silence, except for the howling of the storm just on the other side of the wagon's thin walls.

"It's over," someone else said, low and urgent. "Thebes isn't infected. Look, he's fine, he's not—"

"You're going to drink that," a lady said, "or you're going out in the storm."

Dionysus put his hand over mine where it was resting on my sword hilt, before I could say anything. "Why is it important?" He could speak like they did.

"It's medicine," she said tightly.

"It helped," the first man said, just as obscurely.

"What does that mean?" I asked, somewhere between frustrated and dismayed.

"Just drink it!" they all yelled at me.

I looked at Dionysus, in case any of that made more sense to him than to me. "I can't break my vows just to be polite," I said quietly, only for him. I wasn't sure what I wanted him to do.

"You can if it means you don't die in a dust storm," he said.

"No—"

"Your life is mine. You gave it to me. It isn't yours to throw away for no reason."

I swiped the flask and drank, then pushed it back against his chest and had to sit there with that rancid poison lightness going through my veins.

For whatever insane reason of their own, all the people from Pylos relaxed.

I put my hands over my face so I didn't have to look at anyone.

It couldn't have been that long, but it felt like hours. We kept perfectly still, trying to breathe slowly. I thought we really would all die, even in the shade of the wagon, and I sat there trying, through the molten slag that was my brain now, to piece together what I should say to Helios when I saw him. He'd be livid. *Did you die honourably in battle, knight? No, sir, I suffocated drunk in the back of a wagon like a fucking moron.*

When it stopped, the temperature plunged so suddenly that I felt cold. All my thinking came back; all of us lifted our heads and looked between each other, as though we all hoped somebody else might have proof that it was over, properly, not just pausing. It was Dionysus who pushed open the wagon door first. Cold air rushed in, and I'd never been so happy to breathe. It felt like swallowing ice water. He stepped down first, and turned back to give me a hand, because it was an awkwardly steep step. We both helped everyone else down. The little boy was last and giggled as we swung him down, one of us on either arm. I tried to find something else to look at, and Dionysus was the nearest thing. He was staring towards the city walls.

"They never opened the gates." There was real dismay in his voice. "Why?"

At the gates, there were ragged heaps that looked like old grain sacks, some big, some small, with dust heaped up on their windward sides. The big shapes were dead horses and oxen. The little ones were dead people.

In a strategic way, I could see very well why they'd done it. In a human way, though—I was glad I hadn't been the one to give that order.

"Because there's no food in the city. The choice was bodies inside, or bodies outside," I said. I coughed, because I'd swallowed a lot of dust, which was making cement along the back of my throat. Around us, other people were starting to edge out from whatever had given them cover, but not all of them.

I had thought I'd grown out of it, but seeing the bodies at the gate gave me that tidal bore of panic-relief that comes when you've just marginally not died. Dionysus looked like he might be having it too.

"Thank you," he said. "For helping me."

I gave him a disapproving look, because nobody should thank knights for doing their duty. It was a bleak window into the life of a witch. He expected to be left behind. "Don't be silly," I said, imitating the way he'd said it to me before. I'd never imitated anyone in my life, but I wanted him to stop looking like he thought he didn't have a basic right to be rescued when it was necessary by someone whose profession it was. I hoped he'd hit me.

No; he only smiled. "Do you think we can get back into the city?"

"They should open the side gate if we can convince them we're citizens. They'll be able to hear us now."

We set out that way. The wind was still strong, though blessedly cooler now. After the furnace heat of the storm, ordinary baking was a relief. I smiled when I realized I was entirely in his shadow. It was still an uncanny novelty to be so close to someone so tall. Nice, though. Even around other knights, I was always worried about what would happen if someone made me jump. Dionysus . . . I'd bruise him, but he was big enough to restrain me if he wanted.

Dionysus pushed one hand against his ear, took it away, then did it again, and turned around twice as he walked. The way the wind pulled his clothes made a ghost of the way he'd looked when he danced. I looked right away. "Can you hear something?"

"I can never hear anything," I said, but as I said it, I realized I could. It was just at a pitch that blurred for me. It sounded like a kind of wailing whirring, but what a thing really was and what it sounded like now to me were very different. It was a little while before I heard people yelling, and when I looked, I soon saw why.

In the ground, there was a chasm, just at the base of the city wall. It must have been there all the time, but the wind had uncovered it, scouring away decades of earth and leaving just the rock.

Something was down there among the rocks.

It was something bronze. Bronze statues. People were starting to gather along the edge. It wasn't steep, so I climbed down along with a priestess in red and a couple of young men who were gripping cudgels in the way of people who had never been in a fight before. Dionysus stayed at the top, looking uneasy, as though he would have liked to tell me not to go.

The wind sang through the fissure in the bedrock, and it sang in the bronze as well. There was a clicking I couldn't work out; something, I would have sworn, was winding up.

It wasn't until I was almost down on a level with them that I realized how big the statues were. Twice life-sized, at least, made to be seen from a distance. They were lying down, like they were sleeping. At first I thought they were supposed to be women, but they weren't. They were monsters; all teeth, limbs all far too long for humans. When I started to pick a way through them, trying to work out when they were from, I wished I hadn't. They weren't like any marvels I'd seen before. The joints were all hinged; if I'd known a way it was even remotely possible without hydraulics—and there couldn't be unless these things had their own reservoir that somehow hadn't dried up, buried somewhere beneath them—I would have sworn they were designed to sit up. It shouldn't have been so disconcerting. They were just statues.

Maybe long ago, those hydraulics had worked. Now there couldn't be anything in the clockwork but dust.

They sounded like they were breathing.

Up above us, the wind gusted, and the statues howled. It was loud even for me. The boys shot back up the scree to ground level. The priestess slammed her hands over her ears.

One of the statues twitched, and something in its mechanisms woke up just enough for the clockwork to remember what it had used to do. It was a horribly living twitch. Its shoulders jolted, and I stared, because to move like that, the bronze would have to be as pliant as chain mail, but it wasn't, it was bronze, I could see, it was right in front of me. I started to edge back to the chasm wall. The priestess was already climbing it.

The wind came again, and one of the statues sat up. It was serpentine, snake-smooth, not a mechanical jolt, and it should have been impossible. Bronze rusts. Leave it underground—all of them should have been green with age and damp, but they were as perfect as they must have been when they were put down here.

Then another one, and another one, and I couldn't look away and I was feeling behind me for the wall, which somehow still wasn't there, and right by my boots, something bronze moved too quickly for me to catch what it had been, but I thought it was a tail.

The wind was powering through the statues now, and they were howling a terrible clockwork song. There were words, but I couldn't understand, and now they were sitting up, the bronze things were taller than me, and I had a sudden crushing certainty that whoever had built them, they had never, ever meant for a person to get stuck in among them, because if a single one of these titan machines smacked one arm sideways, I was dead, and there were so many of them juddering upright from the earth now that I would never have seen it coming.

Just as I pulled myself up onto the next rock shelf and Dionysus caught my hand to help me to the top, a tail slammed into the place I'd been standing. It shattered the stones.

Dionysus and I sat on the edge of the pit, staring down at the bronze monsters still screaming their lost ancient words in the wind, and so did everyone else. We were all quiet. The dust and the heat and the storm weren't forgotten but it didn't matter for now.

The marvels were like nothing I'd ever seen. The quantity of bronze was madness. It could have supplied a legion of knights with full armour. The quality of the engineering too. It could only have been a message from a queen or king. Nobody else could have commanded anything like the wealth to build these things. Whatever they were saying, it had been important to whoever had wanted them built. And it was hard not to feel as though, for all they were saying words we couldn't understand, this was what you would make if you weren't building something for now, but for people living a thousand years after your language had been forgotten. That was the only reason to do *this*, instead of just carving it on the city walls. If you carved it, you expected someone to be able to read it.

"Can you tell what they're saying?" I asked.

Dionysus repeated some of it. It was odd, but the Furies' language matched his accent better than ours. "I'd have known what that meant, when I was young," he said, sounding strange, and sad. "Do you ever feel like your whole life happened to you in languages you don't speak any more?"

That hit me deeper than I expected. "All the time. What is it?"

"I've forgotten," he said, apologetic.

I knew what that was like. I'd grown up across half the world, swimming in a hundred languages. I knew scraps of things whose names I didn't know from territories I couldn't remember. Sometimes I said things to myself around the house while I was making bread or pinning back the shutters, and for my life I couldn't have said where they were from or what they meant.

Whatever the marvels were saying, though, it was a warning. You didn't build twenty screaming Furies and bury them in a cavern for a once-in-twenty-generations drought to uncover if you were saying anything good.

"I need to report this," I said, getting up.

15

Queen Agave came down herself. One of our priestesses came too, with a dictionary. It was bound papyrus, a book, not a scroll, as thick as my wrist and so fragile with its reed pages that I half expected it to catch fire in the sun. They said it was Old Cretan, which was what royal proclamations had been made in, long ago. Nobody spoke it any more.

I wondered how Dionysus had known. Maybe there was a tiny pocket of mountain country somewhere where it was still alive, just. I couldn't ask; he was gone already, probably to help the survivors.

Along with our priestess, and another from Pylos, and six or seven Guards, cloaks such a deep purple in the glaring sun they didn't look real, we stood at the edge of the marvel chasm while the statues roared. I was cooking inside my armour, and Thebes's crown of towers really did look like it was burning. Even from down here, the smell of charred meat and incense was so heavy I felt like I'd never be able to taste anything else again. In twenty years, if I had the bad luck to live that long, I'd bite into some bread and it would *still* taste of sacrifice fires.

The priestesses were struggling to hear the Furies' words clearly enough to look them up. It wasn't that they were blurred, just that it's very diffi-cult to hear the borders of words in a language you don't hear aloud, even if you can read it.

Listening for Dionysus's cadence, though, which sang much more than ours did, I could guess. I offered a couple of words I was sure about, eyes right down, not wanting to sound like I thought I knew more than they did.

"Oh, you're right; of course you're right," the Pylos priestess said. She sounded annoyed. I stepped back, out of the way, so that I wasn't looming over her shoulder.

"Gods, Phaidros," the Queen said, as if it really were a genuine skill. "You're going to have to teach me that."

I tried to tell if she was taking the piss. Any sailor speaks a lot of languages, which means we tend to be good at hearing accurately, even if we don't hear *well*.

"It's a loop," our priestess said at last. She and the other from Pylos had just closed the dictionary and exchanged a look I couldn't read. "They're saying the same thing again and again. I think it says sacrifice—"

"Or sing," the other one put in. "It's the same word."

Something heavy settled deep in my chest.

"Sacrifice, or sing . . . to the master of dancing."

I had a powerful urge to get right away from the marvel Furies. They were unsettling enough just in themselves, all bronze teeth and razor wings, but they couldn't, they could *not* be chanting a forbidden song that had begun in Thebes after the falling of a star. They had been underground for—how long? A thousand years? It couldn't be the same song.

"What's that, is that a god?" the Queen asked, looking sceptical that the priestesses even distantly knew what they were talking about.

Our priestess shrugged and the Pylos priestess looked troubled. She was saying the words to herself.

"What else does it say?"

"It's . . . something like, *made in thunder, burner of cities* . . . and then an old word we're not sure about. It could be a kind of clan leader, or . . . ?"

Thunder-wrought and city-razing . . . I could hear it as clearly as if I were in the cells still.

"King," I said, not believing that it really could be. "King of the holy raging, rave and rise again. Is that it?"

Our priestess looked indignant. "You speak Old Cretan?"

"What?" the Pylos priestess said, as if she had just watched me crawl out of a tomb.

"At the Temple of Ares, six knights are singing that song and they can't stop," I explained, clear like I'd always been taught to report, but I didn't feel very clear. Our knights couldn't be singing the same song as some marvels from a thousand years ago which had been buried until this morning. "The priests say it's madness—"

The Pylos priestess caught the arm of a dusty man whose clothes looked like they had used to be very fine, and spoke in their dialect so fast I only just caught it.

"The mad god is here. The knights are already singing to him."

The man looked grim, and shouted an order to some of the people on wagons nearby. I didn't understand the words, but I understood their faces. He might as well have said there was plague here and someone had just arrived coughing. People who had been unharnessing horses and oxen to let them graze on the sparse, straw-dry grass snatched up reins and straps again, and like a ripple, the news started to travel backwards through the great caravan.

"What was that?" the Queen said to me. "What did she say?"

"She said the mad god is here, but I don't—wait! Lady, what do you mean? It's just a song—"

"It is *not* just a song," she said. She came right up to me, and the Queen, and wrenched her veil off. There was a terrible scar down her right eye, inflamed and still new. "It means he's *here*. Our knights sang it too. Half of these people sang it before the end. Half of Pylos went insane. I don't mean they were angry because there was no food and it was very hot, I mean *insane*. They started to sing that song, and they started to dance, and they couldn't stop, and before long they were tearing the Palace down." She looked between us. "Troy was a holy city and we burned it, and *he* is the curse that follows. And now he's here. You need to sacrifice to him *yesterday*, or you need to get out. It's infectious, you probably have it already. I'm sorry," she said again, grim, and sprang onto the back of a wagon that was passing us. The driver was urging the oxen into a trot. Dust rose up all around us.

The Queen glanced at me as people and horses and wagons juddered by. She was still and unflustered, like any good knight in the face of something strange, but she did look puzzled.

"Have you ever heard of a mad god?"

I shook my head. But everyone from Pylos must have thought he was worse than the drought, because right down the length of the road, everyone was moving on, and I didn't see a single person stop. Soon, the only people left on the road were the ones who had died in the storm.

16

The throne room was wreathed in steam from the dragon marvels. It was a relief to walk into the white gloom after the blinding sun outside, but it wasn't just to save everyone's eyes. Here and there in that artificial fog were ghosts—people listening, maybe scribes, maybe Guards, always too hazy to see well. Around the throne itself, the air was clear. People standing in the steam could see us, but we couldn't see them. The vapour was cold enough that I needed my cloak, which was a desperate relief. With the dimness and that cold fog, and the spectres of the watchers around us, the throne room didn't seem like it was part of the rest of the Palace; it felt more like we had crossed a border, and come into that dead hinterland at the gates of Hades.

The Chamberlain had told me to stay, but I didn't understand why. There was nothing useful I could do here, and the longer I was here, the longer I wasn't organising the census.

The other people here were important: the Chamberlain, the captain of the Guards, senior advisers, and even, sitting on the steps that led up to the throne and almost invisible in the vapour, the royal prophet. I didn't know anyone, so I stayed back, standing on the border between the clearer air in front of the throne, and the fog where the watchers waited.

I felt someone's eyes down my left side and looked across to find that the prophet was staring at me, or rather through me; Tiresias was blind.

"Heliades," they said, quiet but clear, even though I was twenty feet away and not making any noise. "Come here."

Disconcerted, I went across and knelt down close to the steps.

There were all kinds of stories about Tiresias. People—including Tiresias—said that they had started out as a woman and been turned into a man by Apollo, or the other way around—now they were neither on account of how Apollo couldn't decide in the end and didn't really care anyway because it was core Tiresias-ness that he liked. They had been struck blind by the force of their visions, and if they weren't immortal then they were at least old enough to remember Kadmus and the dragon. I believed the first two but not the last one. They weren't that old.

Now that I was close, I could see what they were doing, which was sharing an apple with a very happy tortoise. It's hard not to like someone who befriends passing tortoises.

"Prophet?" I said.

The tortoise gave me a narrow look, defending its half of the apple between its paws.

"The Queen," said Tiresias, without any preamble, "is about to ask us all to agree that there's no god at work here, it must be a perfectly ordinary plague or a conspiracy or some rubbish; but I think you and I both know that the mad god is very real, and very much here, in Thebes. You're not going to want to, I know, but you need to say what you think. Otherwise all she's going to hear is a bunch of idiots who always agree with her; and me, a vendor of what she likes to call esoteric bollocks."

"I decidedly do not know that there's a god—"

"Don't be silly," Tiresias said, so similarly to the way Dionysus had said it that I had an eerie certainty that they were quoting him, to prove they could overhear things even when they weren't close by. And—they spoke like him anyway. It was that same accent. Slighter, but they sang their sentences like he did, the ends of words sharp and bronze. "You know him well. He has blue eyes, and wherever he goes, growing things riot, and people lose their minds." They winked at me. "In places where they haven't been so stupid as to forget about him, they call him Bakhos."

That sent a cold spider down my back. It meant "Raver."

"Why would you think I know him?" I asked. No one knew about the boy from the shore, no one.

"Depends, doesn't it?" Tiresias said, glimmering at me in exactly the same way Dionysus had last night. "Either a prophet is a person with an excellent intelligence network, and we make certain to hear things across many countries and decades very secretly, and someone saw what happened to your ship and reported it to me—or, Apollo granted me a vision. But a prophet is *assuredly* a person who would be foolish to let anyone know which it is. Some people will listen only to Apollo, some only to more earthly intelligence. Best to straddle both, I find."

The Raver—gods, what a name.

"Do this for me, sweet knight," they said, more seriously. They took my hand, easily, without searching for it. Because they wore indigo, Apollo's colour, their sleeves had stained their knuckles blue, like the reverse of witches' tattoos. "The Queen is in danger of making the mistake that all clever people make every so often, which is to think she always judges well, and always sees right. Don't let her."

All the things I wanted to say crowded up behind my teeth, so many that I couldn't say anything. If the mad god was the boy from the shore, then there was a severe chance that I had called him here. Only I wasn't dead, so he couldn't be; so what was going on, and why was Tiresias so sure, and was it possible that they were lying to me in order to win the point they wanted to make?

Too late, though: there was a stir across the hall as the Queen walked out from behind the throne, a heavy cloak across her shoulders now, and the marvel crown, with its writhing silver figures of warrior saints, set through her hair.

"What we know," the Queen said into the new, deep silence, "is that a star fell, and some knights close by lost their minds. Shortly after, my son vanished. Several days earlier, Pylos fell, amid reports of the same madness, and the same song." She was standing in front of the throne, not sitting on it. "Several centuries earlier—too early for us to have any record of their building—Fury marvels were buried outside the city wall, reciting the same song as the knights now confined at Ares. If this were any other city, with different folklore, I would have no hesitation in concluding that this is a god. However, as we all know, any suggestion of divine intervention in Thebes must be treated with the utmost scepticism. Therefore, I'd like to hear what else this might be."

A smallish woman stepped forward. She was, like most people who worked directly for the Palace, a slave, but instead of an iron collar, hers was silver, and she was dressed as finely as any Sown lady, in orange: a senior marvel-maker. I only just had time to wonder why a marvel-maker was important for all this before she began.

"It seems striking," she said, "that this madness has emerged in a drought. We must consider the possibility that it wasn't the *star* which caused the madness in the afflicted knights, but something it churned up in the ground. There are many substances that can cause madness, as anybody who's ever worked in a mercury mine can attest. Pylos is likewise in drought. It seems significant that the Furies were uncovered by a dust storm, and were apparently designed for that. Dust storms move soil. If the madness they warn against afflicted people at the time of their building, also in drought, we can fairly safely say this has something to do with drought conditions."

"Why would people be singing the same song, cities and centuries apart?" the Queen asked.

I had a sudden feeling that this had been rehearsed. Tiresias smiled at me.

"Songs can survive for a thousand years. Certainly some of the legends of King Kadmus are that old. If it's in general folk memory, then many people will have heard it outside Thebes. I find it telling that it was *knights* who sang it, not ordinary citizens: the knights have been away from Thebes for many years. They heard all kinds of forbidden things. It is, sensibly enough, a song about madness—and the deranged will tend to say the first thing that comes to mind. It isn't wildly unlikely for mad people in different places to sing a song about a mad king. One starts, another copies them; there needn't be anything divine about it, only ordinary human clockwork."

She didn't, I noticed, say "mad god."

"I think that's a very benign view of what's happening," the captain of the Guards said from beside me. He was as slate-faced as he had been last night when he ordered a hundred and fifty people to be confined for three days in lethal heat. "Something in the ground would suggest this madness is real. It clearly isn't. The refugees from Pylos were very keen to tell us that people there just . . . went mad. There is no such thing as a citywide madness. But there is such a thing as civil uprising. There was never any madness at Pylos, there was treason and an old song about riot and chaos that the ringleaders used to pull people together under one banner, but now it's over, people want to believe something else, and they've convinced themselves that the mad king in the song is a god. As Zoe says, songs have long lives, especially treason anthems. Outside Thebes it could easily have survived from the time of King Kadmus to the present day. And as for the 'afflicted' knights—I'll stake my armour that there was nothing in the ground, and nothing in the star. Someone ambitious took advantage of its falling and *paid* those knights to sing and feign madness."

I wanted to think that wasn't possible. I'd been with Amphitrion when the star fell; but if someone had moved through the smoke and spoken to knights quietly, would I have known? Probably not.

"They would have had to do that very quickly, Captain," the Queen said, "given that it was less than an hour between the star's falling and the arrival of the first knights at Ares."

"Blackmail doesn't take long," he said seriously. "Don't do as I say and I'll kill your sister, do as I say and I'll pay you: it's that fast."

"So. Something in the ground, or opportunistic fraud. Anything else?"

"I can tell I'm going be hurled off the city wall in a sack full of snakes soon, but I'm very old so I don't care," Tiresias said, and in the fog, a few people laughed. It was a strange choice, I thought, for them to be funny: prophets were usually serious people. I would have thought that the less serious the prophet, the less serious the prophecy would sound.

"Tiresias, I already know what you're going to say," the Queen said.

"Really, you know all about the mad god already? Good. You know not to ignore him, then."

He has blue eyes, and everywhere he goes, growing things riot, and people lose their minds.

And about an hour before all this began, I had called him here. It was too close to ignore, but I couldn't make it fit. I still wasn't dead. I wasn't even mad.

The Queen looked weary. "All right, who is he?"

"Long ago," Tiresias said, "there was a god older and greater than Zeus, who is a child by comparison. He was never a god of anything so straightforward as thunder or the sea. Humans are weird animals; partly we're wild, and partly we are clockwork. Unholy devices, all of us—mechanisms bolted onto bone."

I frowned, because they were speaking subtly differently, not in the cheerful way they had before. They sounded less like *they* were talking now, but something else was talking through them; something friendly and ancient that liked them, but nonetheless had its own voice. I'd never been to Delphi, I'd never seen Apollo possess the Oracle, but all at once I knew it would look like this.

"The mad god is as old as human beings, and his function is to guard the border between the clockwork and the wild. When we veer too near to clockwork, he brings the old wildness again; to remind us of what we are, and to save us from much worse. He can be gentle; he is in music and the bards' stories, and in a cup of wine. He can be a shepherd easing us away from the borders of the poison places. But fight him, and he will fight back. He is madness too. At our peril we forget the king of the holy raging, who, like the ivy, never dies."

"Is that," said the Queen, sounding as though she had passed irritated now and flown into a sort of serene hopelessness that she was ever going to get out of this room, "a very impressive-sounding way of saying we should all get really drunk and have a cataclysmic party, or else? Music, stories, wine? What? Is this a bet you've got with your opposite number in Athens?"

People laughed.

Tiresias swayed, like they had been sleepwalking and now they were waking up. I went up the steps fast, worried they were going to fall.

"Prophet?" I said tentatively.

Tiresias blinked twice. "Helios?"

"Phaidros."

They shook their head once, looking disconcerted. "You sound so alike." It was true. If I was being especially obnoxious, all he had to do was swear pyroclastically at a general through a tent wall and blame me, and discipline was immediately restored. "What . . . was I saying?"

It wasn't pretend. They had no idea.

"A masterly performance as always," the Queen growled. "Now we've heard from all sides: send out the heralds. Anyone who sings that song will be condemned to immediate slavery. Anyone caught sacrificing to any new god will also go to the fields, or to the galleys. Anyone spreading rumours of the lost prince will be executed. Thank you all. Heliades, come here."

Tiresias squeezed my arm and gave me a wry look that said, *Didn't I tell you?* "Hand me that tortoise," was all they said.

I gave them the tortoise, and the apple, and watched them vanish into the cold fog for a second before I carried on up the steps to the throne. That voice just now—it hadn't been Tiresias.

The Queen looked me over as though she suspected Tiresias was infectious. "Go to Ares and question the afflicted knights. Find out if they really are mad," she said. "If this is fraud, then whoever paid them will also have Pentheus."

"Yes, lady," I said quietly, but didn't move, because two equal and opposite forces were at war in my head, and the result was exactly no motion in either direction.

What Tiresias had said was sound. I knew it was. I knew there was a god who drove people mad and who had wrecked my ship. I'd brushed his hair once.

But the kind of person who said, *Haha, but what you've got to remember is that humans can't be all duty and honour and rationality all the time, and if you try then there's a special god who'll drive you mad*—that kind of person was usually telling you his grand philosophy while he was four drinks down and about to make his third lunge after the good-looking stable boy. It was laziness, and the need to intellectually justify being a pig. *We're all just animals really, no use pretending we ain't!* Lunge. Cue a huge fight to save the stable boy. Something right down in my soul was embarrassed for Tiresias, that they had said that in public. Even though . . .

Even though I also knew that what had said it today wasn't some hog of an Athenian gone three sheets to the wind. It wasn't even Tiresias.

"Do you . . . need winding up?" the Queen offered, pretending—very kindly, given that she could have hit me—to look for the key to my clockwork.

I couldn't say to her that a god had once turned my ship back into a forest. She would never listen to anything I said again.

"I think it's possible not to see what you don't expect to, lady," I said to the hem of her cloak.

Even that made me sound like I wanted to desert and go to Athens.

"And to see what you do expect to, even when it isn't there," she said. She took my elbows and guided me upright. I kept my eyes on the cloak hem. It had a double seam, stitched in silver. "Why do you expect to see a god, knight? Do you think the story about the lost heir is true, do you think my sister had a child of Zeus?"

"Are you certain that she didn't?"

"Yes," she said unexpectedly. She touched my shoulder and guided me behind the throne, through a low door into a much smaller chamber behind.

I slowed down, because I'd expected a receiving room or somewhere private she could sit by herself and not listen to Tiresias, but it was full of marvel mechanisms. They were built into the walls, and everywhere there were pipes, hot and cold. Things clicked and turned, feeding into the throne. In the middle of the room, looking out of place, were a couple of chairs, a little table with a pitcher on it, a bowl of apples, and box of papyrus documents. She nodded for me to sit down. "Less eerie when you know how it works, isn't it," she said, nodding at the walls and the pipes. "The story about my sister is the same. It was never meant to be a true story, when she said the father was Zeus; it's a legal shorthand. Have you heard of this?"

"No?" I said, wrong-footed.

She didn't seem annoyed; she only sat forward. "When someone has a child outside wedlock, she has two choices: she can hand it over to a temple for adoption, or, if she wants to keep it, she vows that the father was a god. Of course it's very unlikely that that happened, but nobody can say it absolutely isn't true, as you point out, because that would be denying the existence of the gods, which is blasphemy . . . the penalty for which is slavery, you see? We find that with this law, far fewer people end up in cycles of revenge killing that start with infidelity. One of King Kadmus's more elegant legislative solutions to ongoing blood feuds. It isn't a genuine account of meeting a god. It's a legal way to invoke the protection of the crown." She half laughed. "If Zeus was involved at all, it was because he was angry with having his name associated with hers. Hence the lightning."

"I understand," I said quietly.

"You look doubtful."

"What if it's a god who's nothing to do with your sister?"

She nodded slightly. "Maybe. But if I send out the heralds and announce that we think there might be a god, let's sacrifice to him and try to stop the madness spreading, people won't sacrifice to *a* god. They'll sacrifice to *the* lost heir. The more they believe, the more ready they will be to accept the first enterprising fraud who steps forward, and he will. Across my reign, three men have tried. I'm sure there will be a fourth."

"But what if there *is* a god? It's more dangerous to ignore them."

"No, it isn't," she said frankly. "Gods come and go. Thebes can survive the brief and passing interest of a god. What it cannot survive is a civil uprising in a time of drought and oncoming famine. Look at Pylos. Those uprisings very rarely succeed in installing anyone new on the throne. All they do is destroy the throne." She opened her hands where they had been clasped on her knees. "Look, just between the two of us, without any politics or other interests: I don't think there's a god here. I think Zoe is right, I think there's probably something in the ground, and I think—I hate to say it—that Captain Pompous is right as well. Someone's trying to swing this around to look like a good story and climb up to the crown. And I think that even if I'm wrong, even if there is such a thing as the mad god . . . he's far less dangerous than thirty thousand human beings hanging over the edge of bread riots. Do you agree?"

"No, lady," I said, seeing the mast, which had turned back into an oak, smash into the sea.

She smiled. The lines formed round her eyes the same way they had around Helios's. "Good. Kings and queens need to have someone who disagrees with them." She clapped my shoulder as she stood up. "Onward to Ares, knight."

17

The temple courtyard had been tranquil when I brought Amphitrion. Now, it wasn't just full; it was seething. Most of the people inside I recognised from the garrison. Older knights, knights in training, even a general. Some were healthy but bringing commanders and wards; and some were singing or humming, left alone to just spin and spin in whatever corner they could find with enough space. The song was everywhere, different snippets of it, different verses, but it was all the same thing.

I'd never been afraid on a battlefield. It's not that I'm especially stupid, or, I hope not. You can see someone take down the knight beside you with a battle axe and not panic if you know exactly what's meant to happen next and how to do it. It was liturgy: close the wall, step into the breach, spear forward, step, and watch the signal flags. It wasn't easy, but it was simple.

I was afraid walking through that courtyard.

I shouldn't have been. Most people in it were just dancing, and humming, or singing. But it was so away from anything they would ever have done in their right minds that part of me wound up tighter and tighter with a dread of what they *might* decide to do next; and whether there was something in the air that would bring that madness to me too. By an orange tree, two priests were trying to tie someone to the trunk to stop him dancing, and I could see why. He was badly sunburned and he looked like he hadn't had any water, and if they let him keep dancing like he wanted to, he would die soon. But as soon as they caught his elbows, he lashed out with his spear arm, and hit one of the priests so hard the man reeled away with blood pouring down his face.

"Knight?"

The priest I'd spoken to before was just in front of me, looking like he had meant to be on his way somewhere else before he noticed me. He had a cloth over his mouth and nose. I wished I had one too.

"The Queen sent me. I'm supposed to try and talk to some of the knights."

He touched his ear to say he couldn't hear over all the noise. He motioned me into a side building, shut the door, and leaned against it. It was a records room. Clay tablets lined the walls, up to three times the height of a person, with ladders that moved along the shelves on rails. A wheelbarrow full of new records stood in the middle of the floor waiting to be filed, so fresh out of the kiln that they were steaming. He didn't take the mask off. I wished he would; it was much harder to make out what he was saying now I couldn't see his lips.

"Did you say you've been sent here too? You don't seem mad."

"Not yet," I said. "The Queen wants me to talk to some of the knights. She isn't convinced the madness is real."

"Not r—have you *seen* out there?"

I nodded, even less convinced she was right now than before.

He pulled another mask out of his pocket and gave it to me. "Put that on. Why wouldn't she think it's real?"

"There's a rumour about a god of madness," I explained. "And anything to do with a new god looks like fraud to her, because of the story about her sister."

"I'll show you the boy you brought in," he said, sounding angry, but it wasn't anger-anger. He was tired and upset.

He led me outside again, then down through the temple. The hallways were all howling. There were five times more people here than the temple had ever been made to hold. As we passed downstairs, though, into the cellar where the original five knights had been, it was quiet. I was about to ask if the priests had found some kind of drug that worked, but then I stopped, because that wasn't it.

Lined up and covered in sheets, waiting for their pyres, were four bodies.

"They don't eat," the priest said quietly, "and they don't drink, and they won't stop moving. In this heat . . . it's killing people in about twelve hours. We're restraining as many as we can now."

I moved the edge of the shroud on the smallest body. We always say to relatives, he looked like he was sleeping, but bodies don't look like they're sleeping. They look as different without souls in them as coats look without people in them. But it was Amphitrion. I sighed. I'd always known I'd be standing here like this one day, because he had never been the kind to survive long, but I had thought it would be a little further away.

"Have you notified his commander?" I asked, wondering what would happen now to Penelope the Not-Sacrifice Lamb.

"No time," snapped the priest. "There are two hundred others up there and we're trying to keep them alive. None of us has slept. Tell that to the Queen."

"What do you need?" I asked.

"More space. More people. Quarantine measures, for fuck's sake. Now get out, before you catch it too."

I must have been thinking about it behind everything else, but I hadn't be aware of it, so the thought felt like it flew out of nowhere.

There was a very simple way that this could be the god from the ship. I wasn't dead yet because he was going to make me watch everyone else die first.

When I arrived back at the Palace, the Queen was in the cloister, talking to the Guard captain about arrest numbers. Someone else was there too, the abbess from the Temple of the Mother, which was strange, because it was hard to see what she could have to do with the Guards. I stayed back, but like before with the Egyptian prince, the Queen saw me and held her arm out for me to come closer. Once I was in reach, she shepherded me nearer by the small of my back and gave me a little interrogatory look that was asking if that was close enough for me to hear. I could have kissed her hand. Because I could mostly read lips, and partly hear, and I was decent at guessing, most people completely forgot I had any trouble.

"—should get at least a hundred people," the Guard captain was saying. "Our informants in the lower city have reported that the song is already everywhere, even among people who aren't mad."

"And the temple's fields have lost how many slaves?" the Queen said to the abbess.

"Two hundred to starvation, and another two hundred have tried to run," the abbess said.

"That many," the Queen murmured.

"In the last week," the abbess said grimly. "And the rations will only get worse. We'll lose a lot more next month unless the Egyptian grain comes through. What crops we do have will rot in the ground without people to farm them."

"Arrest four hundred people," the Queen said to the Guard captain. "At least. We get them transferred to the fields as quickly as possible. No holding cells: straight into chains, straight out to the estates. Preferably men. Rowdy ones who we can do without anyway. Anyone talking about a new god."

"For those numbers, it would be best to have use of the Hidden."

I twitched. A Hidden ride was difficult enough when you were hunting hardened murderers. To go after ordinary people—there were knights dead enough inside to follow that order and lose no sleep, but not my unit of little knights. They were only fifteen.

"Yes. Inform the duty officer at the garrison."

He bowed briskly. "Obedience is strength, lady."

"Thank you, Captain," she said, and he clipped away. The abbess bowed slightly too and went more slowly. "Heliades, that was quick."

I almost didn't hear. Arrest quotas: I'd grown up with restricted rations and rules, I was used to someone in a palace somewhere deciding how much I was allowed to eat or how much of my time was really mine, but I'd never heard of innocent civilians being arrested for a non-crime just to fill a labour shortage.

"We can't get workers into the fields any other way," the Queen said, as if all my thoughts had etched themselves right across my face. "We can't haemorrhage money paying day labourers to do it. The payments to Egypt for the grain are crippling the treasury. This is the only fast, cheap way to get the harvest in."

"They'll all die," I said, as if she wouldn't have thought of that already.

"If they don't, then all of us will." She caught my eye. I'd been staring at the ground. "Your report from Ares?"

I had a nasty thought. Was she *truly* worried about sedition, and someone making a false claim to the throne—or was she making the mention of a new god a criminal offence literally just to fill the fields? It was ruthless, and it was flawless marvel-thinking. If you didn't consider misery, yours or anyone else's, a reason not to do something, which was the real heart of being Sown . . . it was a good solution. I had to box my thoughts around to what she'd asked me. "The madness is real. It's contagious; there are hundreds of knights there now, the whole place is chaos. They're starting to die from it. Four deceased, so far."

She frowned. "They're dying?"

"Yes. They don't eat or drink, they won't stop dancing, so the heat kills them quickly. The priests are trying to restrain the rest, but it's not going well. They've requested help. More people, more space, quarantine procedures."

"What's your assessment, do they actually need it or can they get by with what they have if they just dig in?"

"They need it if we don't want hundreds of knights to die by tomorrow evening."

She was gazing across to the shrine of her sister, in the lightning-blasted courtyard where the ivy was claiming back all the broken, blackened masonry. More ivy than before. Something in its roots had woken up. "So it's something in the ground. Zoe was right." She sighed. "But the more people we involve, the more people will see what's happening to the knights and call it the doing of the lost prince."

I tipped back slightly, because I had been about to say, *Look, what's more important, the lives of knights or the suppression of rumours about the lost prince,* but that was stupid. I had just watched her order the arrest of innocent people because it would be cheaper than paying day labourers. She would absolutely let a few hundred knights die. I caught myself wringing the red string with the bee charm on it round my wrist, as if it could magically tell me what Dionysus would say, because the gods knew he'd have a cleverer answer than just begging her uselessly not to do it.

"Witches," I said, before I really understood what was behind the thought.

"What?"

"We ask the witches to help. Using witches makes it look like a medical problem, not a divine one. No priests, no prophets, no civilians who'll spread rumours. Witches can't talk about their patients. They belong to the Temple of Hermes, don't they? Hermes is huge. They could fit hundreds of people in there, and none of them will talk about it."

She nodded once, slowly. The sun burned in the crown. My chest went tight. I was standing here giving advice to the *Queen*. Not considered, well-researched advice. Just the first chaotic thing that had occurred to me. Helios had told me once that being in royal service felt exactly like that moment where you've tripped on a stairway but you're not falling yet, and I'd had no idea what he meant until right this second. "There can be only one parliament of witches in a generation. It's part of their vow," she said.

"Why?"

"It's a protective mechanism for the crown. If they ever got together and agreed anything—well, you've met witches. One is bad enough." She paused. "I always swore I'd never do it unless we were in truly dire need."

"We're about to see a full-scale famine," I said quietly. "Pentheus is missing, the Egyptians won't give us the grain until they have a royal hostage, and if we don't find Pentheus, we will need to steal that grain from the Egyptian ships in the harbour, and we'll need the entire garrison to do that, because those ships will be defended by half an army. In what way could the need be less dire?"

"You just want to save some knights. Remember we are also trying to save Thebes."

It was several steps too grandiose, even for a queen. The voice in my head said, *You know, Phaidros, you probably need to shift your tolerance for stupid things up several notches if you're going to work for the royal household,* but the rest impaled it on a spike and set fire to the spike. "When you say Thebes," I said, a bit flatly, "do you mean you and possibly some of your friends? Because you do not mean the rest of us."

She lifted her eyebrow, just a fraction. "You know speaking truth to power is very rarely an ingredient for longevity."

"Do your worst," I said tiredly. It would be her or the god. Either way, I wasn't going to live out the end of this week. I was starting to lose interest in the exact hows and whens.

She nodded once, and motioned across a slave. I couldn't tell if it was going to be about arranging for me to be immediately strangled, or something else, but I couldn't summon anything stronger than a kind of indifferent curiosity.

"Send a herald to Hermes," she said. "Call a parliament of the witches for tonight." As the slave hurried away, she shook her head at me. "That wasn't brave, Heliades, that was suicidal: you didn't know I wouldn't kill you. Can you not throw yourself in front of any more chariots, please?"

"Yes, lady."

"Now take fifty of the afflicted knights to Hermes. I want to know if the witches have any treatment for the madness. Report back in the morning: we'll issue the stay-at-home order at dawn and begin the census then."

"Yes, lady."

I thought she would send me on my way, but she stood still, scanning me. "Phaidros—are you all right?"

Well: I think I might have called a god here, and I think he might be saving me till last. It sounds vain, but when you've been truly wronged, you can stay furious for years. Killing someone isn't enough: you have to do something insane and make them watch. I burned down half the palace at Troy before I slung Andromache off a balcony, and she didn't even do anything that terrible, she just killed a man in battle, which is much fairer than taking care of a child for almost a fortnight and then not stopping a crew of soldiers trying to murder him.

"I've just been out in the sun," I said.

18

Hermes is the god of heralds, travellers, merchants, thieves, and liars. Foreigners always say that makes no sense, because how could you be there for merchants but also for the thieves who were nicking stuff off the back of the cart, and the witnesses who they paid off to lie about it, but the thing is, Hermes doesn't care if things are taken honestly or dishonestly. Gods don't care about what's in your heart. Gods care about what's *happening*, and what's happening in all those cases is a crossing. Something moves; news, whether it's right or not, people, goods, either sold or stolen.

So it isn't very surprising that Hermes is also, in Thebes at least, the god of witches: the best liars in the world.

When the Queen's call for the witches went out, it went from the Temple of Hermes. It was simple. Each messenger was told only to say, *Come at dusk.*

I was there on the steps, waiting with the Palace herald and the Queen's chamberlain, when they started to come. People got out of their way, fast; but some stayed to watch, too, pointing out the temple to children.

More were arriving now, always one at a time.

I'd never known a group of people with so much in common to be so silent. Even on battle lines, people talk. The little knights turn brash and hyena-cackly, to try and prove they're not scared; the officers ask each other if anyone knows whether the slaves have got anything interesting in for dinner, because by the time you're thirty on the line, it's the same as bricklaying for a day. But here, no. Each witch was a solitary thing, never standing too near to another, sometimes nodding once, but not talking.

Most of them were women, but not all. Some of the youngest had only the tips of a couple of fingers marked with the red tattoos; some of the oldest had them right up to their elbows. All of them had their hair loose, which meant not a single one was married, and all of them wore the black veil. Nobody shifted or complained in the last of the ailing sun while we all waited. Other people kept away from them even more clearly than they would have from bloodstained soldiers. It was eerie, and after a while, I started to feel cold.

I didn't catch myself doing it for a little while, but I was looking for Dionysus from the moment the witches began to gather. It was difficult to see in the smoke and the orange evening, and the witches' black veils, which swam in the wind like shades trying to pull away to Hades. Sometimes there was a tall figure who could have been him, but then they turned and the set of the shoulders was wrong, or the tattoos. They were like spectres in the smoke, and the more of them came, the harder it was to tell them apart.

I had just begun to think that he wouldn't come, when I realized he had been on the edge of things all along. I bowed where I sat, not sure he had seen me through his veil, but he lifted his hand to me too. Seeing him gave me a bolt of something between gladness and fear.

He was just a man with blue eyes who liked causing trouble and being kind. He was.

A gong sounded, and we looked up to the temple steps, where the herald came forward to explain that there were afflicted knights inside, and the purpose of the parliament was to devise a treatment.

They opened the gates of the temple, and the witches moved through without a sound. No one spoke, even when the locked wagons and the mad knights came into easy view in the torches of the main courtyard. Dionysus didn't go anywhere near them, and only folded down on one of the stone benches by a fountain to fill up his water flask. I went over to him, slowly, in case he was thinking, but he put his hand out to me; it was the way witches showed you they were smiling under the veil. I took it and he pulled me to make me sit down beside him on the fountain edge.

"Will you not look at the knights, sir?" I asked.

He stretched past me to set a lamp on the next level of the fountain. He didn't take his veil off, but the light made it translucent.

"They'll still be just as scintillatingly mad in a few minutes." He stopped. "I mean . . . tragically mad. I think it's all dreadful and bad because I'm a normal person who doesn't in any way enjoy mystery ailments."

"In fact you're unusually sensitive," I agreed, disproportionately happy that he wanted to play. "Sometimes you struggle under the weight of human suffering."

He looked delighted, and I had to fight not to laugh. "Drink that," he said, and held the flask out to me.

"Hm?"

"You've a headache."

I hadn't been aware of having a headache, but he was right. I must have looked rough. I did as I was told, then tried to give the flask back. He hinged my elbow back to knock the flask into my chest. Tingles went up my arm. I was used to people bashing into me, but nobody was careful. I'd have felt it less if he'd punched me.

"All of it." He was studying me in the new lamplight. I wished he would stop doing that. "How's the search for the person who was lost?"

"Nowhere," I said. "The census is tomorrow, though. Did you stay with the people from Pylos this afternoon?"

He nodded. "They stopped at the springs on the forest border, a lot of them. Five women went into labour at the same time; five. I don't know why Apollo built humans to give birth if they've had a shock, it seems impractical, then you'll be running away from a lion *and* having a baby, but he did."

"Five," I echoed, thinking what a wonderful time I'd have if my profession involved meeting five brand-new babies daily. "Were they all right?"

He showed me his right hand. There were new tattoos on his forefinger, where the red didn't quite go to his knuckle yet: five rings, just below the density of the main tattoo. I hadn't thought I knew what the tattoos meant, but some distant memory reported that yes, that was what it was: one ring for every delivery where the mother and baby both survived. Across both his hands, those tattoos represented hundreds of people.

"Good," I said, much too stiffly in an effort not to sound envious. I looked across the knights and the witches to pry my thinking back to something useful, not daydreaming about starting an orphanage.

The witches were passing cups between themselves, and pouring out what I'd thought at first was medicine, but I could smell it now. It wasn't. It was alcohol, and nothing so mild as wine; it was some savage kind of brandy. It smelled like it was supposed to strip paint. Maybe it was something ceremonial, but—no. They weren't just taking a sip from the cups. They were draining them.

"It's an old ritual," Dionysus said, noticing me looking. "When you deal with madness like this, it's dangerous to have a mind with clear hard edges. You need it to be fog. Far less easy to catch. It's what those people from Pylos were trying to do, when they made you drink."

"What does the catching?" I asked, uneasy.

"Your man in the song," he said, a little concerned, as though it worried him that it hadn't seemed obvious to me.

"You—think the mad god is real, then," I said, so redundantly that Helios would have smacked me over the head. I seemed to be saying a lot of obvious things lately.

"Why, what do you think is happening to them?" he asked, about the knights.

"The Queen thinks it might be something churned up in the ground when the star fell. And the drought."

Dionysus laughed, just the smoke off a blown-out taper, a few tiny embers floating on it. "That's stupid."

I kept my face neutral, because not far from us, a woman in plain clothes but who I recognised from the Guards' barracks was making no particular secret of watching us. I had a bright flash of envy about how unembarrassed he was to say it, though. "No. She thinks it's more dangerous to tell people it might be a god than not. You know the story about the lost heir, who's supposed to be a son of Zeus? She says civil uprising is more dangerous than passing gods."

"It . . . is not," he said.

"No." I meant to leave it there, but it was a relief to sit and talk to him. We weren't friends, but enough strange things had happened to us when we were together now that it felt like being in the same unit. It didn't matter if we liked each other. "It's getting to me a bit. I just told her that she's being a crazed despot and she threatened to kill me and I said bring it on."

I thought he would laugh, but he went very still. He hooked his finger over the string around my wrist. "There is an agreement between witches and the Ferryman," he said quietly. It must have been the angle of the lamp, but I thought his eyes were more blue than before, the blue of very clear water where you see can see fathoms down to where leviathans fin. "Do you know what it is?"

I shook my head.

"If you try to give Hades your life whilst it still belongs to me, the Ferryman will not take you. You will wait on the Black Shore until I come for you, and I bolt your soul back into your body, and it will not matter if your body was burned at a stake by the sea: you will become a puddle of sentient ash, until I say you can go."

I tried to search him through the veil for any sign that this was a long joke, almost certain he was about to laugh and say, *Ha, got you, but be more careful.* He wasn't smiling. "You made that up," I said anyway, because even witches aren't so deinos.

He inclined his head at me, then bent and held his hand close to ground. A snake writhed straight up his wrist. My heart thunked painfully, only half climbing over its next beat, because the snake was an asp, the poisonous kind that could kill you almost by looking at you. Dionysus straightened up and showed me the snake, too close, close enough for it reach me and bite, and when I leaned back, he snapped his fist shut and crushed it. I heard the crunch of its skull. The body went limp, and venom trickled between his fingers.

He opened his hand, and there was a horrible cracking noise that must have been bones resetting themselves, and the snake lifted its head as if nothing had happened. He let it go into the grass again.

I had heard of sorcerers in Egypt who had that kind of magic, but I'd never seen it, and never thought I would see it. I didn't want to breathe.

"I can make it so that you don't remember," he said, nodding to the snake, "or so that you do. Do you understand?"

"Yes," I said, feeling warm and gold, and safe.

I wondered what you had to do, to forge an agreement with the Ferryman. Something deinos. Perhaps more than an ordinary witch could do.

He has blue eyes, and wherever he goes, people lose their minds . . . and I had invited him here, and there had been footsteps in the glass.

"How do you know about the mad god?" I asked.

Sometimes, you have a conversation between two mirrors. Instead of talking to just one person, you talk to versions and versions of them, reflected back and back. Maybe I was talking to a good witch. Maybe I was talking to a thing that had screamed down from the sky and made itself into a man from the cinders. Maybe he knew I was wondering about it, and maybe he didn't, and maybe he would laugh if I asked him, or maybe he would lose interest and I'd be a pillar of fire. Among all the reflections, I couldn't tell which one was really him.

"Everyone knows, except here."

"But you can't just—not notice a god."

"How do you mean?"

"I mean—I know Zeus is here, I've seen lightning. I was a sailor, I know Poseidon; I've been in love, I understand the Lady. I've fought justly, so I know Athena, and I've fought in a blind rage; I know Ares. Wherever I go, they have gods, but those gods are the same as ours really. They have the Mother in Egypt, but they call her Isis, and in Persia she's Ishtar. Everyone dies: everyone has a name for the Unseen. But I've never come across a god we just . . . don't have."

Dionysus was smiling. "You've seen him. You know him well. Knights know him as well as any sailor knows Poseidon."

I looked up slowly.

"On battle lines, sometimes people go blind, don't they? Or they run away, and everyone thinks they're cowards, but later they don't remember. Or they seem like a great fighter, for years, but then one evening, something snaps, and in their sleep they murder fifty cattle thinking those are soldiers; or fifty people. Herakles killed his family. That's the mad god."

He was right. I *did* know all that, very well indeed. I'd seen people hauled off the line blind for no reason. We all knew it had to be a god, but nobody knew which one. And battle madness: I'd always conceived of it as a kind of generalised weakness of soul, not a god taking a hammer to anyone's mind.

His function is to guard the border between the clockwork and the wild.

"The royal prophet said something about how he's to do with wine as well," I said. "That's—a different sort of madness, I can see that, but . . ." I was struggling to say what I meant. "But it's very *specific*. Battle madness and drunkenness? It's not like the sea, or death. They're not important enough to be a . . . to be a god."

Dionysus was watching the other witches finishing their ritual, the figures in black moving straight and slow now through the mad knights in their cages. "Well. They're two things of a great many, none of which people here put together into one idea. There are plenty of others. Stories. Dancing. Masks." A dry wind moved his veil, ghosting it against one of side of his face. "And the trance of prophets, and the bees, and the auroch. He is what makes a beaten wife murder her husband, and slaves kill their owners, and citizens burn palaces." He moved his fist very slightly, miming an upward punch.

None of those things felt to me as if they had anything to do with each other, and I was about to say so, but I recognised the feeling suddenly. It was how I felt when I was learning a language that marked the borders of its ideas differently to ours.

In our language, we have a colour that is the sky, and also the colour of a shield, and we say that's bronze. Then there's a colour that's wine, and the sea, and we call that purple: but that doesn't make sense to anyone from the Tin Isles. If you sail into the north, where the nights are long and you can be fog-bound for days ten ship lengths from shore, and you pull in at Tintagel, by the great mines, people don't understand calling the sky bronze and the sea purple. It doesn't matter if you say, *Well, before you treat bronze it's greenish and where the sun is strong in the south, the sea really is the colour of wine in the afternoon*: they look at you like you're mad, because for them, the sea and the sky are one colour. We aren't seeing different things, but we are thinking of them differently.

The mad god was like that. I was seeing him: but the way I thought meant I didn't put all his parts together into one thing.

When I'd found out about the special Tin Isles colour, I'd spent a week gathering up bits of old glass and jewellery and corroded bronze and thread and asking miners, *Is this right? Is this? Is this?* and eventually, I'd got an idea of the band of things they put together as their sea–sky colour.

It had a been an uncanny thing when the idea had soaked into me enough that one morning, I looked out at the sky and the sea and thought: *Yes. That's blue.*

"I know they all look different," Dionysus said, and I could see him hunting around for ways to explain, but I cut my hand across the air. I didn't mean to, but it was my sign for *it's all right.* It was almost impossible to explain things like that, when you could already see what linked them up.

"I'll see it soon," I said, and explained about blue.

He tilted back a little then, as if I'd said something extraordinary. "That's a graceful way to see a group of things you hate," he said.

"How I feel about things isn't very relevant to understanding what they are and why they're driving half the garrison mad," I said. "You didn't say he was a *good* thing, just that he's a true thing."

"Yes," he said, and looked away again. He wasn't, I noticed suddenly, drinking. Maybe he had had some of that lethal brandy before he arrived, but I didn't think so. He was glacially sober.

"Do you want to get on?" I asked awkwardly.

"You still haven't drunk all that," he said to the flask.

I'd forgotten what I was supposed to be doing. I drank more water.

Bakhos, the Raver, lord of the dance, and madness, and wine, and blasphemous music, and whatever that animal, auroch fury it was that built and built in you when you'd been wronged and one day you just— snapped. Whatever colour it was that ran through all those things, it was something to do with chaos. It was everything we hated here, and everything we outlawed. Wasn't it? Bees, the trance of prophets . . . there was nothing wrong in those. Stories; Helios had told me stories.

"Do you think he's offended, that he's been forgotten here?" I asked.

I thought he was going to say, *Yes. Obviously. He's calling in his debts.*

"No," Dionysus said. He sounded strangely muted now, as though he had found something sad in what I'd said about blue. I hoped not. I liked the blue story; I'd only meant it as an interesting curiosity. "Belief never made a god, and nor did sacrifice. They just are."

"What do you mean?" It sounded close to heresy.

"Well—Poseidon is the sea, and the tide won't stop rising just because no one sacrifices to him. Time is there, death is there, the earth, war, love. Even if there is some terrible place three thousand years from now where nobody remembers any gods at all, there will still be the sea and love . . ." His eyes slipped to the knights again. Even behind the veil, they were starry with the lamplight. "And madness. People will have just forgotten how to talk to them."

It had the ring of prophecy. Even after I'd thought about it later, I couldn't tell why. The words of oracles are delivered in verse—that's why bards sing in verse, because it's the Muse talking, not them, or so they like to say—but Dionysus hadn't spoken in poetry. It still prickled the hairs on my arms. "Then . . . why would he do this?"

He was watching the other witches and the mad knights in their cages now, not me, his shoulders loose and his red-tattooed hands in his lap, trapped between his knees. For such a tall man, he took up almost no space. "Maybe he's like anyone, maybe he's just visiting. Maybe he's trying to make sure some idiot doesn't commit suicide by tyrant."

Either he was reminding me he couldn't possibly know, or it was a way of saying, *Well, you asked me to come.* Back between the mirrors again.

Maybe it was because I was turning feverish from hunger and the strangely comfortable headache, but it didn't feel terrible, to be between the mirrors. It was disconcerting, but sometimes . . . I liked being disconcerted. And I didn't like that I'd made him sad. I hunted around for something that would spark him off again.

"Don't call the Queen a tyrant," I said. "Tyrants *seize* power, monarchs inherit it; if you call her a tyrant it sounds like you're saying there's another rightful heir. I don't think you could make her think she's a swarm of bees, or whatever it is you normally do to people who vex you, before she has you shot. So just—be careful."

"It's squirrels," he said seriously, "I really like squirrels; it's because they have tiny hands and their tails are silly."

I looked away so he wouldn't have to see me grinning. I was still caught up in the novelty of meeting an adult who liked to play and joke and who didn't seem to worry at all about his dignity—and the strangest thing was that he wasn't missing dignity. He had plenty, but it was like quicksilver instead of armour. You couldn't put a dent in it.

He refilled the water cask and gave it to me again. "How's the headache?"

"I'm fine," I said, and I was. I had a feeling it was less to do with being made to drink enough as sitting down and talking to someone who minded so much about what happened to me that he would threaten, convincingly, to go down to Hades and drag me back if I was too careless. "Thank you. Is there anything I can do to help?" I nodded at the mad knights.

He shook his head as he stood up. "I doubt it. Go home, get some rest."

"No, I'll wait for you. The road isn't safe, neither of us should be walking alone at night any more."

"You really think so?" he said. Earlier, with the people from Pylos, I'd thought he was oblivious to danger because he was too tall to come up against any most of the time, but I had a scritching feeling now that it might be because he really, truly never was in danger. I almost asked him. Only almost. If I was wrong, he'd laugh at me, which would be a relief, but if I wasn't . . . I didn't know what he would do. But sure as the Acheron is cold, we wouldn't talk again like we had just now. That was the most I'd talked to anyone in ten years, about anything that wasn't to do with how to smash a city wall open. I could live between the mirrors for a while longer.

"The Guards are arresting people to order, to go into slavery and get the harvest in," I said instead, quiet, because you don't need to be told when some things are secrets. "I don't think they're going to be strict about whether anyone's committed any real crime or not. I think they're going to take whoever's an easy target. Anyone alone on the road."

As soon as I said it, I was acutely aware of the people around us, and how many of them were near enough to listen. If someone tried to drag him away, maybe they would turn into a tree—or maybe he would die in the fields. That hurt to think of.

Dionysus said nothing, but he nodded once and turned towards the mad knights. I did too, wanting to see what the witches would do differently than the priests.

Already, they seemed more precise. None of them were trying to stop the knights dancing or singing with brute force, and not just because it would have been hard for them to. When a priest tried, one of the witches stopped him, fast, and I heard her say it would hurt the knight more than letting him get on with it for now.

I blinked twice when one of the witches took out a mask, one of the ones—or very like them—from Dionysus's dance. It was sculpted and painted to look like an old man, gaunt, with cheekbones that were too sharp and sunken eyes painted dark to make them more sunken still, mouth open so the person wearing it could still speak clearly, beard as grey as the skin, silver hoops pierced through the alabaster ears to suggest a sailor. It looked like a horrible caricature of a person while the witch was holding it. She held it up in front of a knight so that he could see it as he turned through his dance, and then, fast because she had to catch him in one of those turns, she pressed it over his face.

The man stopped turning. He didn't bring his hands up to hold the mask, but he let the witch hold it in place while she tied the cord of the mask behind his head. He just stood there, not moving, not dancing. Then . . . all at once, he seemed to feel the heat of the evening, and how tired he was, and probably how hungry and thirsty, and he buckled down onto the ground. One of the witches gave him a flask and he drank from it.

"How did she do that?" I breathed. There was silence from everyone who had seen. Other witches were moving away purposefully now, opening up their medicine satchels, taking out other masks—masks of beautiful married ladies with short hair and golden coronets, masks of satyrs with wicked grins and tiny horns, masks of old men, but never, I realized, anyone of fighting age. No unmarried women with long hair. No young men. But all the witches had some, as though a mask was an ordinary kind of medicine everyone knew about.

"Do you want to guess?" Dionysus asked me. It should have been irritating, but he said it carefully, and after what we had talked about just now, I understood why. He was trying to show me what blue was, and that worked far better if I had to look for myself. I brushed his elbow to tell him not to worry I was about to swear explosively and demand real answers. He skimmed his hand over mine and I almost said, *Please, please don't*, because I already liked him too much for it to be knightly.

"The masks aren't knights," I said slowly, not quite there.

There was a frustrated shout from not far away, because on another knight, it hadn't worked, and she was still turning and singing. On another, a man from Polydorus's unit now in a married-lady mask, it seemed to slow him down enough for one of the witches to get some water into him, but he didn't stop, exactly; he was still rocking and mumbling, and when she let go of him, he went back to a small, more shuffling version of the endless spinning of the dance.

I couldn't see Dionysus's face any more, and so he was only a tall spectre beside me, but I knew his angles and posture well enough to know he was watching me, though he hadn't moved his head. "Warm," he said.

"What's happening?" the first knight in the old man mask asked, but he didn't sound right. He was about twenty-five, but his voice was cracking and high. He sounded elderly.

"The masks make them . . . what the mask is," I said slowly. "Or, it—confuses them? Just enough, to . . . what, to not be knights, and so the madness doesn't quite—stick, in the same way?" I stopped. "Is this why witches wear veils?" I said it at the same time I thought it, without being able to trace the reasoning properly, but the moment it was out, I knew I was right. It was witching thinking, I could tell that much at least, and maybe even blue. "You can only be a good witch if you're not entirely a person at the time. You have to be something . . . blank."

Dionysus's shoulders went back and he looked down at me with a disconcertion that showed in all his bones. "Gods, Phaidros. If the knighting ever falls through, the witching is waiting."

It was hard not to feel pleased with that, even though I shouldn't have cared what he thought.

It was working on perhaps a third of the afflicted knights. Some were sitting down now; some were even eating, slowly, as though they were struggling to remember the last time they had done it. A girl from my unit in the mask of an older lady was even talking to her witch, almost normally. With a fizzy hope rising and rising inside, trying to crush it down so I couldn't be too disappointed if it all stopped working, I went across to see if she would recognise me, and she lit up.

"Phaidros," she said. Her voice was lower than usual, but that was all. "I haven't seen you for an age."

She had seen me two days ago. It sounded mad, but it was so much better than the singing madness that I could have cried with relief. I hugged her and she laughed, and I asked her if she wanted to see her commander, and she looked a little bit puzzled and asked me if her commander was still alive—she was talking as though twenty years had passed—but when I said that yes she was, she was at the garrison, very worried, the girl beamed and said she'd like that a lot if I really wasn't winding her up. When I gave her some bread, holy of fucking holies, she ate it. I held her masked face in both hands for a second, torn between joy and dismay, because if we had asked the witches sooner, maybe Amphitrion wouldn't be dead. The girl smiled and held my wrists, and told me to calm down, young man, which only made me laugh more. I sounded hysterical; it wasn't knightly, to laugh like that, but just for now, I didn't care.

Not a cure, not exactly, and not for everyone, but so, so much better than a death sentence in the cellars of Ares. Feeling like you feel when you walk into the sea and a wave lifts you and tides you to the shore, I went back to Dionysus and, not caring that it was improper, or that I shouldn't touch a veiled witch, or that I didn't even know any more if he *was* just a witch, I slung both arms around him, dragging him down to that he had to bend forward against me.

"Thank you," I said against his hair. "I would never have asked the Queen for this parliament if it weren't for you and all your—fucking peculiar ways." I was still laughing while I said it and it made me my voice sound completely unfamiliar, even from the inside.

He hugged me back just as tight. I couldn't see through the veil, only the sheen of the strange, liquid fabric in the torches. I kissed him through it, just a scratch against his cheek, playing really, but he went still.

I did too, suddenly needlingly aware that there were people watching us, and why wouldn't they, because probably Tiresias had been a child who knew nothing of Apollo the last time a sane knight had forgotten himself so far as to snatch at a witch in public. I had a searing realization that I'd crossed an unmarked, crucial border.

"I'm sorry, sir," I managed, staring at the ground and wanting to vitrify. I'd always thought I had a great curtain wall in my head between me and anything like that, and there was a chthonic horror in understanding that actually, it was just a tiny moat I could trip over if I didn't look where I was going, and there was evil on the far side, whickering at me through the fog. Helios would have had me flogged. Forget yourself a little, and you're far closer to forgetting yourself altogether than you ever want to think.

"Don't be so stupid," Dionysus said. He sounded shocked.

"I know, I'm sorry—"

"Phaidros! I'm telling you *not* to be sorry, not—this—where is this rancid shame coming from, who *did* this to you?" His voice was a broken lamp, smoking and full of shattered glass, and I didn't say anything, because I didn't understand, and it was so far away from what I'd expected him to say that the sounds of the words hardly hung together into any meaning at all.

He had no time to say anything else, because right through the temple courtyard, there was a sudden, perfect silence. The witches had stopped murmuring. And the knights—the knights, masked and not, were marvel-still, and as if they had heard a command roared across the field, they all turned the same way. It was towards us. No; towards him.

Something took hold of them then. They started to talk. Not to each other. They aimed it at some point in the middle distance, and they all said different things. I slipped past other people until I could catch some words.

"—and they shall rave on the mountainside—"

"She will murder her sorrow—"

"Dance!"

"The High City shall fall when the god goes before the Queen . . ."

Close to me was a scribe from the Palace with a clay tablet. I apologised, stole it, pushed the heel of my hand across the clay to erase the marks, and started to take down what they were saying. It didn't take long before I realized each knight was saying the same thing again and again, but all of them were saying different things.

When the god goes before the Queen, the High City shall fall
She shall murder her sorrow in a crown of ivy

They shall break free and rave on the mountainside
Into ruin shall fall the House of Kadmus, into ruin all Achaea
Flee, children of the dragon
Sing
Dance
Flee.

"It's prophecy," the scribe said quietly.

Dionysus touched my wrist, just over the red string and its bee charm. "Don't write it down," he said, soft but urgent.

He was right. It was treason. *Into ruin shall fall the House of Kadmus*, that was bad, but *She shall murder her sorrow*—Pentheus's name meant sorrow. *When the god goes before the Queen . . .* There was supposed to be no god.

A crown of ivy. I'd called him Ivy.

"I think it's too late," I said, because there were too many people here. Not just the witches, but the priests from Ares who had helped to bring the mad knights across town, administrators from the Palace, the Chamberlain's staff. Some of them would be reporting to the Guards.

The knights kept on, though, all of them staring into the middle distance with something horribly like joy in their faces.

Dionysus was just at the right angle with a lamp for me to see his face through the veil. I don't think he knew I could, though, because when I turned to him, he didn't look concerned or unsettled, or even confused about what the prophecies might mean. He looked annoyed. As I watched, he clenched his hand, the way I always did at Jason to say *stop that fuckwittery right now.*

The knights went silent.

Then they started their ordinary song again. The ones who had been partially cured with the masks went back to eating or talking to the witches as though nothing had interrupted them.

I stared at Dionysus with what felt like gravel in my throat.

Of course it was him.

"Are you all right?" he said. I must have looked bad.

I almost laughed.

Pretending to be friendly, making me feel like maybe I wasn't quite so alone, that someone would be angry if I got myself killed, and that sometimes there were miraculous enraging strangers who came along and saved you from an auroch—that wasn't revenge. That was—

Haha.

Madness.

"Yes," I heard myself say, "I'm all right."

He didn't look convinced. "Let me take you home."

"No," I said, "I can take myself."

"But you just said—"

"I can take myself," I said sharply, just to get away from him, and not even sure why. He knew where I lived. I made sure I vanished into the crowd. On the way, I found a herald and sent a report to the Palace, as dry as I could make it so the Queen wouldn't take it as a frayed knight overstating.

But once I was on the road, I slowed down. The Nothing was there with me again, keeping pace. Like always, it took up the air, and tinted the world darker.

Someone coming for you on a revenge quest is much better than nobody coming at all.

19

A long the roadsides, there were more people sleeping out than ever, sometimes in makeshift tents, sometimes just on the grass. They were the ones who hadn't managed to sell themselves; mostly men, but plenty of families who must not have wanted to split up. There were bits of smashed wine jars everywhere and the smell of stale alcohol hung in the air. Tiny fires jagged gold over people. Everyone was hard lines and bones. Down on a dry stream bed, some girls danced, not in a way that looked like they were choosing to. I couldn't hear if they were singing, but there was a dull thump that might have been a drum. Someone was trying to use it to slow them down. I couldn't tell if it was working.

I felt light and strange from not eating, but even if you had put me in front of a banquet table, I don't think I would have been hungry. I was all churned up like I hadn't been since that huge fight with Helios. Which was ridiculous, because I owed Dionysus all the revenge he wanted, uncomplaining. It wasn't a bad thing at all, either. It was fantastic. He was here, he was all right, he hadn't died on that shore a decade ago. That was all I'd wanted. I was grateful, I was, and I had no right to feel betrayed, or sad, or any of it.

"Wine, sir? Helps keep the madness away, the witches say so!" Someone shoved a jar right in my face.

I shook my head and told myself to get a fucking grip before I walked obligingly into a band of thieves.

A lot of people, I started to notice through the hunger haze, were wearing clothes that were quite good; the kind of clothes I'd have expected from clerks and accountants and the owners of olive groves. A few months ago, they would have been well off.

All along the sides of the road, there were lines of people begging or selling small things set out neatly on sheets. Ornaments, cutlery, jewellery, cloak and kilt buckles, clothes, seal beads, even little marvels, the kind that would pour you a drink if you put a cup in their hands. Some of it would have been valuable three months ago. Now—it was so much junk. I didn't know what a sack of flour cost now, but probably it was more than even the best silver necklace.

As the travellers on the road thinned out, and as the way twisted up to the maze and the mountain, eyes followed me, catching on my armour. Mostly it was just hostile lethargy, but there was speculation too. For the first time in a long time, for all I was so used to it I barely thought about it any more, deafness felt dangerous. I couldn't hear if someone was behind me. I looked back. Only a few other people on the road. Soon I'd be the only one. Very stupid to have come alone.

I was coming up to a great tree now, and it was hung with bright prayer ribbons. On each one hung a clay tab, the kind you scratch a prayer into if you can't pay for a scribe to write on papyrus, and though it was too dark for me to make out what any of them said, I could see there were dozens. Close to the tree, the air reeked of wine and honey: the roots were sticky with it. Little clusters of candles glowed among the roots too, nested in wreaths of ivy. People ghosted among them, lighting more, or tying up more prayers. A man's voice was preaching up there somewhere; he was talking about the marvel Furies, and saying that Thebes had forgotten an ancient god, and the drought and the madness were his revenge.

Dionysus had said sacrifices made no difference.

Sing, sing to the lord of the dance . . .

A clear high horn split the night.

Usually, I was *with* the Hidden when I heard that horn. Inside the ranks, it felt safe. I'd never heard it alone on the road, in the dark, on foot. The hymn to Ares rose into the night after it, horribly slow, and far louder than the mad god's song.

Even though I knew it was slow because that forced the riders to breathe normally, there was a deep primal part of me that didn't hear it like that now. It sounded slow because they knew they were in no hurry. They had all night to run people down, and they would. I could feel the horses through the ground.

Everyone at the tree scattered. The road was instantly empty.

Normally, all I'd have to do was stand aside. The Hidden didn't arrest knights. This wasn't a normal ride, though, and they weren't hunting slaves. They were filling the arrest quota. The Guard captain, for sure, wouldn't care what I was.

I hauled myself up onto the bank, and it was shocking how weak I was after just a few weeks on short rations. I could lift my own weight but only just, and my arms shook.

The shanty camp stretched right down the hillside, much bigger than I'd thought. The whole camp heaved now; people were putting out candles and fires, and running further into the scrub. Barely a quarter of a mile behind me on the road, a battalion of knights in black armour was riding in fast, torches streaming. The ground shuddered, and even from here, even I could hear the noise of their chain mail.

I ran, and I didn't stop until I was much further up the hill, on the last bend before the maze, alone in the deep dark. Back the way I'd come, there was a noise like seagulls finding a feast in jetsam from a wreck, and for whole seconds, I tried to think what seagulls could be doing so far inland, until I understood I wasn't hearing birds, but people, being caught and dragged away.

Although it should have been a huge relief to get home, I didn't want to go into the house. The triplets would be there. I was too stormy inside. So I lingered in the olive grove, on a perfunctory hunt for any more dead things.

I found a hare, killed in the same way as everything else. Wanting to do something simple and useful and calming, I skinned him and stretched the hide on my leather frame, then left the body on the edge of the forest in case whoever or whatever had given him to me wanted the meat. There could easily have been escaped slaves living in the forest, leaving me things in exchange for olives I hadn't even noticed going missing, or apples from the store in the maze. Would the triplets tell me if food was going missing? Probably not. They would worry I'd think it was them. Well, they wouldn't worry, because they were hell automata and probably they didn't worry about anything, but even so.

The forest was dark and silent. I could hear the dryads talking to each other in that low creaking of wood as their bark settled for the night. Nothing faster than a tree was moving out there.

"Thank you," I said anyway.

The ivy was soaring so thickly up the trees now that some of the smaller saplings were losing their shape.

With nothing left to procrastinate with, I turned unwillingly to the house.

Obviously it's horrible to be stolen from your city knowing your parents are dead if they're lucky, or slaves elsewhere. Obviously it's horrible to be taken to some barbarian country where people speak a different language and suddenly you're supposed to spend your life doing housework for some army pig and feeling grateful you're not out in the fields. Obviously I didn't expect the triplets to be cheerful: that would have been stupid.

But here's what happened whenever I went home.

The triplets had always made bread, very good bread, and set the table, everything laid out beautifully. Just for me. And then they stood there in a silent row and watched me eat.

I had tried to stop them doing it. I'd tried telling them to eat with me, or go away. I'd tried asking them why they were watching me. Nothing. They just stood, and watched. If I tried to take my plate away somewhere else, they followed. And so I had to eat in a minutely scrutinised, paralysingly awkward silence.

Then, I retreated to my room to get washed and changed, with the door very firmly shut, but one of them always stood right outside. I could see his shadow in the light from under the door. They did it in shifts, about an hour each. Always. Again, I'd tried to say they didn't need to do that and frankly it was unsettling and could they, you know, sod off and play a game or something? But no.

They didn't talk to me unless they absolutely had to. They rarely seemed to talk to each other. And if I woke up in the night and looked at the moonlight under the door, there was always the shadow of a pair of boots just outside.

Once I'd lit a candle for Helios, I brushed my fingertips against the fili-gree pattern on his helmet, trying like always to remember what he looked like, and failing. The bronze visor had been cast when he was fifteen; the age my little knights were now, a half-finished person, not the man who had laughed to face chariots. I mixed together some wine and some honey and a prayer to Hades to look after him, and poured it into the earth just outside my balcony door, by the shrine. The parched earth soaked it up straightaway. For what must have been at least the thousandth time, I wondered if he had kept his promise and waited for me on the shore.

I didn't expect him to have waited. It wasn't to do with him; it was that generally, I was like sea spray. I slipped off people's feathers. It was the same again and again: I clung for a little while, but before long, everyone remembered their real concerns, shook their feathers out, and flew. I'd tried to make new friends after I found my way back to the legion at Troy, but I never stuck. Every so often there was someone who I would have given anything to stay with, but every time, it was the same. I had no traction.

Except with Dionysus. I hadn't slipped away from him.

Now I'd had time to think, I didn't care what he was doing. I'd go and see him tomorrow, and apologise for snapping, and make up a reason why, and then I'd enjoy him for however much time I had left, until he decided it was finished.

20

I was just falling asleep when the triplets did something they never had
before. One of them banged on the door. I jolted awake and pulled it
open, feeling hard done by. I hadn't slept for years; all I'd ever wanted in
life was my own tent and someone cleverer than me to tell me what to
do, and this was what had come of it.

"What? What stunningly sinister thing have you come up with now,
you creepy little doll-people?"

All three of them were outside. They all pointed to the door down
into the maze. It was down a flight of steps from the kitchen.

"Something's down there," one of them said. "It's . . ." He looked at
his brothers for a word.

"It's banging," one of the others said.

"It screamed," the third said.

They all looked up at me with huge eyes and I realized that they meant
it. They were frightened.

"Something?" I asked. I had to rely on them for sounds around the
house: by myself, I wouldn't know if a thief was making himself dinner
in the kitchen. "What do you think it is, a wolf, or . . ."

"It's not a wolf," the first brother said softly.

Maybe it was the mystery thing that had been leaving dead animals in
the olive grove.

Suddenly the boys looked very fragile.

"Right," I said, quietly, in case it could hear us too. "You all come in
here. There's a lock." I'd put on a lock, so that I knew they couldn't come

in at night and hide under the bed. "I'll go down and see what it is. Stay here until I come back. If anything happens, if I don't come back—run to Dionysus next door and tell him. You know, the tall man, the witch?" The furious celestial thing that will burn me soon—no. No. Shut up.

They all nodded.

"Good. Lock this after me. I'll see you soon." They only looked more afraid than ever. There was nothing reassuring I could say. I had no idea what was in the maze. "And don't do anything unnatural to my gear. I don't want any dolls with pins in or little cursed bundles of sticks or whatever it is you're planning to use this time for." I signed watching them.

Owl stares, but one of them might have smiled: the experimental smile of someone who was just starting to wonder if maybe I was joking.

I smiled back and pressed the door closed.

We never went far into the maze. We kept apples and cheese down there when we had those things, or olives from the grove if the trees grew any edible ones, but we left them just inside the door. It was cold no matter the heat above. The dark was deep, the passages were narrow, and unless you enjoyed being lost and upsetting a lot of bats, there was no reason to bother. I went with my sword in one hand and a lamp in the other, listening. Now I was down here, I could hear whatever it was in the echoes—rasping, breathing. It was loud, but that didn't mean anything. The maze moved sound so strangely it must have been designed to do that.

I clocked the hilt of my sword to the wall to see if I could make whatever it was come to me. It did pause, like it was listening, but then nothing.

"Come on. Come out, come and be murdered like a good mystery thing so I can go back to bed," I said into the echoes.

"Back to bed," said the echoes, "back to bed?"

I tried not to be unnerved by the way they changed my intonation.

"Back to bed," they crooned. "Be murdered."

I decided not to do any more talking.

Painted onto the walls, which were bare, hacked-out bedrock, were pictures so ancient I wasn't sure people had made them. They showed the old goddesses, all wings and teeth. The Furies still sleep under the earth somewhere. I tried not to look. I didn't want to think about whether they were why this maze was here.

"Come out," the echoes whispered, and perhaps because I wasn't hearing well enough or because the twisting ways had changed the sound, it didn't sound like my voice any more.

I hit a dead end and had to double back. The echoes were stealing the sound of my steps too, at a lag, so that it sounded like there were three or four people walking. I had to keep stopping, to check.

The fifth time I stopped, the echo-steps didn't stop. Someone else, something else, was walking close to me. I swung my lamp back. No one behind me, no one ahead, but they must have been only a few bends in the path away from me. I moved faster, and started to concentrate on keeping silent. Still, though, there were steps. Through the echoes, I couldn't tell if the thing was moving on four legs or two.

Something tapped my shoulder.

I spun around sword first, but no one was there. Or no one I could see.

Tap, same shoulder.

Still no one.

I clamped my hand over my shoulder where I'd felt it, tingling nastily, and felt something sticky. When I held my hand to the light, there was something black-red on my fingertips. I shone my lamp upwards, and stared, because the ceiling was bleeding. Slow, viscous streams were creeping down the walls, dripping on the way, through strange patterns in the rock walls that had formed like furrows. They looked horribly biological. A feeling like dozens of spiders ran down my back. Nothing in my training had told me what to do if one day you went down into a maze and part of it turned out to be the insides of a giant.

Something bumped into the side of my head, and I heard a discombobulated buzz.

Bees.

Now I'd seen one, I could see others. They were following flight paths about a foot above my head. They weren't normal bees. They were massive, black, cicada-sized monsters, and the droning of their wings was just at the pitch I struggled to hear, and gods, but the walls weren't bleeding, it was *honey*. Those furrows weren't rock, but hives. I'd never seen them built like that before. I held up the lamp higher, trying to see further, not sure I should trespass any more into the bees' territory.

Another shriek came from up ahead. Further among those great citadel hives.

With honey tapping me all over now, I followed the noise.

The way opened out. It was sudden: the was the narrow beehive-lined corridor, then a turn so tight it aimed backwards, and then a great cavern that swallowed up my light. The bees were everywhere. I'd thought the hives along the corridor had been huge, but those were only little outposts. In here was a whole city. Honey gleamed on the floor and sometimes on the wreckage of broken combs where other things had wanted to get at it, and the bees were out in legions, making the air gritty, and I didn't understand, because there were no flowers down here, but then I saw where they were going. There was a fissure in the roof of the cavern, and through it: moonlight. And a great tumble of flowering vines, completely in defiance of the drought.

There was a light, not too far away; just a single lamp, like mine. Someone was moving among the hives there, a tall slim figure with a knife that shone and hair bound up in a green band. Dionysus: I almost called out that it wasn't safe, but then I saw what he was doing and shut up. He was taking pieces of honeycomb, setting them into a basket, and the bees were seething around his hands. There were so many that they would have killed him straightaway if anything startled them. They were swarming out of the hive, like soldiers pouring out to muster from a ship, under the command of some bee-herald whose voice we couldn't hear, but they weren't flying or stinging or any of it. In among all their writhing, they sometimes made shapes that bees shouldn't know about. I saw shoulders and spines, and ships, and I stopped still when I understood they weren't just looking at him. They were telling him things. Bees are prophets, everyone knows that, but I'd never actually seen them talk to anyone before.

I realized about a heartbeat too late that standing there in that vast dark space with a lit lamp was stupid, and right then, there was an unearthly crowing noise from the darkness. It was very much: *What's that?*

I put the lamp down and snapped to the side, as far away from it as I could get without charging right into onto of those palace hives, and something else prowled into the light.

It was the size of a person. Crouched over, bundled up against the cold in the maze, honey-filthy, hair matted, and I would have said it was a human, but the shape of the head was wrong. Huge, heavy; horns. A bull—there was horror crawling right up the inside of my spine and making a nest in my skull—but no. A bull mask, made from tightly bound straw, the horns crowned in ivy as if the man had smashed headfirst into one of those vine-bound trees in the forest. Whoever it was, he considered the lamp, then kicked it, and the dark plunged in.

There *was* moonlight from up above, and Dionysus's lamp, but both of those might as well have been as far away as the stars. I couldn't see the bull-masked man. I couldn't see my own hand in front of my face. The man must have been able to see, though, because he screamed again, that same mad primordial scream that I hadn't even recognised as human before, and he flung me backwards into the wall. Honeycomb broke under my shoulder, and furious bees roared, loud even for me, and then—

—and then it wasn't bees.

It was the roar of chariot wheels as they thundered in over the plain at Troy. I wasn't in the cold cave. I was in the cold night under sterile frozen stars, and the chariots were coming, making that insectile whickering noise they had because of the razorblades worked into the axles. They only had to drive past you to cut you off at the knees.

Helios was marshalling us into square units, shouting over the noise that he knew we remembered how to do this. Spears down, push, you could flip a chariot, he'd give the horses to the first person to do it (not you, Phaidros, we're drowning in bloody horses, you little show-off) and people were laughing, and then—and then the sweep of the chariots reached the unit beside us and their polemarch was in pieces, and Helios shouted not to look at her, look at him, ready, *and* . . .

"Phaidros. Knight, can you hear me?"

It was such a familiar voice, but it didn't belong with the regiment. It had smoke in it. I didn't have time to think about it, though, because the chariots were right on top of us, and Helios was facing the enemy polemarch at the front, smiling. He loved being on the front line, the way athletes love being in the stadium.

"It's Dionysus. You're in the maze. Come back, knight."

I did know someone called Dionysus. He was kind, or maybe he wasn't, maybe he was dangerous, or both; I couldn't remember.

"Oh, it's the bees," I heard him say, more to himself than to me, and all the noise vanished.

Everything was silent.

No more Troy, no more chariot line. This was the maze, of course it was the maze, and I couldn't believe there had been any question; and now Dionysus was kneeling in front of me, holding my neck to see into my eyes by the light of a new lantern. It shouldn't have been quiet. The bees were boiling all around us, and I was crumpled against the cavern wall beside a hive swarming with upset workers trying to rescue baby bees who weren't ready to leave the combs yet.

I tried to say something but I couldn't even hear my own voice.

Dionysus touched his heart—the sign I always used for *sorry*. I must have used it with him and not realized.

Dionysus: who *was* dangerous, who was the boy from the shore, who was here for revenge, and who I was very happy to see all the same.

In case he had seen me do it before, I made my sign for *thank you*.

He pointed to the gap in the cavern roof, where there was a rope.

It was knotted, so you could stand on the end. He kicked some mechanism hidden by a rock, stepped onto the knot below mine, and put his arm across me. My ribs flickered, not used to that; he felt it and put his hand flat on my breastbone. Easy, easy. The rope began to rise on its own. I saw the counterweight go by; a person-sized wine cask, probably full of stones. Still, everything was soundless. It was a relief. I shut my eyes and let my head rest forward against the rope, which was waterproofed with beeswax pushed deep into the grain of the hemp. Behind me, Dionysus smelled of honey and flowers and hot linen, and I had a spike of embarrassment, because surely I was covered in honey and crushed bees now, and—but it was so good and safe too, his arm across me and his chest against my back. I could feel him breathing. I put my hand over his. I regretted it instantly because I shouldn't have, because he was going to smack it away, but he only hooked his thumb over mine to hold it there.

He always seemed to make me feel two things at once and this time, it was hope and despair. I couldn't go around feeling like this about a witch, if he even was a witch. I was supposed to be on the marriage register. And if he wasn't . . . only, it didn't matter, because I'd forgotten what it was like for someone to think I was worth something, and it was like being exactly the right amount of drunk: shameful and lovely.

At the top was a little gantry. We stepped off the rope, and then there was the moon, and the ruin, and the impossible plants; ivy and grapes and jasmine and olives and flowers, as lush as they would have been in the greenest spring—they were so strong it was eerie, and all of it was silent. I couldn't hear my own breathing. Dionysus led me across to a low flat wall by a water channel and pushed my shoulder until I sat. Some of his glass lamps sparkled there. I'd been right, I was covered in honey. I wanted to get clean, but without being able to hear my own voice from the inside, it was impossible to talk. I could tell the sounds would be wrong.

He touched my shoulder to make me look at him. He had brought his basket of honeycomb too, and now it was gleaming gold beside him. A little madly, I wondered what the bees had told him. He gave me a cup. It wasn't water but deep, black wine that swam with stars from the lamps. I shook my head.

He put my hands around it. "Medicine," he said, clearly, so I could see it.

I could smell that there was alcohol in it, but I sipped it anyway.

It was wine, or at least, mostly wine: but it wasn't like anything I'd ever tasted before. It was sweet but sharp, and I could taste spice and fruit in it, and it was strong enough that it swept right through me straight-away, but there was something else as well. Everything went still, and slow. All the sharp edges of the world softened. Far from feeling drunk, I felt more like myself, like my normal thinking was coming back after that vision down in the cave, and with a new clarity, I understood why he had been collecting honey. This was honey-wine. I hinged forward over my own knees. I'd thought I knew what relief was—coming off a ten-hour night watch, not being wet any more after a screaming storm by the Cyclades—but this was something else.

Dionysus leaned to catch my eye, the ends of his hair coiling over the ivy on the wall. "You're safe."

I heard it somewhere deeper than normal hearing. Some part of me that I hadn't known was curled up tight, backed into a corner, spear out, straightened up and looked around and said, *Yes, you're right. That's all right then.* And relaxed.

I could hear.

No.

I could hear *better* than before.

I could hear an owl a long way away, and something rustling in the forest, and the tiny shush of the wind in the trees. The water was giggling.

Whatever invisible box I'd been in since Troy, he had taken me out of it.

"Can you hear me?" he asked.

I hadn't realized that I was lip-reading as much as I was hearing. He sounded different—richer, clearer, like the low hum of a lyre when no one is playing it, but a cavalry regiment is riding close by, shuddering the strings.

"Yes," I said, and then twitched, because I could hear myself too. I'd thought I could before, but it had been a lot dimmer than I'd realized. I could hear that I was speaking too quietly. "Would you—say something else?" I asked, to check, not wanting to believe it yet in case it was some kind of joy-hallucination brought on by not being trapped in a cave with millions of bees any more.

"Are you hurt?"

Incredible. I started to laugh, and it sounded weird, because I could hear it in the air as well as though my own skull. And there was a lovely shushing sound around us, one I did know, but I hadn't heard it for a long time, and it was—of course it was the leaves of the vines and the trees, swaying in the hot wind. It was nothing, but it felt like I'd finally made it home, for all I'd been home all this time. "I can hear the trees," I said, probably sounding insane. "I couldn't! I couldn't before, I lost most of my hearing the day Troy fell, how did you *do* that?"

He opened his hands, the universal *what can I say* sign. "Witching."

"Piss off, witching! There were falling towers, witches can't fix that—"

"No," he said. "But do you remember what it was you were doing, when your hearing stopped?"

"Nothing special," I said, trying to think. "I was sitting on the steps of the throne room at Troy, we'd broken in about an hour earlier. It was lovely. I went through the kitchens and the slaves had just baked these amazing cakes. They were from the Tin Isles, you know, the ugly people with grey hair, but gods, they can bake. It had strawberries in it."

He kind of laughed, not quite as though anything was funny. "What else?"

"Well . . . some of the little knights were getting a bit overenthusiastic, they'd got the king in the corner, but it was very restrained, for the end of a ten-year siege. I hardly got any splatter. Feral Jason only set him on fire a little bit. Why? Is it important?"

He was giving me a strange glassy stare, the kind that he would have aimed at somebody exclaiming happily about the lovely wildflowers as they skipped closer and closer to a bear that was looking hopeful and getting the good silverware out: it was half dismay and half a dark need to see just how close to the bear I'd get before I noticed. "No," he said, "not important at all, I was just interested in the ugly slaves and the baking."

"I don't know what's happening any more," I said, but I didn't care, because I felt like I might pop. There was an owl in the olive tree behind him, watching us with eyes narrowed against the little lights of the lamps, and running its talons over the bark to clean them. I could hear the scrape, small but clear. I could hear the water laughing in its channel, and the sound my palm, sword-rough, was making against the stone wall, and the miniature shush of his clothes shifting when he moved, and it was all glorious. I'd forgotten there was so much in the world.

From the great fissure in the ground beside us, a voice echoed up. It was eerie, because the words didn't quite sound like the speaker knew the meaning. They broke in odd places, as if they were just noises that came from somewhere past understanding.

I, I am the lord of the dance,
Duty, oath, and law are sacred
Lies, lie down all your sorrow
Dance with me again.

"We can't leave him down there," I said. "If he gets into a house . . . my slaves are children. You're alone. I should ask some knights to come."

"Ah, no," Dionysus said unexpectedly. "I don't think he was trying to hurt you, he was just surprised. He's been here a couple of days already and no harm done. He likes the bee cave, he likes the honey."

"He was screaming."

"Bees sting," he pointed out. "Don't bring the knights. He's better off down there than in a cell, is he not?"

"He . . . are you sure he won't try to hurt anyone?"

"No, but I don't think we ought to chain him just because he might."

He was right. It *was* better than a cell, and whoever it was, the man hadn't really hurt me. I'd wandered into his territory with a sword: it wasn't unreasonable to be surprised.

"Walk you home?" Dionysus rounded off.

All good things kill you, in the end.

"Yes please, sir," I said.

He gave me a lamp. Even that wasn't quite safe on the uneven ground, which was sunken sometimes and full of unexpected exposed steps, or the pollards of broken pillars. I put my hand out for his. He took it and pulled me so that I bumped into him, on the edge of laughing his smoky laugh, and on my other side, the Nothing slunk off into the dark.

Bliss.

We paused for some goats to cross the path ahead of us. They were clearly on a mission to raid his miraculous garden. One of them baa'd at us politely. "So in Scythia, they have a kind of sheep with a really long tail," Dionysus told me. "The wool weighs them down, though, and the sheep drag them along the ground and the wool gets all tangled and dirty; so the shepherds build each one a tiny cart to rest their tail on. They wheel around the mountains like that. If you hear a squeaky axle, it's usually a sheep."

I did my best stern look. "You made that up."

"No, I've been," he protested. "It's a strange place. It rains feathers."

"No it doesn't."

"It does, very cold feathers! I don't know why."

"I expect from the Great Heavenly Goose? Or the Almighty Eider Duck?"

He took a breath, then stopped. "Now we're saying it, I'd like it a lot if Zeus turned out to be a big duck."

We both laughed. It might have been the first time I'd laughed without feeling ashamed about it in years.

At my gate, he looked up at the lemon tree that never made any lemons as if he suspected it was just sulking and not trying hard enough.

"Do you—want to come in?" I asked, raw and somehow nineteen again.

He winced, and shook his head. "I can't," he said. "I'm expecting a runner, I've got two girls right on the edge and if one of them doesn't go into labour tonight then I'm no witch. Although," he added, "before I forget." He took a jar out of his bag and held it out to me. It was marked beautifully with blackwork patterns; bees, and vines, picked out very fine indeed.

"What's this?" I asked.

"Honey."

"Why?"

"Ah. Normal humans who live in proximity sometimes give things to each other; it's a way of saying you'd like to be friends if it isn't too inconvenient. Do you know about friends? It's when you keep talking to another person for a good while but neither of you sets the other one on fire."

I almost laughed, because that was a two-sided joke if there ever was one, given that he assuredly would be setting me on fire soon. "I see, I see. And what's the strategic function of this?"

"It's operationally redundant," he said, just as seriously, "but good for morale."

I did laugh this time, sad and not. "Thank you," I said. "I love honey."

"Welcome." He looked down at me for just slightly too long, and I thought he might come closer, but then he dipped his head and stepped back. "Sleep well, knight." He walked away into the dark, and from a tree, an owl swooped down and flew ahead of him, for all the world like it was showing him the way.

The house was quiet, but there was still a line of lamplight beneath my bedroom door. I tapped on the middle panel. "Boys?" I said softly. "Are you awake?"

The lock clacked, and there they all were on the other side, looking like lost ducklings. I froze when they lurched forward and hugged me, then put my arms around them as well as I could. They were still just little enough.

"It's just a man," I promised. "He's gone mad. Dionysus is looking after him. I don't think he's going to try to come into the house. But you stay in here tonight, just in case. Keep the door locked. I'll sleep in the other room. Wake me up if you hear anything inside the house."

But actually, I'd wake up, because I could hear. It was only slowly breaking over me, all the things I'd be able to do now.

They looked at each other uncertainly, and I realized they wanted to keep up their normal night watch of me.

"Why do you do it?" I asked. "Why do you watch me at night?"

There was a kind of silent conference, and then the one I suspected was the eldest looked up at me properly.

"Because you walk at night," he said. He looked nervous mentioning it. "The mad god possesses you."

A sort of heaviness came over me, like all my bones were turning to lead. "Mad god."

"There is a god who you do not worship here," he said, small, as if he expected me to throttle him. "He has—cursed you. He curses soldiers. He makes you think normal people are enemies, at night. We have seen this curse at home. We watch, because we want to make sure you do not kill us."

I stepped back without meaning to. "What?"

He glanced at his brothers again. "And—this last couple of days . . . you've been killing other things. In the garden."

Gods on Olympus.

"I see." It was hard to talk, because my throat had turned to rock. "All the more reason to lock yourselves in. I'll put locks on your doors tomorrow." I had been going to leave it at that, but I couldn't. "Why didn't you tell me?"

"Because—you don't like us, and we do not know what you will do."

Silence. Horrible things always are simple.

I didn't know what to say, except the only solution I had, for all it was less than bronze-clad. "If you think I might hurt you, bring Dionysus, because if that happens, I'm not in my right mind, and he needs to take me to Ares. Do you understand?"

They nodded.

"I like you fine," I said, lower. "You've been wonderful. I know this is a hard life for you now. You're doing beautifully."

"We are?" the middle one said. He looked like he might cry.

I brushed the top of his head. "Are you joking? You haven't poisoned me or anything, it's all very relaxing."

Something was different. They were just ordinary children now, not guarded and blank. They were caught exactly in the strange half light between childhood and adulthood. I could see how they had been when they were five, all round and tumbling, and how they would be when they were thirty. I couldn't believe I hadn't had the sense to put it together earlier.

"Now off you fuck, get some sleep."

For the first time since I'd met them, they all smiled.

"Night, Phaidros," the oldest one said softly, once the others had gone into the bedroom ahead of him. He gave me what might have been a smile through the narrow gap between the door and the frame.

"Night, Kat."

He looked taken aback.

"Ah, you see? Sometimes I'm not just a pig in a Phaidros disguise," I said.

He laughed. It was still a small-child giggle, deep and involuntary, and it chimed down the corridor, finding its unfamiliar way around the rafters, and the house felt different entirely.

21

I walked up through the city at dawn, and by then, the heralds were calling the stay-at-home order: the census would start at noon. Night market vendors packing up to go home, dusty and tired, looked annoyed about the noise; the homeless people on the road verges barely stirred; and some knights coming back to the garrison after the Hidden ride wondered grumpily if that would mean they had to be awake at noon. It felt like a mad luxury to be able to hear it all. Yesterday, I would have come this same way and not known the heralds were out until I saw them. Now, I could hear five at a time, streets apart. All of Thebes was full of their bells ringing and the clear voices calling. They would do it for an hour now, and an hour before the census began.

I should have felt hazy from the broken night, especially after what the triplets had told me, but I was full of energy. I kept hearing things I didn't recognise and soon found myself playing a game to see how many I could guess. There was a skimming noise that turned out to be a weaver's shuttle as she skimmed it through her loom, a shush that was dead leaves tumbling on the road, and then, incredibly, the hiss of the paintbrush as a man worked brilliant colours into the glaze of a new mask at a tiny table he'd set up outside his pottery shop. It was exquisite, and so were the others drying on pegs on the wall behind him. Word must have been spreading fast, about what the witches had done.

After that, I saw more of them. When I passed the Temple of Ares—where, gods alive, I could hear the disjointed songs of the knights inside—there was a delivery cart with its two drivers unloading and four guards with them. All six of them were wearing full masks, painted in colours and gold, the faces all the blank and beautiful, like young lords and ladies come to a feast.

The census began with a briefing for the census-takers—Palace scribes all—at the Guards' Court. I explained that we were looking particularly for young men between the ages of fifteen and twenty-five, because before long, we might have to start a general army draft, and we needed to know who we'd got before anyone had time to hide. Everyone took it silently. The Guards were standing on the edge of the gathering, watching, and I knew they were looking for anyone who seemed too intrigued and too chatty; anyone who might imagine that the silence order didn't apply if they just told one or five neighbours and a few kitchen slaves.

My part of the grid was the High City; the garrison, where I'd know straightaway if anything was odd, and the Temples of Ares, then the Bronze Court and the Weavers' Court. I always liked visiting the weavers; they hung gigantic bolts of cloth up to dry from dyeing, each one sixty yards long, and they flew over everything like the battle banners of giants.

A census sounds easy. You just have to take details from everyone and note them down. But the logistics of doing that on clay tablets were exhausting. I could fit maybe four people on each tablet, if I wrote small. So I arrived with a crate of tablets—or rather, a burly slave and a crate of tablets—and by the time I'd covered the weavers, the whole crate was used up. While the slave fetched another box of new tablets from the main administration office, I ran the old crate over to the Potters' Court for firing. Their yard was already filling up with crates from other census-takers, the heat from the kilns was already blistering, and potters were working soaking wet from the fountain, because it was only way to stay even half cool enough.

On the pretence of looking for smuggled gold or silver, the Guards searched everywhere we collected information. They, at least, knew who we were looking for. It felt profoundly inefficient. I kept pausing to uncramp my writing hand, fantasising about just putting out a general proclamation: forty talents of silver for Pentheus returned to us safe and well. But then the Egyptians would hear, and Prince Apophis would make doubtful noises about handing over his grain, and the Queen's authority would seem untrustworthy if she couldn't even keep a good rein on her own son, and it would all be a mess.

When it was the garrison's turn, the young knights seemed mutedly pleased to see me, but they were quiet, and I saw why straightaway. At least ten of them were missing. All gone to Ares; all singing that infuriating song. I could smell alcohol in the air, and even though that would have been enough for a garrison-wide lockdown in normal times, everyone was pretending not to notice. Amphitrion's sister was by herself in a corner. Polydorus, Jason's commander, had taken over while I was gone.

"How have they been?" I asked. We were in the mess, each unit lined up and waiting to be registered, either by me or by one of the scribes.

He shook his head. "A lot of them . . . they're having nightmares. All the same thing."

I stopped writing. "The same thing?"

He leaned forward half an inch, his version of a nod. "I have it too. It's a hunt. There's a lion, and the hunters and the dogs kill it, but once it's dead, it turns into a man. It must be an omen, but I asked the priest at the shrine to Apollo and he didn't know."

"A lion that turns into a man," I said, uncomfortable and not sure why. There was something familiar about it.

Polydorus was quiet for a second. Across from us, still in the line, obediently enough, Feral Jason was dissecting something which I hoped had been dead already. Polydorus watched him with the blankness of a person who had given up on trying to protect anything smaller than a dog. "They say everyone dreams prophecy when a god is close."

"Don't let anyone hear you say that," I said, looking around for Penelope now that I'd seen Jason. It was a relief when I realized she was curled up under the table, eating a basket of dandelions. I stroked her ears to say hello. She bleated hospitably.

She wouldn't last much longer. I'd arrived exactly as lunch did, and it was sparse. The bread loaves were much smaller than normal. There were olives and apples that looked like they'd been in the stores for months, still good but not very; some oil, some oranges that must have been imported or pirated because our own groves had failed this year; but no cheese, no milk, not even eggs. Knights only have meat at festivals or after sacrifices, it's too luxurious to give even to the Sown every day, but usually that translated into once a week. It had been a month since I'd seen any here. What was on the tables now were starvation rations. Around the edges of the room, the slaves were watching with a vulture intensity.

I was hungry too. I'd been too busy to notice mostly, but now I was sitting here, it was difficult to remember what I was supposed to be talking about. I wanted some of that bread more than anything. I was entitled to it, it was part of my rations, but I'd be able to get something somewhere else. At least I was on the border of the forest. I could shoot something tonight. I would. There's only so long you can get by on bread and oil. I split one of the meagre little loaves in half and lobbed one half to a little boy, one of the kitchen children, and gave the other to Polydorus.

"You need to eat," Polydorus said to me, grave.

"I'm smaller than you," I said. "And I'm on writing duty, not training." I lifted the stylus.

He stared at the bread and I thought he was going to refuse, because at least among knights, it's shameful to accept a gift from anyone you don't feel is your equal or better—he certainly didn't think I was his equal—but he took it.

"Why *are* you on writing duty?" he asked, in his sniper way. "Jason thinks the Queen is keeping you in a secret harem."

"With this face? No, it's administrative rubbish."

He lifted his chin a fraction. "And it's nothing to do with how nobody has seen Pentheus since the star fell."

Fuck.

"Why would my going blind staring at tablets have anything to do with Pentheus being in a sanctuary?" I asked, making an effort to sound light.

"Because if he has the madness, then he's out of the succession, and you're . . . it," he said. "You're the Queen's brother-in-law. You're on desk duty because it takes you away from anything dangerous. If you're killed, there's no other obvious successor."

I almost dropped my tablet. "Polydorus—gods' sake, I *am not* anything to do with the Queen, and the succession is not determined by some random moron marrying the Queen's younger brother, that would be stupid, the succession is determined by *the Queen*. If anything happens to Pentheus, there are slaves in the fields with better links to the royal family than me. I wasn't even born in Achaea, I'm probably Egyptian."

"You're a good liar," he said, with exactly the coolness and certainty of his own integrity I had aimed at Dionysus when I first spoke to him at the dance, and for the first time, I felt how unpleasant it was to be on the receiving end. It was righteous, in a shut-down way that looked—from this end—cultish. I frowned into that thought, because it was a jellyfish thought: there were things in the tentacles that trailed down deep and shimmered with a nasty electrical sting, though I couldn't see what they were just yet.

"I will stab you in the liver with this stylus."

He tipped his head in a way that said he would have very few opinions about it even if I did, and ate the bread.

I carried on writing names, checking down the tables and counting to make sure I hadn't missed anyone, and trying not to do it too resentfully. Any garrison is a rumour nursery, but because they weren't allowed to listen to bards to get their dose of made-up twattery that way, Theban knights grew bushier and more luxuriant rumours than anyone else in Achaea. I shouldn't have been surprised.

Jason flicked something biological at one of the other boys, who yelled and punched him. Polydorus's stare migrated into the distance.

"Does this need to involve me?" I said, sliding the traditional razor into my voice.

"It was a *lung*! Permission to throw him down the fucking well, sir?"

"Granted," I said, in case there were still miracles.

"I'm going to make a sacrifice to the mad god," Polydorus said, as matter-of-fact as he would have been if he were saying he was off to the market for honey; not suggesting treason. "Do you want me to buy a lamb or something for you?"

"*No!*" I hissed. "Fuck, you'll be sent to the galleys!"

There was a shriek that sounded suspiciously like someone being bitten by Feral Jason.

"I know," Polydorus said dreamily.

By the time I'd finished my grid section, the potters had done a great deal of work, and most of the tablets from the rest of the census-takers were already fired. They were stacking them in the middle of the court-yard so they could be taken down to the archives, so I set up there to see the incoming census-takers as they gave in their tablets. The census was not, said the Queen, entirely irrelevant: it was useful to know how many people we needed to feed. In any case, it was important to pretend the census data was what we had wanted. The Egyptians were wandering around the Palace freely, and if they realized we appeared to have conducted a census but taken no records, someone would put two and two together.

I marked off grid sections as each scribe came back. Everyone said the same thing: no sign of Pentheus.

As the number of open, possible grid sections shrank, I started to feel a dull certainty that the Hidden must have missed something on the road. But I'd seen the report from the unit polemarch. They had stopped every wagon on the road and turned them upside down, but nothing. Of course, someone could have paid her off—not hard when the rations were sinking to nothing—but if that had happened, if Pentheus had been taken to Athens or Sparta . . . surely we would have heard from the Athenians or the Spartans by now, sniggering and demanding ludicrous sums of silver?

Two figures were moving through the smoke more slowly than the potters, one very tall. I went down on my knee when I saw the sway of the Queen's long hair, which, like always, gave me a sorrow-hope twang, because in that first instant I felt like it might be Helios. The Queen bent to lift me up again.

"You remember Apophis," she said.

"Vividly," I said, looking him up and down in a way I hoped would discourage any urge he might have to speak to me.

Apophis was looking at some of the tablets. "Is this writing?"

I wondered what amazing Egyptian misunderstanding I was about to be treated to now. "It is."

"Is it just numbers?" he asked after a moment.

"No. These are names, these are addresses; holdings."

"But there are so few signs. How are you getting down the information?"

Another belter.

The Egyptian view is, as far as I can tell, that if you're not a master artist willing to dedicate twenty years of your life to learning thousands of symbols, you have no business writing or reading anything and you ought to shut up before someone comes along to smite you.

"Each sign is a sound," I explained. "Ta, ke, ka, like that. We only have so many sounds." Forty-two.

"It doesn't seem very sophisticated."

"It isn't. It isn't for temples and monuments, it's for noting things propped against a horse. You write in Coptic sometimes, don't you? That's just lines and dashes."

He frowned. "That's shorthand. *Writing* is sacred. Words can last for eternity. Some effort ought to go into them. Do you not think?"

I wrestled heroically with the urge to shove him in a kiln. "We like it for tax purposes."

He laughed and turned to the Queen. "I was under the impression that you didn't have writing out here, Agave. This is a nice surprise. You must teach one of my scribes, so we can translate your holy texts. Our scholars would like that very much."

That would be hysterical. I'd once tried to tell an Egyptian the story of Athena's birth—she is wisdom, and so logically enough she sprang from her father's head, heads being where wisdom tends to gestate—and what he took away from it was that I had no understanding of reproduction in mammals.

"I'm sure they would," said the Queen, sounding very much like she had the same concerns as me. "Thank you, Heliades."

Apophis drifted away, still looking puzzled.

The Queen switched into Achaean. "Anything?"

"Nothing," I said quietly, aware that it would have been idiotic for the Egyptians to come here without at least one person who could understand Achaean. Still, maybe they were arrogant enough not to bother.

She nodded once. "Well. Thank you."

"What will happen if we can't find him?"

"The grain ships are anchored at Aulis. They're guarded by three thousand soldiers."

"Three *thousand*?" I repeated.

She nodded again. She was beginning to look calm to the point of disinterested. Helios had used to do that. It was instead of screaming and punching someone. "What do you think? Can the garrison take those ships, against those numbers?"

Egyptians are terrible sailors. It's because the Nile is so straightforward. The current takes you to the sea even if you sit on a raft with no rudder and you flounder about like a confused octopus. On the open sea, we would have the advantage; but in total, including my unit of brand-new, barely trained knights, some of whom had never sailed, there were only two thousand of us. It had been five thousand before Troy.

"Yes, but we'd lose half the garrison."

"I might yet have to give that order," she said. She looked grey, and not just from the smoke.

I bowed my head. "Duty is honour."

22

Despite the Hidden raid last night, there were people selling things at the roadside again when I made my way home just after sunset. Lots of wine in rough jars, and lots of straw masks now, cheap ones that didn't need a potter, just string and some imagination. Where the hot wind stirred through the branches, the trees rattled with prayer tablets. The things were everywhere: they had crept through the trees all the way up to the maze. As I came round the corner, I saw someone had even put one in one of my olive trees, on a bright green ribbon.

I slowed down and had a little drop of happiness, because Dionysus was waiting by my gate. He seemed not to feel the heat, or anything else; he was unnaturally still and straight in the shade of the lemon tree, so still I almost didn't see him. When I came up close enough to talk to him, he still didn't move, and I had a strong feeling he wasn't really there.

"Dionysus?" I said tentatively.

I saw him come back, and saw him feel the heat properly, for all the world as if he hadn't been standing in it. I smiled, hoping he was going to tell me about something weird he'd done to an unreasonable census taker, but he didn't smile back.

"So I need you to swear something," he said, without any preamble.

"What?"

"Whatever you see now, you are not going to vanish into the Temple of Ares, because that won't help anyone and you'll die there."

"Why?"

"Swear," he said, with an edge in his voice I hadn't heard before; or, not for a long time. There was pyre smoke in it, and hot ash.

"All right, I swear?"

"On your commander's soul."

"I swear on his soul," I said, much more slowly.

Dionysus let his breath out. "Come inside."

I followed him like it was his house, not mine, five paces behind him. He held the door open for me, and with dread pulling its bowstring tighter and tighter, I looked around for the triplets, surprised they hadn't come out yet.

And then in the corridor: bodies.

The triplets.

Horror welled up in me, seawater in a boot print on the shore, and I felt it well too far and spill over the top of me, and I couldn't breathe.

"Why did you make me swear not to go to Ares?" I asked, very quiet. Maybe this was it, maybe this was the revenge he had set out for me. Maybe he wanted to see it close up. It was difficult to lift my eyes and meet his, because I knew he was going to be smiling, ready to say, *You know you deserve this.*

But he wasn't smiling.

In fact, he looked worried that I wasn't shouting at him.

"Because there's a mad person in the maze," he said. "This could be my fault, not yours. I'm the one who said he'd probably not hurt anyone. So you and I are going to stay here tonight, and we're going to see what happens."

Yes, because then I'd got a little bit of hope, and it would be so much worse when nobody came and we had to agree it was me.

"But it wasn't him, was it," I said.

"Look," he said, and took my hands. He frowned when I flinched. "No scratches. Look at them, they fought, but there's nothing on you."

"Stop witching me. Just let me go to Ares."

"Phaidros! I'm not witching, why would I do that?"

I nearly laughed and listed all the reasons. *Remember that time I stole you off a beach and meant to sell you into slavery in Egypt? Remember how my crew thought they should throw you off the ship? Remember how I didn't stop any of it? Remember how I didn't die with the rest of them?*

Only, only, only, what if he wasn't doing that, what if he really did think it was the mad person in the maze?

Hope is the death of valour.

"Do you trust me?" he asked.

"Of course I don't trust you!" A hilarious thing about me: I look horrifying, but my voice breaks high when I'm not happy and I sound about fourteen. "You tried to convince me it rains feathers in Scythia!"

He hadn't let go of my hands, and ignored it when I tried to pull them back. He was strong. "Look . . . I know you took a vow to tell the truth no matter what, and so I know what that makes me look like to you. But—please understand. I took a vow to lie no matter what, for the *same reason*. The honesty of knights helps people. The lies of witches do that too. When I say, 'do you trust me,' I'm not asking you if you trust me to tell you the truth; I hardly ever tell the truth. I'm asking if you trust that I want to help you, and that my help could be useful."

My breath hitched on the way in, because I didn't even trust that.

He seemed to see he wasn't going to get much more out of me. He gave my hands a tiny squeeze and let them go. "I'm starving. Will you make some bread while I dig?"

"Dig?"

"To bury them. We can't burn them, it will start a wildfire."

"I should bury them."

"Not good for you," he said seriously. "It will hurt you more."

"I *should* be hurt more."

His eyes went up and down me twice, and then slipped past my shoulder. I thought someone was there, but when I looked back, there was no one.

"They don't want you to," he told me, as quiet and simple as everything else he had said.

"Bullshit," I said, but my voice came out tight.

He smiled gradually, as if it were genuinely funny and he was trying not to. "All right, you do what you want if you're so clever."

I made the bread.

Dionysus did it all himself. He dug on the forest border, and carried them there, and he wouldn't let me help. He made me sit down while I waited for the bread to prove, and by the time it was done, the corridor to the triplets' rooms was just a corridor, washed clean.

"Why are you doing this?" I asked him. I was beyond confused now. There was horribly twisted revenge, but burying bodies was something else.

We were at the table in the shade of the shutters, the bread between us, and some of his amazing grapes, and olives, and cheese. The cheese was from the farmer across the way from us, because she was grateful Dionysus didn't mind about letting her goats into his garden—they were yielding the best milk they ever had, she said, so he deserved the benefit. I had to stare at it before I touched anything. Everything on the table between us now was so much better than what was at the garrison. Even though it was only what I would have expected in an ordinary year, it seemed like a feast. I dipped a piece of bread slowly into the olive oil, watching the gold sheen cover the crust. When I bit into it, I could taste that it had grown near a lemon tree.

Dionysus had tied his hair up to work, and taken off the top half of his tunic, sleeves tied round his waist and tucked into his belt. He was sitting flat against the wall now, for the cold in the stone, not moving and breathing slowly while he waited to cool down. He had a deep patience for being uncomfortable I'd never managed to learn, even on the long day watches outside the walls of Troy.

"Because either it wasn't you, or it was but it's not your fault."

"If it's your fist, it's your fault," I said. "If I did kill them then I'm going to a sanctuary."

"Let's see what happens tonight before you decide," he said.

I dragged my wrist over my eyes and didn't know what to say. I didn't know what gods the triplets had, or what they needed. They had little figurines in their room, but I didn't know if those were holy icons or just dolls they had saved from home. They were still little boys.

Maybe about the age Dionysus had been, when I stole him off that shore.

Dionysus poured a handful of water into his palm and dragged it down his arms, and pressed back against the wall again. I stared at the floor. He was a witch. Normally he wore a veil. It wasn't right for me to see him like this, only half dressed; there might not have been a law, but that was only because nobody had thought it needed writing down. And it wasn't right to notice how the light was turning him gold down one side, or how fragile-strong his collarbones looked, or how it would be if I could put my head on his shoulder.

If I had killed the triplets, then I shouldn't be touching anyone ever again.

"You were a sailor, right?" he asked.

My throat locked. He was about to say, *It's nice how you care what you do to children now, because you didn't ten years ago.* "Yes." I waited for the fire.

"So," he said, with a little witching sparkle, "I was in Africa, beyond the desert, where there's a great kingdom which sometimes trades with Memphis, and I was going south, because there are more kingdoms that way and I wanted to talk to their witches. Their magic is better than ours."

"You were not, but all right," I said, and my voice fissured with something between relief and frustration. How long was he going to play with me before he got bored?

"So I get on a ship, and as you know, you sail down the length of Africa with the land on your left and the sea on your right, due south, yes?"

"And the sun rises in the east and sets in the west . . ."

He narrowed his eyes and closed his fist at me. "After about two months' sailing, there's a place where it all turns around. The sea is still on your right and the land is on your left, but now you're going due north, and the sun rises in the west and sets in the east."

"And then I expect you met a sea monster."

"I've never met a sea monster. But."

For a burning flash of a second, I thought: *No one has ever been this kind to me.* Helios had an obligation, commanders and wards are kin, but this was something else. This was ludicrous, painful kindness. Obviously it was a trick and it was going to end with some kind of fresh horror for me, but it didn't matter. I wanted it anyway. I cut another slice of bread, thinking of all those Athenians I'd known at Troy who knew the alcohol would kill them one day and agreed the Theban companies were right to ban it entirely—but drank themselves into oblivion all the same.

"At a port on the coast in Africa, there were ships from another kingdom. They said they had come from beyond India. The ships were . . ." He lifted his hand high above the table. "Fully the size of towns. The people on them look different to us, they're taller and paler and they sing to each other instead of speaking. While I was there, it was one of their holy days, and they made shapes with fire in the sky."

"No they didn't," I said, a laugh breaking through even though I hadn't expected it. "You're worse than the bards. Oh, by the way, I met a cyclops on the way home, he ate my crew, I definitely didn't lose them on that tricky wrecking shore round by the Cyclades."

"If you say so," he said happily.

It should have been maddening. Usually I couldn't stand it if I wasn't sure whether someone was lying to me, but this was different. He didn't expect me to believe it any more than the bards did. He was just showing me bright things.

But the way he was glimmering at me: I had a creeping suspicion that actually, the joke was that everything he had just told me was true. The idea that it might be, and the world really might be that brighter, more deinos version of the one I thought I knew, made me sit back a little, feeling small but in a good way. I was one person with insignificant problems on a rocky barren plain at the end of the world. Maybe, in a kingdom beyond India, there were people who sang instead of talking and painted with fire in the sky.

"You're a good witch," I said at last.

He rested his head on his hand, looking far too pleased with the compliment for someone who was going to murder me soon. "All flowers, cakes, and other tokens of adoration gratefully accepted at the end of the show."

I got up.

"Where are you going?" he asked, wariness inking into his voice.

"I have eggs; I have your honey. I'm making you a cake."

He looked delighted. "Really?"

I pushed him, trying to think when I'd last met someone so easily pleased who wasn't also six. "Really."

As soon as the honey cakes were out of the oven, I knew that the recipe was finally right. They smelled different. They were Helios's cakes. When I bit into one, daring it to be wrong, I was eight years old again, on a beach somewhere around the Kind Sea, and Helios was looking mischievous while he hid cakes behind dead horses and twisted bits of armour. Every so often he'd point at me and yell at me to stop cheating, and I'd squeak from inside his stolen helmet that I wasn't cheating, honest.

"Phaidros," Dionysus told me, "you've missed your calling." Then, because I was staring at him, "What?"

I shook my head, because the part of my mind that usually dealt with words had gone off somewhere else for a little holiday. For years, Helios had been hazing away from me, eroding at the edges, but I could see him again; quite small, laughing, not nearly as immortal as I'd always thought, my age now. It was as if I'd seen him an hour ago and he'd just stepped outside to do something nefarious to the sheep of someone he didn't like.

"I wonder if you can die of cake overdose," Dionysus said seriously to the plate. "Do you think I should see? I think I should see."

"My commander used to make these," I said. "Just like this. I think it must have been this honey. But—it must be rare?"

"He'll have had it from a witch. We use it a lot," Dionysus explained. "It's very good for soldiers, and for mothers who had bad labours. The magic smooths down the edges of terrible memories, so you can think about those things without cutting yourself."

I lifted my eyebrows. "You've made me drug myself with my own cake?"

"I have," he confirmed, making no effort whatsoever not to look gleeful.

"Shut up and eat your cake overdose," I told him, feeling stupidly happy.

Mortals can hurt gods. Aphrodite was wounded at Troy: an entire unit of knights from Mykenai swore they'd seen it, and people from Mykenai are serious. Ares is hurt all the time in fights, and even Zeus nearly died once. I was fast, and if I was up in the night sleepwalking and I caught Dionysus at the wrong moment, I'd do a great deal of damage or worse.

So I taught him some proper knots, and then he tied me to the bed; just by my ankle, but with the knot well out of my reach, looped over the other side. He put a cup of water where I could reach it and a lamp where I couldn't. I saw him notice Helios's helmet, and the bright side and the dull side. He didn't say anything about it, and uncomfortably, I realized that meant he understood what he was seeing much better than I would have liked.

"Do you need anything else?" he asked. He didn't look happy about leaving me that way for the night, but he must have known nothing he could say would change my mind.

"No. Thank you." I was propped up against the wall, feeling like I was never going to sleep ever again. "Are you sure you want to do this?"

"No, it's none of my concern and I've plenty of other friends who bake much better cakes than you." He sat down next to me, on the edge of the bed. If he came up close to anyone, I was starting to notice, he made an effort to make himself smaller. He didn't spread out; he curled up, one knee folded under him. While he'd been digging, the sun had turned him an even more vivid shade of bronze. He was too bright for the drab room. "But for what it's worth, I don't think there's anything wrong with you."

I tested the rope, pulling against it hard. No. The knots were good. "Why?"

He half smiled. "Because if there were . . . you'd not be able to sit with me and stay calm."

I felt like I'd missed a step on the stairs.

That was a confession.

"I'm infuriating," he explained, with a rueful glimmer. "Show me an unthinking murderer who doesn't dive on me straightaway and I'll show you someone who isn't an unthinking murderer."

That was a double joke. *You think I'm talking about being a witch, but ha ha, I could be talking about the other thing.* He liked the ambiguity. Maybe he even liked that I could see it was ambiguous.

I almost told him that if all the humans you know well are fifteen and likely to hand you a kidney at any given moment of the morning, distantly

NATASHA PULLEY

sinister jokes were not only undisturbing, but a sparkling example of refined adult conversation.

"I'm sorry, but your own inability to imagine that you might be slightly shy of unbearable is not evidence of my continued health," I said. "Go over there."

He looked at me as if I'd said something immensely kind, and just for an instant, I wondered if I hadn't got him wrong—if it hadn't been a joke in the way I'd thought at all, but a kind of apology.

It took me a long time to go to sleep. The lamp had burned out by then, and the night had finally turned cool, the almost-full moon making Dionysus silver where he lay under the window. Standing up he was imposing, but lying down, he looked like one of those statues abandoned in the desert in Egypt, built thousands of years ago and forgotten, wearing down and down as the sand blasts by. I had to stare at the ceiling with my hand over my heart to try and calm down and convince myself there was no way I could hurt him. I'd tested the rope. I couldn't break it. If I wanted to get at him, I'd have to snap my own ankle.

When I did sleep, I tipped into the most vivid dream I'd ever had. I was in a forest, the forest behind the house, but I couldn't tell why I thought so, because it was different. The weather was different, and not just seasonally. It was *cold*. It was like Scythia, with that strange ice on the ground—what had they called it, frost?—spinning webs and white tapestries everywhere, and the trees weren't my trees. They were giants, not the struggling olives and ash that I knew now, but massive oaks, the ground thick with acorns, and grazing through those acorns, the greatest aurochs I'd ever seen, twice my size, horns nocked and savage from fights, and more of them than I'd ever seen together. It was a vast herd, and somehow, even though I knew nothing about wild cattle, I knew that this was part of their great journey south for the winter. We were following, and the hunters were leaving diagrams and instructions about the breeding season on the rocks for Those Who Come After, and the going was hard, so hard that the witches said that if anyone fell pregnant now, we would have to give the child to the forest, because there wasn't enough food.

There was a person among the bulls. It was insane, because the aurochs were wildly protective of the little ones at this time of year in these woods where the wolves would always follow, but someone was standing by one of the biggest all the same, tall and sparse, and wrapped in wolfskin. When they looked back, right at me, they were wearing a black mask, and a crown of auroch horn, but I knew the eyes behind it. They were the blue at the hem of the sea, where it turns indigo by the horizon.

He snapped his fingers at me; fingers tattooed red-black.

I jerked awake.

It was the middle of the night. Orion was hanging framed in the window, at an angle, like he was leaning sideways to look inside.

The room was still. Dionysus was exactly where I'd left him. Trying to breathe normally, I sat up and started counting down from two hundred. It was something Helios had used to do; it worked, sometimes. I could feel it wasn't going to work now, but there wasn't much else to try.

I was on a hundred and fifty-nine when, opposite me, the cupboard door opened and someone climbed out, monstrous in the bull mask.

The front of my mind tried very, very hard to convince the back of it that I was asleep and having a nightmare, because there was no possible way someone could have been sitting in that cupboard, but there they were, standing in the middle of the room, just out of the moonbeam. They were looking at Dionysus, standing too bent. It looked painful. Very quietly, they drifted towards him, not quite into the light, and sniffed. It was the way that the bulls studied a thing before they crushed it. And—I could hear hooves. I could hear the thunk of them on the floor, so heavy I was sure I'd see scars on the stone if I could just twist far enough to look, and I could smell that dense, green animal smell of cattle, and now, the way the moonlight was just catching those horns, which I was certain had been straw before, just part of a mask—the shine was the shine of bone.

I had to be asleep. I had nightmares all the time.

The bent figure swung slowly away from Dionysus and thudded across to me. It was so much heavier than it should have been. I could feel the floor shaking through the frame of the bed. The man, the thing, was keeping to the left of the moonlight, so that all I could see was a shadow with the suggestion of limbs and clothes. My sword was in the corner, as far out of reach as the Nile. I couldn't do anything except keep still, and hope that would work on a man-bull like it did on real bulls.

The man-bull was right next to me, leaning down beside the pillow. It sniffed hard again, then powered out the same breath so hard it moved my hair. I still couldn't see it fully, but I would have sworn on my armour that that head wasn't a mask any more.

Fuck's *sake*.

"Dionysus!" I yelled.

Dionysus sat up fast, and at the same time, the person, the thing, let out an animal snarl and ran away, thundering into the next room, and then there was a bang that was the door down into the maze smacking into the wall. I tried to get up but the rope round my ankle pulled me back. Dionysus had stopped in the doorway, hunter-motionless, looking out, into the kitchen, and towards the darkness of the stairs.

"Where did it—untie me? Where did it go?"

"Into the maze." He cut the rope rather than wait around wrestling with the knot. The knife must have been very sharp indeed, because the rope gave with just one slice. Yes—it was *my* knife, the one I'd given him in the wagon with the people from Pylos. He gave it to me, then took the flints out of my tinderbox. Crack, crack, the tiny flashes strobing across us both, eternities between each one, and then one caught on a coil of sawdust, which he held to the wick of the lamp. The orange glow made the room feel safer, even though of course there was no difference at all.

"It was . . ." I pointed at the cupboard. "It was in the house all the time we were. It must have been. I was cooking all evening. I would have seen. Gods, don't go down there!"

"Just to lock the door," he said, fading into the dark at the bottom of the stairs. There was a clank that was the lock. He came back up, fast, and helped me pull off the last loop of the rope. "Are you all right?"

I had to look away, at the open cupboard. "Dionysus, that was . . . in the maze, I thought it was a man in a mask, but—*was* that a mask?"

"I don't know," Dionysus said. "Perhaps not, any more."

From somewhere outside, or perhaps down in the maze, I couldn't tell, there was a weird, eerie scream. It wasn't a person. Dionysus sharpened.

"What?" I asked, uneasy.

He inclined his head and gave me a strange look. "I . . . think he's defending his territory. He doesn't understand why we're in it."

I thought, *Well, if there's anyone left who understands the Hunt, it's you.*

And then I thought, *Where the fuck did that come from?*

"Then why didn't it try to hurt us?" I asked.

"We're bigger than your boys."

I breathed out slowly. "I need to catch it, once there's daylight. See if it can talk. I want to ask it if it killed the triplets."

He had been tying his hair up, but he stopped halfway through the last turn of the green cloth, his elbows still bent above his shoulders so that his shadow looked like it had wings. "You can't still think it was you."

"If that thing thinks it's a bull, then it's bad-tempered but it's a herbivore."

I should have gone after it then. It was stupid to sit around and wait for it to come back, but I was too tired. I'd been tired for days. I hadn't slept properly since before the Hidden ride, and although I could function well enough for ordinary things, beginning a hunt for a wild— monster—would be idiotic. I was the kind of tired that makes wrong decisions, that catches on little worries but ignores real threats, that hesitates when you should never hesitate. I'd catch nothing in this state. I'd only hurt myself, or worse, get Dionysus hurt.

"Right." Dionysus hinged down on the windowsill again, and something about the way he said it made me think he hadn't really heard me. Now that everything was over, he didn't seem at all as collected as he had a minute ago. My heart was thumping too. It was good that neither of us was hurt, but I kept having to look at the cupboard and check nobody was on their merry way out of it again. Maybe there was a secret tunnel. Maybe there was more than one. Maybe we should move to Italy.

"*How* is he a bull now?" I asked, or maybe it was more of a demand. "Have you cursed someone?"

"No!" There was more force in that than I'd expected. "This is old magic. It's the mask." He was saying it to his own knees, not me. "Even in normal times, if you give a person a mask, the mask changes the person. When there's a god close by, everything is . . ."

"More," I said dimly. Jasmine racing up the mast of my old ship. Knights like me who had been seeing things and wandering at night anyway but functioning, just, now swerving into madness. It was as though something of the god was in the air always, in the way the vapours of the great volcanoes must always be in the air, all across the world, but now—we were all on the edge of the volcano, staring into the caldera, but instead of making people dizzy and faint, these vapours made miracles.

He nodded, very slightly, as though he still had a strong instinct not to move.

Too late, I noticed that he was shaking. It was subtle, but even in the moonlight, he had the tight paleness that everyone does after they come off their first battlefield. It's what happens when you stare right down the spear-shaft of being murdered. Not generally, not like when you feel ill or you realize that there's going to be an imminent supply problem, or even something dangerous but impersonal like the dust storm. It's different when the Unseen is in the doorway and you're so near to the Ferryman that you can hear the creak of his oar.

Even gods must be afraid sometimes.

I held my arm out, in case that would help.

He went very still for a second, then dropped down next to me and put his head against my shoulder. He was fear-cold. I snagged my cloak from the other chair and put it around him. He stayed quiet, not moving except how my breathing moved him. I shut my eyes, trying not to think about what I'd done next, the last time I'd held him wrapped in my cloak.

I rubbed his hair. It was warm, and I could feel the difference between the black and the grey. Despite everything, it gave me a little glow of joy.

"Drink time," I said. "I've got some wine. It's not as good as yours, but I mean, medicinally . . ."

"Yes please," he said. "Yes. Hold on, you aren't meant to have—"

"It's emergency wine, all right?" A few days ago, I would have thought that drinking with a witch in the middle of the night was one step away from turning into a slob who spent all his time beating his wife and staggering home at dawn in yesterday's clothes. I'd never met anyone who had poise without austerity. I hadn't thought that was possible, but here he was, spun of poise, and not a thread of austerity. "You don't know about it and I never mentioned it."

"Yes please." He pressed his hands over his face. "Sorry."

"No, that was frightening," I protested, not liking that he thought he needed to be sorry.

I'd never thought I'd see him look ashamed. I'd thought shame would just ping off him. But he did look ashamed now. "You're not frightened," he said.

"The . . ." I shook my head as I poured out some wine from its slim little jar, because the cups were distracting. I only had four, one for me and one for each of the triplets, and I felt like I was robbing them to use one. It paralysed me for a second and then I had to switch them round, so he had mine and I had the old one we normally kept spoons in.

I brought a plate of the honey cakes from yesterday too, because he was right about his honey: it did help. Anything sweet did, but this all the more so. The bees must have been a special kind. Maybe they were witch-bees.

"I've not had any monsters climb out of my cupboard before, but midnight ambushes are ordinary after-dinner fare, you know? We used to make it into a game. We had a scoreboard and everything."

"A scoreboard?" he repeated, his voice smoking. He sounded like he was trying hard to calm down and I wanted to tell him to try less, because it would go away faster, but instructions wouldn't help. Distraction was better.

"You earned points for acting stupidly," I explained. I set the cups down and lit a lamp. The tiny light made everything seem safer. Everything in the room had been grey and silver before, but now, there was a pool of colour, and it was reassuring. "Five for dropping your sword, twenty for letting someone take it off you, thirty for being asleep on watch, fifty if you let someone burn your tent down. And then we had a special Moron of the Month ceremony. The prize was a jar of really old cheese. You had to keep it in your tent the whole month. So, when some Hatti cavalryman rode screaming at you, you didn't freeze, which is normal; you went, *oh fuck, what if they give me the Cheese of Shame?*"

It was a relief when he laughed.

I touched our cups together. "To eventful evenings."

He smiled, but it was pretend. He was looking at the cup, the one that was usually mine. Helios had given it to me. It was supposed to be a special-occasion wine cup, because it was fantastically made, the glaze flawless, and it was inscribed for me. It said *kalos Phaidros*. Kalos means "beautiful." At the time I'd assumed it was my due and I fully deserved a commander who had things specially made to toast how lovely I was, because as I've mentioned, I was vigorously unlovely. Now I had to wonder if, not at all unlike Dionysus, Helios had been telling useful lies. He wasn't blind, he hadn't failed to notice I was about as kalos as a homicidal pig, but I'd never fought better than I had when I knew he was watching.

"Don't laugh," I said, about the cup.

Dionysus glanced up at me, not laughing. "Are you sure it's all right for me to use it?"

I almost asked why he said so, but then I saw it. I clearly didn't live with anyone, but I wouldn't have kept it if Helios had left me. He had seen the helmet in the other room too. "Of course it's all right," I promised.

He held it carefully all the same, in both hands. "This wine is so bad," he said, but he was smiling.

"Witch it into something better then. Come on, what's the point of you?"

"All right," he said. "Will I show you some magic?"

"Yes please," I said, curious, because I'd expected him to pour it in a plant pot.

He held the cup in both hands and closed his eyes for a second, then held it out to me.

"Piss off," I said.

"Taste it."

I did, and then looked up at him. It was gorgeous. It was his wine now, the black honey-wine that fizzed. "*How* did you do that?"

"Witching," he said, with a muted spark.

I'd never been so happy to have such an annoying answer.

He turned my cup around in his fingertips. It was painted with figures of knights in formation, with Athena watching from the end of the line. At first I thought he was going to ask if it was strange to end up in a marriage to someone who raised you, and I got ready to say that goats are strange if you don't grow up with them; and then I thought he would say something about the war, and whether anyone really did see Athena there like so many of the stories said. He didn't. He looked sad, as if he were holding the relic of something precious that had been stolen from him long ago.

"You must have a hundred of those," I said. Even Feral Jason probably had a kalos cup, either from poor suffering Polydorus or some ill-advised lord who didn't realize what he was getting into.

He sort of laughed. "Not one."

I had a vivid impression then that I was missing something important. I felt like I'd boasted about winning the Oracle Games to someone who had lost a leg.

"Witches don't marry," he said. "If you have a family . . . you're not strange enough for witching to work properly."

"It only works if you're strange?"

"The more deinos the witch, the more deinos the magic," he said. "Be deinos enough, and even the snakes believe you." He smiled just enough to show his teeth. "Even the Ferryman."

I had a dangerous, crossing-No-Man's-Land feeling that according to his vow, he probably shouldn't have told me that.

"Isn't that lonely?" I asked, quiet.

He inclined his head. He was thinking about it, really thinking, which meant he hadn't said it before, or at least, not recently. I was afraid to move in case he remembered he wasn't supposed to tell me. "It is. But it is the vow."

"Is it worth it?"

"Is yours?"

I smiled, because that felt like a really beautiful, deft uppercut that he pulled so well it didn't even knock my teeth together. "Fuck, no, it's fucking dreadful, but it's who I am and I can't be anyone else now."

He touched his cup to mine.

A howl came from outside. His eyes ticked to the window. The shutters were open, because it was far too hot to close them no matter the danger. Anyone outside would be able to see the little lamp between us from way up the mountain. There was nothing between us and everything else except the agreement that a door requires permission to open.

"The Palace needs to stop people wearing masks," I said, only level enough to think it out properly now. "They're everywhere. They're selling them in town as a kind of medicine against the madness, and—" I stopped. "And you did that too."

"What?"

"Before the madness really began," I pushed, shocked now that I hadn't taken him up on it before. "The first night after the star fell, *you* brought people here to that dance, and you gave them masks, and wine. You did it before anyone, you knew something was coming." Stop, stop, stop, of course he knew something was coming: he was the something. I pulled it back as much as I could. "Didn't you? But—you . . . knew that masks could be . . ." I trailed off. "Why? The masks make it *worse*. This is so much worse; that man . . ."

"No, it isn't." He looked wrung out in a way that was nothing to do with needing to sleep. He let his arms unhinge slowly across the table, his hands open, wrists facing up, so that he was almost touching me. "The song, the one the Furies are singing, and the knights; they're singing about the holy raving. That is . . . how . . . cities fall." He said it slowly and with great care, his eyes flicking up to mine and begging me not to hear it as hyperbole. "The holy raving is what happened in Pylos. The only medicine for it is what you've seen. Wine, and masks, and the dance. A little madness can keep away great madness."

Exactly like it had with Tiresias, the well-greaved and garrison-trained part of me snorted and said, *Don't be ridiculous. Only Athenians and hysterics talk like that.* That made me fall still. I'd always listened to that voice. It had been armour against so many things: idiot decadences and superstitions, laziness, the urge to abandon duty when it was inconvenient. It was my favourite part of me. I was proud of it. Nothing could get through it. Now, though—it was getting in the way. A god was talking to me, and I couldn't understand, because of that bronze helmet that I'd forgotten how to take off, and the visor that wouldn't hinge up.

"How does that help? How does being drunk and partly a bull help anyone, at all, in the face of a *thing* that eats cities?" Even as I said it, I could tell I was trying to see it through the bronze helmet, with no peripheral vision. "That sounds as arbitrary as saying we need to befriend a hedgehog and then put three pebbles on the doorstep."

He took a breath, and then shook his head a tiny fraction. "It's blue," he said softly.

And there was yet another thing I didn't understand. He was talking about trying to prevent this city-burning madness that was coming, but he *was* the madness, so what was he doing?

Somewhere deep in the maze, the thing screamed again. Dionysus flickered. His hands were still open in front of me. I didn't take them, because of what he had just said about his vow, but he gave me an impatient look then, like I was being cruel, and took mine. It was like how a cat would have got cross I wasn't paying it enough attention and shoved its head under my palm. I didn't know what to say, because what I really couldn't do was say that that tiny thing had made me a lot happier than it had any right to, and that I'd never met a person more confusing. I wanted to say, *But what do you mean?*

"Do you really think it was that thing that killed the triplets," I asked in the end, "or are you just witching me so I won't panic and go to Ares, and then you won't have anyone to wind up with your sheep-and-feather-rain stories?"

"I'm witching you," he said. Some of his usual spark flashed back to life. "There's not another soul in Thebes I could delight with my fascinating and educational and extremely true stories. You've gone irredeemably nuts, and we should be careful about the legions of squirrels coming for you as we squeak."

Which was another could-mean-something-nice, could-mean-something-terrible joke. I was tempted to start scoring him out of ten for them. I gave up on answers and ate my honey cake. If he was back to his double-edged jokes then he felt better, and that was all I'd wanted.

23

We were still awake to see the dawn come in past Harper Mountain. All night, we sat watching the front door, expecting to hear something bang into it, but everything was quiet. When I tilted it open, I eased out first and looked to either side in the glow of the sunrise, the blade of my sword tinted pink and violet. No one was there, and nothing looked out of place. I went out a little way to see up to the roof, waiting to see a horned shadow crouching up there. No.

Dionysus pinned back the doors to let the air in. There was no reason to think the danger was gone just because it was morning, but it was hard not to feel like we'd reached a safe border wall. At least now if the thing came back, we would see straightaway.

Like it was an idea that had travelled a long way to arrive in my head, I realized I was going to have to put on the red cloak and go to the Kadmeia again, because despite everything, I hadn't found the prince, and I was no closer to anything useful.

It was only gradually that I noticed what Dionysus was doing. He was cutting up some oranges.

"Where did you get those?"

He pointed with the knife. "Your trees."

"But they're dead," I said, twisting around, and then blinked twice, because in fact the twin orange trees that marked the way through the olives weren't dead. They were very much alive, verdant, and full of oranges. Not quite believing what I was seeing, I strayed out to look, and it was only when I'd picked an orange and peeled it and found it was real that I turned back to the house and saw the ivy and the honeysuckle surging up the old masonry. There were bees looking into the flowers, and tiny bright birds perched in among it all. Two days ago it all been as barren and beige as everything else.

"They must have found some water deeper underground," he said, doing very good work of seeming distracted. "Eat that, you need something alive, you can't be living off bread."

I didn't say anything, because I was too puzzled. He could have said, *Yes, that was me, you'd better get used to it, but don't worry, you won't have to live with it for long.* In fact, he could have done that all along. When he first saw me with the bull on the edge of the crater, he could have said right to my face, *Watch this: I'm going to make you like me, and I'll only kill you once you do, and it will be satisfyingly terrible.* There was no need to hide behind witching, or pale excuses about underground water. That was bizarre. He hadn't cared, years ago, whether anyone realized what he was, and I couldn't see why he cared now.

And, *and*: half of Thebes was looking for a god to give the crown to. It was his for the taking, but he wasn't taking it. If he had done something huge and deinos, and turned the Queen into a deer or the Palace into a great tree, then he could have been king by now.

But no. He was in my kitchen.

He noticed the silence.

"I do not," he said, "get in trouble with the Temple of Hermes for frivolous witching, and I'm not in the least worried about what would happen if you report me to them." It was one of those lies he lit up like a signal for an incoming army.

I was starting to notice that whenever he did that, there were actually two lies involved: the one he was lighting up, and the one that fell into shadows that were much deeper because of the light. The first one, you were supposed to catch. I was supposed to sit here and laugh and think, *Ah, well, so there is a rule at Hermes.* But the second one . . .

I pretended not to have seen the second one. "I won't tell anyone. This is lovely. Thank you."

He looked pleased and sat down around the angle of the table from me. I watched him as well as I could without staring, filling up with a honey happiness. For years, I would have given anything to have him back and see if he was all right. And here he was. Grown-up, healthy, vengeful maybe, and a bit crazy, but not broken. He was the least broken person I'd ever met.

"May I ask you for more advice?" I asked.

He snapped some grapes off a bunch where each grape was fully the size of a plum, and as dark. I didn't ask where the grapes were from. Probably there were brand-new vines growing out of my bedroom wall. "You stayed up half the night calming me down about a mad person in the cupboard, I think you can ask me for as much as advice as you like."

I nodded slowly, feeling confused about that now too. I'd just accepted it last night, but in the clearer thinking of the morning, it seemed bizarre that any of it could have frightened him. He hadn't been frightened of being stolen by pirates: one madman in a cupboard was startling, but that man could have been ash floating on the breeze by now if Dionysus had been genuinely worried. So what: he was pretending to be frightened? I didn't think so. I'd spent my whole life around frightened people and he hadn't been acting, last night.

All the odd things—that he seemed not to want his crown, that he was finding excuses for his miracles, that he had been scared yesterday— they were starting to make the outline of a shape. I was missing something, and it was sizeable. I felt like I always had done when I did a cargo stock take and found myself staring at a big empty space where *something* was supposed to be, but it wasn't on the manifest.

"Why *were* you afraid?" I asked, hoping he wouldn't mind now in daylight when he could see any monsters coming. "I don't mean you shouldn't have been but—you can tame real bulls, never mind a pretend one."

He watched me for too long, and I had a creeping sense of having said something stupid. "For sure, knight: why would I have been afraid when I think it was fifty-fifty that you *almost didn't* shout. I think you almost lay there while he tore you apart. Never did a witch struggle more to keep a healthy person alive, Phaidros, I swear it."

"I—right," I said, because that wasn't what I'd been expecting at all. Me, he'd been frightened *for* me, and that had been real fear, the way he'd gone so cold; it wasn't soldierly irritation that I'd been careless, nor witching. He cared what happened to me. To *me*.

218

Because he was the one who needed to kill me, and it would be enraging and rending if someone else did first. The gods knew I'd felt like that about Andromache. I'd once shot at my own knights to keep her alive towards the end—anyone watching the way I was in those last few battles would have thought I loved her, the way I protected her—but I still felt like he had just taken me in from the winter and wrapped me in a blanket.

"I'm sorry, sir," I said.

"Ah, so," he said neutrally, sinking back in his chair and still watching me over the rim of his cup, which put pressure on a part of my brain that hadn't been built for pressure. It creaked dangerously. I looked down and tried to think about something reassuring and boring that wouldn't make me want to choke into humiliating grateful tears, like how we used *so* differently. For him, it was more like "then"—it was a ghost of some rhythm in an older language, but I couldn't trace how I knew until suddenly, uncomfortably, I realized I knew that in the same way I knew about the Hunt, and the god in the mask, and the Ones Who Come After.

Fuck, pull yourself together.

"The census didn't work," I said. Yes. Reporting. I knew how to do that. "The person I was looking for is still missing. It's going to cause problems. He's crucial to a deal for grain from the Egyptians, but it won't work if he's fucked off to fucking Sparta. I really thought he was still in the city, but I just don't . . . know any more."

"An alliance," Dionysus said. "We're not just talking about a nobleman, are we?"

"No. It's the prince. I die if you tell anyone that," I added.

Dionysus looked into a plant pot which had had some dead mint in it for about three months, and planted his orange pips in it. "Even if I told someone, they'd think I was making it up."

"True," I said, reassured.

He thought about it. He had his hair tied up in a knot with its green cloth, and he had never looked less dangerous. He looked like he was about to take some laundry out to the springs. "So the problem is that the Egyptians will be offended."

The mint, I swear, had perked up. There was green on it.

"Yes. At best they'll think we're incompetent and at worst they'll think the Queen is lying so she doesn't have to hand him over. Either way, there's a danger they won't let us have the grain."

His eyes went over me twice and I thought he seemed unhappy about something. "Can I ask why it's *you* looking for him?" He sounded unusually serious. Normally, his ashy laugh was only arm's length away, waiting in the corner, but it had gone away elsewhere for now.

"The Queen thinks he ran away, and that he might come with me willingly if I find him. My commander was the Queen's brother. I'm his uncle by oath."

"Her brother," he echoed, and there was something strange in the way he said it. There was hopelessness in it, and however I tried to look at it, I couldn't see why.

"What?" I asked.

"No, I was going to say you should leave it to someone else, but—I can see you can't."

"Why should I leave it to someone else?"

The way his eyes brushed over me then, I could see that he had watched the centuries turn, and knights like me serve queens like ours again and again, all different, and all the same. "The Queen will kill you in the end."

"She might, she might not," I said. "But duty is honour."

He looked like he would have liked to punch whoever first said that, but he didn't argue with me. Instead he stayed quiet, studying the edge of the table. He wasn't thinking: he had already had a thought, but he wasn't sure it was a thought he should say. It was extraordinary to read a person like that, but he was like watching very clear water. "Hold a funeral."

"Hold a . . . funeral," I repeated experimentally.

"The Egyptians can't be offended if he's dead."

I had to stare at it for a while, because my instinct was to say, *No, that won't work, because what if he turns up again?* Immediately there would be problems for the throne, because people would say the real prince was dead and this person might look like him but he was clearly an imposter, and there was nothing the Queen could do to argue against that. People love conspiracies. And even if that wasn't a difficulty; it would be a hard,

hard thing for the Queen to arrange the funeral rites for her son without even knowing if he was truly dead or not.

No, said the little voice in my head that had always belonged to Helios but increasingly sounded like Dionysus. *She's a Sown lady. Duty comes first. She won't refuse to do something just because her feelings are hurt. That's the reason she clashed with Pentheus in the first place. She doesn't understand people who aren't* like that.

I expected to spend an hour waiting around at the Palace. I could walk around the shrine to Semele among the ivy and try to think of a good way to suggest a funeral, without sounding as though I had given up hope for Pentheus. I wanted that wait. After barely half a night's sleep, my head was full of fog. I was still nebulously scared that Dionysus was wrong, and I was the one who had done that to the triplets, and scared that I only believed him because that was so much nicer than not believing him. It was making me prickly and twitchy.

"Ah, good morning, Phaidros," said the Egyptian ambassador, clipping down the steps with the happy energy of a person who had slept for ten hours and had a lovely long morning to himself to think things over, without being interrupted by any mad people in the cupboard at all. Even worse, it wasn't the kind of *good morning, Phaidros* that planned to stand alone. It sounded horribly like it was bringing lots of friends. "I was just wondering—"

"No," I said, before he could get going. "Fuck immediately off, I am not explaining writing or marriage, or . . . *shoes*, or whatever normal thing has mystified you now."

He was smiling. "Breakfast. Would you like to have some?"

"In general or with you?"

"With me."

Sometimes vows of honesty aren't difficult to uphold. "I would rather get in that fountain and drown."

Fortunately, for some Egyptian reason of his own, he looked delighted and went away laughing.

"You didn't sleep very well then," the Chamberlain said dryly at the top of the steps.

"You look me in the eye and tell me you'd have bloody breakfast with him."

"I can't," she admitted.

"May I see the Queen?"

"Go straight in," she said.

"You are not a reliable person!" I growled.

It was early, but there was already a stack of clay tablets on the Queen's desk. She was ignoring them. Instead, she had turned her chair around to face the courtyard, and she was making chain mail. It was fiddly and boring, and I knew exactly why she was doing it, because I'd used to do it for the same reason. It kept your hands busy and your mind in a straight line, because if you didn't pay it enough attention, you stabbed yourself in the hand.

I'd made chain mail, when I was waiting for the witches to tell me if my ward would live or not.

"Did I just hear you giving the Egyptian ambassador a considerable dose of Theban honesty?" she said.

"You did, lady," I said to the floor.

"Good, keep doing that. I don't think he's ever met anyone who doesn't pretend to like him before. He keeps talking about you."

That sounded dreadful. "Any chance we can discourage that, lady?"

"No. Duty is honour, and so forth. You look terrible, what's happened to you?" she said.

I went down on one knee near the chair. Even doing an ordinary thing that any human would do waiting for news of a lost son, there was a holy-mechanism quality about her. It was a stillness and a precision, a sense of perfect counterweights working and springs blessed by gods long ago. It made me worry less about what I was going to have to say. She was a marvel queen. She would carry on no matter what. "Someone broke into my house in the night. He's been in the maze for a while. But . . . then he climbed out of the cupboard."

"That's exciting."

"It was," I agreed, and loved her for that. She would never say, *Gods, are you all right?* Of *course* I was all right, and if I wasn't, I could take myself to the garbage well and get in it, thanks. It was a reassuring vote about my capabilities. "He was . . . turning into an auroch. He was wearing a bull mask. But it wasn't exactly a mask any more. He had hooves."

She didn't do me the indignity of asking if I was sure. Instead she nodded slowly. "Yes. There have been other reports. Tiresias is doing an experiment at the Temple of Apollo."

I wanted to ask, but it wasn't my place. If I needed to know, she would tell me.

She coughed. She was getting ill, from the weather or the strain or both. Of course, she would sit there and disintegrate before she said anything. I could see her attendants hovering in doorways, not sure if she would defenestrate them if they gave her something for it.

"You look like someone hit you with a rock and left you under a hedge," I said, because I was probably too heavy to hurl from the balcony. "Are you going to let them make you a tea or something?"

She snorted. "I'm fine."

"I'm the Queen of Sparta," I said, and nodded to the closest boy to say it was probably all right to make that tea now.

"Are you here for a reason?" she asked me, putting arrowheads in her voice, but she was only play-fighting.

I shifted to go down on both knees rather than just one. "I think we should consider a funeral," I said, and heard how flat it sounded, but I was so tired I couldn't think of anything better.

I thought she would hit me. She didn't move.

"I was going to say the same thing to you," she said. "At least it will mean we're blameless, in the eyes of the Egyptians. Perhaps if Apophis is sympathetic enough, the agreements will go ahead even without a hostage."

I looked up at her and wondered how many people ever had the luck to serve under a just and careful monarch. Not many. Not many people at all would be able to kneel beside the throne and *want* to be kneeling there. But I did, then.

"Can the Treasury *afford* to hold funeral games?" I asked. "Do we have anything spare in the warehouses?" Even as I was saying it, it felt improper. I was talking as if we were family, a widow and a widowed brother-in-law awkwardly joining households and trying to find ways, without offending each other, to get some idea of the other person's finances and how things were going to look until winter. I regretted it straightaway. I sounded like I was trying to shoulder my way into royal decision-making.

"No," she said, astonishingly unoffended, and I sank down onto my heels with relief. "If we properly supply the games . . . we'll be perhaps a week off famine conditions even for the Sown." She was studying me as if the answer might be in the scars on my face. "But that's why it's a good idea. Apophis knows we're close to starving. We wouldn't stretch to the expense if it wasn't real. If we can make him believe it, he'll rene-gotiate the grain deal. Meanwhile—all garrison units will be drilling war games this week. You need to rehearse how to take a heavily defended cargo ship."

"There's really nothing left, then," I said.

She sighed, and tilted a tablet at me. "This is a Guard report. They found an old lady on what used to be a successful olive farm. No crop this year. When the census-takers visited, they saw a man's shoes and coat by the door, but no man, and she wouldn't admit to there being any in the house. They thought she was hiding a fugitive, but when they looked into the shed . . . anyway, the Guards are having to go around the outer estates to make sure nobody else has eaten a tax collector."

I made a noise I've never made before or since and smacked my hand over my mouth.

"I'm glad you did that as well," the Queen said, tapping my shoulder with the tablet. "But that's what we're looking at now. There will have been more cases that have not been reported." She was studying me again. "You think I should have sent the garrison out raiding months ago."

"I did think that, when the rations went down. But . . . did we even have the means to supply more long sea voyages?"

"No. It cost more to fight at Troy than we gained from any plunder."

I wasn't surprised. A fully fitted warship cost acres of silver. We had lost so many on the punishing voyage home. It shouldn't have been that way. It wasn't that far. In fair weather, you could sail from Achaea to Troy in about two weeks. But Troy had fallen in winter. Our word for winter is the Storms. It had taken five months to get home. Harpies had raged all the way, spinning the wind and the water into terrible cyclones that had hauled ships right from the sea and dropped them from the air. Whole crews had drowned. I'd never known a season like it—my unit had tried to wait it out, but after two months stranded, we ran out of food and we had to sail. Probably some ships were still wrecked on little islands, trying to make repairs.

"If all else fails," she said, "it's going to be Athens. But that will be scant gain for a lot of effort. They're barely better off than we are."

I nodded once, soaking all that in. When I'd said it—when Dionysus had said it—I'd known funeral games would be a political gamble. That wasn't the same as gambling the lives of everyone in the city on the very last of the food.

"So," she rounded off, "we'll need to find a body that looks more or less right, though I'm sure that won't be difficult." She said it with the same dispassion as everything else. Then, suddenly, like a splinter in glass, "Would you ever have just run away, when you were his age? You had a difficult life. I imagine you never got anything you wanted. Did you ever think about desertion?"

"No," I said slowly, "but . . . I had everything I needed. I had Helios, and my unit, and a profession I was good at. It didn't matter that I didn't always get what I *wanted*."

"Are you saying Pentheus didn't have what he needed?" Arrows again, but not quite play-fighting this time.

"Yes. I don't think royal heirs ever get what they need," I said, looking at the neat rows of chain mail, the pliers still resting on her knee, how she had her hair in a long rope over her shoulder, like a knight.

The way she stared at me then: I might have punched her in the gut and she would have been less hurt. I tilted back, because I hadn't meant it to hurt her at all—I'd thought I was saying something obvious that we both knew but that she couldn't say herself.

"I'm a bad mother, aren't I," she said quietly.

I wanted to hold her hands. Of course I didn't do it. "You're Sown."

She looked down at me with the fossil of a smile around her eyes. It was the kind of smile I'd always imagined that Athena aimed at the people who died under her banners; the sorrow of immense might, capable of going into a frenzy of grief that brought cataclysms, but far, far too restrained to do anything but smile that sad smile.

24

It took only a week to organise the funeral games. That didn't seem like nearly enough time, but it turned out that the contracts for state funerals were advanced and updated depressingly often, so that they could be held at short notice. In the garrison, the younger knights volunteered to compete, especially the ones who were hoping to marry soon (suddenly the old saying that a good match comes with victory laurels was everywhere), the banners went up through the town, and the vintners and farmers shipped what was left of their dwindling stock up to the Palace supply offices.

I took over my unit again from an exhausted-looking Polydorus, who gave me a thousand-mile stare and said he was just off to die in peace now. The little knights seemed happy to have me back, even Feral Jason once I'd given him a dead mouse to feed his snakes-for-hair and pretended that looking at him had turned me to stone, but more of them were missing, too; gone to Hermes or Ares. I'd only got two thirds of a unit.

It was becoming rare to see anyone moving between Palace courtyards without a mask. They were all different, and though they were mostly shaped like human faces, not animals, I kept catching myself going tense whenever I saw a new one, waiting to hear that thunk of hooves, or to catch the sun gleaming on real horns. Outside the Palace, there were more and more of the unsettling straw masks—cheaper, stranger, all bound into different dead-eyed shapes.

I stopped the little knights wearing them. I told them about the man who was halfway a bull, in the maze. Some of them laughed at first but when it was obvious I wasn't joking, most of the masks vanished again, or at least, they did until I went home at night.

We were supposed to be conducting war games—how to take cargo from a docked ship—but that was sporadic. What took up almost all our time, the whole garrison, were patrols of the major roads. I'd never done that before in Thebes. We were drowning in thefts, robberies, sudden attacks, especially outside the bars, which were heaving like I'd never seen before. Every street corner was littered with broken wine jars.

But we were coping, more or less, until the night before the funeral.

I thought it was going to be a quiet night. My unit was patrolling Harper Way, the long main road to the mountain and the maze, and it was boring, because after nightly Hidden rides, it was deserted. A few masks lay discarded at the road sides, and every so often, forgotten things winked and gleamed—dolls, necklaces, even abandoned bags—but the people had melted away.

Ivy was forcing its way up between the paving stones of the road. In the deserted quiet with the wild creeping back, I could see what the road would look like in a hundred years, or a thousand, when Thebes was a ruin after all the fine clockwork melted down for swords long ago, and nobody remembered there had ever been marvels.

We were almost at the end of our watch when a battle horn sounded, high and eerie in the night.

The little knights all looked at me, confused. Inside the city: it had to be a mistake, or a drill, or someone taking the piss.

It wasn't. It was Polydorus's unit, formed into a shield wall at the top of what was usually a quiet road, full of airy houses where trader families lived. I couldn't believe what I was seeing at first. A whole mob of people in those straw masks were hurling wine jars at the knights.

"Phaidros, fucking Zeus alive," Polydorus said when I locked my shield with his. "It's something about flour, the traders are using short measures—"

A wine jar smashed against my shield. There must have been a lit rag in it, because the thing exploded. Burning brandy vapour hissed up around us both. I had to tear my cloak off as fire rushed down one side of it.

There was a hush. Not far away, my cloak blazed by itself. Getting angry about flour was one thing, but trying to kill a Sown knight was something else.

Between the shields and through the smoke, I saw a slim figure standing on a wall. For a lightning bolt of a second I thought it was Dionysus—but it was just a man in a bronze mask that looked a bit like him. I should have been thinking about the fight and the order to advance, but even as the crowd of masked men realized they didn't have much choice now but to charge at us, I found myself checking every few steps for that man on the wall. He was very still, but watching, like a general.

Afterwards, I sat on the edge of a fountain in the road, washing blood and soot off my shield. The fire had done something interesting to the filigree, and now it had oxidised rainbows in it. I quite liked it. I was in a sunny mood now. Things had seemed a bit too much earlier, but sometimes what you need to remember is that everything is fine as long as you aren't currently on fire. Around us, the traders were edging out of their houses, bringing us cold water, which was kind of them, and helping to move the bodies.

"Sir," Jason said, sounding uncertain. He was frowning at something off to our left.

Polydorus looked over at the same time as me. He was halfway through plaiting his hair over his shoulder to keep it damp and cool for longer. Mine, wet too, was coiled up on the nape of my neck. The stone roads seemed to soak in the heat all through the day, and breathe it out again as soon as the sun set. Some of the little knights were lying flat on the paving, staring up at the sky and trying to keep still until I had to give the order to move.

Jason hesitated in a way I'd never known him to do, and then like a much smaller child, took one of our hands each and towed us to the shadows around the other side of the fountain, where there was a dead man. Or I'd thought it was a man.

Polydorus knelt down slowly. He tugged one of the feathers—huge, white pinion feathers—gently at first, then harder.

"Is it glue?" Jason asked.

"No." Polydorus pushed the cloak aside so we could see.

The man had feathers right down both arms, tawny and white. When I took the owl mask off him, we all recoiled, because the face underneath was not altogether a man's any more. The eyes, open, were orange. We all stayed exactly still for what felt like a long time. Other knights came to see what we were looking at, and then stood there in silence too. Some people made the bull sign for good luck.

The body was changing in front of us. It was like watching a flower wilt. Now that the mask was off, the beak was softening, and there were tiny snaps as the feathers began to fall away. They didn't vanish. They stayed there on the ground, offensively, still being feathers. When Jason picked one up, it looked heavy. Polydorus smacked his hand to make him drop it, like he'd touched something cursed.

"Pardon me, knights?" said a light, polite voice.

There was a young man waiting far enough away to be respectful. Someone held up a torch so we could see who we were talking to; slim, small, probably a slave, but strange-looking, because he had blue eyes.

"Yes, sir?" I said.

He was the man from the wall.

"May I take my friend away?" he asked, and he was starting to seem odd, because although he was being polite, he didn't seem afraid of us—even though most of Thebes would have waited at least an hour to interrupt still-bloody knights, particularly if it was civilians who had just tried to set one of them on fire. I started to get a tickle of unease.

"Not yet," I said. "You'll need to wait until the morning. I have to take him to the Palace to show the Queen his—condition. You can come for him then."

The young man stayed where he was. "But the Queen will have the body destroyed. He must have a real funeral, and real honours. He was undergoing the Holy Change, after all." Still calm, still unafraid, as though there were an invisible wall between us that would stop anyone hurting him. It was how Dionysus was.

Something in my thinking, the part that was beginning to understand witching, went *click*. I looked down to his hands, knowing he would be holding that bronze mask from earlier. It was beautiful, cast to look like very wealthiest, most cultured sort of Egyptian gentleman; except that in the eyes, there was blue glass, and wound through the hair was an ivy crown.

Wearing a bull mask would turn you into a bull now.

Wearing a Dionysus mask would . . . what?

A little crowd had gathered behind him. Some of them were the same people who had just run away from the battle. Most were wearing masks, but under them, they were still ordinary: young girls and boys who had just come straight from kitchens, still in aprons; an older lady in an orange sash that meant she was a marvel-maker; a man who still had dried clay on his hands, who must have been making vases—or masks—at his wheel an hour ago. They were all keeping back from the young man with the bronze mask, though, and not in the practical way they would have kept back from a knight. It was the way people gave priestesses space—and witches. Reverence.

I was glad, for the hundredth time, that I sounded so unlike what I was. I sounded like a temple chorister only just old enough to grow his hair long. It was a voice to keep the peace with. "Holy Change, sir?"

The young man nodded once, all restraint and grace. I could have been speaking to a king, not a slave. When he spoke again, it sounded airy, and he aimed it at a point somewhere just above my head. "This is a most sacred thing, and it will change all Thebes before the end." He was speaking with an accent now. It was old. It was how Dionysus spoke; or it would have been if Dionysus had said the things people *expected* gods to say, and not stories about be-carted sheep and feather rain. "It is part of my rites, which I must not be denied."

The little crowd behind him, which was broadening now—some of the traders had come across to look, some drawn with worry, some kindling with what seemed to me like a terrible sort of hope—murmured and nodded. I heard a couple of people say something that might have been *all hail*.

Fuck fuck fuck.

"Your rites? I'm afraid I don't know your name, sir."

Don't say it, don't you fucking say it; channel Dionysus enough to have his foresight, and to realize what I'll have to do if you say it.

He put the bronze mask on. "I am the Raver."

Some people knelt. Murmurs skittered away in every direction— through the crowd, through the knights.

Sometimes, you can see the future. Sometimes there are two ways, laid out as clear as parallel corridors in a maze, and sometimes, you can look down through the ruined places and see both paths.

I could try to keep the peace. I could take him to the Queen, and these people would come too. They'd send their children running to bring relatives and friends and there would be a mob, and the Guards would have to let them into the Palace or end up trampled. There would be no order to fire or draw swords, because nobody wanted to massacre civilians. When the Queen appeared, though, the witching that is all that maintains the royal house would be very weak. Rather than a great figurehead seen from a balcony, she'd be right there in front of them all, a tallish lady who looked like a knight and just as easily wounded as one. And someone would risk their life, because they were desperate and hungry and the only way out was a god, and they would snatch the crown. Maybe they'd fall, maybe there would be a massacre then, but even if the crown didn't reach him, this man would be king then. There would be knights who obeyed him—I could see some even now with hope-stars in their eyes—and maybe, if he wore the mask long enough, he would be god enough to convince the rest.

Sometimes you can keep the peace. Sometimes you can't, and then the only consideration left is whether smashing it yourself with as precise a blow as you can will end with fewer people dead than letting the Fates do it. The Fates are never precise: they use sledgehammers.

There was a dusting of grey in the man's hair, just like Dionysus's.

Part of me locked up. It was the part that had finally breathed when Dionysus lifted me at the dance, and the part that had believed him when he said I was safe, and the part that secretly loved his mad stories— or rather, that he told them to me.

It said: *I can't. I can't. He's too like him.*

I wasn't wearing a helmet, but that didn't matter. The one on the inside was there, and now, I pulled the visor down.

"We'll see, sir. Gods can't die," I said, and slit his throat.

———

He did die. He crumpled into a little heap on the ground, and where his blood poured onto the flagstones, poppies bloomed.

Poppies grow on battlefields. They like blood. The fields in front of the walls at Troy had been full of poppies, every summer. I tried to stop that thought, because like one of those hull breaches on a ship that start out tiny but prise themselves open wider and wider as the force of the sea crushes into them, I could feel I was about to lose where I was and when, and I'd be back on the plain again, with those gruesome poppies, and that it was going to be worse than before, and it was going to happen in front of everyone.

Something that wasn't me waded through the flooded corridors, and closed a watertight door.

I couldn't hear.

The crowd was writhing and I could see people were shouting, or praying, or crying, but all I could glean was a kind of hum. It made me feel like I wasn't really there, even when some people pushed forward to pick the poppies and soak cloths in the blood, it all felt more like seeing it in a painting than living it.

The Kadmeia was overrun with ivy. Everywhere slaves were working with garden shears, trying to cut it back where it grasped up the pillars and sprayed around the window frames. It wasn't just ivy, either; honeysuckle, swathes of jasmine, growing right out of the flagstones, wrecking door hinges. In the courtyard where the shrine to Semele was, the pomegranate trees were in full bloom, and already growing pomegranates. For me anyway, it was as silent as moss.

I wanted to curl up in a corner and stare at the wall, or anything that wasn't the way the man had fallen, his hair like incense smoke. There wasn't time for that. We were waiting for the Queen. We had the body to show her, and the mask, and the story.

Jason and Polydorus had come. I must have looked wrong, or ill, because Polydorus had put his cloak around me, and Jason wanted to me to sit down. I was glad of the cloak, because even though I was nearly sure the night was still hot, I was freezing; my fingernails looked like glass. All my thoughts had gone spacey and strange. I didn't feel bad, just distant.

It was quite nice really. It was a relief not to be collapsed in a heap thinking I was at Troy: this was maybe not ideal knightly function, but it was all right. I wished they would stop looking so worried, but the way they kept looking at each other, it was like they thought . . .

Like they thought I was going to lose it and murder someone if nobody intervened. Of course they did. Jason had seen that once already, with his old commander. Polydorus didn't want him to see it again.

People were turning, looking and talking towards the right; the Queen was here.

Someone must have just turned her out of bed—it was an unholy watch of the night—but she was dressed, her hair bound up in a knot like mine because of the heat. If she was surprised to find her receiving room full of knights and dead bodies, she didn't show it. We all knelt. Polydorus was explaining something, his eyes trained respectfully on the hem of her dress. Like Pentheus's robe at the Bull Ceremony, it was stitched with a slim band of embroidery that from any distance looked like a plain ribbon, but up close, like this, showed Hatti gods. I loved cloth from Hattusa. I wasn't supposed to: it was all amazing colours and much too gaudy for us, or at least the way they wore it: whole cloaks covered in brocade, temple curtains brilliant with stitched scenes, sometimes in patterns so spectacular that the weavers probably went blind at thirty. If it was just up to me though, I'd have filled the house with it.

The hem came closer, and she took my arms and drew me upright. I kept looking down, but she touched my chin to angle it up, so I could see what she was saying.

"You did the right thing," she said. "Well done. What's happened to you?"

"It's battle madness," I said, and with shame screwing a way through my skull, I knew that it came out strange and flat, in that accent that all deaf people have because you modulate your own tone so much as you speak, and when you can't, it shows. I hated it: it made me sound like I didn't belong here. "I'm sorry, lady."

"Bring the witch," she said to someone past my shoulder. I felt something through the floor that might have been footsteps. Then to me again, "You're freezing. Come on." She took me out to the courtyard steps, which were still warm, and pushed my shoulder until I sat down.

She sat next to me to wait, and took off the crown. She spun it between her hands the way athletes spin laurels. It made her look like a girl who'd just won a boxing match, one she hadn't enjoyed very much. The crown flashed silver and gold, the figures of the warrior saints dancing around the band.

"Lady, I'm all right," I tried to say.

"Oh, shut up."

I did, gratefully.

"So, it seems Apollo has forgiven us," she said, at the green everywhere. "Do you think?"

"No, lady," I said.

She snorted. "You don't need a witch, you're clearly fine."

I felt a bit better for that.

"You really believe there is a mad god?" she asked. "Why?"

"Because everything that's happening—it's all the same and what it adds up to isn't Apollo. The wild, and the masks, and the madness, and the song . . . it's all . . ." I told her not very coherently about blue.

I thought she would tell me not to be so stupid, but she only listened. When I finished, she nodded. "I understand. I don't . . . see it, though; they don't seem the same to me. Perhaps I was wrong about something in the dust, perhaps the madness is a curse, but if so, it's from Ares, as punishment for excesses at Troy. The drought is from the Mother. The magic in the masks—that seems like Hermes to me. God of witches? But something's changed for the better. All this green. They say we'll have a pomegranate harvest tomorrow. I think the sacrifices are working."

I nodded slightly, though I didn't think it was about *better* or *worse* at all. It was the wild, taking back Thebes, and it wasn't doing that to benefit or hinder anyone. Dionysus was brandy, and these miracles were the fumes, and the longer he stayed, the drunker we, and all the land, would be. I couldn't say that.

The Guard was coming back with a witch who moved like she was very old. The Queen was talking to her, and I couldn't tell if the witch spoke back because she was wearing her veil. She came to sit on the next step down from me, directly in front, so I could see her properly. The red tattoos on her hands came almost up to her elbows. I wondered how many mothers and babies that was. She'd seen whole generations into the world.

The Queen said something else and the witch took her veil off. She had bright black eyes.

"My name is Circe," the witch said to me, "and I am ninety years old. I've served in the courts of queens and kings from Tintagel to Memphis, and my magic is far greater than the power of any of them. What's happening to you now is a blessing from the mad god. He's taken part of your mind away to keep you from doing anything else that's going to hurt you."

"Can we perhaps not invoke imaginary gods," the Queen murmured.

"Just because you don't know him in Thebes doesn't mean the rest of us don't," Circe said, unmoved. "Drink this." She gave me a bronze cup of that feral brandy.

"No," I said, because I couldn't do that in front of the Queen.

She put it aside, but gave me a look that said she couldn't do much to help me if I wouldn't accept any help. "You're going to go home, and eat something, and see your family, and sleep like the dead, with no dreams. When you wake, you will hear again."

No; I wouldn't. I could see the trick. It was the way she'd told me who she was. The more deinos the witch, the more deinos the magic. She was trying to make sure I knew she was deinos. She was doing exactly what he had done, she was telling me I was safe, only it wasn't going to work, because I didn't believe her.

If you know how the witching works, it stops working.

"You can come home with us," Polydorus said to me. He had knelt down on my other side. "We're much nearer than the maze."

"No," I said, because he didn't like me, and because he had a wife who would surely not enjoy a whole extra human in her house when she already had to put up with Jason—especially not a deaf battle-mad one she wouldn't even be able to communicate with. And they had children: two little girls still too tiny to join the garrison. Polydorus had married the second he was eligible to on his mother's orders, and his wife was . . . I thought she was a knight too, invalided out of service because she'd lost an arm, and now something influential to do with the Temple of Athena.

And his commander was still alive: he was an official in the Assembly. I had a distant feeling that they were all one household. I knew the house, on Copper Street—it was one of a row of beautiful Sown mansions, built for exactly that sort of extended family. They all had courtyards with orange trees, and if you looked down at them from the Palace, you could see them because of the oranges that fell in the gutter channels in a bright line.

"It will be worse by yourself," Circe told me, severe.

I nearly told her she didn't know what she was talking about. I didn't have it in me to stay with a family. Even if it turned out Polydorus's wife and commander didn't mind me at all, they would still be one thing, all joined together and belonging, and I would just be me. When I tried to go to sleep, the Nothing would be there, filling the room, where my little boy and Helios and his wife and children, and mine . . . weren't. It would be worse than going home by myself. That was good, dark loneliness, not the kind horribly illuminated by someone else's happiness.

"All right, everyone get out," the Queen said, to put an end to it. She looked tired. "Not you, Heliades."

"Come to Copper Street after," Polydorus told me urgently.

"I'm fine," I said again. "But thank you."

The Queen watched them leave. She seemed like she was struggling with something. "They're right, you shouldn't go home by yourself. I imagine you'd be easy to steal. You're very manageably sized."

I snorted without meaning to and mimed punching her in the head. She caught my fist.

"Come on. You're staying here. Where there is not a lovely family you don't belong to," she said over me when I started to argue.

I must have looked taken aback, because she shrugged slightly.

"I don't like visiting families either," she said. She looked like she'd wrenched it out from under a grindstone.

If she had handed me a fistful of rubies it would have felt less important. I couldn't think that she said anything like that more than twice in ten years.

She tipped her head towards the long cloister to point out where to go. I followed her. We had to walk carefully, stepping over vines—ivy, wisteria, things I didn't know the names of—growing right across the flagstones.

"I'm sorry," I said.

"It's an injury, it isn't your fault," she said. She seemed muted—she was too restrained to complain, but I knew why. Before now, she'd talked to me as though we were more or less made of the same stuff. Now . . . she was being careful of me, because it was obvious that we weren't.

I wanted to punch something.

"How are you like you are, lady?" I asked. "Like a marvel?"

"I didn't spend twenty years at war and raids, for a start," she said, smiling a bit. It was regret, that smile. She wished she had served. She was ashamed she hadn't.

I filled up with a sort of helpless devotion then. Nobody had expected her to stay with the garrison. It would be idiotic for a queen to die in a field a thousand miles from her city and hurl the succession into disarray. She knew that too, I knew she did, but if she was so deep-down Sown that she felt ashamed anyway, in the face of all reason, then we hadn't had as true-hearted a knight on the throne since Kadmus.

"No, you would have been fine at Troy," I said. She would.

"You have to say that."

I let the silence fill up with all my suicidal opinions about how she was a mad despot and how her fish were stupid.

"True," she admitted, as if I'd said something. She thought about it for a little while. We were halfway along the cloister, with gardens on either side, and ivy bursting up the pillars. The slaves were still trying to cut it back, but as we went by, I saw one of them stop and unwind a vine that had grown around his ankle while he'd been standing there. "I lost three children before Pentheus. It was because I had them when I was too little; I was fourteen and babies are big, so it was a bit silly."

Nothing ever made me feel sick. I could watch a witch do surgery on someone's brain while I was having dinner and have no reaction at all except general interest, but I had to slow down now.

"Don't look like that, it's how just things are for married girls, it's part of growing up," she said, as if that wasn't worse. "But the point is, if the mad god was going to come for anyone, it was me. He didn't, though. He didn't take my mind away to make anything easier. I was in my right mind for every second, no one tried to help, not a god or a person, which is a thoroughly good thing, because I learned to fulfil my function. My mother said something I'll always remember. She said, being Sown is about being hammered out in a furnace. You suffer, and if you're not careful, you crack on the anvil. But not if you learn to love the anvil. In the end, really, cracking or not is a choice. It isn't a god; there's no mad god, he's just a story to make people feel better about letting themselves break. Love the anvil, and what it can make you, and you'll be a marvel knight."

I stayed quiet for a long time, so long that she must have thought I had nothing to say about it, because she moved on.

"But Phaidros—I thought you could hear this week. You were deaf before, or a little bit, but this week, you've been much better. What happened there?" She said it carefully, and with a surprised little drop I realized she was worried about prying.

"A witch," I said.

"What did she do?"

I didn't want to talk about Dionysus, not to anyone, but especially not to her. It felt like I was drawing a thin but crucial thread between them, one that might tighten, and reel them nearer and nearer, until they crashed into each other. "He told me I was safe and I believed him."

"Why? You didn't believe Circe just now."

"He's deinos. He doesn't try to be, he's kind and he laughs, but—he is."

I thought she would grumble about mummery, but she grinned. "Enchanting."

The Nothing caught up with us, stretching.

"I'm too old for that," I said, as much to remind me as her.

"Oh, fuck off, Phaidros, you can't say that to someone ten years older than you."

It was the first time I'd heard her swear properly and it cheered me up a lot.

"No, I mean too old for men. I should be on the marriage register."

She looked interested. "Why aren't you? You must be paying a fine."

"I punch things that make me jump. I kill things in my sleep." I pressed my teeth into my lip. I didn't want to say it, because if it was only Dionysus

238

who knew, then it was a sort of shared dream, but once I told her . . .
"Maybe my slaves. They're dead."

"Oh. Well, the Palace can supply you with new ones, the Egyptians brought us some as gifts. There are some big men you'd struggle to sleep-murder."

"Not quite the moral of that story, lady?"

"Yes it is, knight," she said, smacking my arm. "Gods' sake, get new slaves, get on the marriage register, and get a fucking grip. And sacrifice to Athena, to apologise for all the grip you haven't been getting."

I laughed, then put my hand over my mouth, because it was wildly improper, but then she laughed too, and I actually heard it sing around the cloister. For the first time all week, I felt like I'd done something good.

A minnow of a thought said: *Blue. Dionysus tries to make you laugh, and you have this deep-down sense that she needs to laugh sometimes, and that's . . . blue.*

"Here you are," she said, about a doorway open and filled with candle-light. There were lamps everywhere, and food set out on a table, and a marvel cup-bearer by the door, holding a jug of water. The Queen put a cup in its free hand and it hinged forward to pour out the water, beautifully calibrated. Once the cup was full, she gave it to me. "Get some rest. I'll tell the Guards you might sleepwalk, and one of them will bring you back."

"Thank you," I said, and relaxed. She was right. It was safe. I couldn't hurt the Guards. They wore full armour. Slowly, because there was time now, I started to feel the bruise down my shield arm from earlier, and the place where my cloak had been on fire, and a cut through my eyebrow I didn't remember getting. After all the hazy dislocation of the way I'd been thinking before, it was lovely.

"No, I should be thanking you. You might have saved my crown tonight."

"What are you going to do, lady? If anyone who wears a god mask now starts to turn into . . ."

"Oh, Tiresias is ahead of us both," she said, with an absolute absence of urgency. "I'll show you, it's interesting."

I hinged a couple of inches into a bow, too tired to be curious, just relieved she'd already thought of it.

"Sleep well, knight."

"And you. Though—lady?"

"Mm?"

"What you said, about how no one came, and what your mother told you. I hope she's eaten by wild fucking dogs in Hades for the rest of eternity."

At first, she started to nod, which was a response to whatever bland good night she'd thought I was going to say, and then she stopped and looked at me properly. Different things went over her face then. It was hard to track them, but when they stopped, the one left closest to the surface was something very brittle. She didn't say anything, but as though I were the king and she were the knight, she took my hand and kissed my knuckles, and turned away into the dark.

25

On the day of the funeral, the knights marched in the procession through the city, just behind the Queen. The roads were frosty with scraps of cloth cut into the shape of flower petals, in the absence of real ones. They were everywhere, piling up in drifts on the waysides and spinning in little whirls where the hot wind played with them, catching on laundry lines and along the spokes of cartwheels, and in the high plumes and horns of the generals' helmets.

Some of my little knights looked glassy and strange. I found myself counting heads over and over, to make sure nobody had drifted off to dance in an alleyway. Two units ahead, I saw Polydorus, obvious because of his grey hair, turn back often, clearly checking exactly the same thing. He looked even more exhausted than he always did. I didn't blame him. If anyone was going to go mad soon, it was Jason.

The people lining the roads looked just as bad.

Usually, important funerals are like dark carnivals. I could remember sitting on Helios's shoulders to see the parade when a famous king was killed in battle, excited because they were giving out free food and a state funeral is the only time you'll ever hear the Hymn to Hades, which felt special and magical, and in a way specially for me, because of our line's words—*be Persephone, always negotiate.* All the children had learned it the night before so we could be part of the choir and we'd all loved it.

There weren't any excited children today. There were children, but they were standing quiet and dusty with their parents, some slumped on the ground where there was a bit of shade, but mostly just stuck in full sun. Everyone had scarves crossed under their collars so they couldn't burn worse than they already had. The heat was a sledgehammer. Some people looked upset, perhaps to see the royal line broken, and all the uncertainty that brought—or perhaps just that it was miserable to stand out for so long, breathing the ash. When the Hymn to Hades began, some people did sing it with us, but some just stared at nothing.

Everything still sounded dull and woolly. I could hear a little bit more than yesterday, enough to function, just—but still not even as well as I had done before Dionysus cured me.

Someone, not that far away, wasn't singing to Hades. I would have sworn I heard—*raving wild and riot raving* in one of the pauses, but though we all looked, it wasn't obvious where the voice had come from.

In the alleyways between houses, there were people sitting, avoiding the procession, and they had gone still in the dead-eyed way people do when there's nothing left to do except sit there and die.

The gods willing, Dionysus was right: if Pentheus was officially dead, then the Egyptians couldn't be offended, and perhaps we'd have to pay more for the grain, but we would still be able to have it. If they turned around now—I'd really hoped to hold onto my little knights for longer than this.

I kept scanning the crowd for any more masks that looked like a god, but so far there was nothing. The Guards were searching people, just in quick scuffles lost in the crowd. I wasn't sure because I couldn't hear, but I thought it was those masks they were looking for. I didn't think there would have been an official proclamation. If it were announced that putting on a god mask turned you into a god, everyone would try it. The Queen had seemed so calm about it yesterday, though. I still couldn't tell if that was because she was pretending to be calm, or because something about that experiment of Tiresias's had given her a good reason to be.

When Dionysus met me at the stadium gate after the parade, waiting to the side of the streams of people, he was lifting linen petals out of his hair, the fall of it pulled over his shoulder so he could see. The grey in it made him look—now he was in funeral white—as though he had been standing close enough to a pyre for the cinders to have settled on him.

"Good morning, sir," I said, trying hard not to let it show that I'd just had a gigantic burst of happiness to see him. There was part of me that was writhing like molten iron after yesterday, but the sight of him poured water on it and in all the steam, I could breathe properly again. I couldn't tell why.

"Good morning, knight, how strange to see you upon the road," he said, and fell into step beside me. He was giving me a witching study and I thought he was going to say that he'd heard I'd lost my hearing again, and was I all right, and I'd feel stupid and humiliated all over again. But he didn't. Instead he put his arm around me and pulled me close. "I'm so happy to see you," he said against my hair.

He had on a silver bracelet, and it clinked against my armour. It was oddly unsurprising to find that I could hear that now. Around us, the world turned loud and clear. I was out of my box. I could hear people talking, actual words, not just a distant buzz.

He hadn't done it on purpose. I doubted he even knew. It was just a function of—what?

Calming down. Feeling safe. Something—easing.

Blue, maybe.

I put my arm around his waist and squeezed. "Why?"

"I was lonely." Like we had been married for years, he took my shield for me. It was a relief, because it meant I could pull my helmet off and carry it.

"You see people all the time," I protested, wondering what it must be like, to be so unembarrassed and so open that you could just say that to someone. I unclipped the helmet's visor and put it down the front of my tunic, where it stayed in place because my breastplate was buckled on close. I'd been doing that for years. Things get stolen. If someone wanted that visor, the only image of Helios ever made, they'd have to take it off my corpse.

"You can be lonely in a crowd," he pointed out.

"Well. Not today, strange one," I said.

"What does that mean—strange one?" he asked.

I heard it from his point of view and realized how odd it was. The word is *daimonios*; like a daimon, a spirit. It was another one of those words like *deinos*, that means several things—"inexplicable" and "wondrous," "uncanny" and "precious." "It's like 'my dear,'" I explained.

Inside, the stadium was much bigger than I'd thought. Around the outer edge, marvels of nymphs held up a canopy that covered the sun-side half, and everything smelled gloriously of wine—his wine, all black and honey—because there were stewards taking it round to everyone, free.

"You must have sold your whole stock to the games master," I said.

"Me and every vintner in the city," he agreed.

Although everyone was dressed in white and it was still broiling, people didn't seem so grim now as they had on the parade route; there were people laughing, groups of girls taking turns trying to juggle apples—for some reason everyone was learning to juggle this year—and old men clustering together to compare news, and I had to take it in bit by bit, because I'd not seen so many people all in one place before since Troy, but it wasn't like seeing battalions form up. There was no one giving orders or directions. Everyone seemed to know where to go, and it was strange watching them, because from a distance, they made patterns, a lot like bees.

The seats were stone, and they'd soaked in the sun all morning, so they were warm, and everything must have been scrubbed clean yesterday or this morning, because it all looked brand-new.

Dionysus lifted two cups down from a steward's tray and gave me one.

I hesitated, feeling uncomfortably like I was rule-breaking even though I wasn't. In the story, they always said, don't eat anything; don't drink anything. If you take something, you owe something. I'd always wondered why Persephone ignored it, or forgot it, but I was starting to see. It wasn't that she was ignoring or forgetting anything.

I took the cup and tapped it to his, and for all it was blazing out here, his wine tasted of winter. It made me remember that dream about the frozen forest and the man in the mask and the crown of horns.

It made me even warmer too.

"Can you help me?" I asked about my armour. Theban armour laces tight down the back: you can't put it on or take it off by yourself. It's a way of making sure commanders and wards overlap twice a day, in theory. In practise, for me, it meant I inconvenienced a lot of a slaves.

He nodded and undid the lacing, which was straight, designed not to be tugged open fast. I looked at my knees, trying not to feel it too much as his fingertips skimmed the nape of my neck, but I did; much more than when one of the Palace valets had laced it up for me this morning. When the two sides opened out, I eased out of it, clipped Helios's mask against my belt instead, and set the breastplate down on the ground, along with my sword. I'd propped that against the seat, but a little girl in front of us lunged for it, wanting the shiny thing and Dionysus had to catch it awkwardly just as she knocked it over. It tilted partly out of its sheath on the way. I tensed up, because it was honed so sharp it could cut falling cloth, but of course that was stupid: he knew knives, and he held it safely. I swallowed, waiting for him to ask about the inscription. He was looking, but he didn't say, *Why is your sword named after a Trojan princess?*

"Can you read?" was what he actually said.

I could have crumpled onto the floor and put my head on his knees. "Mm. All senior officers have to."

"I can't." He was still looking at the letters. "Is it worth the effort?"

"I don't know how I lived without it," I said, a lot more effusive than I would ever have been if I weren't bathing in relief at not having to explain how Helios had died. "It would be brilliant for you. If you wrote down your magic it would be much easier to keep track of everything, and to teach new witches, and . . ."

He looked uncomfortable. "But it could last longer than me. I haven't anything to say that should be around longer than the time it takes me to say it."

"That's silly," I told him. "You're silly."

"Look at Pylos. You think you're just an accountant noting down someone's tax payment on a bit of clay you'll wipe clean at the end of the day, but oh no, everyone goes mad and riots, the archive is on fire, the clay all bakes, and suddenly *Achilles the shepherd, fourteen oxen and three barrels of apples to Poseidon* will be all that's left of you and the entire city."

"Well—"

But he wasn't finished. "And after all our world is gone and there's no trace of us or marvels or Pylos and nobody knows if the war in Troy even happened, there it'll fucking be, and priests thousands of years from now are going to have huge gatherings about whether or not their ideas about us are supported by *fourteen oxen and three barrels of apples to Poseidon!*"

"Or," I said, concentrating to keep a straight face, because I couldn't just burst out laughing in public like a little boy; it was probably conduct unbecoming. "When you go shopping, you write down what you need and take it with you, and the writing remembers for you, and you'll never forget the milk ever again."

"Oh, that is clever," he admitted.

All at once it occurred to me that he absolutely could read, and all that had been a way to make me stop being afraid of questions about Andromache. I felt like an old candle that had sat forgotten on a shelf for years, frozen into the same lumpy awkward shape, dull with dust, but now here was the fire again, and I was softening and changing and finding I didn't have to be that cold shape forever, and the wax was turning warm and bright again. He'd burn me away altogether before long, but it was worth it.

A horn sounded to warn everyone the games were about to start. Dionysus scooped me sideways so I could rest back against him, one arm across my ribs. I held his wrist, wondering how this factored into what he had said about his vow. No family; no name; no one who knew him true. Well. I didn't know him. I never would. Maybe that was why this was all right.

He put his cup on the ground and held my knee instead. It felt like a glimmering half-promise that maybe there was more that would be all right too, maybe later, after more wine, after walking back up to his garden in the dark.

The quality of that half-promise was a lot like the half-promise of xenia I'd made to him on the ship.

He was lying to me, of course he was. That was fine. It was a lovely lie.

There were some young men behind us, knights, making their way down to the patch of red around the Queen, and not being very quiet; they were already drunk and making a lot of effort to be more drunk, all of them carrying wine cups, one with an entire pitcher at the ready. I geared up to telling them to keep it down, but I was too slow. One of them knocked into Dionysus, hard enough to jolt him forward.

"Watch where you're going," he said.

"You watch where I'm going," the young knight snapped, vicious out of all proportion, and yanked Dionysus's head backwards by his hair. "How about you come with me, kalos?" *Kalos* had never been more of a threat.

It was Feral Jason. Of course it was Feral Jason.

All the people around us went instantly, deeply silent.

I broke his nose, then caught him by the strap of his cloak, meaning to drag him down to Polydorus. Later, I couldn't decide if Jason realized that it was me before he pulled the knife. I did hear his friends scream at him to stop, but then it was too late, and the nasty little blade was hilt deep in my shoulder. I lifted my eyebrows at him, meaning to say, *My gods, assault of an officer, you little fuckwit, let me see your rich uncle talk you out of that one*, but I didn't have the chance.

"Stop," Dionysus said, not loudly, but he had stopped bulls, and it stopped knights too.

If someone else had said it, perhaps even if I had, Jason and his friend would have been on them like wolves, but they went still. It looked involuntary. It looked like what had happened to the knights at the Temple of Hermes, when they began to recite their prophecies.

I pulled my red ceremony sash off and shoved it against the wound, then pulled out the knife. The sash soaked straightaway, and blood sheeted down my arm. Because it was so hot out here, the blood didn't feel warm, just wet. I had a bleak vision of the next few weeks. I wouldn't be able to lift a shield properly. I'd be twitchier than ever, seeing knives everywhere, I'd have a string of thoroughly entertaining panics in the middle of the night, and I'd feel ashamed and useless and like I'd left all my dignity on the floor of this stadium.

"Sit down," Dionysus said, so soft and controlled that it couldn't have been anything except almost-panic. It was how I talked when I knew someone might die. "Lying down would be better—"

I saw Jason realize that I was hurt badly enough that he might actually stand a chance of killing us both, running down to Polydorus and telling his story first, before anyone else could say that he had started it. If he could say I was drunk and I'd grabbed *him*—it would only work if I wasn't alive to defend myself but even so it was better than what would happen to him now, if I lived—

"Diony—"

He didn't even turn around. "I said *stop*."

Even though Dionysus spoke no louder than he ever did then, I felt his voice whiplash through everyone in that stadium. It was the way that lightning will strike an officer on the end of a front line, but then blast through the whole shield wall, hurling the knights backwards, burning inside their armour before they even hit the dust: Zeus's last resort if the generals ignored signs from the augurs not to fight.

Something vanished from inside Jason's eyes.

Tiresias had said that humans are clockwork welded onto a soul. Jason's clockwork smashed, and all that was left was something wild.

It went from the boys behind him too.

Down closer to the arena, there was a weird stir that sounded like the bees had sounded when I crashed into one of their hives, and I looked back, knowing something was wrong but not able to pin down what I was hearing. Around the Queen and the Egyptian delegation, a swathe of red and purple was vivid against the white crowd, because all the knights and Guards were sitting together; now that swathe was writhing. People were standing up, reaching for swords . . .

Jason tore into the boy next to him from nowhere. One of his friends screamed and went for him teeth first, and down by the arena, there was a roar, because it was happening down there too. One after the next, the knights were—snapping, like invisible lightning was tearing through them, rippling out around the stadium, and then the air was made of yelling and screaming, and the whole crowd in white was abandoning everything and running for the gates in a human surge, and everything closer to the arena was heaving mass of red and bronze.

I waited for it to happen to me too.

Dionysus levered me down on the closest seat. Chaos howled around us, but no one touched us; nobody even came near. He pulled the veil out of his hair and bound it around my shoulder, leaning hard into the knot until my arm went numb.

I stared at him, waiting, because surely if he had cursed all the knights then I was soon to follow, and any second now he was going to say, *Well, you know what you did,* and my mind would snap.

"Just stay still," he said, as people hurtled past us. Down by the arena, the shocked Guards had got themselves into some order, and they were pushing back against the heaving mass of the mad knights.

I took a breath to demand that he stop this, right now, and I didn't fucking care who he was and what I'd done to him, because this was insane.

But he had gone; he was four rows down from me now, helping up a woman who had fallen in the crush and whose arm looked broken. She looked relieved to see a witch. Once he had bound her arm against her chest, he moved on again, to a boy who was bleeding. It was happening around the stadium now; that first river of people was gone, leaving just tributaries now, and witches ghosting around the fallen.

Down where the knights were, the Guards were locked into place around the Queen, and there was a different quality to the madness. People in red cloaks were losing interest in the strange, absent way that distracted animals sometimes do. Some were leaving. Some might have been coming back into their minds. I saw Jason straighten up suddenly, blood on his face, paralysed for a second, and then he ran for the south gate.

I picked up my sword, because my sword arm was still fine, and started down.

"Phaidros," Dionysus said when he saw. "Don't."

He's playing. This is it. This is where he kills everyone and you watch, and then you're last.

Strapping my shield on, the weight of it pulling against the new wound but duty is honour, I ran down to help the Guards move the Queen.

26

If, like Dionysus, you could ask a hawk if she would lend you her eyes, and fly above Thebes, you would have seen people running away from the arena, some with their white clothes stained red, and towards the Temple of Athena.

As the arena emptied, Athena's courtyards filled. The priestesses were confused at first, but when they understood what had happened, the sacrifice fires flared and slaves leaned into the great bellows, and as the water that ran beneath the altars boiled and steamed, the great marvels of the goddess lifted their heads, like they were waking, called to attention by the howls from the crowd. The black-plumed helms gleamed in the punishing sun, the greaves and gauntlets whispered. Sometimes, you can tell when the ghost of the god is there in the holy devices. You can feel that something immense is close by, listening.

Before you start a blood feud, you sacrifice to Athena. It's a way to show her that you understand your duty, and that even if it takes you years to get revenge for the person who was killed, you won't ever forget. It's important that she knows. If you fail in that duty, she will curse you.

I did it when Helios was killed. I took Athena a black ram, and I had the name of the Trojan princess etched onto my sword to prove that however long it took me, it was destined for her. It was still there. It was what Dionysus had seen earlier: ANDROMACHE.

Hardly any of the people whose relatives had been killed were soldiers. There were young girls and old men, and nobody had a sword to swear on, but that didn't matter. The priestesses hammered out silver bands in the furnaces where they usually repaired armour, twisted the bands into torques, and sealed them around the wrists of the survivors with Athena's sigils—the spear and the owl. War and wisdom, strength and justice.

It took twenty of us to get the Queen out of the stadium. The road to the Palace wasn't much better. When people saw the purple cloaks, they threw stones. The second we were on the stairway up to the High City, the watchmen slung the iron gates shut behind us. For the first four flights—within arrow-shot—the stairs were covered, and we all eased.

"What *happened* to them?" It was the first time there was enough quiet to ask questions instead of bark instructions. The Queen unstrapped a shield from her arm too.

"I think we can safely say that was the displeasure of a god," said a slim older man whose name I was nearly sure was Lord Halys. I liked him distantly for reasons I couldn't remember; I had a feeling he had been a general when I was little, and that Helios had liked him. Sometimes you inherit liking people.

"Why only the knights, why not everyone? And why not even all of the knights? Phaidros is all right, some of the others too. I saw General Alexandra, she isn't mad."

"Lady, we can't guess at divine reasoning—"

"Halys, if I didn't question what appeared to be divine reasoning, I would have been overthrown by frauds four times now."

I couldn't concentrate. After the howling in the stadium, the sudden quiet didn't seem real and everything had turned strange and dreamy, and I was teetering right on the edge of one of those insane moments where I was convinced I was back at Troy. I had my shield strapped on my injured arm because I could still lift it a bit, and I couldn't stop staring at the little picture of a tortoise etched on the inside rim. I must have seen it every day for years, but I hadn't really been *seeing* it. I'd etched that on when my boy was alive, because baby knights need a gauge for how high to hold a shield and for reasons I can't remember, tortoises are supposed to protect you against bad magic. *Hold it up, remember you have to be able to see the tortoise, tiny knight . . .* it had just been a game. He had been too little to use an adult-sized shield, but he'd loved playing dress up with it.

Divine reasoning, had they just said?

I wanted to laugh. I wanted to say, look, of course he didn't *choose* the knights. Dionysus is lightning and we're kites.

"More pressingly," the Guard captain said, "the knights aren't coming back here. I saw some of them just wandering in the street, they weren't in their right minds, and the ones who are were running away. We can't even begin to resolve any of this until we have them back."

By resolve, he meant execute some of them and hope it was enough to satisfy the families of the victims. There was no other way around it.

"People will think they're here, though," Lord Halys said. "We're going to be under siege soon."

If the Queen had heard them, she seemed not to have. "Captain, you and your soldiers need not make the climb. Leave your cloaks here, go the underground way, and report to the twenty largest Sown estates. Tell the ladies of each house that their children have dishonoured the garrison."

The captain bowed briskly. "Yes lady."

I watched him go, at a loss. Of all the things she could have used the Guards for, informing the knights' blood relatives didn't seem like a very important one. Maybe she thought the knights must have been going home, if they weren't here—maybe that was right, even. I must have looked confused, because the Queen knocked me gently. On the wrong side: pain burst right up my shoulder. It was hurting in a very urgent, inconvenient way now.

"You don't know your mother, do you?"

"No, lady."

"Most knights are not so fortunate," she said, and didn't elaborate, already climbing the stairs.

I looked at Halys in case he understood what was happening, but he was grey and staring at a space of air beyond my shoulder.

Sitting like a rock in my throat was the need to tell the Queen she was wrong, it was a god, he was back in the stadium and he was doing all this in the way a cat will play-pounce on a mouse and then pretend to lose interest before shredding it.

At the top, she sent more Guards down to defend the stairway if the gates broke, and then bronzesmiths to assess whether the gates might break, and then slaves down through the same underground passages as the Guard captain, but this time to the temples. Why the temples, I couldn't tell, and I couldn't ask, because she was surrounded by people. I had nothing to do: none of my little knights were here. Hardly any knights at all. The few red cloaks I could see belonged to people who hadn't been at the stadium. They'd drawn the short straw for guard duty at the garrison here, and everyone looked confused and worried. I asked one of the officers of the Guards if there was anything I could do to help, but he only snapped that I could sit still and try not to murder anyone important.

So I sat still, shield propped against one knee, on the wall that blocked off the sheer drop down to the lower city. On this side, it was about a hundred feet. People were swarming around the gate, yelling, and hammering on the bronze: it wouldn't be long before someone organised enough of them to get a battering ram. On the other side, where there were no stairs, it was a rocky and jagged slope. Only mountain goats made the climb there. A rank of Guards stood at that wall anyway, in case anyone tried. Maybe they would, because since I'd last looked at it properly, it was tangled with ivy.

I'd never been on the inside of a siege before. It was difficult not to think of those people I'd used to see on the high balconies at the palace in Troy, and how much I'd hated them for having an *inside* to go to, and food, and baths.

Beyond the heaving crowd at the gates, I could see down into the streets. There was some looting—unless those boys were running with sacks of flour just for the exercise—and up where the night market would be later, something was on fire. Every so often, there was a flash of red that might have been a cloak, but I never caught it for long before the knight disappeared under their own mob.

"Heliades," the Queen's voice said right behind me.

I stood up fast.

"Why didn't it happen to you? Why are you different?"

I pressed my teeth together against a thirty-year instinct to report exactly what had happened. My friend wasn't an ordinary person; he had snapped, just for a second, because anyone would lose their temper with

Jason. And I hadn't turned because I'd wronged him badly long ago, and he was saving me until the end.

"I don't know why, lady."

It was the first outright lie I'd told to anyone in seniority since I'd taken my vow. I wanted to scrub my skin off.

She shook her head once, then paused. "You're hurt."

"I've already seen a witch."

Dionysus was still down there somewhere. I was probably never going to see him again.

"And you're not . . . drunk," she said gradually.

I blinked twice, wishing I could say, *This is an astonishingly irrelevant thing to be asking me about when either we're all about to die, or a lot of other people are.* Of course I couldn't say that. Even if she had asked me what I thought about the courtship habits of red badgers, I couldn't have said it. "I'm never drunk, lady."

"It's a festival day, you didn't want to relax?"

"I had half a cup of wine but then all this . . ."

"Half a cup," she said thoughtfully.

"Lady?" I asked, desperate for her to say something that would explain why she seemed not to mind about the raging crowd, why she'd sent the Guard captain to the Sown estates, what anyone's mother had to do with anything. The first rule of the legion is that you trust the orders of your commanding officer even if they seem openly crazy, but it had been a long time since I'd had a commanding officer whose reasoning I couldn't follow.

She studied me for another second. Despite everything, and despite how everyone else in the courtyards was drawn and grey and anxious, she had a glow: she was full of energy, exactly like Helios right before a battle. It was that zing that great knights get right before they're finally allowed, after weeks and weeks of paralysingly boring night watches and drills and being forced to care about stock-takes and ship maintenance, to prove that they are great.

I don't know what I thought she was going to say, but it wasn't what she did say.

"Have you ever seen inside the mechanisms of a holy marvel?"

I baulked, because that was really asking me whether I'd committed sacrilege. "No!"

"Come with me."

On the roof the Palace is a great marvel of Apollo: lord of all Thebes, of marvels, of order and logic and everything we are. It's about the size of the Herakles marvel at the Amber Gate, but you wouldn't know, because the roof is high enough that it looks like it could be the size of a human. I'd always thought it was a statue, not a working marvel, because I'd never seen it move, and I'd never known that you could even get up to it. You could, though. Behind the throne, leading up from that complicated chamber full of the mechanisms that made the dragons run, there was a stairway. It was a narrow helix that coiled up inside the old watchtower, and at the top, a low door led outside, and a thin flat path went along the runnel of the roof to the feet of the marvel.

Covered by a roof but open to the air, except for its four posts, was a kind of cabin. Inside was machinery. There was a heavy lever, and something complicated that connected to the marvel, something like a flue.

"Only the royal family know what this is, and how it works," the Queen told me. She leaned hard into the lever, which ground forward. Somewhere below us, steam surged and rattled, powering upwards through the pipes to the marvel. I stared up at it. I'd never been so close to one this big before. There was a hatch in the back of the left ankle that was big enough for a slim person to climb into. I had to fight the need to back away. Not because it was intimidating, though it was, but because I shouldn't have been close enough to start guessing how it worked. That was sacred.

"Can he move?" I asked, thinking of all this gigantic weight of bronze right on the Palace roof.

"No. But he can speak. That's what you're going to do." She held her arm out to make me come closer, and showed me the flue. "You're going to speak into that. It will make him speak too."

When you were younger, as a prank, did anyone ever do that trick where they put their fist on top of your head and smack it with their other hand, and then drag it down your neck to make it feel like they've broken an egg, and it's slimily realistic and then because you were an irritating little prick, you immediately did it to all your other friends too? I felt like that. I felt like she'd done the egg trick—not just that she'd broken something nasty on me, but that it was inappropriate, a kind of stupid, childish prank close to this great thing that was holy. I waited for her to laugh and say, *Ha, not really, of course you can't make Apollo talk, that's silly, nobody knows the real magic inside marvels.* She didn't.

"What you're going to say, when I tell you, is: 'This is not the work of a god, but a man, and poisoned wine. Justice is in the hands of the daughters of the dragon.'"

"Poisoned . . . wine."

"Yes."

"This is—lady, this is sacrilege, you can't just make a god say whatever you want—"

"Phaidros," she interrupted, almost laughing. "I'm not making Apollo say it. I'm making a machine say it."

"A *holy* device," I said, appalled. "I can't—"

"This is how they work," she said over me. "This is how they all work. There's no magic in marvels. Apollo doesn't care what you make a machine say. I need you to say this, it needs to be a man's voice, and it can only be a member of the House of Kadmus. You're family, Phaidros."

I was suspended in honey again. Drowning, but in something sweet. I'd never felt like that before this week, no one had ever made me feel like that, and now two of them had come along at once.

I must have looked like I was about to hurl myself off the roof, because she slowed down and came back to me, although she had been on her way to the edge to see out over the city.

"I know it's hard to hear," she said, more gently—but not, I thought, like she really did know. More like she knew that it was the best thing to say in order to make me gut up and do as I was told. "I know. It's reassuring to think the gods are with us in holy machines, but they're not. It's just priests and oracles. And sometimes, desperate queens and kings who need to find a way to bring order back to a city that's eating itself."

I couldn't tell what it was in me that was breaking, but something was. The way I understood the world, and Thebes, and everything in it—it was too big to have a name.

"Tell me what you have to say, knight."

I swallowed it all down. "This is not the work of a god, but a man, and poisoned wine. Justice is in the hands of the daughters of the dragon."

"Good. Stand here." She looked up at the marvel, leaning back to see the heights of it against the sun. "It's almost ready." She was right: the steam was singing inside. She went to the edge of the roof, saw something that made her smile, and knocked her fists together. That zing she'd had before in the courtyard was even stronger now. She was Helios on the front line, waiting for the advance order: it was pure joy. I'd thought it was deinos enough in him, because even among knights, it's rare to genuinely love battle once you understand what it is. I only have it sometimes. To feel the joy of war in the face of not just a chariot line coming at you, which is straightforward, but an entire city howling at the edge of uprising—that was something else. "They're here."

I went to the edge too.

At the hem of the crowd now, there was a red band. I couldn't work out what I was seeing at first. Not serving knights.

They were women, all of them, Sown ladies dressed in ceremony red. Every one of them, and there must have been about a hundred, had come on a war chariot, with a full team of horses, and with younger girls behind them to serve as the squires—just like in the story, where Hera and her daughters got Athena's chariot ready. They had surrounded the crowd without trapping them: there was enough room between the chariots to run past. Each chariot glittered with the combat lineage crests of each family; each of the women would have once been a serving knight, before marriage. From up here, I couldn't make them out, but I could see the blinding shine off the bronze and the filigree. The horses, bred from the same lines as the garrison's chargers, were bad-tempered in the heat and the crowd, snapping at anyone who came up too close to them. A weird, uneasy murmur went through everyone.

The Queen gave me a look of absolute delight, and shoved another lever in the marvel, hard.

A noise like I had never heard before tore right across the city. It was like a battle horn, but it was so much louder than any horn. I had to smack both hands over my ears. It shook the roof under us, and vibrated in the bronze of the marvel. If someone had told me that it was the signal that sounded when Athena and Ares rode out from Olympus, I would have believed it.

The crowd turned, looking up at us, and the Palace, and the great marvel.

The Queen put me in front of the flue, close, so I was breathing into it. Even that tiny sound echoed impossibly, so loud I was sure people down in the streets could hear it. She grasped my shoulders to keep me in the right place.

It was sacrilege, but it was an order from the Queen, and duty is honour. Duty *is* honour.

"This is not the work of a god, but a man, and poisoned wine. Justice is in the hands of the daughters of the dragon."

Some device inside the marvel took my voice and changed it into thunder that crashed over the whole of Thebes.

The Queen tapped me and pressed her finger over her lips, and then, still full of joy, mimed giving me a round of applause. She pulled me to the edge of the roof, pressing my shoulder to keep me low. We both knelt down at the edge to see into the crowd below, where the angry chants and shouting had gone silent. I had to push my fist against my heart, because my ribcage had gone stiff with the knowledge that—just like when Dionysus had lifted me up and I'd lost sight of why I shouldn't dance—I'd crossed an invisible border, and there was no true going back. Only with Dionysus, it had been a relief, in an unholy kind of way. This was just unholy, and what was leaning its boot right into my chest was the opposite of relief. Pressure, that felt like it would be rib-breaking soon.

The Sown mothers, a good two feet above the ground where they were mounted on the chariots, all held up something. They had one or some-times two each, small things, the size of an oil jug or a head, and it took me entire seconds to understand that the things weren't just the size of heads. They *were* heads.

I forgot everything about the marvel and sacrilege and the Queen and Dionysus. Jason's mother was down there. I recognised her, she was my age, we had been in the same unit, but she had gone home to Thebes to marry before the ship was wrecked. The head she was holding was Jason's.

When they spoke, they all spoke together, and it clear even from the roof.

"Pardon us for the dishonour our children have brought to you, citizens of Thebes, and pray that we shall give you better knights in the years to come."

If I was shocked, the crowd was stunned. Nobody moved. Nobody said a word.

The Sown ladies climbed down from the chariots and picked up baskets. The baskets were full of gold and silver, the spoils of war from Troy—not money, but plates and chalices and jewellery. They began to hand it out to everyone in the crowd. On any other day, they would surely have been mobbed, but everyone was broken-marvel still, and the red figures moved through in peace, trailed by their younger children, who had brought water, or wine.

And then people just . . . began to leave. It began at the edges of the crowd. It effervesced, and people misted away into the alleys and the squares, moving slowly, without any of the rage from before. The faces I could make out looked numb, or confused, or sometimes relieved. One man was sitting on the ground, staring at a severed head as if he were trying to work out what he was supposed to do now.

"You didn't know why the Theban legion is called the Furies, did you?" the Queen said.

In the top of my mind, I'd thought it was just because we were fierce. But somewhere in the deep under-strata, I did know. People had told stories around campfires about what happened if Theban knights tried to desert, or worse, if they killed a Theban civilian. I'd thought they were just trying to scare the children. The Furies—the real Furies, from the holy stories—come for any truly unjust murder.

Down in the crowd, people began to sing. It was the hymn to Athena; the thanksgiving for justice.

The Queen patted my back and I followed her to the stairs, down through the tower—all the way down, the hymn swelled, even though the walls—and then out past the throne, onto the balcony that looked out over Thebes, and over the singing crowd. Her chamberlain was waiting, with the Marvel Crown. The Queen lifted it from its velvet cushion in passing and paused while slaves fitted the royal silver armour over her clothes.

"Borrow your sword?" she said to me as she came into view of the crowd.

I gave it to her.

She unsheathed it and held it up high, and there in the sun and the burning sky she looked like Athena, and the crowd exploded. I twitched, because for a split second I thought they were about to surge at the gates and start firing poisoned arrows at her, but I was wrong. It wasn't rage. They were cheering.

27

In the garrison dormitories, commanders, wards, or sometimes mothers were collecting the gear of the executed knights. Armour, clothes, kit; sometimes boxes of dice and games, or worse, toys. It was all so quiet I might as well have lost my hearing again. I opened one door and then snapped it straight shut again, because one of the mothers had hanged herself inside. I called for some slaves before anyone else could see and then, because it was all I could think of, I went down to the kitchens and told the cooks to use the last of the eggs and honey, and get some cake into everyone.

Few by few, I found what was left of my unit. The little knights were coming back one or two at a time, ashen, and sometimes disguised as civilians, in case people decided they hadn't quite finished wanting to lynch anything in a red cloak yet. I got them sitting down in the mess, where they stayed exactly where I put them, looking like lost ducklings with no duck. Some of their commanders, the surviving ones, came through to find them. Some didn't. Polydorus sank down next to me, silent and wooden. I didn't know what to say. I had a feeling he was prob-ably as much relieved as anguished, and probably the guilt from that was worse than anything I'd ever felt about Helios. I swallowed down the need to tell him what had happened with Jason. It wouldn't help. It would break him in half. It was still like trying to swallow needles.

"She's arresting all the vintners," Polydorus said, nodding out to the courtyard to show me where he'd heard it. "Have you ever heard anything so stupid?"

What would Dionysus do if someone tried to arrest him? I didn't have enough brain leftover to think about it.

"Help me look after the little knights," I said, because Polydorus needed something to do other than stare at the ground. "Do you remember the rules of that pirate game?"

"Pirate game—oh, Ares. I can't forget."

It was a board game that everyone at Troy had used to get very intense about on the long, miserable night watches. It was to do with sirens and sea monsters and pirate kings, and it was stupidly complicated, which was perfect. Between us, we roped in all the little knights. Whenever anyone new came to join us, there had to be a Ceremonial Recitation of the Rules. After a little while, they were squabbling about whether sirens beat pirates and could we explode the sea monster or was that cheating.

One of the generals slowed down as he passed by, and I thought he was going to tell us to stow it, but instead he asked if he could play.

"Sir?" one of the little knights said to me suddenly, sounding alarmed.

"Hm?"

"You don't look very . . ."

I had forgotten to do anything else about my shoulder. I cast around vaguely for anything I could use as a new bandage. "I'm all right."

"You realize you took a vow of honesty," Polydorus murmured. "Is there a witch anywhere in . . ."

"I've seen one. I'm fine. A lot of blood doesn't mean a lot of hurt."

The general had overheard. "Go home, Heliades. You can't do anything else now. I'll send a couple of slaves with you, make sure you don't collapse on the road. Take some horses." He sighed. "You're one of only two polemarchs left. Do take care not to die of that, would you please?"

"Yes, sir," I said, staring into the near future. Home: I'd probably see Dionysus there. What was I meant to say? *Would you mind not playing with your food quite this much?* I had to say something now. What had happened today—I couldn't call it disproportionate. It wasn't. Cross a god at your peril. Apollo and Artemis had murdered all sixteen of a woman's children because she boasted too much. Gods aren't meant to be reasonable. But I couldn't keep pretending he was just a witch.

"Oh, that reminds me," the general said. "There's a witch looking for you. Tall, good-looking? Arrestingly weird voice? He's outside."

Fuck.

I heard Dionysus before I saw him. The courtyards were quiet. The haze of smoke that hung in the air, dancing with tiny ashes, seemed like maybe it didn't come from sacrifices, but from those pyres in his voice.

"So what you do is, you get a racing camel, and you go out into the desert in the very hottest part of the day. It's so hot that this is incredibly dangerous; the way is strewn about with the bones of people and camels who didn't go in and out quick enough. If you drop water on the ground, it boils."

I came around the last corner from the cloister, and from there I could see down into the Knights' Court, to where Dionysus was sitting on the edge of the fountain with a whole group of people sitting around him. More were pausing in the colonnades, leaning against pillars, some setting down baskets and boxes. Usually anyone telling anything even approaching a story would have been dragged away on suspicion of being a bard (penalty for singing unlicensed accounts: slavery) but perhaps the red tattoos were his shield here. Or maybe nobody had enough heart left to stop him.

"And you know when you reach the right place. Because everywhere, all through the sand, there are tracks a foot broad of gold dust. Under the surface, as the ants tunnel through, it gets pushed up, and you can see it everywhere, just like you can if you see an ant colony when you lift up a stone."

I had an eerie vision of a great desert plain all laced with gleaming veins of gold.

"So, the gold-hunters leap off their camels, and scoop up as much as they can. But they don't have long at all before the sun starts to sink and the air starts to cool, and the ants come out again. Every single ant is as big as a dog, and you've not seen quick till you've seen these things."

I strayed closer, not quite sure what I was hearing, but I was definitely hearing right.

"And then it's back on the camels with the gold dust and they ride hell for leather for home over the desert, all these giant ants galloping after them, and if your camel isn't quick as Artemis herself—" He leaned down and snatched up a tiny little boy, who squeaked joyfully. "Eaten!"

Little voices laughed and exclaimed: they were all children. Who belonged, of course—finally my bashed-about brain clicked around to what was going on—to people who hadn't yet come back from the stadium, or who wouldn't, or to slaves who were working past the usual hour to try and get the Palace back into some kind of order. I kept to the back, worried I was going to scare them, and waited for him to see me. He put the little boy factually in the fountain, which made the boy laugh like I'd never seen a human being laugh before. Children clung to him and asked for details as he made his way across, and he made up answers that made them laugh and tumble away to play.

The ghost of my little boy laughed through my memory, chasing a foal in the sea.

"I've your armour," Dionysus said. "I couldn't find anyone to give it to."

"Thanks. Listen. You and I need to have a talk, so . . ." I stopped, though, because he looked terrible. He was holding one arm close his ribs—his wrist was sprained or broken—and as he reached me, I saw the bruise just under his hairline; there had been a fight, or something. Once he was within arm's reach, something in him shut off, like he'd managed to last just long enough to reach me, and he collapsed. I caught him before his head could hit the ground. His hair pooled on the flagstones.

"Excuse me," I said to a passing slave who looked like she might work for the stables. "How possible is it to borrow a carriage?"

She smiled. "Borrow? You're Phaidros Heliades, right?"

"Yes?" I said, waiting for a new bargain to do with my hair or something worse.

"The Queen assigned one to you. I'll have the horses brought around. Do you need some help?"

"No." He was lighter than he looked, and all at once, I didn't want anyone else near him. "If you can show me the way."

The driver went slowly. Despite the chaos that had overtaken the streets a few hours ago, the ways were clear now, hundreds of slaves still out with wheelbarrows and brooms. I kept Dionysus propped in my lap, one arm across his chest to keep him steady. I'd never been in a carriage before, never mind one that purported to be my own, and it was strange to see the world gliding by so smoothly outside—and to travel so easily, without feeling tired or hot. I was glad not to be in the sun. More glad that Dionysus wasn't. I'd thought I was angry with him, but I couldn't reach it any more.

He wasn't out cold. He was awake enough to know where we were. How he'd stayed upright and telling stories to children all that time was beyond me. The bruise on his temple should have knocked him out. No doubt it would have, if the person who hit him hadn't had to reach so far upward.

"What happened to you?" I asked after a while; after we were leaving behind the busier streets, and pulling onto the road that led up the mountain.

"Just some knights." He was looking at the floor. I waited to see if he was going to spin me some mad story, but he didn't, and he didn't offer any more explanation.

"Why would you let anyone do this to you?" I said, not sure if I was angry or dismayed. "People don't see you when you don't want them to, why the fuck would you . . ."

"Witching doesn't work so well in a riot," was all he said. I was sure it was a lie, but it wasn't enough of a lie to highlight where the truth might be.

I let my head hang for a second, almost touching his. I'd worked myself up for a fight, but I couldn't do it. "Can you tell me what I need to do about your wrist?" I asked instead.

"I can do something at home."

"Like fuck you can, tell me what to do or I'll guess and then you'll be fucking sorry."

He might have smiled a little bit. "It just needs a splint."

I squeezed his good hand, worried that he still wasn't looking at me. I felt his breath judder. "Is there any magic for pain that will work on you?"

He shook his head. We sat quietly for a while. Outside, the city fell gradually away, until there were more trees than buildings, clacking with prayer tags. I watched the woods thicken, and I thought that maybe, lurching from shadow to shadow much too fast for a human, there was a thing with horns following us.

The driver tapped on the roof. "Sir? Is it this gate, or the next one?"

We were outside my house, under the lemon tree. "It's this one. Thank you." I pushed the door open. "Come on, you're staying with me," I said to Dionysus.

"No, I can—"

"Shut," I said, "up. Can you walk?"

He nodded and eased down after me. The carriage driver said the carriage and the horses were mine now, he could stable them here, he was happy to stay, but I sent him home, not wanting to think about what I could do to four sleeping horses if some new insanity overtook me while I slept, or what the mad bull thing would do to someone else in his territory. The carriage driver looked like he might die of gratitude.

"Bless you, sir."

That was uncomfortably extreme. I wondered what had happened to him today. Maybe he had been at the stadium. I wished him a safe journey back and turned back for Dionysus, who was—of course—picking some brand-new, beautiful, perfect lemons from the lemon tree which had previously never made any lemons.

"Lemon cake, then, strange one?" I said to him. Maybe I should have been demanding answers, and even a cessation of hostilities, but he was the boy from the sea; *my* boy from the sea, and whatever he'd done and whyever he'd done it, being a guest is the same as being kin, and kinship doesn't stop just because someone has done something terrible. There are laws older than the laws of a city. Taking him up on the right or wrong of it all could wait.

He did laugh, at least, and let me put my arm around his waist. I had a vivid memory of helping Helios, fuming, off the battlefield after he got someone's javelin through his thigh. Being injured had always made him furious: he took it as a mark of personal incompetence. I couldn't help feeling glad that Dionysus didn't seem to.

"How are you feeling?" I asked, suspecting that if I didn't ask directly, I wouldn't hear about it until he collapsed again.

He was shaking with the effort of standing, but he managed to make his voice easy. "I'll be happy as long as no one's living in your cupboard."

28

I did check. I checked the whole house twice, and parts of the ruins to either side. I put another bolt on the door down into the maze. That didn't mean no one could get in. It would have been easy to climb in through the windows, whose shutters we had to leave open to circulate some air through the house. I put broken pottery under them, though, so that at least it would be loud if someone did come. Across the outer walls of the house, ivy and honeysuckle rioted richer than ever. The goats from before were grazing on some fallen olives from my suddenly exuberantly healthy olive trees.

Meanwhile Dionysus was, like all witches, a terrible patient. I had to threaten to recite Athenian poetry at him before he settled down and let me bind up his wrist.

"What do you think happened today?" I asked at last, to give him a way to it if he wanted one; or a way away, if he wanted that.

His eyes ticked up. They looked black in the lamplight, except for the very edges of his irises, which hinted at deep water. Like she often seemed to if he sat still for long enough, his snake had found him, and she was coiling across his shoulders. There's nothing like a venomous monster to make an already brittle-seeming man more fragile. "I didn't do anything to the wine," he said.

"I know." I concentrated on tying the knot in the bandage around his wrist. "There's a god in Thebes. I don't understand what happened today, though." I risked looking up, feeling like I was between those mirrors again. "He destroyed the garrison today. He could take the throne right now, there would be nothing to stop him. He could incinerate the Queen, pick up the crown, say, *This is mine*, and everyone would kneel. But . . . nothing."

He looked down at the snake, who was sitting in the crook of his elbow, and shook his head. Not much; it must have hurt. There were bruises around his neck in the shape of hands. "You're seeing it like a soldier. You're talking about destruction and ruin, and stealing crowns."

"What else is it?" I said, nearly indignant.

In other languages—in yours too maybe—medicine and magic are different things. Perhaps like the Egyptians, you have physicians, and those are different to your witches; the one sets bones and the other sets minds, and rarely do they cross over. But in Achaea, no. They are the same, and that combined thing is what our witches do, and we have one word for it. I have to tell you that, because there's no other way to tell you what he said without making it sound like something far longer than what he said.

"Pharmakeia," he said.

"What?"

He was quiet for a second. "There are two kinds of pain. One is . . ." He nodded at his wrist, where I was just tying off the bandage. "We all know what that's for. It stops you doing things that kill you. If we couldn't feel pain, we wouldn't live long. We'd walk into fires because they look interesting and we'd have scratches that we don't notice and that go bad and we still don't notice; pain is useful."

I hadn't thought of it having a purpose before, but he was right. "Right?"

"The other kind is unhappiness. Not—passing discontent, I mean real unhappiness, the kind that lasts. And . . . that's for the same thing. It's there because you need to *stop* doing the thing that's making you unhappy, or it will kill you."

I looked at him sideways. "It definitely won't. Lots of things make me unhappy. I'm not dead."

He laughed. "No, but you've been trying very hard."

"What?" I said, wrong-footed.

"Your little knights say you called the prince a whiny little prick. You told the Queen she was being a crazed despot. All the Palace slaves think you're hilarious because you told the ambassador from Egypt, who holds everyone's fate in his hands, that you'd rather drown in a fountain than have breakfast with him. You were stabbed today and instead of sitting down you went straight into the fighting. You want to die."

"No, I—"

"You didn't care," he said over me. "And what, you made friends with a witch because you like me? Of course you don't. I'm a chronic liar and I'm dangerous, and for all you know, I did poison the wine today. You don't care what happens to you. You stay in the garrison, you keep riding with the Hidden, you murder anyone you're told to, you keep training children who are mostly going to die by the end of the year: all those things are tearing gouges in you—"

"They aren't, I'm trained to do those things—"

"Your training isn't armour, it's anaesthetic!" He didn't raise his voice, but there was rage under it, hot as the glass in the crater of the fallen star. He let his breath out and the fight seemed to go out of him at the same time. His focus slipped to the air somewhere between us. "So the function of the mad god is to break your mind, before your mind breaks your soul. Pharmakeia."

I kept quiet for a while. It was the most fragile quiet I'd ever sat through. I wasn't saying, *I know it was you.* He wasn't saying, *I'm trying to explain why I did it.* I couldn't tell why he wasn't. I'd thought he was playing with me and he thought it was funny, but he didn't think any of this was funny. "Savage kind of pharmakeia," I said eventually.

He nodded once. "Kill or cure."

He had set down three lemons between us. In one of those vivid, not sane bolts you get when you're worried for someone else's life or you're waiting to hear if yours will be shorter than you expected, a thought that didn't feel like my own used me as a lightning rod. It was that if you have three lemons, you have some lemons. But you're also seeing the shadow of *threeness*, traced out in fruit. It's an idea, three; but not one that needs a human to think it. It just *is.*

He was like three. I would never see *him.* Only his shadow, traced in a man, and sometimes in madness. *He* was . . . somewhere else, as well as here. I couldn't see in the right way to see him true.

I could see, though, that it was lonely.

"You're wrong," I said.

"About what?"

"Me. I do like you." I had to look at the floor. It felt like heresy to just say that to him flat, even though it was exactly in accordance with my vow. "You're not entirely unpleasant at least two fifths of the time."

He smiled gradually against his hand. He didn't believe me. It was written across him. He was doing what I had been too, all this time: enjoying it while someone was insincerely nice to him, because it was better than the Nothing. "I bet you say that to all the boys."

He was hurt, and younger than me, and there was a chance I'd try to kill him in my sleep. Even if it was what he wanted, even if revenge had become a strange kind of precious to him, and even if I didn't touch him otherwise in case I pressed a bruise—if I went around the table and kissed him to make him believe me, it would be dishonourable at best and dangerous at worst.

Only, the way he'd looked at me before, when I hadn't taken his hands—it had put roots down in me, and it had turned out to be something I did recognise, with dark flowers I knew very well.

Helios's death had hurt, but what had hurt much more, for years, was his chivalry. For years, he refused to touch me, because he was just such a fucking good knight, and I *hated* it, because after a point, chivalry like that is just cowardice.

Feeling like I was trapped in one of those bright weird Troy visions, and half expecting Dionysus to punch me and say, *No, I didn't mean that at all*, I got up and leaned on the back of his chair rather than his shoulder, and kissed him once, very light.

He stayed exactly still, then put his hand around my throat to make me lean down again, not for much longer, his other hand set over my ribs to tell me not to bend too far. He was tall enough, even sitting down, for me not to need to.

I hadn't thought as far as *after*, and now I was burning and hazing away and relieved and despairing all in one lovely, horrifying whirlpool.

He tipped his head at me, still holding my ribs; he was pressing slightly and somehow that dulled the pulsing ache in my injured shoulder. "You're going to ask me to lock you in tonight, in case it was you, and not the man in the maze. Aren't you?"

I nodded.

He didn't argue, but he did stand up and put his arms around me. It felt like a way of reminding me that he was tall and strong, and I'd struggle to do him much damage. I put my head on his chest, not convinced. He *was* tall and strong, he could lift me without trying, but he didn't like defending himself—not with the bull thing, not with Jason, who he could easily have just punched in the face, not with the knights at the stadium who had put him through such a wringer. "All right, my knight."

I made Dionysus give me the strongest sleeping draught he had, then lock me in the front room to sleep on the couch with the storm shutters bolted from the outside, and himself in the bedroom. If Asleep Murder Phaidros really made an effort, it was possible to get through two locked doors or a set of storm shutters, but that would make a fuckload of noise. Dionysus would wake up far enough in advance to get out or hit me with something heavy. It was hot with the shutters closed, but whatever was in the sleeping draught, it was good. It knocked me out so quickly I didn't make it to the couch; I was still blowing out the lamps and ended up curled in a heap on the floor.

I couldn't tell when, maybe soon after that or maybe hours, but I woke up just enough to notice it when he came in and lifted me up off the floor. That was an odd mix of humiliating and nice, being carried; I wanted to stiffen and get up and walk myself, but I was too asleep. It occurred to me after a little while that it seemed to be going on for a long time. I was sure I'd only been a few yards away from the couch. Maybe he was stealing me. Gods steal people.

Well, that was fine. I didn't mind being stolen.

It was cold.

There was a thunking noise as well, like something hard and heavy on flagstones, and something . . . breathing. An animal, something big, lungs like bellows.

Tap. Tap tap.

Where had I felt that before? Honey, that was it, I'd thought it was blood but it was just honey. I didn't want to be covered in honey again, though, it was sticky and it took ages to wash off. Oh, and the sodding bees. I shifted, trying to wake myself up enough to say, *No, no more bees, I don't think I like the bees.*

He put me down on something soft—moss—and put a cloak over me. I curled up under it, shivering now, because it was freezing in the maze.

The maze.

What?

"Phaidros!" *Phaidros, Phaidros, Phaidros? Phaidros . . .*

That was Dionysus's voice, slung weird by the echoes. He sounded frantic.

And far away.

So who had carried me?

Then I was *awake*, and the sleeping draught was holding me down like a swamp and it was the most muscle-wrenching effort to haul myself out of it and even halfway free, and fuck, there were *bats*, blasting through the corridor, keening in their strange high voices as they looked for their way, and something big snarling at them, swinging its horns, hating the noise and the rush of webbed wings that made the moonlight through the fissure in the cavern strobe.

I pressed back against the wall. The bull thing was almost as tall as a real auroch. It was stamping, snapping at the bats. All I could do was stay out of the way of those hooves, which scarred the ground. I eased upright, waiting for it to turn more away from me. If I was fast then I might be able to run. I'd have no idea where I was going, but lost in the maze alone was much better than not lost with this—thing.

There were handprints on my tunic, made in dark honey. They weren't right. The fingers were fusing, maybe into something like hooves, but I thought maybe it was talons. I eased along the wall, not thinking about it, watching the bull man. I had to strangle down a yell when he jumped to snap at a bat, and what I'd thought was just the hump of his bull-spine snapped open into wings. The pinions brushed me, massive things, as long as my arms. I stared. What else was he? Was he going to turn out to be like the bats too, did he even *need* to see me to find me in the maze, or could he just shriek and coo and find the shape of me in the sound?

I could only see him clearly in flashes, and only then by the draining moonlight. I watched, willing him to turn away just a few degrees more to take me out of his peripheral vision, which had to be restricted under the mask. He was covered in weeds and—no, they were flowers, he had taken vines and made a kind of cloak from them, some old and wilted, some new. Under that, he was still wearing ordinary clothes, honey-grimy now, with a ribbon of what was still quite clearly Hatti embroidery around the hem. In places it winked with silver thread.

Only two people in Thebes could wear Hatti embroidery.

He turned just far enough, and I could have run then; only, I couldn't. The last of the bats flapped away.

"Pentheus," I tried, very quiet, to keep the echoes from hurling it everywhere and startling him.

The bull thing paused, and twitched. It huffed to find that I was awake, then took me by the shoulders and put me back where it had left me to start with, on the cloak on the ground, like I was a little clockwork doll that had wandered off. He had hands, still, but they were something like hooves and claws too.

Be Persephone. Always negotiate.

"Hello again. What have you stolen me for, hey? I'm ugly. You didn't want Dionysus?"

The bull huffed twice, and under it, as though the air were passing through some extra chamber, there was a soft, birdish twitter; I thought it might be a kind of laugh. Gods, so he was human enough, even now, to understand. Very gently, one massive hoof-claw-hand patted me on the head. *Don't be silly. You stay there.* It was sticky from old honey, and strands of my hair stuck and pulled. It was absolutely not the worst thing that ever happened to me, but I'd never more powerfully wanted to yell and run away.

"Thank you, for this," I said about the cloak he had put me on. It was much cleaner than he was.

Behind the hollow eyes of the mask, serene bull eyes watched me.

"Were you lonely?"

Thump. He had sat down, more like an animal than a person, his spine wrong for sitting upright now. He made a very, very deep sound, a kind of croon, with a whicker of birdsong behind it; it wasn't a noise anything in the world had made before.

Those enormous wings were folded up now. And there was a tail, a lot longer and stronger than a bull tail. More like a lion. The mask—what was it? I was sure it had been a bull when I saw it first, but it had feathers on it now, and sharp, sharp teeth. I couldn't see. There was hardly any light.

"I wonder," I whispered, "if I could take this mask off you. They're dangerous. There's a god here, and . . . we're all turning into our masks."

He only blinked at me. He let me take the mask and set it aside.

In the dark with only the moonlight to see by, I couldn't make out much of what was underneath, except fur and eyes that were too golden to be human. I forced myself to look, because I had a feeling that if I flinched, the spell would break, but I let my eyes blur so I wouldn't see, because if I saw I'd never unsee. I could cheerfully look at someone with all their insides on the outside, and I'd watched witches dissect hearts, that was all normal, but this—I didn't want to dream about this.

The heavy head went down in my lap, which pinned me, and there was a clack of teeth meeting. I rubbed the patch of fur between the horns, trying to sing the hymn to Ares in my head, because it was so slow, and it made you breathe. A minute, five, ten. Be a marvel, just slice out the hour. If he was like the others, he would change back into a boy soon. *Ares, golden-helmed, bronze-clad . . .*

There was less weight than before. At first, the tip of the nearer horn had been right by my eye, but it was smaller. He was changing. It was about the speed the flowers round his neck were wilting.

Steps, from the maze. Light.

"Here," I whispered, which as much noise as I dared to make. Pentheus wasn't asleep, just resting, liking having some company. "It's the prince."

Dionysus came around the last turn with a lamp. My heart tried to lunge right out of my chest. "Oh, Phaidros," he breathed. "Are you hurt?"

"No. No, it was like—he wanted a doll. I don't know."

He knelt down next to us. Pentheus stirred and rumbled a deep sound at us. Maybe I was impatient, but I didn't think he was changing any more, or not nearly as quickly. Dionysus touched the back of his head and it seemed to settle him.

"What—has *happened*?" Dionysus whispered, taking in the horns, the wings, the tail—the teeth. "The mask was a bull."

The tail lashed playfully over his throat.

"He's not changing any more," I said, sure now, and worried, because my idea had been to walk out with him once he was himself again.

"Masks go on the inside too," Dionysus murmured. "Where is it? The mask, do you . . ."

I gave it to him.

Dionysus flinched when he saw it. As though he didn't want to see, he tilted it to the light of his lamp, and what went over his face was about the same as what went over mine if I'd just seen a spider skating around the rim of a wine cup.

With the new light, it was easier to see. There was a pair of wings fastened to either side of it, smallish, bluish brown, maybe a pigeon's. And there were teeth—a whole jaw. The original bull mask was only the upper half of the face, because all the witches' masks were designed to let you talk, but someone had used tough dried grass to graft on the bone. It was parched, probably from something that had died in the drought.

"Cuckoo," Dionysus said softly, about the wings, and then he touched the teeth. "Lion." He lifted his eyes. "Phaidros, he's been making his own spell. He's been . . . experimenting. I think he's trying to make himself into what he needs."

"I don't understand," I said, but I did understand there was something unholy about that mask, even to Dionysus. He was holding it slightly away from us both. On my knee, Pentheus sighed, and there was the echo of birdsong in it again. Cuckoo; cuckoo.

"An auroch is strong," Dionysus said, touching the horns of the mask, which had been mostly destroyed by the real horns growing up through them. "But quiet, and—if it isn't near people, it's not aggressive. This should have been a good mask for someone who wanted to forget and to hide. It should have kept him to the forest, made him able to defend himself if he needed, but otherwise he'd have been no harm to anyone. But—then—maybe he didn't like strong and quiet." The lion's canines shone yellow-white, nearly as long as my hand. "Phaidros, the dead things in your garden. He's been courting you. Leaving you presents, things with nice pelts ready for skinning." He looked up. "Like cats do."

"But the triplets said that was me."

"You walked at night and they found carcasses in the morning. But did they *see* you kill anything?"

I shut my teeth. I didn't know. Dionysus was right, though; it was what cats did. The lion tail tickled over my leg. The part of me that still wore its bronze helmet visor down stood between the rest of me, and believing it. Dangerous to believe it.

"Why a cuckoo?" I asked instead.

"I doubt he knows it's a cuckoo, do you know what one looks like?"

"No, I thought it was a pigeon."

"He just found a thing with wings. Maybe he was just trying to fly away, but . . . it *is* a cuckoo. You know what cuckoos do? The young ones?"

I thunked my head back against the wall. "They're put in another bird's nest, and they throw out any chicks that are already there"—Ares alive, fucking hell—"Dionysus, the triplets—"

"Right."

It should just have been sad, but I had huge rush of relief and joy and hope, because if it wasn't me, then I was so much safer than I'd thought, and it wasn't dangerous to stay in the same room as someone else overnight—it wasn't dangerous to stay with *him*.

When I looked at him, he was looking at me too, with that same unspoken half-promise as he had at the stadium.

Pentheus sniffed and, like a cat, ranged over me and bumped down to claim Dionysus as well. He was smaller than he had been with the mask, but he still wasn't small.

We both sat looking down at the thing that might still be a boy; spoilt and undutiful and determined and lonely. If I had the Fates' view of time and all the ways it could go, and how the warp and the weft wove; to what extent had this happened because I hadn't taken him seriously when he asked me for help? I'd thought he could learn to be stronger, but what if he was just made brittle, and he couldn't, and he'd . . . what? Bought a mask from a witch to hide his face and accidentally ended up like this? Or had there been a witch who realized what the star was, and what the magic would do, and who had said, *Choose one of these masks, and decide what manner of thing you would like to become?*

"We can't stay down here," I said. "If anything happens with the bees I'll lose my fucking mind again, and he's one startling bat away from eviscerating us both, I think."

"Yeah," Dionysus murmured. "Let's see if he'll come up with us." He stroked the place between the horns. "Pentheus, sweetheart. Let's go. Phaidros is cold and he doesn't like the bees. This isn't a good place for knights, they need quiet. Will you help me take him back?"

The answer was a snarl and teeth snapping at his hand, and claws sinking right into my leg.

I pushed my hand over my face. Of course, Pentheus wouldn't be doing anything that would help anybody except him. "Right. Pass me that rock."

Dionysus led the way and I carried Pentheus. I was only just strong enough, and I had to stop halfway up my cellar steps, shoulders on fire, before I could make the last lurch to the top. I put him on the couch—there were hoof marks on the floor beside it now—and once that was done, I felt disconcerted, because moving him had seemed like such a titan task that anything beyond it had had a bit of a fairy-tale quality, not worth thinking of, and now it was here. My back hurt.

Now—ugh—I'd have to tie him up and slog over to the Palace, and give him back to the Queen, and try to explain that yes, he had been living under and sometimes in my house all along but I was much too stupid to have noticed, and hope that there were witches who could turn him back.

"Could *you* turn him back?" I asked Dionysus, who was standing next to me and looking down at Pentheus in exactly the same logistically troubled way I was.

He frowned, like that was an odd thing to say, and because I knew him enough now, I had a pricking sense that we were coming up against something else we saw so differently we couldn't reconcile. Madness, pharmakeia; blue. I could feel the shadow of it. "Why?"

"He's got to go back to the Palace. It was would much easier if he was coherent and boy-shaped?"

"No, he doesn't have to go back to the Palace," Dionysus said, quite slowly. "He—Phaidros." His voice dropped into deeper smoke than usual, as if I were suggesting taking him to a torture chamber. "We have to take him to another part of the forest, where he can't hurt anyone."

"*What?*"

"He asked for help. He asked *both* of us for help. He asked to forget everything. He found a way. He put the mask on, and he made adjustments to it, he chose this."

"Yes, because he's a useless spoilt coward and now it's time for him to be a prince again," I said, confused.

"He is a maltreated and neglected *child* who ran away."

"Maltreated and neglec—he's Sown!" My voice was doing its breaking-too-high trick again. "His function isn't to do what he likes, it's to do his fucking duty."

Dionysus was breathing in slowly, and I recognised the way he looked, because it was exactly the way Helios had looked when he realized he was going to have to fight someone a lot bigger and stronger than him, but he would do it anyway, because he would die of shame to retreat. It put me on edge. I didn't want to fight. I already hated arguing even this much. If he tried, though, he was going to crush me.

"His duty was hurting him, and this is the medicine, and the only reason you think that's unreasonable is that *your* duty has hurt you much more, there never was medicine for you, and you don't see why other people shouldn't be hurt the same way."

I wished he had hit me. It would have hurt less than hearing what he thought I was like, and how embittered and terrible. "No," I ground out, "the reason I think he should do his duty is that it is necessary. I don't want to make anyone suffer, I don't take some foul joy in it—"

"That isn't what I said—"

"Yes it is. You can think what you want about me, you can think I'm some vengeful cruel monster, but I took a vow. Duty is honour. My duty is to return him to the Queen, so that he can do his."

He was shaking his head. "And I took vows to do what was best for the patient, not for someone else."

"So it's fine to just let him go on the odd murderous rampage?" I demanded. "The triplets' lives don't matter? He's dangerous like this, and he is required as he was. How can you possibly think that it's better to just leave him be?"

"For the same reason," he said, and this time there was a flint edge in his voice, "that I didn't chain *you* to a wall when you thought you were killing things." He picked up a pomegranate and held it out, close to me. It turned to dust in his hand. "Because it wouldn't help you. Only me."

It wasn't what he was saying, exactly, that grated so badly. It was the way he was saying it. It was that—absurdly—he had wasted a pomegranate, and that that little trick was clearly meant to show *I* could have been dust by now if he had wanted. It was patronising, and it was hammering a nail with a sledgehammer, and worst of all, it scared me in a sharp immediate way I hadn't been scared since I was little and staring at certain death under the hooves of a Hatti charger. My whole body only knew one thing to do when I was scared like that, because anything else, all my life, would have meant going down under that charger.

I punched him so hard he collapsed in front of me, and instantly, I realized it was too hard. He didn't move, and nor did I. I had to just stand there, staring at the window, because if I looked at him, it would be real. A child-part of me was convinced that if I didn't look, he would get up.

He didn't get up.

I sank down on my knees and pressed my temple against his chest, trying to find his heartbeat. Nothing. No thump; no lift of his ribs.

Reasoning insanely that it wasn't too late, I could find another witch in town who might still be able to help him, I lifted him up. Dead weight is so much heavier than you ever think it could be. Carrying a dead person is like trying to carrying the same weight in sand. I knew what that felt like and it felt like that now, but I had to be wrong, because I couldn't have just murdered the last of my family for no reason except that he had argued with me, I couldn't be *that*.

I reached halfway down the olive grove before I had to buckle onto the grass, the newly lush grass, under the newly beautiful lemon tree.

As soon as he touched the grass, it died. It withered, like it was burning, shrivelling up, rippling out from us, to the bases of the trees, where, even by the moonlight, I could see that the olives were dying too, the lemons, the leaves desiccating half to dust.

He breathed in.

I started to cry. It was shock and relief and horror and fear all at once.

Dionysus punched my arm. "Fuckwit! Look at the fucking trees!"

I couldn't speak.

He sighed. "It's all right. Don't . . . we should be able to save the trees."

"The *trees*?" I yelled at him. "I'm sorry. I'm so sorry, I . . ."

He took my hand and held it in both of his against his chest. "No, I'm sorry. I made you do that."

"You didn't make me."

He made a soft impatient sound. "I did." He sighed. "I wanted to remind you it isn't a choice."

"I killed you."

"Briefly."

I touched his chest to feel his heart. Yes; going again. He was warm. I didn't ask how. I could see how. The trees were dead instead of him, the grass, the vines. I didn't know what to say. I had a stone in my throat. Distantly, I could feel I was still crying, my breath coming in shudders.

Dionysus put his hands through my hair to make me look up.

"I'm sorry," he said again. He looked distraught now.

I hugged him hard. He was much stronger than I thought as he hugged me back. I could feel the muscle moving over his bones. It was such a paralysing relief that I had to drop my head against his shoulder and try to soak him in, the feel of him breathing and the glassy loop of his hair I had clenched through my hand. "My fist, my fault."

"That's stupid."

I choked on a laugh. He guided our foreheads together. I had to keep hold of his wrists just to make sure he was really there and not a vision Apollo had sent to save me from the truth.

Dionysus really did seem all right. He seemed nervous, though, and with an anvil sinking through my insides, I realized we had circled back to where we had started.

"What are we going to do about him?" I asked, nodding at the house.

He bent his neck for a second. "Say he does turn back. He won't thank you. He will turn slowly to clockwork, and you'll have a marvel king who has no pity because no one ever had pity on him. Is that what you want running your city?"

"We have a marvel queen now and she's working beautifully."

"She's killing you," he said, simple and very soft.

"She's heroic," I said, flatter than I wanted to. I sounded angry. I always sounded angry when I was upset. "Thebes has held together this long because of her. And—I know what you think, but madness is *not* medicine." I looked down at the ground. "I'm taking him back to the Queen. It's for her to decide, not us. Turn me to dust or don't."

"*This* is what you choose?" he asked, quiet. The way he said *choose* made it sound not only important, but the only important thing.

"I'm not choosing! I don't *have* a choice, he doesn't have a choice, that's what I'm saying to you, we're Sown!"

"No. You are choosing honour over a boy's life."

Something deep in my cellars said: *Gods don't care what's in your heart or what compelled you. Gods care what you have* done.

"He won't die, he's going to the Palace!"

"He won't be living either."

"Why is *this* the hill you want to die on?" I demanded, somewhere between infuriated and helpless, and betrayed, because he was choosing some obscure ineffable principle he had never properly explained over—

I caught myself.

We weren't friends. I just *wanted* to be, for all I knew perfectly well he was going to kill me in the end. But that was just life, for him. I'd seen him dance. I'd seen dozens of people catching at him as if their lives depended on touching him. He probably thought everyone being a little bit in love with him was normal. It was just the air.

"No, all right," I corrected myself. "Fine."

He frowned. "You'll leave him?"

"No, bizarrely," I snapped. "I'm taking him without you."

So I took Pentheus down the mountain, then up to the High City. Halfway, I had to take a horse from the public stable at the Temple of Poseidon and lash him to it, because I couldn't carry him once he started to wake and kick. The stable master gave me a frightened stare, and I said—not that it made things any better—that the snarling kicking bundle was an escaped slave I was taking home. As I led the horse through the streets, people looked away, crossing over to get away from me.

All the way, what Dionysus had said churned angrily round in my head. Sometimes madness is medicine—medicine for who, for Pentheus? But not for literally everyone else. Everyone *else* would be fucked. The royal line would be broken; the Queen, the noble, clever, deinos Queen, would have to risk her life having *another* child; but no, that didn't matter, he was in Thebes to watch it eat itself and call it pharmakeia—

"Phaidros, why have you got a person in a bag?" the Chamberlain asked me slowly. I was at the Palace steps.

"It's the prince," I said, almost absently, more wanting to say, *Listen to this ludicrous thing a witch just said to me, tell me if I'm being unreasonable.*

"It's the what?"

"There's something wrong with him, he keeps . . . don't undo that," I suggested. "He needs priests. Or witches. He's . . . not himself."

After that, the morning was a chaos of priests and priestesses from half a dozen different temples, surgeons, witches, half the court. I had to explain to least twelve different people how I'd found him, where he had been, what he had been doing. I explained he had killed foxes and a wolf, maybe people, and that he had been foraging honey. It was horrible, because they had to chain him up, and though he kept fighting at first, he retreated into a corner in the end like a frightened animal and curled up in a miserable ball. Those great cuckoo wings were out, trying to mark out some space around him, the way birds of prey do when they've got food or chicks to protect.

"How did he get like this?" the Queen asked at last, after everyone had finished interrogating me, and all the theories exploded around her. The Egyptians have a saying: put six Achaeans in a room together and you'll have twelve opinions. That it's annoying and patronising doesn't stop it being right. "Who put the mask on him?"

Some witches were murmuring. Someone tried a different mask on him, the mask of a young man; it didn't do anything. He just tried to bite the lady holding it. Of course it wasn't changing the mask on the inside; like Dionysus had said.

Like me. Visor down, spear out, even when a god was telling me I was wrong.

Pentheus was watching me over his knees, looking utterly betrayed and beaten under all the dirt. His eyes weren't quite human, but they were his. He wasn't looking at me like a young man looks at some older man he barely knows. Anyone seeing this would have thought I was a god he had worshipped for forever and who had then personally hurled him under the wheels of a chariot. I wanted to kneel down with him and ask why, when I wasn't at all what he seemed to think, I had no power to change the mind of a queen, or to help an unhappy prince; I was just a used-up shadow of Helios, and he couldn't expect me to be more than that. I couldn't save him, I couldn't clash with the Queen, I couldn't do any of it.

Very useful that he thinks you can though, remarked a voice like Dionysus's.

Something deep in me clicked into place then.

The more deinos the witch, the more deinos the magic. That was really just another way of saying that the magic of a witch works because people—or other things—believe in the witch.

Pentheus believed I was more than I was.

Nine-tenths sure it couldn't ever work, I knelt down in front of him and held his hands. One was mostly talons, one was halfway a hoof. It was much worse, the boy-animal chaos, here in the bright light at the Palace. At least there had been plenty of good, ambiguous darkness in the maze.

"Pentheus. It's time to remember who you are. Wake up."

And he just—did.

He pushed his hands over his face and sat up without that terrible animal hunch, the one that said he was ready to bite if someone upset him enough, and all at once he was just a boy again, dirty and ragged, but a boy all the same.

I sat back, shocked.

"Phaidros," he said, sounding confused. "Where . . . what's happening?"

"You've been asleep, sort of," I explained, trying hard to sound normal. I knelt forward again and put my cloak around him. The wound in my shoulder stabbed me, but I felt it less than before. Distantly, I had a sense that something in me had shut off after fighting with Dionysus. "We're in the Palace. You vanished for a little while. Your mother asked me to find you. It's been eleven days."

"I don't remember," he said, his eyes wide and glassy. He looked bewildered. "Eleven . . . days, how? Where was I?"

"Out by the forest, in the maze."

I should have been more relieved. No: I should have been relieved, generally. I wasn't. I wasn't anything. I couldn't feel anything. Some lever had gone clunk in my clockwork and I was only half here. I was looking at a lost boy who had been through some kind of strange, savage curse, and I didn't even feel happy to have him back. Just—blank.

"I'm sorry. I didn't mean to cause you any trouble, I don't know what . . ."

Well, I'd have to fucking pretend.

I hugged him carefully. "It's all right. I'm just happy you're all right. Your mother's here," I added, nodding that way. Nobody else had noticed he was all right yet, still arguing.

His confusion dropped away, but not like I'd hoped. I saw the weight of the whole Palace sink onto his shoulders. He straightened up under it very slowly, and a neutral, adult veil came down over his expression. He looked like someone who had had a wonderful, convincing dream, but woken up in a prison cell again.

"Yes, of course."

I unlocked his chains. "Let's see her together. I'll get in the way if she goes—you know. Full Medusa."

He didn't laugh. "You can't say that."

"No, *you* can't say that."

A very thin smile.

Sometimes madness is medicine.

I tried to kick Dionysus's voice out of my head, but it wouldn't go.

"Up you get." I helped him up, and put my arm round him as a partial shield when everyone went quiet. Not because I was worried about him; it was because in a cold dead clockwork way, I'd assessed him, and concluded that the course of action most likely to end in the objective, his eventual transformation into a functioning king, was a strategic display of protective kindness.

Part of me thought: *This is it. This is what being a marvel is.*

I hated it.

People got out the way so that he had a clear path to the Queen. He bowed stiffly.

"Lady."

"Sown." She smiled, bowed back, and there, in her, I saw exactly what was happening in me.

She didn't care either. She had learned not to, because it would have been agony, all the time.

"Come on," I murmured, less and less sure I'd done the right thing. "Let's get you away from all the audience."

The way he gripped my arm, he might have been drowning.

As the Queen's attendants began to see people out, Apophis clipped up the steps and, because he was six feet tall and twice their size, brushed by them without seeming even to see that they were there. His own retinue of slaves was behind him, half a battalion of them, all just as immaculate and polished as he was, most of them far taller than any of us, gleaming with turquoise and gold worth more than most Sown estates. I must have been more tired and more hungry than I'd really known, because seeing them made me think about a story I'd heard a bard sing at one of the wayside places on my way from Troy. It was about a great knight, dead in Hades, and what he said to a living man who was visiting. *Better to be the meanest slave in heaven, than a king in hell.* I'd tried not to remember it because I needed it not to be true, because if it was true than Helios was miserable, but the echoes of some stories echo around inside your head long after the lyre strings are quiet. I couldn't tell why I'd thought of that. No; Pentheus, going to Egypt to be nobody, but getting away from being a king in a madhouse.

"What," Apophis said to me, enunciating precisely, "in the name of Ra is this supposed to be? You held a funeral and now you appear to have resurrected your prince? Or was he never dead, and you were trying to avoid your agreement with the Pharaoh? What?"

"He was missing," I said. I put my hand on his chest and pushed slowly to make him stand further away from me. "And we didn't tell you because people here are already starving to death and we need your grain. We were hoping to find him. We didn't: we assumed he was dead, hence the funeral. But we've found him. I know it's stupid and messy, but that's what it is."

"People will think you've swapped in another boy."

"When you say people, do you mean you?" I asked.

"Yes," he snapped.

"There he is, you can see him."

"You *know* you all look the same to me."

"Apophis . . . we just held some extremely expensive funeral games. If we'd swapped him, there would have been no funeral. You'd never even seen him. It would have been easy. This is just what a giant fucking cock-up looks like."

He did seem to think about it at least. When he spoke again, it was quieter. "It's a marvellous narrative. A young prince back from the dead to save his city. It will combat these superstitions of a lost prince and a mad god coming for the throne."

"Sir," I said, "I have no doubt that's what the Palace will say happened, you're right, but it isn't what anyone planned. He went mad, we lost him, we've found him. It is very embarrassing; it is not a conspiracy."

"Either way, you've all been lying to me. According to you, the prince was in a sanctuary all this while. I am astonished; the duplicity is shameless. I am inclined to leave, and let this—insane city eat itself with its mad god and its vanishing princes!"

I looked up at him for a few seconds, not seeing his face, but the future where I had to take my little knights into battle, and see how well they could manage that left turn against Egyptian soldiers who outnumbered them. "Then . . . the next time you'll see me is when I'm killed on the deck of one of your ships."

"Don't be absurd, I have three thousand men guarding those ships, you can't possibly mount an attack, you'll lose your entire garrison."

"I know," I said. "But we'll have to anyway. All this green? Even that can't save us now."

Something opened in his expression. He touched my shoulder, tilting me away from the Queen and Pentheus, and the Guards. Unlike me, he was clean. Somehow his white clothes had stayed white, even with all the sacrifice smoke. "Are you swearing to me that that boy is indeed the prince, and all of this was just—a mistake that got out of hand?"

"I swear, sir."

"Then . . . I'll take you at your word, knight."

That caught me out. "Why?"

He smiled. "Among ourselves we have been calling you Honest Heliades."

"You . . . might not be entirely a prick," I admitted.

"Isn't it nice when we get on?"

"No. I still don't like you, you loom and you've got pretentious earrings."

He laughed. "You're a wonderful, wonderful man," he told me, and walked away looking cheerful, followed by his retinue of increasingly confused slaves.

"Well done," the ubiquitous Chamberlain said to me, with an unusual failure to broadcast her normal suspicion that I was a wild pig in a clever disguise. "That was . . . very good."

I looked around. "Are you feeling all right?"

"The Queen wants you to stay," she added, signalling the last of the slaves to leave, and to close the chamber doors.

"What happened to you? Do you remember?"

The audience hadn't gone, just shrunk. Now, we had a priestess and a physician, and in the background, Tiresias, standing in the archway that led outside to the shrine to Semele, which was crowded with candles and offerings; slaves were out gathering it all up in hessian rubbish sacks.

Beyond that, down on the plain, the dead land beyond the Fury marvels and the last outpost of green that was the Temple of Apollo looked strange: like a god had combed ash into the air in slim tines, much smaller and much more numerous than the titan pillars of sacrifice smoke that still poured into the sky.

Funeral pyres. It was hundreds and hundreds of funeral pyres.

The Queen was watching Pentheus intently. I'd tried to say that it might be better to give him an hour, but she had looked at me like I'd spat.

"No. The last thing I remember is seeing the witch enchant the bulls, with Phaidros." He was sitting very straight, hands clamped into his lap to hide the grazes and the grime under his fingernails. They hadn't even let him wash yet, or eat. I looked at the Queen, wanting to say that if a beggar sought hospitality here then they'd be treated with more ceremony, but I already knew what she would say. *Princes have more duties than beggars.*

"Why had you gone to see Phaidros?" the priestess asked.

He didn't look away. There was a strange calm to him now. It was the one I'd had after Helios had been killed. The worst had happened: there was nothing to be afraid of any more. "To ask for help. I didn't want to go to Egypt. But he said I needed to do my duty."

The Queen caught my eye and tipped her head ruefully.

"Then what happened?"

"I don't know."

"Lord," the priestess pushed, "you ended up in the woods running wild in the mask of a bull: something happened. Someone gave you that mask. Did you see anyone, did you talk to anyone?"

"No, just Phaidros."

That wasn't true; he had spoken to Dionysus, they had walked away together. Still, if he didn't remember, then he didn't. I pushed my hand over my face—thought to the side of everything else that I needed to shave—and wondered why it hadn't occurred to me, given that anyone even a little wobbly in their own mind completely lost it anywhere near Dionysus, it could have happened to Pentheus too.

Dionysus could have spoken to Pentheus, sent him away, and never known that Pentheus's mind had shut down straight after that.

No; that didn't explain the mask. Pentheus had had his before anyone else—before the witches tried it at Hermes, before everyone else tried it.

Gods, had he just . . . picked it up at the dance? The servers there had been in animal masks. Was this just a horrendous mishap?

"And how did you turn him back?" she asked me.

"I don't know. I just said wake up and he did."

"But what made you think that would work?"

"I . . ." I sighed. "I know a witch. He says things with authority and I always believe him even when it's stupid because he's deinos; it seemed worth a try."

"That's enough," the Queen decided. "Madness overtook dozens of people who saw the star fall; Pentheus too, clearly, and the only mystery is how he ended up so far from the Kadmeia."

That felt like missing a step on the stairs at night, because now I'd heard her say it, I could see that it was true and it wasn't. Whatever had seized Pentheus, it was a very different kind of madness. Everyone else sang the song and danced, but he had run wild, killed things, maybe people, and he'd been conscious enough to eat and to drink, and take shelter in the maze from the heat. And if anyone else could have been cured with an order from someone believable to wake up, then the witches would have done that.

"You can go," she said to the priestess. "Not you," she said, when I started to get up.

I sat down again and looked across at Pentheus, who was still straight and stiff, gazing at something in the middle distance now. Because someone needed to, I caught his shoulder and scooped him sideways. I was surprised when he let me. He just dropped his head against my collarbone and stayed there, motionless. He still smelled of the forest, all crushed grass and honey.

I still wasn't relieved or happy, and I still didn't feel sorry for him. I just knew it was important to pretend I felt all those things, because if I didn't, then . . .

Then his mind would kill his soul, now that I'd taken away the mechanism that had been stopping that.

"How did you find him, exactly?" the Queen asked me. She had made everything seem less formal now, but the question was as precise as any of the others.

"He broke into my house," I said. "He was in the maze underneath. He was there all along, I knew someone was—we talked about it, when you were making chain mail—but I didn't realize."

She only inclined her head, which made her hair fall over her shoulder. Helios's had used to fall in the same way. I had a sudden painful vision of combing it out for him, after a battle and he couldn't move his hands. Hold a shield for long enough and you can't open and shut your fingers.

"I'm sorry I broke into your house," Pentheus said to me. "I don't remember."

I hesitated. "Do you remember me bringing you here? You fought."

"No."

I rubbed his shoulder, not knowing what else to do. He was still too thin, but it wasn't as bad as before. He felt stronger. He had run around out there, at least. "I'm glad. It wasn't very nice."

The Queen was watching us. I had a feeling she found it distasteful, that I was being gentle with him. I watched her back, and wondered how different she would have been, if someone had just been kind to her at the right moment. I wanted to say, *Trust me, I know how to build a human. This is how Helios built me.*

"Pentheus, what made you go to Phaidros in the first place?"

"He was sworn to Helios. I'd heard he was honourable. The knights my age all like him. I thought he might honour an oath-bond, even though we're not blood."

"Yes," the Queen said. "So why didn't you?" she asked me.

"Because I couldn't help," I said. "I'm in no position to negotiate for anything from the crown."

"But," she said, steady and gradual, "you live above the maze. You know very well how to get someone out of the city in secret, because you police it. Why didn't you say, well, come home with me, no one will look for you there, and even if they do, no one will find you in the maze, particularly not in a mask, and even better, the Queen is likely to ask me to help find you, and I can make sure she never does? As soon as the weather cools down, you can be in Corinth, or Sparta."

"Oh, fuck off," I said wearily.

"I beg your pardon?"

"If I wanted him out of the city, he'd be gone, I wouldn't be keeping him incriminatingly in the fucking maze for the first fucking poacher to find, fuck me."

She blinked twice.

"He's fun, isn't he?" Pentheus said. He sounded, now, the way he had been trying to sound when he spoke to me on the parade ground: clear, cool, lightly interested in a way that said he was here talking to us because it was an acceptably engaging way to pass half an hour, and certainly not because anything important rested on it. He didn't care about the outcome. She could execute me if she wanted. Or him. He was free for the rest of the afternoon anyway.

"My lady, I can quote what Phaidros said to me when I asked him to help me. I said, 'I'm scared she's sending me to Egypt to start again,' and he said, 'Are you certain she isn't sending you away because you're a whiny little prick and no one likes you?' Half the regiment heard him say it. Ask them."

The Queen frowned. "Did you really say that?" she asked me.

"Nope, I am famously mellifluous, ask anyone," I said. Usually I had a lot of patience for her let's-kick-the-mooring-lines-and-see-if-anything-comes-loose approach—it was only wise—but today I was tired and upset, and I had growing feeling, like mould, that Dionysus had been exactly right after all.

"I know you didn't help me," Pentheus said, "but I think I might love you."

"Oh, thanks," I said, wondering how long I'd have to enjoy that. Maybe even a whole hour.

Pentheus shook his head once. "We all know what happens to kings and queens who make a habit of accusing those most loyal to them of treason. Generally they that find nobody wants to be loyal any more. I assure you, lady, if it had been my choice, I would have stayed mad in that maze. The only reason I'm here is Phaidros's unquestioning and unswerving loyalty to you, which I think he should reconsider before you kill him for no reason."

"I think you're aiming for louche and rakish, but the note you're hitting really is more towards whiny little prick," she remarked.

"Needs work," he agreed, and smiled a bit at me.

She looked more puzzled with that small show of level-headed maturity than anything he had said before. She almost smiled. "Get yourself cleaned up. The Egyptian ambassador is here and we need that grain yesterday."

Pentheus got up without arguing, bowed precisely, and left. I stared after him, and then at her, completely unable to tell if she was about to send me home, or send me to be executed just in case. I wanted to say, *You can't make him go to Egypt now, he needs some time to recover at least*, but I didn't, because if I was about to be executed, then anything I said to try and help Pentheus would only achieve the opposite.

She studied me for a long time. "I'm sorry," she said. "I just wanted to see what your reaction was."

It wasn't a question, so I kept my eyes on the floor.

"Gods, I've really upset you—Phaidros, this is just what being the ruler of a city is, it's . . ." She let her breath out, frustrated. "I'm not used to seeing anyone have a genuine reaction to anything I do. The court is all calculation. You have to see it like a battle. Nothing anyone says here is personal, it's all strategy." She paused. "Usually you're good at knowing when that's happening. Is something else going on?"

I shook my head slightly. "Lady, you don't have to pretend to care what I do outside the Palace in order to make me function better."

She shifted, and it looked amazingly uncomfortable. "The other day, you said something simple, but it . . ." She hesitated. It was a brittle sort of silence, a glass one that someone had just tapped with a hammer, vibrating. "I'm not asking you in order to make you function better, I'm asking because you're even more openly suicidal than usual and I'm worried about you."

"Oh," I said, and nothing else arrived, except a rock in my throat.

"So what happened?" she asked.

"My . . ." What did I call him? "There's man who lives near me, he was a guest a long time ago so he's kin, but we disagree about everything. We found Pentheus together. He didn't want me to bring him back here. We fought. I hurt him, very badly. I don't think he's going to forgive me."

"Why didn't he want you to bring Pentheus back?"

I sighed. "He's a witch. He thinks the madness is pharmakeia."

"He sounds horrifying."

"He's . . ." I had to look fixedly at the floor. Being hit by a chariot is hard and sudden, and I wished that being hit by the truth was like that, but it wasn't—it was hard and slow. I'd been angry, and then I'd gone numb for a while, but now what was smashing into me, very, very slowly, was that Dionysus really wouldn't forgive me. Whatever game he had been playing with me, he would be finished with it now. It had been so good to see him again, and to have the chance to make things right, but instead of doing that, I'd done him even more wrong than I had the first time. "He's like wine. If you describe what he does, he seems awful, but if it's happening to you, it's lovely."

"There speaks an intoxicated man."

"Yes," I said greyly.

The glass silence was back.

"I wanted to talk to you about something else," she said. She had taken off the pin that attached her cloak to her dress and now she was bumping her thumbnail across the design. It was ivory, and it showed a tiny image of Apollo and Artemis, holding their bows, with a dead lion between them.

"Lady?" All at once I was tired. I was so tired I could have tipped sideways on this couch, fully dressed and covered in dust and sacrifice smoke, and gone to sleep right in front of her.

Her focus tilted into the middle distance, which was where, I was learning, she tended to read strategy in the air. "With Pentheus going to Egypt," she said, "my position here is difficult. An heir is what seals a crown. I have to marry again. I'm still young enough to have more children, just; probably." She sounded like I did when I was gearing up for a battle I knew would be awful. I'd do it, because I had to, and I'd never even think of not doing it, but there was a good chance of ending up maimed or dead.

"Who will it be, lady?"

"I was thinking of asking you."

"Oh. I don't know anyone who could be king, everyone I know is fifteen."

She was starting to laugh for some reason. "I didn't mean I was thinking of asking you *about* it, I mean I was thinking of asking *you*."

"What?" I said blankly.

"You've behaved with great honour, and distressing honesty," she said. "I can't think of better qualities in a king consort. Nor in a father. I'm older than you, but what do you think?"

Without meaning to, I stood up, and I realized it was because most of me had decided independently of the rest that it would be good to run away. I'd never more wanted to run away. I wasn't safe to live with anyone yet. I'd hurt Dionysus and he was a head taller than me. More than hurt. I wanted to say, *No, please, you don't understand, I can't do this, what if I kill someone who isn't magic—you, or Pentheus, and what about the slaves, there are hundreds of people who have to overlap with the king in the palace, even if he's just an ornamental king*, but it didn't matter. If I killed someone, I did. It would be a minimal price to pay for the security of the House of Kadmus, whatever my personal feelings about it were, because my feelings were irrelevant.

Can't just meant, *don't want to.*

And anyway, after what I'd done to Dionysus, I didn't deserve to do things the way I wanted.

"Of course, lady. Duty is honour," I agreed quietly, and knelt down.

She touched the back of my head like she was stroking a favourite dog. "Yes. It is."

29

Lots of things happened at once after that. The news that Pentheus had come home was already whipping around the Palace, and with it, all the confusion I'd worried about when we first decided to have the funeral. I heard some slaves murmuring that it couldn't be the real Pentheus, the Queen must have just found someone who looked like him. She took him to the throne room to show everyone, and to tell what was more or less the truth: he'd been found on the forest border without any memory, but by the grace of the gods, it had been restored. Skirting the edges of the hall, I noticed I was getting speculative looks.

"People think you might be magic," Tiresias told me, appearing as usual from nowhere. I was starting to think that maybe they materialised when it was useful but spent most of their time floating around in the ether, eavesdropping. "Plenty of people were there when you turned him back."

"It was just witchcraft," I said.

"If I were you," they said seriously, "I would not tell people it was witchcraft. If I were you, I would not say anything that makes you sound like anything more extraordinary than an honest knight."

"I don't . . . understand."

"Phaidros, you are about to marry the Queen, and you come from an unusual background in that nobody has any idea what that background is. It is standard protocol to consult the oracle at the Temple of Apollo in situations like this, so that we don't have another Oedipus episode."

"Who's Oedipus?" I asked, increasingly at sea, and watching land bob further and further away. It was one of those old-sounding names from when people gave a child a brief once-over and said what they saw. Oedi-pos: sore foot.

"King of Thebes a long time ago, accidentally married his mother."

"How do you accidentally—"

"That isn't the point, the point is that as of at least an hour ago, but probably days ago given how clearly the Queen has been auditioning you for higher duties, the intelligence network of Apollo has been gathering information about you, and if you think I'm well-informed, you haven't seen anything yet. You do *not* want to give them any reason to think you're in any way magic."

I still didn't understand, but I'd fallen down a peripheral rabbit hole. "The Temple of Apollo has . . . an intelligence network."

"Has one? It's *the* one. How do you think the oracles know what to tell people?"

"They're possessed by Apollo."

Tiresias rolled their head despairingly. "They are *sometimes* possessed by Apollo. He doesn't come on demand; you don't ring a bell and there he is. He's a god, he's wild and greater and stranger than anyone can ever know. But people need answers on demand. And so?"

"And so they . . . have spies," I said, feeling that same dull loss I had when the Queen explained the Apollo marvel to me, and understanding more and more why she was so flat about never even considering there might be a god in Thebes. Almost all the things most people could point to and say, *There, a god working*—none of it was anything to do with gods. It was clever artifice and good intelligencers.

"When someone says *oracle* to you," Tiresias told me seriously, "read *spymaster*. There will be at least twenty people in this room who report to *someone* from Apollo, whether they know that someone is from Apollo or not. Do *not* tell them you brought Pentheus back with magic."

After that, they left a significant pause, the one that means *we both know why*—even though they hadn't given me nearly enough data for me to know why. I'd always hated the Pause. I'd heard it from generals again and again, and its only real function was to force you to do a mental uphill climb in order to look like you knew what was going on, the effect of which was put you off balance and make them feel all clever. It had been a point of honour for me, for years now, to force them to climb down and get me. The Pause never works if you're clever enough to know that asking a pertinent question doesn't make you sound stupid.

"Explain why, please."

"Phaidros, you sound like a child. Go away and think about it."

I tipped my head, about to ask why they were trying to make me feel stupid rather than just answering a straightforward question. But then I saw why. They were frightened of me. I was going to have a great deal of power soon. Tiresias had only survived this long at court because they were strange enough and right enough, often enough, that the Queen didn't feel safe getting rid of them. They wanted to make me feel small, so that I would never feel safe enough either.

I hunted around for something penetratingly unfrightening to say.

I poked them gently. "Look, either you tell me, or I'll tell everyone that your secret passion is Athenian poetry and if people want to get on your good side, they should insist, no matter your protests, on bringing you to special poetry-writing evenings where everyone gets together and talks about trochaic hexameters. And people will believe it, because you're so sweary and pragmatic: they'll all go, *Aha, so it's a front to hide the soft and fluffy soul within, we knew it all along, we shall henceforth communicate only in epic metaphor.*"

Tiresias laughed as if they hadn't expected to. I saw their shoulders sink a little as they relaxed. "You're a monster, knight, that's the worst thing anyone's ever said to me. Come on."

They took my arm and tilted me away from the crowd, towards the cloister and Semele's shrine, where the ivy was out of control. Offering candles and sacrifices were nestled through it everywhere. The slaves were still out there, trying to collect it all up, but—actually, no. They were *pretending* to collect it up. They were putting things in hessian bags, but then taking them out again and setting them down in different places, expressions tight with the knowledge that if anyone noticed, they would die; they must have decided it was worth dying for. I didn't blame them. They looked very thin indeed. They would die soon anyway.

I wondered if Dionysus knew about this. What did it feel like, to be a god when someone sacrificed to you? He had heard my prayer, or felt it, or something. Was it like someone talking to you? Could he hear an increasingly loud crowd of voices behind everything now, all the time?

"Phaidros," Tiresias said softly, "if anyone thinks you can do magic— even if you and I both know it was very standard witching—then some people will say, you know what else was magic? What happened in the stadium. The masks. The ivy. And who is this Phaidros person anyway? We don't know who his parents are. All we know is that the Queen's brother was his commander and they look rather alike, in some lights. He's young. What if he's the lost prince?"

"What?" I said. It was true, we *did* look alike, but that was because we were both medium-sized dark-haired dark-eyed explosively swearing men in the same armour. "That's stupid."

"And the Queen would still kill you for it," Tiresias said quietly, "because if the lost prince is indeed alive, then he owes her a blood debt for the murder of his mother." They looked towards the courtyard too, and the light fell strangely across them, so that I could see what they'd looked like when they were Pentheus's age. Slim, sharp, long-necked, one of those swan people who never hurried. "I'm not trying to tell you I think it's credible. I'm trying to tell you that if someone were to feel resentful of your frankly meteoric rise at court, *that* is an efficient way to shoot you down. Be very careful."

They were right. I'd been an idiot not to think of it. "Thank you. For warning me."

"I serve the crown," they said, looking exhausted.

"Come and sit with me for a bit; let's pretend to be talking about important things."

"Why?"

"So they won't talk to us about anything else?" I said, feeling increasingly like a real prick for having made them stand up all this time. I was hungry and tired, but I was trained to be hungry and tired, and I was only thirty-one. They were leaning on their cane, and for all they weren't old, they weren't going to see fifty again either. "Tiresias, this news has been in circulation for about an hour and I'm already up to *here* in people asking me for favours and money and jobs; please just tell me something fun about tortoises?"

Tiresias laughed. "You are a ludicrous outdated piece of chivalry that . . ." They trailed off, and something in their expression went glassy.

"Prophet?" I asked, wary.

When they spoke again, it was their voice, but it wasn't them. "Sweet knight, do not lose your faith in holy devices. The messages might have been bought and paid for, and manufactured by human beings, but there is yet holy transmutation in the great machines, and the god will speak true, even when he has been paid to be false."

Tiresias blinked twice. "Right, so, something funny about tortoises. You're in for it, Phaidros. I know a lot of tortoise jokes." They paused. "I feel like you're looking at me funny."

"I—no," I said, not daring to touch it. "Nothing."

The Temple of Apollo was just outside the city. It sat in what was usually a lake, on an island, but there was no water left. The lake bed was baked, and strewn with the bones of fish and eels, and even birds. What had used to be banks of reeds were more like coarse straw heaps now. Around the struts of the ancient causeway, coins and brooches and tiny messages in tiny bottles gleamed dully in the sun: old offerings. The temple itself was so white it was hard to look at in the morning glare. Beyond it, the plain was blasted, and swimming with dust trails. No one, and nothing, was on the road. The green that was engulfing the city inside the walls wasn't here. I watched the Queen. She must have been talking to her advisers, even Tiresias, about why that was and which god they thought had been appeased. An attendant was carrying a basket of pomegranates that had grown overnight in one of the Palace courtyards to give the priests. I wondered what would happen if even the Oracle said, *Sorry, that's the Raver.*

The Queen's retinue was flying the black flag of the royal house, and once we were close, the temple's bronze gates swung open by themselves. As we passed the bronze panelling, I felt the heat ricocheting off it. The edge of my armour was already burning my neck, even though it had been barely a quarter-mile walk under the shade of the canopies eight slaves had kept over us the whole time.

I kept two paces behind her, the same as Pentheus, so that the three of us made a moving triangle with her in the lead. We weren't married yet, and even when we were, I wasn't going to be a reigning king, and I didn't want anyone to imagine for a second that I thought I would be.

She glanced back at me. "Ready?"

I bowed a little and stepped off to the side with the stewards and the Guards while she went on into the sanctuary.

The way it would work, she had explained, was:

The Oracle would receive her in the sanctuary. That was a place only for the supplicant, to hear the official question to the god. That was the theatre side of things.

But there was backstage, too, and I was it. If I waited in the courtyard for long enough, someone would come out—a priest who didn't look anything much to ask me inside for some water, and we would talk, and the point was that he would find out what exactly was behind the official request, and if I could remember how to be amenable enough and charming enough, he might be the way I could find out what the temple knew, and maybe even how they knew it, and what their answer was likely to be.

Like all supplicants had to be, the Queen was dressed in white. As she climbed the steps, the wind pulled at her dress and tugged her hair sideways over her shoulder.

Flash, headache, and I was at Troy again, struggling to put up the tent with Helios in the wind, which was pulling at his hair too. There had been storms and everything had fallen down in the night, and everyone was nervous, because now was the perfect time for the Trojans to raid us while we were in such disarray. And I swear that he looked at me then like I wasn't the child I'd been at the time, but who I was now, staring at him down the passageway of the years.

Although the lake was dry, there were working fountains in the court-yards, and shady cloisters, and trees that were still alive. I sat down on the edge of a fountain, beneath an ancient olive tree, and scooped up a handful of water. I was so thirsty it tasted sweet, as if someone had put honey in it. I let my head bow until the ends of my hair brushed the fountain rim, grateful for a few minutes by myself. I'd been surrounded by endless people since going into the Palace—gods, that was only yesterday morning—and it was amazingly wearing, after being alone for so long. It wasn't the same as the tight-packed total lack of privacy in the legion. There, no one cared about me particularly, or what I was doing. Now, people were watching me all the time.

Pentheus came to have some water too and shot me a look that was full of apology for existing. I flicked some water at him. He flinched and didn't laugh—he didn't understand I was playing, he was reading it as *fuck off*—so I got him in a headlock and wrestled him sideways across my lap, and then he did laugh. I pushed him gently upright. Then, a bit brilliantly, he splashed me back.

"That," said a cheerful voice, "is a superb scar."

I looked around. There was a man sitting not far from me. He was about my age, maybe, but not sea-battered or worn out from living in camps and ships, and light like you can be only when you work indoors. He was dressed in blue; a priest here, then. Short hair. And he was smiling, because there was a scar across his face too, different to mine but just as noticeable.

"So is that," I said, full of approval. I don't like priests who haven't been in the world but he had clearly, thoroughly been in it.

"How'd you get yours?"

"Run over by a chariot. You?"

"Dunno, I had it when the temple got me. I want to think it's something good like a chariot but probably I just annoyed a cat."

I laughed. "I'm Phaidros."

He gave me a sideways look and smiled. "Very appropriate," he said, pointing upwards to the sky.

We give our gods titles. Apollo is almost always called Phoibos Apollo, "Shining Apollo," which comes from the same word as Phaidros. Anything that's phai or phoi is to do with light.

"Me too," he said.

"Sorry?"

"Phaidros. Is my name as well. That's why the temple adopted me. Would you like to come inside? It's a bit cooler."

"Can I bring this other unobtrusive and manageably sized human also?" I said about Pentheus, who smiled.

"Of course."

I followed him gratefully. He was right, it was cooler inside, and when he showed me to a marble table inside the cloister, the surface of it was nearly cold. I put my arms flat to it and felt like I might die happy. Pentheus sat down silently in the window, which was wide and unshuttered, just one step up from what had used to be a flower bed below. It made him look like he wanted a straightforward escape.

"How are you finding it at the Palace?" Other Phaidros asked as he poured us both some wine. I passed my cup back to Pentheus, and Other Phaidros held his hands up to say he'd just realized that of course knights couldn't have wine. He gave me water instead. "It must be a change from the legion."

"It is a change from the legion." I paused, because I did understand what he was asking: whether I was happy to tell him a few things about the Palace, on the understanding that he might be able to tell me a few useful things back, now or later. Whether it would be worth my while for us to be intelligence friends. "I'm worried about this grain deal with Egypt. If it falls through, then we'll have to go raiding."

None of that was secret. That Pentheus didn't want to go to Egypt was public knowledge, at least at court: Other Phaidros would have heard it before, but it was still true. All I had to do here was be honest without handing over unnecessary information. His work now would be to try and edge me towards more, and mine was to push back, politely. I liked things like that. It was subtle and delicate, and it was the nearest to dancing I could decently go.

In the window, Pentheus had tightened as if I'd pointed at him and said, *This useless fucker won't do as he's told.* I made an internal note to give him some translation lessons. He was right, people didn't always say what they meant, but assuming that they *never* did, and that when I spoke about factual strategic problems I was criticising him personally, was just as counterproductive as taking everyone precisely at their word.

"Go to Athens," Phaidros suggested, "Athens is a hell pit."

I love priests who don't talk like priests. There are two kinds, in my experience: boys made of elbows who spent a lot of their time being bullied, and who signed up with the nearest sanctuary to talk loudly about How I Am Growing Under the Eye of Apollo in order to convince everyone they weren't doing it purely because they'd given up on trying to interact with other humans; and priests who were genuinely cut out for it, and managed to be holy but ordinary at the same time in that fine balance that always reminded me of a well-made sword. "My first choice too. Have you been?"

"I don't know." He looked into his wine like he was hoping to consult it for helpful images. "I think maybe I did once, before I was given to the sanctuary. I remember . . . being somewhere with no women on the street. It was scary."

"That's the one. Better off if it was a hole in ground."

"Khaire," he said, and touched our cups together. "Well, good luck."

"Thanks if you don't tell *their* Temple of Apollo."

"Bunch of bastards," he said easily. "So. The Queen is here to ask the god about your bloodline. There's no record of it?"

"No. I'm from the Furies, they were all over the place. Sometimes my commander said I was the son of a noble lady but I honestly I think he found me in a swamp somewhere in Egypt."

He snorted, and so did Pentheus. "So your commander was Helios Artemiades. The Queen's brother. Do you think you could be his son? I mean his blood son."

"No, he didn't have any children, even unofficial ones. He was a real knight. I'd stake my life on it."

"Mm." He was looking at my armour as if something about it was troubling. He didn't say what. "Did you ever have siblings—other knights, whose commander he was?"

"No, there's only ever one."

"Sorry. I meant before you, boys before you."

"He . . . no, I don't think so. He was only fifteen when he got me, he wouldn't have been assigned a ward before then—fifteen was pushing it, even in those days. I was the first. Or he never mentioned anyone else."

Other Phaidros was quiet for what felt like a long time. "And that's his armour."

"Yes."

"Ares on the front. Persephone on the back," he said. "Be like Persephone. Always negotiate."

"Yes," I said, more slowly, wondering how he knew that. It was a known thing in the legion, but I wouldn't have expected a random priest to know it any more than he would have expected me to speak Old Cretan.

"How did he die?" he asked abruptly.

"He was killed in battle ten years ago."

"But how?"

"He was shot by a Trojan general. Andromache."

Recognition ghosted over his face, the puzzled kind. "There's a Princess Andromache the bards mention. But she was just the prince's wife."

I shook my head. "Our generals ordered the bards never to tell the real story, it was too demoralising. She hunted Achaean officers, she killed dozens. It's in the name. Andro mache, fighter of warriors? That isn't her real name, that's just what we called her. Her real name was something Hatti."

"Did you get revenge?"

"Yes. Nine years later, but—yes." I felt like I was lying to say it, though it was true. "I said, 'You killed my commander,' and she said, 'If you say so,' I threw her off a balcony, and that was anticlimactically that. You sound like you knew him. Helios I mean."

He didn't seem to hear the last part. "I see." He sounded tight and strange, and not at all as though he had asked from general interest. "I need to show you something." He put a knife on the table.

It was a fantastic piece of work. Like my armour, the bronze was worked with a scene in silver: Hades leading Persephone down to the underworld, Persephone holding a pomegranate. Down the length of the blade, lost souls wandered, and right at the end was the hint of the Ferryman's boat.

"Is that his?" Other Phaidros asked.

"It is," I said, delighted, and perplexed. I looped the cord of my seal bead over my head and held it out so he could see. It was exactly the same design. "That's the sigil of our combat lineage. But I don't think I've seen—where did you get this?"

"I don't remember. It was left here at the temple with me, when I was little."

In the window, Pentheus looked over properly for the first time. I held the knife out so he could see.

"It is, right?" I said, because he knew all the sigils of all the Sown lineages as well as I did.

"Yes," he said, then gave it back. "How strange. Maybe it was stolen."

"Or maybe he picked up a foundling on the road and left that to say who to ask about it all, later," I said. Helios was a prince: it was just part of his duty to sponsor temple orphans—although maybe not to leave something so valuable. It was odd the temple hadn't sold it. "Did you ever go and find him?" I asked the priest.

He shook his head. "No. No, the Oracle . . . I was advised against involving myself in the House of Kadmus."

"Probably sensible," I said, disappointed. I'd wanted a story about Helios I didn't know.

"Well. Thank you." He stood up. Talk over.

I stood up too, uncertain, because I still didn't understand why he had asked me those questions, none of which seemed to have anything to do with who my parents might have been. He saw me to the door, and I thought he might do that old trick where he asked his last and most vital question after an "oh, by the way, before I forget . . ." He didn't, though. I'd been prepared for a lot, but not just to leave with no idea what was going on. The way Pentheus twisted his nose at me, though, said that this was only normal.

As we left, I looked back, and I was sure the priest—sitting at the table again, the lovely knife between his hands—was crying.

The Queen was outside again by the time I came out, facing into the wind, towards the Fury marvels. We couldn't see them from here, but they were audible. They were still screaming their warning.

"How was it?" she asked me.

"I think I upset him," I said bleakly.

"Is it because you told him you were going to make him eat his own lungs?"

"I told him about murdering a Trojan general," I mumbled.

She wrinkled her nose. "*Murdering* is a strong word; is it murder, at war? What did you do? Is this Andromache?"

"I . . . threw her off a balcony and left the body outside the city wall to be eaten by wild dogs."

"Gods, Phaidros."

"I know! I know—"

"What had those dogs ever done to you?"

"Ah," I said, basking in relief. On my other side, Pentheus made a snorking noise. "What happens now?"

She nodded slightly. "We wait. It's usually an hour or so."

We all looked at the holy calendar ticking on its waist-high column in the middle of the courtyard. They were the most sophisticated marvels I'd seen, and it had been a bit of a revelation to me when I came back to Thebes and first realized that they were how people knew when the festivals were going to fall, and how the hours were measured. I'd always thought an hour was just a shortish spell of time that meant "a little while," but it didn't at all. It was exact, and these were the machines that said so. This one was a cube, filled with clockwork that you could see through the patterned fretwork in the sides, and dials, and jewels, and little figures and spinning bands etched with constellations. It measured hours, and days, and months, and years. It could tell you what time the Oracle Games should begin fifty years from now.

The hour marker seemed like it was moving very slowly.

"You asked me a few days ago about what happens if someone puts on a god mask," the Queen said. "Would you like to see?"

I looked at her properly. "That—lady, tell me there isn't someone in a cellar in an Apollo mask," I said softly. "What if—"

She was shaking her head. "It's all right. Come and see."

It wasn't a cellar. It was a pretty room inside the sanctuary, one where a priest must usually have lived. There was a desk and a chair and a wide window with a nice view of an inner courtyard, and a huge stripey cat that said hello to us as we came in, and an indigo cloak draped over the back of a couch, and scrolls everywhere. And, reading one in a sunbeam, was someone in a bronze mask of the god. The mask had a laurel crown and curly hair worked in gold. Under it, the man's hair was gold too, the kind of gold nobody has really. Not red, like the north islanders, and not that drab grey colour people had in Scythia and the Tin Isles: it glowed in the sun. I stopped, wanting not to go one step closer, but the Queen squeezed my elbow.

"Good morning, sir," she said to the masked figure. "How goes it today?"

"Oh, good morning, lady," he said, and I jolted backwards, just by a tiny fraction, because he didn't sound like a person. He sounded like Dionysus did when he wasn't pretending not to be who he was: like harp strings, and whole choirs. It was beautiful, and frightening. He lifted his head and saw me, and seemed interested even through the mask. "Ah. Who's this?"

"Do you think you can guess?" she asked.

He shook his head. "I'm still no prophet, lady. Although—you do look awfully familiar."

"He looks like Helios sometimes," Pentheus offered.

I wondered how he knew what Helios looked like.

"No . . ." the masked man said, sounding a little frustrated he couldn't place me. "Never mind."

"We're waiting to see if the mask will bring any deeper qualities of the god," the Queen explained. "He started to *look* like Apollo very quickly. Tiresias put the mask on him immediately after the witches had their success with the knights. So far, there's been nothing else. No ability to prophesy, no particular affinity with a bow, nor a lyre. Any change at all?" she added to the masked man.

"Not that I'm aware of," he said, and under the eerie Apollo voice, I could hear the scholar he really was. "I keep trying with the bow, but I couldn't hit a target to save my life. Lots of dreams, but I think all of us have been having strange dreams. A forest, and a great Hunt, and . . . a man who's also a lion."

Pentheus looked uncomfortable.

"The Hunt, of course, is sacred to the Raver," Not Apollo added.

"Artemis is the god of the Hunt," the Queen said.

He tilted up a scroll. "Of hunting, now. I mean *the* Hunt. The old way, before cities. Before the taming of the herds, and farming, and harvest. Very old god, this one. Tends only to appear when things are terrible anyway. You know. Famine, drought, falling cities; he isn't, contrary to what you might imagine given the alcohol business, a god for good times." He shrugged, and somehow it was clear he was smiling a bit even under the mask. "Hard to tell what he is, really; the collection of things is quite strange. Music, dance—but not music like Apollo's—holy trances, stories, masks, wine, madness, bees, ivy, the auroch. I've got a scrap of an old manuscript here that calls him He of the Trees, and Polyeidos." *Many-formed.* "Difficult to pin down, isn't he?"

All that was blue. I could see it but not quite grip onto why.

"General chaos," the Queen said.

"Chaos, yes," Not Apollo murmured. "But not always. A cup of wine isn't chaos, and nor is a nice story. It's more to do with . . . what . . . all of those things *do*. For people, I mean."

Yes. Gods care what's *happening.*

"The position of the crown," Pentheus said carefully, "is that there is no such god."

"No, well, I see why you have to say that, what with usurpers and the lost prince and so forth," Not Apollo said. "But . . . you can't deny any more that he *is* here. The Kadmeia is so bound in ivy that it grows faster than the slaves can cut it back, everyone says. That isn't Apollo, I'm afraid. Nor is the magic of the masks, nor the madness."

There was a certain freedom, I thought, in being locked in a room with four Guards. Nothing he said would leave, so he could say what he liked.

"What does he want, do you think?" the Queen said quietly.

I made an effort not to look at her, and not to show that I'd noticed this was the first time she had even come close to admitting that there really might be a mad god.

"Want?" He sounded sceptical. "I couldn't speak to his *desire*, but what he *does* will become more and more intense, because it's like drinking more and more wine, until what comes is the holy raving."

"Would sacrifice stop it?"

"No." He laughed. "You might as well pray to wine not to make you drunk, it isn't the nature of wine."

"Well," she said. "Thank you, sir, it was interesting to speak to you."

We left in silence, and in his sunbeam, Not Apollo went contentedly back to his manuscripts. I looked back at the door, though, and as I did, I caught him looking at me. There was something quizzical about the tilt of his head.

"Oh, *that's* right," he said, to himself, not me. "The steersman. No wonder."

The Queen was waiting for me a few paces ahead. "Phaidros? You look like you've seen a ghost."

I felt cold and prickly. "What he said about the holy raving."

She paused. "I know. I know. But . . . here's . . . what I think. The madness began when the rations went down. I think it might lift once they go up again. And once we have that grain—which will be tonight—we can supply ships. There can be raiding again. Whatever this is, whether it is this old god of madness and the Hunt, or just the displeasure of our own gods—it seems to be a function of crisis. Get rid of the crisis, and the rest will go too. Is it now?" she added, because an acolyte in indigo had stopped near us and bowed.

"It is, lady. The Oracle will speak to you now."

I looked back for Pentheus, who was giving me a speculative look. He didn't say why, though, and only fell into step with me behind the Queen.

We walked slowly down the length of the long hall, towards the altar; the Queen ahead, and Pentheus and me behind. He looped his arm through mine, more like a grown-up—more like a knight—with every passing hour.

He smiled at last. "You know, you do sound like Helios. Not just distantly, I mean really like. If I shut my eyes I'd think you *were* him."

"When did you meet Helios?"

"He came back to Thebes when I was little. He was kind."

"Oh, right," I said, not convinced Pentheus could possibly remember him properly, given that I barely did, but not wanting to say that. "Tiresias said that. I can't hear it."

"You even look like him."

"Dogs look like their owners," I agreed.

He pushed me, and laughed when I pushed him back.

The Queen glanced back, and although I had argued with her before, she looked at least halfway to pleased, and I realized that even if she didn't feel she could act on it, she did prefer it a great deal when Pentheus was happy. As we drew near to the altar, I looked between the two of them. I hadn't had any family for ten years, and I'd forgotten what it was like. I didn't know them, either of them, but it didn't matter. I belonged to someone and although it wouldn't last for long, I was glad to have it for now. Despite that, I could hear my heart again.

Where are you, where are you.

On the dais behind the altar, the sacred fire flared, and a glorious marvel of Apollo, twice life-sized, opened its hands, and the moving bronze was silent even as the joints and hinges worked. When it spoke, its voice was echoey and golden from the chambers of the holy devices hidden inside, not human, though somewhere, of course, it would be the Oracle talking. I stared up at the marvel. A few days ago, this would have been holy. It was older than the Furies outside the walls, older than Thebes, probably, maintained down the centuries by priest-smiths sworn to never to tell anyone outside their order how the mechanisms worked, if they even knew themselves. And somewhere in that clockwork, sometimes—or I'd thought so—moving those fine bronze springs in the same way he had once moved matter to make human beings, would be Apollo. I'd used to feel that sometimes there was something mighty here in these holy machines.

Tiresias's voice came back to me. *There is yet holy transmutation in the great machines, and the god will speak true, even when he has been paid to be false.*

No; they must have just said that to make me feel better. They must have, because the alternative was that Apollo was actually talking to me, and that was . . . somewhere between ridiculous and cosmically arrogant.

Whoever was speaking through the marvel breathed in, and it sang through the mechanisms.

"*Agave of Thebes, Shining Apollo greets you, and answers your question. In marrying this man, you both condemn yourself to and save yourself from the prophecy of the boy who should have been king.*"

The silence was so deep I could hear the slaves behind us breathing. When I looked at the Queen, trying to tell if she understood, I caught her giving me exactly the same look; and the slaves; and the Guards. But you can't ask the Oracle what the message means.

The only person who didn't look confused was Pentheus.

"Did you understand that?" I asked him.

He was quiet at first, and then he leaned up, close enough that he had to hold my shoulder. "They mean it's you," he whispered. "They think you're the lost prince."

30

We were supposed to go back to the Palace, but Pentheus took hold of my elbow and said with an authority I'd not heard from him before that we were going out for a little while. The Guards looked perturbed and four of them came with us, without the purple cloaks, so that they might have been slaves, not that they were fooling anyone. Pentheus was dressed like a king in waiting. He took a pair of horses from some grooms at the gatehouse of the city wall.

"Where are we going?" I asked, confused.

"To see a witch," he said, and the second I was mounted too, he urged his horse away, to the mountain road, where there were no real houses. Only the maze.

"Pentheus, wait, this isn't . . ." I broke off coughing, because there was so much dust in the air from the horse's hooves, and the wind.

All I could do was ride after him.

It was with a gathering dread that I followed his dust trail up the slim path. This wasn't my usual way up—it was further east, and steeper. I went slower than he did, worried about the horse, who was a thoroughbred, but streaming sweat before we were halfway. It was the middle of the day, too hot to be moving anywhere fast. Before the end, I dismounted. I'd never run a horse to collapse and I wasn't going to start now. Every extra second dragged like hours. I wanted to just get up there and get it over with. Whatever *it* was. I didn't know any more. Fire, madness, an almighty row. The way I'd left, in such absolute pissing righteousness . . . I wished I could melt into the rocks.

I'd never come up to the maze from this angle before, and I was surprised by how much of it there was before I reached the familiar riot of flowers that marked Dionysus's garden. I tethered the horse in a shady patch where there was still some grass, and climbed the last, eroded stairway.

Pentheus must have slowed down at the end too, because he was just dismounting beside a huge spill of wisteria, and looking back for me.

"Pentheus, you've got it wrong," I said, scanning around for Dionysus. The coward in me hoped he was out. "I'm not—"

"It doesn't matter! They *think* you are—"

"—and the man here is not going to want to help me. I know him, I live along from here, he was with me when I found you. He didn't want me to take you back to the Palace, so we fought, I mean really fought, I hurt him—"

"Probably you should apologise to him then," Pentheus said, undisturbed. "We need advice, and not from anyone at court. Dionysus is new in Thebes, and he has deinos magic. Tell me who better to go to?"

"How do you know who he is?" I asked, because he hadn't mentioned Dionysus when the Queen asked him what had happened after the star fell. "Or where he lives?"

"He saved you at the bull sacrifice ceremony, remember?"

"I remember, but I thought you didn't."

"Yes, well, you'll learn it's a good idea to curate whose name you give to the Queen if you want them to live for very long," he said dryly. "And he told me where he lives. Hello?" he shouted across the ruin. For the first time since I'd met him, he put some power in his voice. He wasn't afraid of being heard any more.

I jumped when something dropped out of the tree next to me. It was a basket of grapes. I looked up. Dionysus was sitting in the fork of a branch. The tree was wound about with grape vines, and he had been harvesting them. Even if I had looked straight up at him before, I wouldn't have seen him. The shadows and the light made him look like he belonged to the tree. His hair was bound up with its green cloth, and around him, ivy writhed the same green.

He didn't come down. "What's this about advice?"

"Apparently the two of you have met?" Pentheus asked him.

Oh, gods, he was an *apparently* person now. I shouldn't have noticed, it was the last thing that could ever possibly be important, but it was reflex.

Dionysus was resting his head against the tree trunk as though he was half listening to things the dryad inside was whispering. "You look different."

"Phaidros took the magic away."

Dionysus's eyes slipped to me again. "Phaidros should take the Witches' Vow soon, then."

I let my breath out. "Phaidros is . . . very much regretting all of it."

"And you're here to present me with a special Dionysus Was Right cake?" he asked, and I couldn't tell if he was joking because he forgave me or because he didn't.

"We've just come from Apollo," Pentheus explained. "The Queen wanted to find out his blood lineage for the marriage, and the oracle said—"

"Marriage?" said Dionysus, sharp.

"She asked me," I said, struggling against the need to apologise to him for agreeing. After everything he had said, it felt like I was doing it to spite him.

"He'll be a good king," said Pentheus, as if that was a normal thing to say about a person. Dionysus was looking at me hard, and I wished we could have this conversation without a teenager between us. "Anyway, the oracle said to my mother, *In marrying this man, you both condemn yourself to and save yourself from the prophecy of the boy who should have been king.* It means Phaidros is the lost prince. The Queen doesn't know, yet. I came to ask you: how do we keep it that way?"

"It doesn't mean that," I said wearily. "It's just—"

Dionysus came down. He did it cat-silent. I don't think he broke a single leaf. He looked exhausted. "Come inside and you can both say what you think."

It had been years since I'd tried to speak and been this thoroughly ignored. "We don't need to—"

Pentheus wasn't going to be left out. "He *is*—"

315

"You're here now," Dionysus said over us, and in another sharp, point-less *apparently* flash, I noticed that his accent was stronger when he was irritated. "I'm not standing out in the sun listening to a shouting match. Hurry up."

I glanced at Pentheus and he looked as awkwardly chastised as I felt. We both bowed a little and did as we were told.

I had never been inside Dionysus's part of the ruin, only the old stair-ways and gardens outside. I expected it to be much the same as my side, but I was wrong. The livable parts, here, were not above ground, but under. He led us down a stairway almost fully carpeted in moss, into a set of vaulted chambers where the light speared down through skylights, and the roots of the trees flooded down the walls. There were plants and flowers everywhere, some in pots, some growing through the walls. In comparison to the blazing afternoon, it was dim down here. As he came in, all the lamps—dozens, delicate glass things hanging among the flowers—lit themselves.

In the centre of the chamber was a fountain. It must have been fed by a deep spring, because the water was incredibly clear, and very cold. He gave us each a cup, and then sat down on the fountain's edge to let Pentheus and me sit together on the couch opposite. What I'd thought was a cushion sat up and turned out to be a leopard, looking annoyed.

"She'll not hurt anyone," Dionysus said. She jumped up onto the foun-tain beside him and sprawled half in his lap, purring.

"How?" Pentheus said, looking daunted.

Dionysus didn't smile. I had to shove down the need to turn straight back around and leave. It shouldn't have mattered that he didn't want to see us—I'd spent my whole life breaking into the houses of people who didn't want to see me—but it was horrible to sit with him like this exactly because that was what I'd always done. I felt like a raider again, and like he was one of those rare people who, upon seeing the city burning and the priestesses falling from the tower, don't run, but open their doors and say to the blood-soaked maniac outside, *Come in, you must be exhausted, my house is your house.* When I was young I'd thought those people were cowards, because nothing's stopping you taking them into slavery and stealing all their things, but that isn't how it goes, if they walk the line between unafraid and polite. It's witchcraft. You end up sitting on someone's couch and telling them how you grew up over a plate of cakes served with tiny silver tongs, not wrecking anything or kidnapping anybody, because after months and months of living in a tent and never being clean, all you want is to feel, briefly, like a human.

Even though you know, and they know, that you're nine-tenths vindictive bloodthirsty animal by this point. There must be a word for that, somewhere: that weird double lie you both perform when you both know something terrible is true but you both pretend it isn't because it makes life fractionally more bearable just now.

I felt like there was blood in my hair.

"Witching," Dionysus said, with none of his normal joy in it. "So, what's happening and why does it involve me?" He didn't have to say, *Given that you don't give a fuck about what I think.*

"Pentheus wanted to come," I said, anaemically.

His eyebrow flickered. Again, he didn't say, *You didn't care what Pentheus might want yesterday.* I wished he would. Hearing what he wasn't saying clang around in my head was much worse than hearing him say it aloud.

Pentheus didn't seem to realize he was suddenly sitting in Arctic conditions.

"We went to consult Apollo about Phaidros's bloodline," he explained, "and the Oracle said to the Queen, *in marrying this man you condemn yourself to and save yourself from the prophecy of the boy who should have been king.* It means Phaidros is the lost prince. And now we don't know what to do, because if she puts it together like that, she's going to kill him."

I took a breath to argue and Pentheus, preemptively, did as well.

"No, it means the Queen paid them to say that," Dionysus said over us both.

"What?" Pentheus and I said together. It would have been funny on an ordinary day.

"Apollo doesn't go around having opinions about the blood lineage of Theban knights," Dionysus said, looking tired. "It's in her interest. Lost heir restored. End of debate. No civil war required."

"No," Pentheus said, "because if it's true then Phaidros owes her a blood debt. She murdered her sister. Everyone knows she did. And anyway, he wouldn't *need* to marry her to be king, he could just be king!"

I realized suddenly that he sounded more excited by that than afraid. I stared at the leopard to keep from staring at him. If he hated her this much, no wonder she had decided to send him to Egypt. He was seventeen and coltish now, but in two years, or five?

I saw Dionysus catch it too, and I saw him—thank the gods—decide to pour cold water on it.

"Phaidros would have to believe he was the lost prince for that to matter, and he doesn't," Dionysus pointed out. "All this does is consolidate power. It's fine. Go home."

"You'll bet his life on it?"

"Sure," said Dionysus, quite slowly, with a lift that could have meant either *Trust your witch, please* or *I don't care that much about his life lately.*

"No, but he *could* be the prince," Pentheus pushed. "He could be. He looks *just* like Helios."

"I'd have to be twenty-seven," I said. "That's silly. Look at me."

"And since when can any of us accurately judge ages to within ten years?" Pentheus said, with enraging placidity. "You've been through a war and famines and you've had a horrendous life, you could easily be twenty-seven. Who's that poor knight in the garrison with grey hair who always looks like he's seeing the gates of Hades? He looks a decade older than he is. As for you," he said to Dionysus, sort of laughing. "Gods alive, you could be twenty or forty."

But probably twenty-seven. Or at least, the man was; Olympus knew how old the god was. I wondered how that worked. Was it dying and rebirth, or did he just flit between humans in the same way he could flit between animals? Had he been *born* exactly, or had he just, well, *arrived* for a look around in a form that didn't have its own soul yet, and then stuck with this particular body because interesting things kept happening around it and probably he wasn't going to find a better one anyway?

"Helios did not lie to me for fifteen years," I said. "Come on, Pentheus, we're leaving. Witches have more to do than talk to idiots like us, there will be mothers in labour waiting."

Pentheus ignored me, and I let my neck bend, frustrated, because I couldn't just drag him down the mountain this time. Dionysus's eyes caught across me with a flint-strike spark. He was not, of course, going to help me.

"My mother told me," Pentheus said, clear and level, "that Helios came to see her on the night of the fire, when the lost prince vanished. You were there. Or, his ward was."

Dionysus looked interested. "You were there?"

Fantastic. He wasn't even going to be neutral; he was going for active sabotage.

I sat straight and tried to set my mind into its night-watch gears: the ones that let you sit and wait, usually in the rain, for hours. And I would just have to sit here and wait. I couldn't leave without Pentheus. There were no Guards with us. All of Thebes knew what he looked like, and an increasing portion of Thebes was desperate. Everything we had thought had happened to him before—kidnap, ransom—could still happen. From here to the Palace was about three miles. That was a long way, for a young man alone and untrained.

"Tiny Phaidros met the new prince, who was a baby. You played, it was funny."

"I remember," I said to the far wall.

"You don't think that's odd?" Pentheus said, tipping his head. "Nobody clearly remembers being four. Are you remembering what happened, or just what Helios told you?"

"If you call Helios a liar again," I said, something very deep down in my clockwork creaking and hurting, "I will hit you."

Dionysus shifted uneasily.

"He *was* a liar," Pentheus said, laughing a bit. "He was known for it. Even my mother calls him Helios Polytropos."

I was just going to have to stare at a wall until it was over. Helios laughed in my memory. *Find the lady, tiny knight! Round and round she goes . . .* I'd loved that game.

"That night, the lightning struck," Pentheus ploughed on, "and Princess Semele conveniently exploded. My mother made sure she did. The baby belonged to the King."

"Did she tell you that?" I asked.

"No, but I've met my mother," he said. He turned back to Dionysus; that was who he was really talking to, which was grating on me, because it made it seem like he didn't think I was bright enough to understand. "Then, the baby disappears. So does Helios, and his ward. My mother

319

always thought Helios took the baby. She thought he took it to a temple somewhere, and she had all the temples searched for a child of the right age. They were all brought to her, about a hundred boys, but she never found the right one. Eventually, she realized he must have taken it back to the legion with him. She sent people after him, but they never found anything, and he never said what he'd done. When he came back to Thebes—I was six, I suppose this was just before Troy—they had a huge row about it."

I frowned. "They did?"

"She said he had undermined the royal line. He swore to her he had no idea what had happened, and that he'd fled Thebes because he didn't want to be caught up in any of it. I mean he got down on his knees and swore on his oath," Pentheus said, looking hard at me, and I realized he was daring me, now, to say that Helios wouldn't have lied. "I don't know how he did it or how he hid you, but Phaidros, you look like him. I can remember him as clear as the morning."

"Or are you just remembering what someone else told you?" I said vengefully.

"Nobody tells me anything about my childhood," Pentheus said. It could have sounded plaintive, but his tone was dry and factual. "I'll always remember him. It was spring, there was apple blossom everywhere. I'd never seen armour like his. I was scared of him at first, but he saw my tutor getting angry with me, and he rescued me, and we stole some pomegranates from the orchard together, and he told me fairy tales." He tipped his head. "I remember I asked him why he was being nice to me, and what he did want, and he looked at me like—I don't know. Like he'd just seen me lose an arm. When he took me back to my tutors, he told them I'd said that, and he was *furious*. He put the fear of Zeus into them. Still not sure why," he reflected. "I was getting a perfectly reasonable education, and my mother told him he was being hysterical, but . . . I felt like Ares himself was on my side for the day." He delivered that in the same slow, thoughtful way as before. "So yes. I remember him very well indeed."

I'd wanted to find something inaccurate in that to pounce on, but there was nothing. In fact, it dovetailed very well with what *I* remembered.

Helios had still been furious when he came home again. We had been posted on the Nile, and it was swampy and cold and I'd never been so overjoyed to see anyone—I'd convinced myself he had died at sea—and that night, even though we were already hovering around our you're-too-young-for-me fight, I snugged up next to him at dinner and he let me, his cloak around us both.

"Something wrong?" I'd asked, because he seemed honestly glad of it.

"No. Nothing." But he'd winced. "I'm lying. Sorry. It's just—Agave's little boy. It's horrible. He's going to kill someone one day."

In the context of a legion encampment getting ready to siege an Egyptian fortress, that had sounded odd. "He'll make a good knight then."

"Knights are a nemesis to our enemies and a blessing to our friends," he said seriously. "But the way they treat that little boy . . . he's going to be a nemesis to everyone."

I frowned then, because I didn't understand, but I was getting good at knowing how to not understand things. I spoke bits of four languages by then, and that gives you a long, long patience for what you don't understand. It would make sense eventually, once I'd been in it enough. Instead of asking him to explain something he probably couldn't, I poured him some water and fetched us both some more bread from the clay ovens, and when I came back, he hugged me so hard it hurt along the scars from the recent Delicious Phaidros incident. Helios had killed the crocodile to get me back, but unspoken between us was that he'd left for Thebes when he had because he needed a few months of not being responsible for a moron who, upon finding a log with eyes, poked it with a stick.

"I love you, dore." Blessing.

"Are you having a stroke?" I'd said.

In Dionysus's chamber under the maze, the leopard lashed its tail to and fro and snapped at a tiny bird that had flown through the gap in the ceiling to drink from the fountain. Dionysus was giving me one of those long looks that I was still wasn't used to, the ones that read all my thoughts etched onto the inside of my skull.

"Do you remember anything about the baby?" he asked, and I had that weird between-two-mirrors feeling again, because I would have sworn he was daring me to say, *of course I do, and you know, he had blue eyes too.*

"Helios did take him," I said, still partially stuck back on the Nile in the camp with that bread still too hot from the oven and one knee cold where Helios's cloak didn't cover it. "But he didn't bring the baby with us to the legion. He vanished for a while, he left me at a temple, but he came back, and . . . I don't remember the journey. I just remember being at home in our tent. That was in Phoenicia somewhere. Where there was definitely no baby."

"Apollo above, I know what happened," Pentheus said suddenly.

"No, you don't," I said, my springs starting to shriek.

The leopard sprang down and pushed its head against my knee. Dionysus trying to make sure I didn't murder anyone. I stroked the leopard's head and its purred and batted companionably at the leather strips that made up my kilt, though it was Dionysus who half-closed his eyes.

"He *swapped* you," Pentheus exclaimed. "Of *course* he wouldn't make it across the country with a child and a toddler, not with the Hidden out looking for him! He left *his* Phaidros at Apollo, and took the baby. The baby was his nephew, it was his duty to protect his own blood, not to mention the royal line." He was all alight. "Phaidros, that's why you don't remember the journey! You were too tiny to remember much at all! And *that's* why the priest at Apollo has Helios's knife!"

The leopard shoved its head under my hand again.

Worse than unwanted, the memory of that terrible row I'd had with Helios when I was nineteen came back. *You're too young! You're too young . . .*

What if I really had been? What if I hadn't been nineteen at all?

"But the legion would have noticed," Dionysus said, and with a distant sort of smugness I realized he was regretting having started all this. "That he left with a child of four and came back with a baby of . . . how old?" he asked me.

"Eighteen months maybe," I said, staring into the past.

I'd been small for my age for so long. It was why he'd kept me off the line. I'd always thought it was because of the famine years.

No, it *was* because of the famine years.

"No, but that's why it's clever!" Pentheus insisted. "He went back to a *different* unit! He came here from Egypt. You just said you went back to Phoenicia, Phaidros. That's the other side of the world! Think about it: it would have taken him about three months to get there at that time of year, and even when he did get there, who was going to know? They would have said, 'Goodness, your ward's a bit young isn't he,' and all he would have had to say is, 'Tell me about it, society is broken,' and that would have been that—"

"Pentheus," I ground out. "Please shut up. That didn't happen."

"But think about—"

"I was not *married* to my *uncle*."

Pentheus gave me a shining, tone-deaf look full of triumph. "There were never going to be children, though so . . . would it really have mattered?"

I slapped him so hard it snapped his head to the side. The leopard jumped, startled, and Dionysus lunged across to catch me in a bear hug before I could do anything worse, which was just as well, because I would have.

"All right! It's all right," he said, I think to both of us. He had got behind me, his arm locked over my chest, pressing me back against his. "Enough. Pentheus—anything broken?"

Pentheus was silent, and very still. The side of his face was bright red. Nobody would ever have hit him before. He pulled his sleeve over his mouth. Nothing was broken. He wasn't even bleeding.

"Are you going to apologise?" he asked me stiffly.

"No. I'm going to gouge your eyes out with your fucking tunic pins," I explained.

Pentheus snatched up his horse's reins and ran back outside.

I didn't care. He fucking deserved it and frankly I would have felt better if I could have catapulted him off a building.

Dionysus didn't let me go, sensibly. "He was just trying to help you, knight, he's worried his mother will kill you."

"I could live with him expressing his concern *some other fucking way*," I snarled, rising towards the end so Pentheus would hear it where he was running up the steps.

"And he will, you'll teach him, but not if you beat him into sludge first. Sludge is generally a slow learner."

It should have been stifling, but being trapped against him with his arms crossed over my ribs was—safe. All the razor edges of everything were dulling down again. "Helios didn't," I said. "He didn't do any of that."

There is yet holy transmutation in the great machines, and the god will speak true, even when he has been paid to be false.

No no no, shut up shut up shut up.

"No. But I think you have a story that could be convincing in very dim light." Dionysus put his head against mine. He was holding my wrist now over the red string and the bee charm. His fingers were a joint longer than mine and he could circle it comfortably, which made me look— despite all the scars that went up to my elbows, and the sword hilt calluses on my hands—strangely delicate. "I think the Queen approached you because of it. If you can't stop people making up rumours about a lost prince and the son of a god, channel them towards someone whose loyalty you already have. It's what I'd have done."

I was finally breathing more normally again, and the horrible blind rage was almost gone. I felt like I was coming up from a fever. I had to squeeze my eyes shut, though, because now I could think again, I couldn't tell if he was agreeing with me because he thought I was right, or because he just wanted me to calm down. "You don't think she's going to kill me then?"

"Not over this."

I went slack so he would know he could let me go. When he did, I sat away from him, and put my hands over my face. "I'm sorry," I said. Fuck, what had I done? Pentheus wasn't a knight. A punch in the eye wasn't a normal way of saying "I disapprove" for him. For him it was . . . what even was it? How was he translating that? Probably that I really did mean to stab his eyes out with his tunic pins.

Dionysus was straight and still, though the leopard came around to nudge itself between my knees to make me stroke it again. I did. After a little while, Dionysus poured us both some wine and gave me a cup. I took it and touched the cups together. The wine was cool, and a mouthful of winter.

"Thank you," I said. That I was supposed to refuse seemed like a very long ago, distant thing now, and strangely childish.

"Phaidros . . . you're sitting here asking me if I think she's going to kill you. This is not what a marriage should be."

"For gods' sake, Dionysus, duty is honour."

"When you say duty is honour," he said, "it always sounds amazingly like *suffering* is honour."

"Oh, fuck off," I growled.

As always, he ignored what I'd said in favour of his unshakeable, unevidenced, unhinged, but completely correct belief that I didn't mean anything bad. "Suffering doesn't make people good or noble. A little bit gives them perspective. A lot turns them cruel, and too much—you get a murderer or a marvel, and neither of those are really people any more."

"I know what you think, but I don't know how to explain to you that it doesn't matter," I said, ragged now. "I can't leave behind my duty any more than I can leave behind my arms, it's part of me. That's just what this is, it's what being Sown is—"

"It matters to me," he said over me, but not loudly. He could cast the smoke in his voice under and around anything else.

I looked across at him. "You don't need to witch me."

He kissed my cheek, so light it was just a scratch. I couldn't move at first, honey-suspended again, and when I could, it was only just enough to do the same. When he touched my throat and guided me closer, it wasn't the kind of kiss I was used to. I was used to the rage-lust you get from battle and from being covered in blood and frost and dirt, and zinging with victory. It was the most careful anyone had ever been with me.

He drew his thumb across my cheek. I didn't know I was crying until he did that.

"Don't go back," he said. "Come away. We can go. Now, together."

I understood. This was it, the revenge he had waited for. I'd made him hope, on that ship, that I would help, and then I'd betrayed him. This was the same. He had just been waiting until I hoped enough. If I said yes, he was going to laugh and I'd be a pillar of fire.

Which would be an end to it. If he'd had his revenge, he would have no reason to stay in Thebes. The madness would lift, the magic of the masks would stop. The terrible pressure leaning and leaning on the

Queen would be gone, and whatever the holy raving was, whatever had happened to Pylos . . . would not happen here. Thebes might just scrape through.

Down in the city, the horns were calling. That was Apophis's grain coming into the city, escorted by soldiers. The horn meant *make way.* Tomorrow, Pentheus would go to Egypt.

Fuck, but I had been such a coward. How many people could I have saved if hadn't played this stupid game with him? What if, right after we realized that the madness was spreading out of control and the masks were wreaking their weird changes, I'd tapped him on the shoulder and said, *Look, enough's enough*?

"If I said yes," I said, knowing I must have turned grey and halfway to stone, "would you make all this stop? Is that the trade? You let Thebes go if you get me?"

I thought he would half smile and say, *Well, do you really think that's so unreasonable?* I thought I'd have to admit that no, it was entirely fair enough.

He didn't do that.

I didn't understand what he did.

He tilted right back from me, then got up and stepped back too. Someone coming in just at that moment would have thought I'd punched him.

"No," he said.

"Then what do you *want*?" I demanded. "What do I have to give you, to make it stop? I'm here, Dionysus, just take it and then for fuck's sake, fuck *off*!"

He didn't say anything. He stood for a second, then nodded once, and then walked away into the maze, to do what I had no idea, but the leopard stalked away too. I waited, but nothing happened; except that slowly, I started to notice that the room was different. There was no water in the fountain any more; no ivy; no jasmine surging and flowering up the walls. It was all dead. There was dust in the fountain, dust on the ground. The wine cups we had drunk from just a few minutes ago were still there, but they were dry, and cracked, and they looked old, as if someone a hundred years ago had abandoned them here.

I thought maybe I'd burst into flames on the steps up to the surface, but I didn't. Nothing happened except that I came out into the daylight, and the heat, and the faint smell of sacrifice smoke. I had to stand there and try to remember what I was doing and why I'd come, and what the point of anything was.

Pentheus was still trying to persuade his horse to let him put the reins on, but the horse was a battle charger and Pentheus was a Pentheus. When he came too close, it snapped at him. I guided its head away. It tried to bite me, like any self-respecting horse, but grumbled around in the right direction as I clipped Pentheus's reins back onto the bridle.

The garden was already dying. The leaves of the vines already looked dull and dusty, the grapes starting to wither in the sun. As though they knew something was happening, the birds that had been taking the nectar from the honeysuckle and jasmine lifted into the air and flew away, like they were one thing that had made one decision.

What did that mean? Dionysus wouldn't just have *gone*. If you could make a god drop a revenge oath just by telling them to go away, then the world would be a much more populous place.

"I was trying to help you," Pentheus said tightly.

"I know," I said to the bridle.

He glanced at me sideways as I swung up onto my horse. I recognised it from the garrison; it did whatever it wanted, including murdering the unwary, but usually only when nobody was looking. "You would have broken my neck if he hadn't stopped you."

"If I'd said to you what you said to me, and you *didn't* try to break my neck, I would think you were a worthless little cockroach."

"You're not going to apologise, are you."

I looked over at him. "Do you want me to push you off that horse?"

He paused. "You're—really angry with me."

"I . . ." I had to push my hand across my face. It was like trying to be angry with a holy calendar. It was going to click around on its mechanisms no matter how badly timed. "No. It's all right. Do you want to hit me back?"

"Will it help?"

"Mm."

Part of my thinking lit up and said: *Blue, that's blue actually.*

He did, quite hard.

"See?" I said.

"That was good," he admitted.

"Brief and concentrated violence is very therapeutic, I always find," I agreed, quite enjoying how the ringing in my head and the lovely muted pain in my cheekbone was drowning out everything else. "I recommend it generally. Get in at least one fight a month, or you go neurotic and peculiar."

He snorted and I relaxed. He sat rubbing his knuckles for a little while. "What did Dionysus say?"

My throat closed up and I had to stare at the road. I wished I could stop seeing an imaginary future where Dionysus wasn't lying or playing games, and the sun rose in the west.

Already too dry, some leaves cracked off their vines and fell on the ground.

Maybe it was what happened when Dionysus was angry, in the absence of hundreds of knights to run mad. Only—he hadn't looked angry. He had looked . . . what?

Tired. Very tired, the kind of tired you can only be after centuries of being tired.

Pentheus touched my shoulder. "Phaidros. Why did you say yes to the Queen? I . . . can see she must remind you of Helios, but that isn't a good reason to marry a marvel who just thinks she's a person. If she doesn't kill you for this, then she'll do it for something else. It won't even be execution, she'll just throw your life away on whatever seems worth it at the time."

"Why does no one listen to me when I say that doesn't matter, because I'm Sown and this is what I'm for? Our duty is part of us, we can't just leave it on the side of the road."

Pentheus thought about it for a little while. He had his hair over his shoulder on his sun side to keep his neck from burning, and with the gold beads threaded through into their half-crown, he looked like Helios. "I thought that too. But then . . . when I was in the maze, duty didn't feel like a part of me at all. It was just chains. I suppose if you're born in chains and so is everyone you know and you never, ever see them come off, then you would think they were part of you and something awful would happen if you found the key, but it didn't feel awful. I felt like I could breathe."

"We can't think like that and be Sown at the same time," I said.

He gave me a look then that would have been strange on a grown man, but it was eerie coming from someone who had so recently been a child. It was pity. Not the patronising kind people sometimes aim at relatives who only appear when there's free food. The kind you have for a beautiful war horse wounded past saving—something glorious and brave, and almost dead.

31

I thought maybe that when we came up the steps to the Palace, there would be people waiting to arrest me, and the Queen, to give me a regretful look and say sorry, but if there was any doubt then the only sensible thing to do was have me immediately killed.

They weren't; nobody was thinking about me at all, because the Egyptian grain convoy was in the main courtyard. Wagon after wagon, painted with the turquoise seal of the Pharaoh, accompanied by soldiers to keep people from stealing on the road—their soldiers, and ours. The Egyptians were all men, so they were bizarrely uniform, and all of them were tall and impressive, looking a lot like they were trying not to openly enjoy the whooping, cheering crowd. There were already grain sacks being passed out, queues behind the wagons, and the Egyptians were laughing with our knights, because probably they hadn't seen people in Achaea queue before for food rather than the traditional mob. Palace clerks were checking ration tablets, running seal beads over clay, trading receipts. It was joyful and loud, but it was meticulous too. Every so often, someone tried to steal something and went down under a knot of soldiers.

"It's you!" A lady with a baby slung both arms around me, then laughed away before I could ask why she was so happy to see a stranger.

Someone else saw, an older man, one of those quick sparky people who always make brilliant bosuns on ships, with a voice like a carnyx. He grinned. "It's the King! All hail the King!"

All hail the King burst around the courtyard. Even the Egyptians standing on the grain wagons saluted, smiling.

Royalty is such a strange thing. To look at a city and everyone in it, you would think the only rational reaction to the richest people in it, who struggle the least, and who have fossilised that unfair economy around themselves so well that you can't change it without a war, would be a sort of weary hatred.

But a royal house is spun of witchcraft, between many mirrors. People *are* their kingdoms—we say we're Theban or Athenian or Spartan before we say anything else about ourselves—and the crown stands for the kingdom. Put some undeserving autocrat in charge who abuses people and loses all their battles, and everyone will resent it not just because their lives are harder, but because crowns are like battle standards: people care when they fall in the mud. In one flat way they are just silver and cloth: it doesn't matter. Only people aren't seeing silver or cloth. They're seeing the kingdom, which is a reflection of who they are. The function of a queen is not just to rule. It's to arrange the illusionary architecture of the royal house between those mirrors in the hearts of its citizens into the strongest structure she can, because though you can't touch it, it is real: it's like *three*. Arrange it beautifully and gloriously and magically enough, and your city in the ordinary world can sit in a dust bowl slowly starving . . . but you won't get weary hate for the crown. You'll get adoration.

The prophecy had tilted people's heart-mirrors at precise angles, and now the royal house was glittering.

I looked at Pentheus, full of dread, because it was a good few notches *too* fucking glittering, and he looked nervous too, but the Guards were already seeing us inside.

Half a regiment of beautifully dressed slaves took me into a set of chambers big enough to house five families, with a ludicrous fountain full of nymph marvels in the middle of the floor, and I hunted around for someone who might be able to say what was going to happen now, but everyone like the Chamberlain must have been busy with the grain.

"Can someone please tell us what's going on?" Pentheus said to the room generally.

Everyone laughed. That seemed like a good sign, depending on what they thought of us.

The Queen, someone explained in the severe way that said we would know this already if we hadn't absconded earlier, was calling the court together for a feast: a celebration of the betrothal and the success of the grain deal, and I wasn't allowed to go in armour.

I wondered if the Queen had seen what had happened in the court-yard just now, and how she was feeling about Apollo's arrangement of the mirrors.

"I need to see the Queen," I said.

"She's coming," someone said. "Stand still."

I couldn't tell if that was good.

There was a bath with rose water. Then gold combs with fine gold chains sank through the base of my long army braid, so heavy that I had to hold my head exactly straight or it was uncomfortable. Gold clamped round my neck, like a very cynical, beautiful version of a slave's collar. More gold all the way up my arm, made nearly like mail but not. Every-thing else in black and red, the colours of the House of Kadmus.

The thought that Helios might have lied to me thundered round inside my head like a charioteer with a bronze whip.

He had told me lies to make life easier, about foreigners having gills, and every time I'd asked him where he got me, he made up something new. But this—this was like saying that just because someone liked having bunches of peonies in the house, he must have run away to tend the Hanging Gardens of Babylon.

Tiresias had mistaken me for Helios. Pentheus thought we looked enough alike that he had added up the prophecy that way straightaway.

I had thought the courtyard didn't look like I remembered. And Pentheus was right: nobody remembers coherent sets of events that happened when they were four. I remembered because Helios had told it all to me. Maybe I remembered *only* what he had told me. It felt real, but what did real feel like? As vivid and clear as I had it—or wouldn't it feel vaguer, rougher, wouldn't there be bits I couldn't catch so well now, wouldn't it be contextless flashes, like the rest of my childhood?

It took me a second to notice that all the slaves were kneeling.

The Queen was in the doorway. I knelt too. She came and pulled me up.

"Aren't you hungry?" she asked towards the silver tray of beautiful things the kitchens had sent.

"Er—yes, but if I leave it then the slaves can have it," I said, distracted, and feeling like my cogs were in the wrong alignment for simple questions.

"Are you all right?" she said, more carefully.

"I'm . . ." It was no good. "There is a priest at Apollo with the same scar and the same name as me, with a dagger from Helios. Pentheus— thinks Helios swapped us years ago. I think maybe all those people outside think that too. Do you?"

"Do you?"

"No! He was a tricky fucker but he didn't lie to me for twenty years!"

She smiled with the same joyful gleam she'd had on the roof during the riot, and I stayed very, very still, because for the first time now, I could see just how finely calibrated a game she was playing. Dionysus was right: the best thing she could do for the safety of the crown was make everybody think the lost prince was *already wearing it*. But if *I* thought I was him—then I had a legal obligation to murder her because she had killed my mother, and I was infamous for paying my blood debts. I was the psychopath who had waited nine years to hurl a Trojan princess off a balcony and burn down her palace. The Queen was balancing between the benefit of everyone else thinking I was the prince, and the risk of tipping *me* into believing it.

And she was enjoying every pace of it, because this was her battle-field, and nobody else was as good as her.

"No," she said. "Me neither. He would never have done that to you. Yes, there's a priest at the temple who he sponsored, but he sponsored hundreds of children, he was a prince. I paid the temple to make that prophecy. It solves our god problem, see? I can hum and say the meaning is obscure, everybody else will put it together and feel clever, they'll rally behind you; meanwhile, we both know it's not you, we all win, and Thebes survives. Hurrah. Do people say hurrah?" she added pensively.

"Only Athenians say hurrah," I said weakly.

Even if she had bronze-clad evidence that I *was* the prince—she wouldn't tell me. That would be idiotic. Of course she was going to say . . .

I couldn't hold onto all of it properly any more. I couldn't do what Dionysus did, and lean back and see it all from far enough away that he could see what was coming. I was jammed right up close to it, and there was nothing left to do except decide if she was doing it all for a good reason or not.

"Phaidros," she said. "Lovely knight . . . if I genuinely thought you were the prince, you'd be dead. I loved Helios, I love that you talk like he does and that you even look a bit like him, but that wouldn't stop me. I think—you know that."

Or you realized I was harmless as long as I didn't know, and you kept me in reserve for a crisis. Like Pentheus vanishing, or a god falling . . .

Did I really look like Helios? I was actually the least qualified person to know. I didn't have a mirror, only rich idiots in Persia had real mirrors. I saw myself reflected in armour or water sometimes, but not clearly.

Sometimes you just have to admit you're in a storm and stop trying to make any difference to where you're going. The wind is the wind, and Poseidon is mighty.

"I . . . gods, I wish you'd said," I said, and it was a sort of relief to stop trying to strain against that internal rudder and just let myself spin into the current. "Pentheus and I were just having an Olympic crisis about it."

"I would have told you both if you hadn't buggered off straightaway," she said, laughing. "What were you doing?"

"Uh," I said, half laughing too now. "We went to see a witch for advice."

"Is this your kinsman witch who thinks that madness is medicine?"

"Yes."

"Glorious, and what astonishing piece of insanity did he say this time?"

"He told me to get out of Thebes."

"I'm glad you don't listen to him," she said, patting my shoulder. "He sounds fun though. Should we invite him to the wedding and enjoy the inevitable fireworks?" Her eyes lit up. *"What if we introduced him to Tiresias?"*

I hugged her. It was the first time I'd touched her rather than just standing still if she touched me, and she stiffened, so that it was like holding a statue with real clothes on, but then she put her arms around me, holding the back of my head. I shut my eyes against her shoulder, breathing in incense. It was a miniature crack in the edifice of my certainty that Dionysus was going to kill me soon, but he had let me go, and now I could see a tiny snatch of a future beyond next week. It was family, and there was someone I belonged to. I shouldn't look, it was dangerous to look, but . . .

"Phaidros." She sounded shocked. "What's wrong?"

"Nothing, lady. I'm just—I didn't think I'd ever have a family again."

She drew her thumbs under my eyelashes. She was smiling, or almost, caught between that and something much sadder, the same as me. "Me neither."

I held her wrists. She didn't wear bracelets, just little sword-slash marks up her arms from garrison training when she was young. Even though I was happy, something deep down in me locked up, because we were close enough for her to kiss me and I didn't want her to, really powerfully, involuntarily didn't want her to, because I was still getting used to the memory of Dionysus doing it, trying to cradle it close and hold it for later, and if she did, one would blur into the other, and somehow that would be worse than being shipwrecked.

She didn't, and only bumped our heads together.

I'd never been more grateful for anything. "Shall we go?" she asked with a carefulness that took me off guard, one that felt like she wasn't just talking about whether to leave the room. I almost said that the way this worked was that she decided and then I followed, but I stopped, because she was watching me in a way that made me realize I was wrong. That wasn't right, not any more. She would decide, and then, mindful of the terrible gravity of the crown, she would ask me if I was going to follow, instead of wrenching me into orbit.

It was like when Dionysus lifted me up at the dance. She was much stronger and greater than me, but courteous. It was frightening and safe at the same time.

"Yes."

Around us, the slaves were smiling, and not even trying to hide that they were. It wasn't until I looked beyond them I realized Pentheus had been waiting in the doorway, looking awkwardly at the floor. He was freshly dressed in feast clothes too—he must have gone and come back again in the time it had taken them to dress me. Just in time to contemplate the full bleakness of his mother remarrying and starting again while he was sent away.

"Didn't see you," I said to him, holding my arm out, in case that would help.

He didn't come. "Did you just say Dionysus is your kinsman?" he asked.

It was well to the side of what I'd expected him to say, but maybe he was grasping at the nearest thing that wasn't to do with the betrothal. "Yes," I said, not knowing how to explain. "He was my guest a long time ago."

"But—I thought he only recently came to Thebes?"

"I wrote to him," I said, which was kind of true. "I invited him."

When I blinked, I saw Dionysus in the maze again, and how exhausted he had looked. Not angry. That was what made it horrible.

I needed to go back. I needed to apologise. I needed to get on my knees like I should have done all along.

After the feast.

Pentheus stared at me with raw pain across his face.

"What's wrong?" I asked.

"I—nothing," he said, but he turned inward and glassy, and strange. He turned away and walked ahead of us.

I looked helplessly at the Queen. I taught people his age all the time, and usually they were clay tablets: all their unhappinesses were easy to read, and easy to sweep smooth and write over. Pentheus's was there too, but it was another language.

She shook her head once, no wiser.

I didn't have any more time to think about it, because one of the Queen's secretaries ran in. *Ran*, even though none of them ever moved at a pace more urgent than an elegant glide, and not the earth shaking nor a god falling would make them sign their beads at anything other than a dead ninety-degree angle.

"Lady! Lady," he gasped, and he was laughing. I'd never seen any of her secretaries laugh. "Lady, it's the knights, you have to come and see—"

"What's happened now? If we need to summon the Sown mothers again—"

"No! They're coming in from Ares and Hermes, they're all—they're *cured!*"

She looked at me with the same wariness of good news that filled me up then too, and then we both started after the secretary, joining a quickening stream of people all going the same way. Pentheus let himself be left behind and ignored me when I put my hand back for him.

Around the pillars, the ivy was dying.

When we poured through to the Knights' Court, along with an interested comet tail of Egyptians soldiers and people who had come for grain, it was already crowded. There were sudden overjoyed yells when wards recognised commanders who had vanished into Ares days ago, laughing, little knots of people thunking together, crying. I saw Polydorus's commander, looking sunburned and worse for wear but very, very sane, scoop him right off his feet and spin him around. Even the Guards were looking happy.

I stared over everyone, at the sky, waiting for something else, something as terrible as the howling madness at the stadium or a star hurtling right at us, but the sky was only the sky.

It smashed into me very, very slowly. Whatever minds have instead of bones, I could feel mine splintering.

Dionysus was gone.

No. He couldn't be.

What?

That wasn't how any of this worked. A god didn't scream down from the heavens for revenge and then just leave when you told him to.

Where are you, where are you, where are you?

"Phaidros," Pentheus said beside me, as though I'd missed something urgent.

People had noticed us where we were standing at the top of the steps in our red and black and gold. A strange quiet was falling. It wasn't until people started to kneel that I understood what was happening.

None of them knew about Dionysus. All they knew was that the Oracle had made a prophecy that made me sound like the lost prince, and now, the *hour* a crown was going on my head, the madness was gone.

The Queen was looking at me with a reserve that had not been there earlier when she told me it was just a trick. She didn't have her war-joy glow. She was thinking. Really thinking. I saw her clockwork click around to the only workable solution, for now. She took my hand and lifted it over my head.

"Sown: your king!"

The roar was like being deaf again—I could hear a portcullis of noise and not hear anything in it. It was cheering, but not the normal kind. There wasn't any ceremony or any duty, or courtesy—it was a visceral relief, and belief, and disbelief.

"What have you done?" the Queen said close to me, sounding strange.

"Nothing!"

"Nothing with your witch."

"He isn't my witch, he's left." I sounded as though somebody had tried to hang me, and for a few seconds my neck had taken my whole weight, but the rope had snapped.

She gave me a sceptical look, one that was reassessing me, clicking through possibilities and risks, and calculating whether or not she had just made an enormous mistake.

I felt sick.

The feast had been an occasion anyway, and the Palace was filled with bright banners, but now it was about two hundred people bigger than we had planned, and no one cared; it was a laughing chaos and I'd never seen anything like it inside the Kadmeia. Usually, the court was an austere place. Sown nobility dressed well but plainly. Anything too extravagant was usually out, automatically, because the first thing anyone would say was, *What are you doing, you look like an Athenian.* But for some very special occasions—the Festival of Athena, coronations, big weddings—there was a certain willingness to let the usual rules slide. There were people here tonight who I'd never seen out of legion uniform wearing bright silk that must have come in all the way from Hattusa, and gold-embroidered cloth, and those gems from India that look like they're on fire on the inside. Lord Halys had gone the whole way; he was wearing trousers, like a Persian dandy. I had to give him some credit. I'd have died of shame. Maybe they were ironic trousers. Apophis, all in gold, looked like a god.

All I could do was sit next to the Queen and stare into the middle distance. Nobody seemed to think it was unusual. Bridegrooms are supposed to be nervous, and probably people thought I was just trying to get used to the enormity of what had just happened to me. Scum of the earth in the garrison last week, king now. King *consort*—though that was not what people were saying. They were saying king.

On the Queen's other side, Pentheus looked like I felt, and I didn't blame him. He was seeing his future vanish. If the Queen had my child now, his claim was gone. He was going to Egypt. In twenty years, if there was a choice between some half-forgotten dilettante from a mansion in Memphis and a true-born Sown knight raised in the garrison—as all younger royal children were—who people thought was the grandchild of a god, then it was pretty clear who the Assembly would back.

People were coming up to talk to us. I must have said things and smiled and deferred to the Queen, but it all hazed together and the second each person was gone, I couldn't remember anything. All I could hear was what the Queen wasn't saying. *What if the madness really was a curse that lifted once we gave him the crown? What if he gets rid of me? He could. The garrison will do anything he says now.*

Horribly, it was clear that a lot of other people were thinking that too.

For me, power had always been fixed. You obeyed the Queen, and you obeyed the general, and your commander. That was the order of the world, and the only way it could go if you didn't want it all to collapse into screaming chaos like Pylos. I'd never seen what it looked like when the foundations of power shifted.

I'd never really understood before that this was all it was: people deciding whose orders to follow. The only real reason everyone obeyed one queen or another was that it would be too difficult not to. But when it *wasn't* difficult . . .

The Queen could see it too.

If I didn't do something very fucking rapidly, I was going to be dead by tomorrow morning.

For a little while, I tried to decide if I cared. Dionysus was gone. I'd really expected to explode some time around now. I'd planned on it for so long now that the idea of living beyond that was a bit dismaying.

Along from me, Pentheus was staring unseeing into a cup of wine. His eyelashes were too dark. He wasn't crying, but he was right on the edge of it, and tipping. On a ship, to gather in the sails when a storm is coming, you have to climb up the rig and edge along the top yard, which is about thirty feet off the deck. That's hard enough in a strong wind.

But it's worse when you get to the sail. There's a footrope under the yardarm, looped along, slack, utterly fucking treacherous, especially with five people moving along it, as they have to. If you're slightly the wrong height—slightly too tall—then you can't hold the yard very well as you go. It's awkwardly at hip height, and in order to tie the knots to bind up the sails, you have to lean *right* forward, curling over it, so that your balance tips too far forward and you feel like you're going to fall, and this always happens in dangerously strong wind, because that's the only time you need to urgently take in sail. One wrong twitch of the rudder and you fall. More than once, Helios had clamped one hand onto the back of my collar at exactly the right second.

Nobody was holding Pentheus's collar.

"Lady, can I ask for a wedding gift?" I said.

"If I can give it," the Queen said slowly.

"Don't send Pentheus to Egypt. Send me."

"What?"

"This, all this, whatever just happened—it makes me a danger to the crown. I don't want to be. I'd rather die. Maybe you'll decide I should do that. But Apophis wants a royal hostage and now you have a choice of two. One, the heir. Two, some fucking idiot from the garrison who's only worth anything because of a prophecy and a well-timed—" I couldn't call it a miracle in front of her. "A well-timed easing of mass hysteria. Send me away, where I can't do any damage."

She didn't say anything at first, but an invisible chisel was marking a frown deeper and deeper between her eyebrows. "Phaidros, you're volunteering for exile."

"No, I'm volunteering to be what buys you grain for the next decade. This is the only efficient solution, lady. I think Apophis will take me if I ask him to."

She watched me for a long time. "This is the wedding gift you request, knight?"

"It is, lady."

"Then . . . speak to Apophis." She blew her breath out slowly. "You are a marvel knight."

"Duty is honour," I said.

My hair was fastened up with some complicated gold things, and when she touched the back of my head, her signet ring clinked.

"Can I tell Pentheus?" I asked, still very quiet.

Beyond her, Pentheus was still looking his wine. He had no colour, and now, I thought he was sweating; he looked ill. I went round to his chair. He flinched when I put my hand on the back of it.

"I need to tell you something," I began.

He stood up suddenly. "Everyone, I have something to say on the occasion of my mother's betrothal."

The long table went quiet.

"I've tried to keep my silence, for the good of the kingdom," Pentheus said. He wasn't holding back the strength of his own voice any more. He was talking like he had in the maze with Dionysus; like I did, I realized suddenly, pulling the sound from low in his chest to give it the strength to carry over a room, or a training yard. "But I can't. I vanished because I was kidnapped and drugged, and brought back to the Palace when the benefit would be greatest for the man who took me."

I stood back from his chair. Someone had spilled some wine and a little of it soaked dark into the hem of my cloak.

"I didn't understand why he did it, but today at the Temple of Apollo, we were given the answer. The Oracle said to the Queen, *In marrying this man, you both condemn yourself to and save yourself from prophecy of the boy who should have been king.* I don't think the meaning could be clearer. Twenty-five years ago Princess Semele's son vanished from the Palace during the lightning strike. Twenty-five years ago, my uncle Helios joined a new legion with a child of unknown origin, and now, everyone who might have known who he was is dead. And then in a time of crisis, I was taken, and given back only once my return would assure my captor great rewards from my mother. The oracle means that Phaidros is the lost prince. And it was Phaidros who stole me, and Phaidros who brought me back."

Someone dropped a spoon. The little clang sounded like an explosion.

"No," I said. "What? Pentheus—"

"No," Pentheus said doggedly to his mother. "They did this together. Phaidros and his fucking witch. He wants to be king and when I asked him for help he saw an opportunity, and handed me over to the witch to be enchanted out of my mind. He just said they've known each other for years. It was a trick." His voice sounded like his throat had locked. With a levee-breaking rush, I realized he wasn't lying: he *thought* he was telling the truth. I'd told him I knew Dionysus, and he'd thought that meant we had planned it together. "The witch took me and together they worked out how best to put Phaidros on the throne."

The silence was dead, like the entire room had taken an opium overdose. I looked at the Queen, because there was nothing I could say. Either she believed Pentheus or she believed me: there was no evidence to give her. Or—no. It wasn't even about who she believed. It was about choosing who was least dangerous now. Everyone else watched her too.

The Queen stood up slowly. She looked utterly weary of the whole thing, and with a sort of fever flash, it went across my mind that this was how brilliant monarchs were pulled down. Bad luck and people reacting just a few minutes too soon, and witches trying to protect their friends, and king consorts who couldn't find a way to make an angry, frightened prince less angry and frightened.

"Arrest him," she said to the Guards, about me. "And find the witch."

As she said it, she watched Pentheus, and this time, I recognised what she was doing. Kicking his mooring lines. She was seeing just how sure he was, waiting for him to say, no, stop.

Pentheus only stared straight back at her.

For the first time, I understood what Dionysus had been trying to tell me all along. I'd seen what happened in the stadium when he smashed everyone's clockwork and all that was left was the wild thing at the heart of a human, but this was what happened when the wild died, and all that was left was the clockwork. It looked different—the opposite, absolute blank calm, oceans from the madness of the knights—but it was horrible in equal measure. I felt like I was seeing someone who had been mutilated past all repair.

The Queen lifted her eyebrow, but that was all. She didn't change the order, and only nodded at the Guards. It was fractional, but I just caught it: she looked approving. She *wanted* Pentheus to be ruthless.

Ruthless is Sown.

32

Traditionally, kings and queens have to be healthy and whole in order to serve, because they're reflections of their kingdom: if the king is sick, the superstition is that the kingdom will soon follow. It's a stupid law. There are generals with one leg or one eye, or with the falling sickness, and I always preferred them, because someone who's been wounded or who's grown up struggling knows a lot better than some hale brash giant what it's like to be scared. But, it was the law. So, the traditional way to rule someone out of the kingship is to blind him, castrate him, and shove him on a galley to be a slave at the oar until he dies, probably about three days later. It's bad luck to execute a king. I don't know why they think it's less bad to do the other thing, but there you are.

I had a cell to myself. It was a dark oven. I could stand on tiptoe and see, just, through the long narrow window into the market square, where slaves were picking up empty grain sacks and people were out in the sunset with freshly baked bread and jugs of wine, and the jubilant ease of people who weren't going to starve any more. Knights newly reunited sat out on the steps together, talking about what the madness had been like. And I could hear the heralds everywhere, yelling that at dawn, Phaidros Heliades was going to be blinded and sent to serve at the oar for high treason.

I'd never been this afraid before. It wasn't like the fizzy energy you get before a battle, the one where you have to bounce up and down and make unfunny jokes. It wasn't like anything. I would have been less scared of being straightforwardly executed, but this was dread stacked on dread.

Be Persephone. Always negotiate. See Death coming, see him leaning against the door, and say, aha, you're coming with *me*, thank you very much. Only there was no negotiating any more. The Guards had been told not to come even within shouting distance of me. The whole prison was silent. The Queen knew all about *Be Persephone*.

The ground juddered; Poseidon smashing his fist into it from far away. I put my head against the wall, hoping I could die in an earthquake before they got the knives out.

A few minutes after the little earthquake, some people came out of the Palace, grumbling about old ceilings. When another tremor came, this one big enough to make the ground look like it was breathing, a lot more people arrived, carrying lamps, still—gods, it felt like a thousand years ago—in their feast clothes, some with cups and plates. It still wasn't enough to really alarm anybody. Achaea is earthquake country. I'd been getting used to it since I came back to Thebes. I watched, grateful to have some people to look at. It was a good distraction from how horribly fucking *alive* I felt, now I was on my way to dying.

Not like invigorated. Just—healthy. All my joints were working strong and smooth, the stab wound in my shoulder was healing wonderfully. I was working like I was supposed to, I was the strongest I could be and probably had ever been. Like Helios, laughing that day on the line, before—before.

I wasn't even going to get that kind of death. What was going to happen in the morning was unsayable. Some things are so poisonous than even the names are poison, and anyone who understands the word ends up sick just from the knowing of it.

There was a knot of Guards, escorting Pentheus.

"The Palace has stood a thousand years, I think it can stand another few hours," he was saying tiredly.

There was a stony but nonetheless concerned shifting under the purple cloaks.

"When the god goes before the Queen, the High City shall fall?" he guessed, quite gently.

He sounded like he had grown up since I'd last seen him an hour ago. The last of his childhood was gone. He had stood up and fought, and now he knew how strong he was . . . he was being careful of other people.

"There's no god here. As my mother said, there was a witch with some poisoned wine and some tricks, and an ambitious knight. It's just an earthquake."

"Pentheus," I said.

The Guards tightened and looked like they wanted to stop him going near any walls, but he waved them off.

"Phaidros."

"You're wrong," I said. "I didn't take you."

He came closer to the bars, but not very. The torchlight slung gold over him. He looked older, and harder. "What's more likely? That I spoke to a witch, who knew a knight with a very convincing claim to being the lost prince, and who just—didn't mention it? And then that knight just stumbled over me, and in the line of his duty, because he's just that fucking dedicated to his vows, happened to take me back at the opportune moment?"

"Pentheus—"

"Or," he said over me, "I spoke to a witch who knew a knight with a claim, and he said, *I have an idea.* You both hid me. You took advantage of the madness and the drought. He kept me drugged in the maze. He poisoned the wine at the stadium. You brought me back when you were certain the Queen would reward you as she did. You tell me, Phaidros. What would you believe?"

"You know if you'd waited another quarter of an hour, it would have been me going to Egypt and not you?"

"What?"

"That's what I was talking to the Queen about. She had agreed. You were to stay in Thebes." What was so fucking aggravating here was that there was no objective obstacle. There was no god any more, there was no army at the gates, nothing clear and clean to fight against. It was just politics, and a broken boy, and a piece of flamboyantly terrible timing. If someone had put all this in a report about some other kingdom and told it to me, I'd have said, *Don't be so stupid, no group of thinking humans can misunderstand each other* that *badly, go back and find out what really happened.* "Sometimes people aren't out to screw you over."

He looked at me like I'd slapped him, but then he shut that down and half laughed. "You know there's a story doing the rounds at the moment? It's new, it's everywhere, you'll have heard it. It's about a prince whose father went away to the wars when he was a baby, and his mother ruled for a long time alone—but now the wars are over, and still no king has returned, suitors are closing in to marry the Queen and take over the kingdom. You've heard it?"

"No," I said.

"Her suitors—lords from all the kingdoms all around—make everyone's life hell. They take and take, they all assume the kingdom is theirs. She's holding them off, but really it's the prince's responsibility to do something, but he's too young to know what to do and he thinks he's going to be killed. Yes?"

"He sounds like a useless little prick, doesn't he," I said flatly. I didn't like monologues even when the setting was a nice campfire on the shore.

"And then . . . his father comes home, and says, it's all right, I've got you now. Leave it to me. The boy doesn't believe him, because there are dozens of suitors and they're all pigs. But then his father kills them all. He just walks through the Palace with a longbow, like Apollo. And after that, the king and the queen and the prince are a family again. Nice, right?"

I waited, though I did wonder what the fuck kind of queen wouldn't have just poisoned them all by then. I suspected an Athenian story.

"I *hate* that story," he said flat and hard. "It's fantasy. Fathers don't come for you when you need them. Fathers are wolves who only don't hurt you for as long as you aren't inconvenient." He inclined his head. "So don't try to tell me you came to save me."

Dionysus had told me this would happen. *Take him back now, and he'll become merciless, because nobody ever showed him any mercy.*

I had to thump my fist against the bars, very slowly. I'd never met a single soul who got in his own way so much. "Gods, Pentheus. Even if there was a father who adored you trying to get into the Palace, even if he was knocking down the gate and offering to kill anyone who had ever wronged you, you wouldn't fucking hear him for crying that no one is coming."

Horrible pain went over his face. He thought I was saying it just to hurt him. "I hope the knife is blunt," he told me, with a knot in his voice.

Rancid ghost pain shot right through me.

You can know someone turned out bad because nobody loved them enough, and you can understand, and empathise—and you can still hope that a building falls on them.

Obligingly, the ground shivered again. One of the Guards came to guide him away from the building, out into the open again. He didn't look back. I thunked my head against the bars.

The tremors had disturbed some bats. Now, they were chittering right through the empty prison, just like they'd gone through the maze when Pentheus stole me. A couple even got through the bars on the door and ricocheted around the cell. One crashed into me. I had to pick it up and edge it outside through the window bars. It didn't try to bite me; it just sat in my hands, looking strangely happy, and when I put it outside, it just sat there too, wings folded and fur fluffed up. It made a little squeaking noise so it could see me, and I had an odd feeling that I was getting a good-natured bat survey. Then it flapped away.

The ground heaved, and I fell over. There was a collective yell from the courtyard as everyone else did too.

I pulled myself upright by the window bars; snatched my hands back, because they felt wrong; then stopped.

Ivy was forcing its way up through the flagstones outside, vivid and green and impossible. I had to stand there with my hands still out, a few inches off the bars. I could see the ivy growing.

Terrible, terrible hope swelled up inside the chambers of my heart, enough to hurt.

A stream of purple cloaks flowed down the steps from the throne room, surrounding the Queen. They Guards had their shields raised overhead, covered in dust.

Another tremor, and the flagstones rippled. I swayed with the quake, riding it, and feeling crazily as though I wasn't really there: I was just watching or dreaming, and my pulse was going *where are you where are you where are you.*

"Let's evacuate the Palace," the Queen called. She sounded calm, like she always did if things were getting dangerous. "Everyone out, into the courtyards. Make sure the fires are out in the kitchens. No lamps left burning inside. Where's Pentheus?" It was hard to see by the torchlight and the confusion of people hurrying away from the buildings.

"Here," Pentheus said. "I've got Apophis and Lord Halys too."

I only saw him then because I was looking for him.

Dionysus was sitting on the edge of the great fountain of Apollo. He had been all along. He was wearing witch black, but unveiled, still as a tomb. Ivy and jasmine had exploded over the Apollo marvel already, the shape of it lost under the density of the vines. No one had noticed. He was there and not there.

"What about Phaidros?" Pentheus asked the Queen.

They both looked towards the cells. They could see me. There was a torch above the barred window.

"Leave him. It's up to the gods."

Dionysus stood up. Nobody seemed to see him cross the courtyard. People got out of his way, though—slaves, Guards, knights, *right* out of it, leaving empty space around him, as though they did know on some level that something was there. A few puzzled looks fell onto the ground where, in his wake, flowers were blooming up through the cracked flagstones. Even though they couldn't really see him, even though he was only there like three is there in three apples, the Guards looked dazed. One of them started to spin.

Sing, sing to the lord of the dance . . .

"What's happening?" Pentheus snapped suddenly. He wrenched a coil of ivy out of a crack in the ground.

"Shouldn't have lied, should you," Dionysus said in passing, and somehow I heard it even though he was still fully forty feet away.

Pentheus heard it too and spun around, but Dionysus was already gone, and all around them, the Guards were going mad, turning into the dance, singing. So were other people. Looking hypnotised, a Guard handed Dionysus the prison keys.

The Queen had seen. She stood in his way. "Stop. Who are you?"

"I'm the one who took your son. He asked me to. He asked to forget everything, so that's what I did."

"*Why?*"

I thought he would explain, because she was the Queen, and even gods listen to kings and queens. I thought he would tell her about how he had been ancient before Zeus was even thought of, and how these forests had been his long before Kadmus and the dragon, and maybe even threaten her, to try and make her remember the old ways of the Hunt before it was too late. In the bards' stories, he would have. They do a thing called an *aristea*, in stories—it's where the two people who are at odds but equally matched meet. It's always long. They always talk to each other. It's always clear that neither of them are wrong or right: it's just that circumstances have forced them to fight. One always dies heroically; usually, the other one goes mad. It's always huge, and sad, and lovely.

He didn't. He didn't care about her. He had seen the passing of a hundred queens.

He just switched her off.

Her and everyone else. They all just fell. Everyone in the courtyard, every Guard and slave, the Queen, Pentheus . . . they all collapsed. I stared. He couldn't have just killed them. Surely he hadn't . . .

He knelt down outside the window and gave the keys to me.

"Are they dead?" I rasped.

"Oh, fuck off, Phaidros, of course they're not fucking dead, they're asleep," he said, his voice smoking crossly. "Meet me round the other way."

I was shaking nearly too much to get the keys into the lock. Just as the lock gave, the ground bucked and I staggered against the wall, half running and half falling into the corridor.

I knew he was coming before I saw him, because the wooden door into the Guards' common room was splitting, the dryad inside stretching, growing, turning back into an oak tree. She was already as tall as the room, branches creaking across the ceiling. Acorns rained across the floor. Something in my chest tied itself into one of those monkey's fist knots we had used to put on the end of heaving lines to give them more weight, because what had he come back for, after what I'd said to him?

Then there he was. I thumped into him and thought, *There, that's fine, set me on fire now*, but he didn't. He crossed his arms over my back, both hands clenched over my shoulders. He curled forward over me, and around us, all the doors turned back into trees, the branches shielding us both, locking together, battening out the torchlight and the falling chunks of stone from the ceiling. We would never have been fast enough if we had tried to run anyway, but I wasn't even sure I could have. I was crying, not just crying, a horrible wracking kind of sobbing, and I couldn't stop, because it was raw relief. I'd never cried like that before. No galley. No hot irons, no knife. All the horror was tearing its way out of me and all I could do was grip onto him like he was jetsam after a wreck.

The trees had made us a shield above, but the walls were falling now. The torchlight was gone and the dark and the dust plumed everywhere. Something slammed into the locked-together branches over our heads and the wood shrieked. We both fell onto our knees at the same time, heads down against the roaring, furious masonry.

When the noise stopped, everything seemed completely silent, though I knew it couldn't be. There was light, though: moonlight, very bright, and it was only in stages that it occurred to me that I shouldn't have been able to see that, because we were supposed to be inside. There was no more inside. I coughed as the dust got into my lungs, and put my hands down. The floor, which had been stone before, was soft with moss. Dionysus straightened up slowly. Where he'd been holding my shoulders, and I'd been holding his arms, there were clean handprints; otherwise both of us were covered in dust. He coughed too and brushed me off, or pretended to; he was seeing if I was hurt. I wasn't.

There was movement beside us. There were horses running past, some still saddled. They must have escaped from the stables, and now they were getting away from the worst of the damage, just like they had years ago when the lightning came. Dionysus put his hand out to one of them, a savage battle charger I'd seen kill Trojan knights entirely by himself, but the stallion stopped and leaned down to nose at us both, a Horse hello.

I gripped the bridle and swung into the saddle. Dionysus climbed up behind me, tall enough to see past my shoulder. The horse cantered away, down to the lower city, through the roads filling with worried people looking up at the ruins of the Kadmeia, speculating, wondering about the ivy growing anew up the houses, the orange trees bursting to life, the pomegranates falling in the gutters, and not seeing us.

33

My house had been set on fire, and it was still burning. It must have been a message for anyone who thought helping me might be a good idea. Whatever they'd used for fuel, it was considerable: the heat from the blaze was powerful even fifty yards away on the path. The smoke was choking, and my poor olive trees were burning. Normally I walked past them every day and didn't feel anything at all about them except distantly grumpy, because at least since I'd been here they hadn't so much made olives as green rocks, but now they were on fire—they seemed like people. Where the fires were hottest, there was a yellow glow and mirages in the air, and just for a few seconds, I would have sworn I saw Hephaestus, limping as he moved bronze into a forge that was there behind the wreckage of my kitchen just like three could be there behind some apples. He looked right at us and offered Dionysus a small, fiery bow. Dionysus tilted forward too, and courteously, the cinders stopped settling on us, stopped trying to set our hair on fire or catch in our sleeves.

His side of the maze was far enough away that the fire wasn't there yet. On the way around, I worried that it would be soon, because the sparks leaping from one patch of scrub to the next were tinderbox bright, but when we came into his garden, I realized I didn't need to worry. There was water everywhere; water running through the channels, in little falls across parts of the ruins that sprayed the paths and made at the old stone smell of the beach at Troy after rain, and of course, in the vines and in the trees, all alive again. No sparks were catching. To get down into the chambers where he lived, we had to step over a stream.

"Pentheus knows where you live. They'll look for you here," I said. It was the first time the bellowing of the fire was quiet enough to speak over.

"He doesn't know where to go once we're in the maze."

"But it's right—" I stopped, because I'd expected to come out in the airy chamber with the fountain, but instead there was just a corridor, and a branch in the ways, and then another, and a weird feeling we were going in a spiral, and then down again. More turns. It would have been hopeless without him. I would never have thought anything was down here, except more ruins.

Then there it was, the same chamber, which I would have sworn was much more straightforward to reach before. The fountain was chattering to itself, alive with spring water, and with tiny birds who had come to drink. They whirred away when we came in, but quickly seemed to realize there was no need to worry, and flitted back.

"Witching?" I said.

"Magic," he said.

I sank down on the fountain edge, which was cushioned with moss, and dipped my hand into it. The water was cool: genuinely, blessedly cool. I scooped up a handful to drink. Sweet and clear. Up above us, the sky was darkening, and there was the smell of smoke, but it didn't feel dangerous any more. The earthquake hadn't broken anything, either, not even a plant pot.

Dionysus sat down a little way from me, out of reach, scanning me in a way that made me worried I looked like I was thinking about murdering him. From our clothes, there was the smell of smoke and of baking, from the burning olives and lemons; we both looked ten years older. The inside of my skull was still echoing.

The leopard sat down nearby, swishing her tail.

I swallowed, and tasted cement. "Does it make you dizzy, seeing through her eyes and yours at the same time?"

He smiled a little bit. "Something wicked. Bees are awful."

Bats, I thought; he had been in the bats.

Another little silence. It rolled around the fountain edges.

"Are you going to kill me now?" I asked.

"*What?*"

"You told me you would come back for me in the end, for revenge," I said, a bit flat, not liking being played with.

He sat as if I'd handed him something incredibly heavy, graven with something important in a lot of languages, like the law stones the Egyptians leave everywhere. He looked like he was trying to find a language he knew. When he did, I saw something break in his expression. "I told you I'd come back for you," he said, very soft. "Come back . . . *for* you. If you needed me. To help."

"Oh," I whispered.

"You called me here," he said. His voice broke smoky again, but he wasn't angry this time. "Why would you do that if you thought I was coming to *kill* you?"

I had to look into the water. "I'd had enough. I . . . I wanted to see you, even if it was just for revenge. You were my guest on that ship, you're my family, even if I was the worst host there ever was." I swallowed. "Why didn't you say anything?"

"You were frightened, at the dance. I thought you'd changed your mind about asking me. No one wants to see me twice. But . . . you did call, and I wanted to stay, and lots of people have blue eyes, so at least to begin with I thought—well, if I pretend not to know what's happening, maybe he'll think I'm someone else." He closed his teeth for a second. "I can't seem very normal for very long, but even when it was obvious, you didn't say anything, so . . . I didn't either. I feel like there must be a word for when two people both know something but they both pretend not to know because they're worried the other one will leave."

I realized I was sitting there with my hand pressed over my mouth and had to concentrate to take it away. "Why? I betrayed you. I should have fought for you."

"What are you talking about? You were a child. They would have killed you."

"You were a child too. You—we *took* you."

"No, you didn't. I let you take me. I wanted to see what it was like on the interesting pirate ship." He laughed, or he started to, but it made him cough, after all the smoke and the dust. "I only meant to be aboard for a few hours, I was going to leave you all alone once I'd looked around, but . . . then you started talking to me like I was a real person and not a pretend ghost thing that used to be a person." He paused. "And you still did that, even when the ivy grew and the slaves went mad."

"You didn't . . . feel . . . ?"

"As though a boy with a sword should have protected me, when I'm older than Zeus and I run people mad even if I just sit quietly and do nothing, and I wasn't in danger, or frightened?"

"That isn't the point."

He paused. "Are you sure?"

I had to hunch forward, because I hadn't expected to laugh. When I raised my head again, he was watching me in the way I always watched a shore as I was leaving when I knew I wouldn't see it again for a long time.

"I . . . am sorry, about—earlier," he said. "I would have spoken to the Queen instead of . . . all that, but there was nothing I could have done to prove Pentheus lied."

"Oh, well; I don't think he thinks he *is* lying."

"Oh, he knows he is," Dionysus said with unexpected acid.

"You—did you say *you* took him?" I asked, trying to tell if I remembered that or if it was just something I'd half-dreamed in all the chaos.

He put his hand over his own throat. I saw him squeeze—enough to hurt. I knew the feeling; the truth was a thing with pincers clawing its way out. "I can't turn down someone who asks for help, it's the Witches' Vow. I told him what he was asking for. Then I gave him the mask. I put him into the maze." He shook his head once. "Then I went back up to the High City and lied to you. I've been lying to you all along. The census, the funeral, all of it, I was trying to steer you away from him."

I had to laugh. It came out very low, from a lot deeper down than my normal voice did.

He looked at me with so much dread I stopped. It knocked me sideways, that he minded so much about what I might say. I could have forgiven him anything then, because he minded.

"You've never made a secret about lying," I said. "You told me from the start."

"Phaidros—"

I had to take his wrist and move his hand, because I couldn't watch him do it any more. There were red marks around his neck. "If there is anything I understand in atomic fucking detail," I said, "it is the upholding of a vow."

We sat quiet for a little while. Behind us, the fountain chattered. The room was cool. Little by little, I started noticing ordinary things, like how there was a pin in my hair sticking into me, how there were anemones growing in the moss between us, and how *yellow* the leopard was, more yellow than any other sort of yellow. How the soot felt gritty under the neck of my tunic.

I looked around for a bowl and pitcher—yes, he had a bronze set, burnished so well I could see the two of us in it, and yellow of the leopard—then drew us both some water to wash with, and watched him from under my eyelashes as he rinsed through the length of his hair. It was such a normal, homely thing; it made him look like a boy at a laundry pool. Around us settled all the things we hadn't said yet.

"Why did you come back for me?" I asked. "After what I said to you."

"It was a reasonable thing to say," he said to the water. The leopard was looking at me worriedly. I stroked its ears and it put its paw over my wrist, unexpectedly heavy. Dionysus swayed. "Things like me . . . snatch at people all the time. It's always terrible and it's never a choice, for you. Hades stole Persephone and Zeus stole a king's son and Aphrodite stole that poor man from Troy. I shouldn't have touched you. I came back to apologise."

"That isn't what I meant," I said, hating that he could ever think I'd think that, and dismayed, because it was a bitter way to see those stories. Stories are stories, and they're brief, because they have to fit into the amount of time a reasonably drunk person will listen by a fire, so they leave out things, like whether the young prince was frightened or whether the Trojan man had a choice—but the way I'd always heard them, the way Helios had told them, was with a kind of gentle wryness. These things were phrased as seizing and thefts, and violence, because the people being stolen could hardly turn around to their families and their kingdoms and say, *Look, I'm terribly sorry, but you can all shove it, thanks, all your duty and your honour: I'm off.* So Zeus said to the prince's father, *No, I stole him*; and the Unseen said, *Well, she had the pomegranate seeds.*

"I thought you were drawing out a revenge quest. I was telling you to get on with it. I thought you were just . . . I thought," I said, trying hard to say it in a straight line, "that the only reason you were being kind to me was to make it worse when you murdered me."

He lifted his eyebrow a tiny fraction. "You're fucked up, Phaidros."

"I've been noticing that lately." I put my hand over his and squeezed. He let me, though he didn't touch me.

"I'm not going to be angry," he said, "if you don't want to stay here. I'm a hell of a thing to stay with. There are other parts of the maze, or . . ."

He let it hang, but I knew what that *or* was.

It was my duty. That was to go back up to the Palace and see if the Queen was alive, to negotiate, to persuade her it hadn't been me, there really was a god, there had been no plot, nobody wanted her crown; it was to go and help, because the High City was in ruins and they would need all hands to move the wreckage, to find places for people to stay, and then the long slog of salvage and rebuilding. I had sworn my oath to Thebes and the call of duty meant I should go back, even if Thebes had wanted me half dead by now and sent to the sea.

"No," I said.

It was much too unobtrusive and quiet for what it was, which was the cracking of a shackle I'd always worn.

He smiled, not enough to show his incisors. "Look . . . however ill-advised I think it is, you're in love with the Queen. I'm not going to snarl at you if you want to try your luck, going back."

"I'm not in love with the Queen. I love her, but that's different to *in* love. She is everything my duty is, but . . ." I struggled, and realized it was the first time in my life I'd ever said anything like this aloud. "If the choice were mine, if nothing else depended on it, if I could just . . ." It sounded utterly wrong and shameful and ridiculous and forbidden, but something was lifting too—there was a mask coming away. "I would never have gone anywhere near the Palace, or her. You've got it the wrong way around. I *want* to stay with you. What are you going to do now?"

"Leave. I can't stay here, everyone will lose their minds."

"You . . . don't care."

"No, but you do, and this is your home, I don't want to wreck it any more than I already have."

"This is not my home, I've lived here for six months and never before that. Let's go together."

"Really," he said, not as a question. He wasn't convinced I was choosing so much as appeasing the horrifying wild thing that had just destroyed half of Thebes.

I brushed a twist of grey-black away from his face. He was very still, and he looked afraid. It was the fear I had around anyone I could hurt by accident. "I'm not some boy you stole, strange one. I stole you, remember?"

He tipped his head a quarter inch, the barest kind of agreement. He had his hands clamped in his lap. I cradled them between mine and kissed his knuckles, then the red marks on his throat.

When he kissed me back, I felt like I'd finally been allowed to sail into a safe harbour after too long at sea. It was like I'd never managed to get home after that shipwreck. I'd come back to land, but there was no anchor, just wandering and waiting and watching the storms, and now—it all went quiet. Shelter. It made me cry, which made me worry he was going to think I was saying no, but he understood and just lifted me sideways into his lap. I felt strangely panicky. It was too long since anyone had done that, I was too old, there was something terrible about a beautiful witch worn down by the world to paying any attention at all to beaten-up knight who should have died years ago.

He set his hand against the side of my skull as if he'd overheard the thoughts, the way you put your hand to a glass to stop it ringing after someone's smacked it. It worked the same way. I turned my face against his hand and listened to all the quiet come down in my head.

It was little by little that I started to notice I could hear things and feel things I didn't generally. Not far from us, there were tiny, busy balls of thought, preoccupied with the logistics of dismantling what I knew was a crust of bread but for them was a mountain, and getting it home, and how nice it was to snug up close with the others in the nest, all brothers and sisters, and sleeping below somewhere was the Queen, who was good and gentle, and whose eggs made such strong soldiers.

I thought I was dreaming, and when I opened my eyes, it was weird to find that I was the size I was, with hands and elbows and eyelashes, and for a whole second, I had no idea what to do with any of those.

I wasn't dreaming. I sat up in the dark, taking in the bedroom, trying to remember where I was. It only came to me slowly. Dionysus's room: his side of the maze. We were down deep, at least three storeys. Moonlight came down through windows that were cut carefully to line up across the levels. We were well below my cellar, and it was cool enough that I could nearly have called it cold. Above the bed were the spectacular roots of a tree, alive with ivy and honeysuckle and some kind of trailing flower that swayed in the little breeze that came down to us from the stairway. Climbing vines with tiny white flowers hugged most of the far wall, full of the glass lamps he had used at the party—all alight, even though he hadn't lit them and there were no slaves here.

My sitting up had made something else near the doorway jump, another mind that had thought nothing big was alive down here and that built its idea of the world with sounds, not light, and it called back to the others, mimicking the shape of what it had heard with the noise so the others would know what to look for. And somewhere above us: great slow ageless thoughts, not seeing or hearing, but delving in the earth, and feeling the hot wind, and keening quietly for water. Even though I couldn't hear any sound at all.

"It's the trees," Dionysus whispered. "They cry when there's no water."

I was so aside from myself that I didn't even find it odd, and I sat there wondering if there were some ants now who were having confused dreams about being a giant.

Dionysus seemed smaller than he was, lying down. He was curled up now. I touched his shoulder to ask if it was all right to lie back down where I had been or if he'd rather I stayed on my side. He held his arm out for me and pulled me back against his chest, and fitted his knee between mine. Somehow he didn't have any difficult angles, even though I'd slept alone for years and I wasn't used to another person any more. I held his hand where it rested on my waist. My fingertips were too rough to feel where the tattoos stopped, but just by my hip, I could. It was a tiny slight difference, and such a meaningless thing to know about him, but it was important, too.

I could feel him waiting, with genuine dread, for me to ask why I was suddenly hearing a lot more of the world than I had done a few hours ago.

I was happier not asking. It was here now. It wasn't unpleasant. I didn't need to know the clockwork of it; knowing wouldn't change anything.

"Blue," I said instead, shifting to face him. "I think I know what it is now. Wine, and stories, and the dance. Madness; masks, and . . ." I didn't want to say it, because it was a kind of holy, the way I was feeling now: weightless, like when he'd lifted me, and the before-remembering moment of waking up. I pressed my hand very gently between his legs to show what I meant, though, and he made a tiny sound that sent a painful, lovely ache through my groin and up my chest. "It's release. It's all . . . things that take you away from yourself, and into something—truer, and wilder. Some of them do that a very small way. Some of them do it entire."

"Yes." He laughed the littlest ghost of a laugh and I understood why: he'd thought I never be able to see it, not really. "Yes."

From up above, a knitting needle of daylight came around the window frame. I shut my eyes, not wanting to think about the next time we were going to be able to sleep. Out in the forest somewhere, hopefully on the far side of Harper Mountain, towards the border with Corinth. Maybe to keep me from saying anything horrifying about getting up and getting started, Dionysus gathered my hair into one hand, twisting it over his knuckles. I held his free hand.

I could feel that *my* hand felt small to him, and rough from sword hilts, and he could tell where the bones still weren't quite right after I'd broken my last two fingers in an oarlock years ago. I'd been ashamed before because I was so used up and worn down, but that wasn't how he was seeing me. He thought I looked the same as I had a decade ago on the deck of the ship as it turned to trees. He was holding, the way people hold moths rescued from candles, the memory of me looking puzzled—but not scared—about the ivy growing around my wrist. It was a little shock. I would barely have recognised myself.

He must have noticed me noticing, because he said, "You haven't . . . you haven't asked me what I am or where I came from."

I shook my head once. "None of my business."

He was quiet for a long time, his fingertips just moving to and fro between the vertebrae in the base of my back where my spine always hurt if I lay still too long. I'd twisted something after falling off a horse once and it had never entirely untwisted—except, now, it didn't hurt. It made me want to laugh. Increasingly I had a sense that he just sort of tidied up as he went along, putting things right, growing things, healing old fractures, in the same way other people stacked crockery and folded blankets.

Yes: pharmakeia.

He touched our heads together. "I can't tell you what I am, I don't know that; but I can tell you how I came to be, and what I'm for."

"You don't have to."

"I do. You need to know what you're making promises to."

34

A long time ago, when only a few hundred people lived along the banks of the Nile and everyone else flitted in the deep forests, before ploughing, and before anyone ever prayed to the sky for rain to save their crops—before crops—what mattered was the Hunt.

They called Her Mother, the god of the earth, but *mother* is one of those words whose meaning shifts depending on who you are. For him, then, it was a flint word, hammered to an arrow point. Mothers were the ones who killed the newborns the Hunt couldn't hope to feed; mothers were the ones who burned the bones, and read the future in the shapes of the cracks the fire made in them. Mothers were more dangerous than the mammoth.

Mothers decided who the sacrifice would be.

He was young but not very. Very young men didn't know anything and they didn't make good husbands. The mothers kept him unmarried, because the bones told them early on what he was for. Everyone knew but no one said it. If you were that tall and that finely turned, you couldn't expect anything else. So he went to the witches when he was small, like the sacrifices always did, and learned how to read the forest. He learned how to feel where north was, even after being blindfolded and spun around in a strange grove. He learned how to follow the deer, and understand the bees, and because his face wasn't meant for anyone but Her, the mask stayed on always.

It was lonely and he hated it, because it didn't feel like living at all, just watching other people live. They always said, *Don't worry, you'll live forever*, but that sounded nightmarish. He had a good idea of what She was now, and mostly it was horrible. It was ripping out the hearts of the deer and skinning wolves and always being up to your elbows in blood, and having no time to think anything or do anything except the endless Hunt.

"You can't live if you don't kill something else," his own mother said, but that was why he liked the bees. If you asked them right, they would let you have some of the honey, and you didn't have to kill anything at all.

Honey had a fizz to it if you left it in water, and once you left it long enough, it took on a kind of magic. It changed people, made them bright and merry, even the witches. So when the Hunt led them back round every year to the caverns, he went to see the bees in their cave. He loved the way they danced to each other. He still couldn't tell why they did it, but they did. And he loved how they built things. They didn't wander endlessly, following stags or the herds. There were hives the size of a tent; mountains, if you were a bee. Instead of killing things, they all had their own jobs to do, and they harvested their pollen, and made enough to feed everyone. He had spent a lot of time wondering how much better the world would be if people were more like bees.

Bees didn't sacrifice anyone to keep the Queen happy. He had watched the bee queens. They were stronger than the rest, and bigger, but they were gentle. They had lots of husbands and, even though the husbands were useless and idle, they didn't hurt any of them. Not unless the hive was starving.

He left the casks in the cave next to the bees to sit for a year while the clan moved on, and then every year he came back for them. A year was good; it tasted nice anyway. That morning, though, there was a bit of an impediment to getting to them, because a bull had got there first. Not at the wine, but the bees. It was munching its way through a giant honey-comb, not looking like it meant to move at all soon.

He looked back towards the camp. He should tell them it was here. Or better, he should kill it and then tell them. Very risky, to do it by himself, but frankly he was quite open to being killed by a bull given that he only had a few months left before the witches killed him and left him in the holy cave. But he didn't want to kill it. The bull was incredible. It was gold, gleaming in the last of the light, and mighty. It must have been twice his size, its horns as long as his arms, and nocked from fights with other bulls. They had enough food already. They didn't need a huge feast.

So he sat down to wait for it to go on its way, and propped up the little leather bag with its grain offering for the bees. There was corn growing in the grove by the camp. He'd planted it last year, not that he'd told anyone. If anyone had caught him doing that, the witches would have shredded him. Folly to rely on the sky for rain. It'll never rain when you want. Don't waste your time scrabbling with seeds. Make your arrows.

You couldn't say: *You know actually, I've been watching it, and corn needs minimal looking after. You just plant it and leave it. It's like a weed.*

But no. You could only make bread when you found a whole grove of the corn, and then everyone celebrated and said how bountiful She was, as if you couldn't do better than that if you just dug over the earth yourself and brought it a bit of water sometimes. No, because that would tie you to a particular part of the land, and what would you do when someone else found you, or when the bulls trampled it, and on and on they went, as though twenty determined people and a fence couldn't look after most of that.

Blasphemy. Fences. The earth isn't *yours*. She'll curse you. Shut up and go hunting. Or do you think that all the mothers there have ever been have somehow been wrong about how to get food into you?

"No," he said, prodding the corn, because he couldn't say it to anyone else, "but maybe when you spend every moment of the day running after something and putting up tents and killing spare children, you're not giving yourself time to do any *thinking*. It's not blasphemy to say there could be better things. Is it?" He aimed this at the bull, who had heard him and looked round.

It clearly didn't think he was worth worrying about. One of the two-leg things with their sharp sticks was no more worry to a bull than one irritable hedgehog would be to him.

"Hmph," it said.

He got up to see how near he could go to it. The big ones were vicious, but they were—because they were so big—sometimes very calm, too. They knew you couldn't hurt them. This one was honey-drunk already, all sticky and happy. He put his hand out slowly. It eyed him, not too impressed, but when he touched its side, it seemed not to mind. Close to, it was even bigger than it had looked before. It had left great prints in the earth, and whenever it moved, he felt the ground judder.

The bull studied him, looking almost interested.

It was so strong. If a person could cut into the earth a little way with some flint and then plant seeds, you could clear whole groves if you could persuade a bull to help you. A whole plain. How much corn would there be then? More than the clan could eat in a whole year, even if they ate nothing else. And if the bull brought his wives, and they agreed to help too, and there were the bees . . . you could live without ever killing anything. Milk and honey, and bread. The Hunt could end.

He could see himself in the bull's serene eyes. He was just a man and it was just a stupid daydream. Nobody would ever tame the herds. They were the wildest things there were. No bull would ever help plant corn.

And anyway, they weren't wrong, the witches. The bees and the herds and the earth weren't just tools. Even good axes had names. To try to make a bull into something so tame as a thing that just helped you plant seeds . . . that was unholy.

But just yesterday morning, he had had to ask Henna which of her twins she wanted to live, because everyone knew they couldn't feed two extra. Barely one. She chose the girl, of course she did—women lasted far longer in times of famine, men were strange fuel-hungry luxuries for times of plenty—and so he'd had to take the boy out into the woods to the altar.

The witches called that the balance. But that was unholy too. He had never said so to anyone, he would have been shunned, but he was sure that he couldn't be the only one who thought so. The freedom of a bull was worth as much as anyone's, but that little boy had been worth something too.

The wind shifted. It was cold, colder than it should have been. The season was turning early. Tomorrow there would be frost. The bull noticed it too, and turned away.

Someone touched his shoulders, and he froze. No one could touch him. It was forbidden. So he didn't turn around. It wouldn't be anyone he knew, and there was no one else in these woods. These were clan heartlands. The totems kept others away.

"Already?" he said.

She paced around in front of him, and he closed his eyes, because you weren't ever meant to see. But She took the mask off him, and his lungs seized up, because no one had seen his face since he could remember.

"Already," She said, and She sounded like She might laugh. She; they. It was lots of voices, many women, young and old, some half singing, but really there was only one, in the same way that there are many bees but one swarm. "Other things to do, have you?"

"No, lady," he whispered.

"You're shaking. Are you frightened?"

He set his teeth and shook his head. "No, lady, it's just—cold."

A heavy fur cloak settled over his shoulders. It was better than anything he'd even heard of before. He couldn't tell what the fur was. Maybe a bear. He had seen bears, but no one in the clan had ever killed one.

"What courtesy." She was laughing now. "It was interesting, to see your dreams just now. You can see far. Plains of corn and tame herds. A land of milk and honey."

"I know it's stupid," he mumbled. "I know it's heresy. Forgive me."

But She didn't sound angry when She spoke next. Those voices, that great choir, just sounded . . . speculative. "Do you understand how the world would change, if that dream came to pass? Do you understand how quickly they would forget the Hunt and the earth, and the honour of their mothers, and the necessity of the witches? Crops need rain, not witches and trackers and readers of trees. They would worship the sky, not the earth. It would be a turning of gods, as well as minds."

"They wouldn't dare."

"It is good to be courteous with each other, I agree with you. But not to lie. They would dare and you know it. Their memories are small. They would forget. You want them to leave behind the Hunt, and perhaps it is time, and enough children have died; perhaps I am old and there should be new gods, but tell me true, husband: do you not think the price is too high?"

He had to clench his hands under the cloak. She could see what he thought anyway, but She was seeing if he was brave enough to say it.

And—She was right. Lying would be a bad way to start. "I was raised by witches. I bring children into the world and I bury most of them on the same day. If the price for changing that is that they forget the earth and turn to the sky—it's worth it. But they need not forget. Not if you remind them sometimes. We don't last long, but our stories do. I know stories from my grandmother's grandmother. We remember what's important. Or—we can."

She put both hands around his neck, and he thought She was going to strangle him, but She didn't squeeze. "I won't remind them, husband. You will."

"What?" he whispered.

All the voices rose, and sighed, and sang.

"You are the forest and the earth. Yours are the hives, and the honey, and the great bulls; the things that mean living without killing. You will die and rise, and die and rise, as evergreen as the ivy. Yours will be the border between the new world, and mine. Down the ages they will try to stray too far, and forget their nature, and their limits. Wherever they transgress, there you will be. You are the watchman, and the memory, and the madness. In the times that are to come, humans will need a god to make them remember what human is."

She took Her hands away.

"Open your eyes."

35

We set out early, while it was still cool—or almost—and the sun hadn't broiled everything yet. It would have been cooler to walk under the shade of the trees, but neither of us even discussed it. Helios had told me the story of Actaeon, who had tried to go into the sacred woods to hunt, and ended up turned into a stag himself. The stag's head was still on the wall at the Palace.

It was the strangest thing, but as we walked uphill, I could feel things that didn't belong to me. I kept wanting to rearrange my feathers, or get a burr out of a tail I didn't have, and every so often, the sun was blinding through eyes that were meant for moonlight. Once, I tried to reach up to pick an orange, and it was Dionysus's hand that moved. He winced.

"Sorry."

Something in my head vanished, and I was just me again. Which felt small and uncomfortable and trapped. I'd been—bigger, a second ago.

He was looking at me like he expected to be shouted at.

"But that was nice," I said.

He hesitated, then took my hand, and it came back; not so strong. I wasn't seeing through anyone else's eyes any more, or feeling confused about wings. But I could feel that we were surrounded by lots of star-points of tiny minds that didn't even notice we were alive, just funny moving hills, and great, slow, strange minds I didn't recognise, for whom we were strange flashes, babies one minute and then dust. Those were dark, under the earth somewhere, but they could feel us walking above. Off to our right was a disturbed-hive thrum that I realized after a little while was Thebes. It was eerie, but only in the way that floating underwater above a reef is eerie, knowing you're seeing things humans can't normally see, and that you could drown, but you won't.

"That's lovely," I said, and for a split second, I heard how my voice sounded to him, which was dizzying but not horrible.

He smiled as if I'd said something immensely graceful, not just the truth.

The sun was creeping up higher, the air already warmer. The way was getting steep, and rocky, and dry. Whatever that great presence was that lived under the ground, it died away here, and the world seemed too quiet. No water; even the trees, though they delved deep, were gradually dying.

"Might take longer than we'd hoped," I observed, not feeling very optimistic about the springs. If they were still there, the water would be hard to get to.

"There are lots of animals up there," he said, pointing more or less north. "That usually means water."

Another hour or so proved him right. The springs had shrunk, a lot— there were smooth patches on their banks where the water had used to be—but there was still water, and it was full of birds and animals that must have come from all around the forest, including what I was almost sure was the same leopard I'd met before. Some of the birds were amazing, brilliant green, with red crests, not normally to be found at all in Achaea, or not that I'd ever known; they must have come a lot further.

As if he were opening a door, slowly, in a way that felt very much as though he was hoping I might not notice, I started to hear all their minds, little bright things delighted with the water and stealing shiny things from the big featherless boring birds and their stone nests down in the plain below, and feeling the tug of north, where there would be cooler weather.

I lifted my eyebrows at him, pretend-stern.

He faltered. "Too much," he said.

I pushed him in the pool. "What sort of *moron* doesn't want to make friends with the adorable birds, Dionysus? Who have you been talking to for the last thousand years and why did you put up with such a luxurious selection of dickheads? Fuck!"

He laughed, and incredibly, much more incredibly than finding myself able to overhear the interests of birds, he blushed. I couldn't see it, he was too dark, but I felt the blood rush. I pretended not to notice and started refilling our flasks, a little away from the smaller animals who would have been frightened if I got too close. The leopard sat down opposite me, coiling her tail and thinking how useful it would be to have the weird claws that could carry things like water, even when you were away from a pool; very ugly, though. Imagine being that ugly all the time. Amazing how more of their fathers didn't just eat them at birth to spare everyone else the unpleasantness of looking at them.

"Yes, well, I hate your ears," I told her. "Look, they're all wonky, someone's eaten one."

Funny noises they made as well. Still, probably anybody would make all sorts of distressed noises if they had go around all bald and minus two legs and with stupid prey-teeth that weren't any good for anything except—urgh—*vegetables*.

I flicked water at her.

Probably, *probably*, the One from the Trees wouldn't mind if she ate his friend, just a little bit. It wouldn't be very delicious, but it couldn't be flicking water annoyingly if it didn't have its weird claw things.

"Dionysus, the leopard wants to eat me." One from the Trees; it was like she knew, somehow, about the Hunt and the forests, and where he had come from.

He pretended to bite my shoulder. It was only when I twisted back that I realized twisting should have hurt. Yesterday the knife wound had been raw and barely closed. There was just a slim scar now. I looked down and pushed my fingers against what had been most painful place. Nothing. He saw me notice and this time, he pretended to look stern, which doesn't work so well when you're beautiful and half your face hasn't been minced.

I smiled. "Got enough water?"

He nodded. "Shall we go?"

"Very slowly," I agreed.

His dark eyes strayed up ahead. "I've never walked so far in this kind of heat, is it . . . ?"

"Miserable, but it'll be fine. I'll tell you riddles. You'll be too annoyed to notice it's hot."

"I'm . . . very old, I know all the riddles."

"Oh, not that old, surely," I said, filling up with the glee of someone who can see victory laurels waiting right there on a plinth.

"I'm trying not to think too hard about it, actually, given how recently you were a baby."

"So you won't mind," I said, trying hard to sound boyish and innocent, "if I bet you dinner in Aulis I can tell you a riddle you don't know?"

"Lovely, I'll take free food."

"You *promise*?" I really do sound about sixteen if I half-try, it's dreadful.

He shrugged. "I promise I will eat the dinner you are assuredly going to pay for with the silver you will somehow have to acquire between here and there, yes."

I grinned. "I like scallops, by the way, they're very expensive."

He watched me for a second, hunting for whatever he'd missed, and then hissed. "Oh, *fuck*, you're a fucking sailor!"

"Too late! Dinner in Aulis, old man!"

He started to laugh, but then stopped, and touched my arm to stop me walking. "Phaidros."

It wasn't anything he'd seen. It was that down in the city, something had shifted, and minds sharp and well-fletched were turning their attention towards the mountain.

It wasn't like having a god's-eye view. I'd always thought the gods knew things because they were looking down from Olympus, maybe with some kind of holy device to help them focus on the people of specific interest, but the way he saw—the way he was making me see—was the same way I always saw, but with lots of different eyes. It wasn't only seeing, either. I was hearing, and feeling the heat, and noticing things filtered through different minds that perceived everything a little bit differently to the way I did.

A few miles behind us, the Hidden thundered out of the Palace gates. It had taken this long to go through the wreckage of the prison and find the trees that had been doors and the safe hollow space where I conspicuously wasn't.

It wasn't a young unit. It was everyone who was left, who could ride. I could feel Polydorus, or rather what had used to be Polydorus. When he had seen Jason's mother hold up the head from the chariot, he had broken. It wasn't a great, grand, spectacular breaking, just the tiny but definitive snap of a bird's hyoid. He felt strangely free now. All those years aching and worrying that he wasn't going to be able to see Jason through, even though that was what he had sworn to do when he found that tiny little boy hiding behind a dead sheep after fucking Ajax's fucking insane rampage, and all those little fires of hope when Phaidros, who wasn't actually the unmitigated curse everyone said, realized that the way to help Jason was to play with him, not flog him: gone. All he was now was the shield and the spear, and the narrowed vision from the inside of a helmet.

Amphitrion and Allecto's mother was there too. She had retired from the army fifteen years ago when she had the twins, which was a waste of fucking time it turned out, because the boy had died of the madness and she had had to kill the girl with her own hands after the stadium. Children were only yours for seven years, everyone knew that, and they had been in the garrison now longer than they hadn't, but when the order came from the Queen—she had almost packed a bag and run for Aulis. But then her husband had said, *Please, we need to run, you can't do this*: and she had locked up with scorn and said, *We are Sown. We* are *this*. And then down deep somewhere, there was a little snap, and suddenly, amazingly, she didn't care any more.

As they rode down through the lower city, priests and slaves were everywhere, digging in the rubble for survivors, helping people into shade, handing out bread. Everyone looked grey and exhausted: not much better than the refugees from Pylos.

The Queen was with them too, because even if monarchs and heirs did not go to war, they did hunt. It was good to hold a shield and spear again. What had happened yesterday had a dreamy quality now, for her and for nearly everyone. She remembered the earthquake. The Guards had gone mad. And then, in the prison, that weird glade, formed of great oak trees that hadn't been there before. Tiresias said, *Look, they were the doors*, but . . . that couldn't be true. What was true, though, was that there was no Phaidros. No body. He had run. Or been taken. Had there not been another man, a tall man in witch black, who had stood in front of her, terrible and entirely unconcerned in a way human beings can't be, and . . . ? No. That memory felt untrustworthy. It was a sort of mirage, born of the earthquake and all that suffocating dust that had knocked everyone out. Dust, of course it was something in the dust. It didn't matter. What mattered was getting Phaidros before he crossed the Corinth border, because after a disaster like this—well. People would think (already thought) the earthquake had happened *because* he had been imprisoned. They would drown her and give him the crown just to apologise.

She'd thought she had killed everything but clockwork in her, years ago. But it wasn't dead. She had beaten it into coma, but this last week, it had been waking, and a tiny voice had said, *What if he's* right, *what if it* was *monstrous, what your mother said to you, what if* this *was what family really was, this one modest man who was savage and kind at the same time . . .*

It was like brandy.

Heady, and wonderful, and poisonous.

Somewhere down on the mountainside, Pentheus was struggling up the path in the heat, trailed by Tiresias, who was trying to tell him—begging him—not to go. I could see them through the birds and the ground, and I felt it when Pentheus almost fell and pulled himself up against a rock.

"Pentheus! Pentheus, stop, you can't go up there. It's dangerous, *he's* dangerous! If your mother corners him—don't you understand? He's a god!"

Tiresias remembered what had happened because they always saw true, although just now, they wished that wasn't the case. It would be a lot less awful, not to realize what was going to happen in about a quarter of an hour. It would have been less awful to stand in that courtyard after a god had shut down everyone's minds and grown trees though a prison, watching everyone come around and feel puzzled and just . . . look at those trees and the hollow inside big enough to hold two people, and brush it aside like peculiar weather, seeing and not seeing at all.

"Of course he isn't a god," Pentheus said stiffly. "He's just a witch and he was helping Phaidros to the crown, no doubt in exchange for a lot of money. I don't know what's so hard to understand."

"You're lying, Pentheus. You *know* you're lying."

Pentheus didn't know that, actually. What he did know was that there had been an earthquake, and something about it had done something to everyone. Just like when the star had fallen. Sudden madness was unsettling, metamorphosis was very unusual, but . . . the holy machines weren't gods talking, just people. The story about the lost prince was just a misunderstanding of the fact that *child of a god* was royal code for *born outside wedlock but let's not have a blood feud.* Wherever you looked for a god, there was just a collection of dull, human things where one wasn't.

And that was because . . . there were no gods. There were forces, like the sea and death, and madness, but they weren't *conscious.* They didn't want things, or plan. That was all witchcraft, and once you know how the witching works, it stops working. He could see it all. What a god *really* did was marshal people together under a banner, and help them get things done. Build palaces, win wars. Otherwise nobody would ever agree about anything, but if you said the magic words, in the name of Zeus, or in the name of Ra . . . you could make people build things so great that their grandchildren wouldn't see the finished temple. The gods were ideas, a great, sparkling lie to oil the clockwork of the world, and priests were only witches.

When you came down to it, nothing was anything except itself. A crown was a band of silver. An earthquake . . . he didn't know, but he would have bet anything now that it was just some arbitrary shift in the mantle of the world, no more significant or meaningful than a tree shaking in the wind. And sure as clockwork, madness wasn't a god. It was just human minds, malfunctioning, like faulty marvels. Nothing divine breathed through it.

The reason he knew that was true was that he didn't want it to be. It was terrible. But in his experience, the worst and bleakest explanation for a thing was the truest one.

"Pentheus," Tiresias called again, coughing. They had breathed in a lot of dust, in the earthquake. "Pentheus, what do you mean to *do?*"

Pentheus didn't say anything, because there was no point, and he'd had enough. A whole lifetime of enough, even though he'd hardly lived at all yet. All this time, everyone had been trying to tell him to be Sown, even though they wouldn't let him *learn* to be Sown: no garrison, no commander like everyone else, no training, he was supposed to know everything by magic. And then the Queen was angry when he—shockingly—didn't understand how to do any of it. But the strange thing was, he had learned. Whatever the witch had done to him in the maze, it had switched off the thinking part of his mind, and now that it had switched back on again, he could see much, much better. Everything was right in front of him and as clear as the morning.

If you wanted to be in Thebes, and not go to Egypt, and learn how to be a good king . . . then that was what you did. You didn't rely on the Queen, who thought, not very secretly, that there were caterpillars who would make better kings. Or Phaidros, who said one thing to your face and did something else, as cunning as all good knights were supposed to be.

What you did was, you shot Phaidros *and* the Queen, blamed a witch, and took the throne.

That was Sown.

36

There was nowhere to hide but the forest, but even so, I slowed down when we came up to the border. I'd never crossed it. Men hadn't, not for a thousand years. Not since Actaeon had seen the dryads, and turned into a stag, and been ripped apart by his own dogs.

The next step would mean easing over the roots of a great oak that had pushed up my side of the road. She would know, the dryad who lived in the oak. It must have been a slow kind of fury, the rage of the trees, but all I could think of was how it would feel, when the bones of my hands started fusing together into hooves, and the horns started grinding up out of my skull.

Dionysus stepped across it like he would have his own threshold.

"It's all right," he said. "Listen." He took my hand to give me a tiny pull over the border, and he was right: I could hear them if I listened.

I'd always thought of dryads as people who also happened to be trees, but that, I realized then, was a very human way of imagining. They weren't.

They were under the earth, sometimes shallow, sometimes deep, and they knew we were there. They could feel us walking, the weight of us, the length of our steps, and from that, they had quite a good idea of us, though not the same as mine. And they didn't know enough about humans to know what type of humans we were, any more than I would have known types of dryad, or even if there were types. They were minds that stretched for miles through the woods, knowing every inch of those miles, and they were dreaming: huge, slow, ancient dreams, because they had been here as long as Dionysus and longer. Those dreams were about the taste of the soil, and the festivals of the ants, and strange, creaking acquaintances with roots and branches that lasted a thousand years. I was like a sudden spark; the things down deep noticed me in the way I noticed fireflies. It was brief interest, and that was all. They didn't care if I walked in their woods, because humans weren't important enough to think of at all.

"But . . . Actaeon," I said, confused.

"Witching," Dionysus said.

I didn't understand, but then, maybe because I just knew him well enough, or maybe because I could think through his thinking now, I did.

If you've got a city full of professionally violent, angry men who go out to the wars and trudge home battle mad and uncontrollable, you have to make sure there are places they cannot, cannot go. Only, there are no fences that a strong enough, angry enough person can't rip down in the end, so what you do is, you build the fence in his head.

The dryads were there and these woods were holy, that was no lie. But they didn't care. Of course they didn't care. They were older than people, and long after people had blasted themselves off the face of the earth, they would still be beneath it, dreaming.

The dryads could feel hoofbeats.

A hundred horses, more, heavy with people on them. And ahead of them, dogs. The dogs knew exactly where we were.

We started to run, aiming for the rocks up ahead, under the shade of the great trees and into a gloom and unevenness of ground that the horses would struggle with, and Dionysus did—something, I felt it, but I couldn't understand what exactly—and birds exploded from the forest, gritting the air so that even someone very close to us would have been hard put to make out two running figures among the chaos of feathers and wings.

The horses were still coming. The dogs called to each other. There, over there, over there.

Dionysus turned back, and I felt the thoughts go through him this time. He could have made all the riders forget what they were doing and attack each other, but that was cruel, and for him, it was the same as hitting a child; he couldn't send them to sleep, because a lot of them would be killed as they fell over the horses' hooves, and he didn't want to do that either—just warn them again, and so he made the horses panic, just for second: just enough to make them rear and throw a lot of the riders, and no more.

Some people fell, but some didn't.

The trees were growing, pressing closer together, the branches closing the way. The dryads remembered him, He of the Trees, the little witch who had faced the Mother and told her his dreams of honey and fields, and an end to the great Hunt; of course they would help—but even with a titan effort, even at a sprint, they couldn't move as fast as humans did, and though the bark was creaking and reaching, it was slow.

The birds were still thundering. Everything was wings and claws.

Through a brief gap, though, I saw the Queen, in silver armour, with a silver bow.

Just like Andromache.

I did what I'd been much too stupid to do all those years ago for Helios. I didn't try to pull her off her horse. I just got in the way of the shot.

It's strange how there can be stillness in the middle of a storm of birds and falling horses, but there was. Her mind was right there in front of me, and I could see myself through it, and how tired and sad it made her. Even though she *knew* it was hopeless and stupid and irrational, there was a fluttering scrap of her that wanted me to say something that would make all this unnecessary, so we could just go home. I even knew what it was.

I'd say: *No, he stole me—he stole me. I don't choose this. Let me come back. I choose duty and honour, and you, I choose you.*

The tree branches were creeping closer together, and by tiny fractions, or it seemed so because time is so slow just before you die, some of the riders were turning into wild animals, but none of it was quick enough.

In that split second, I realized I'd rather die now than say that.

Some final fragile thing snapped.

She shot me straight through the throat, and I felt whatever that vital crucial thing that makes humans humans go out, and then I was just . . . gone.

37

What's most confusing about being a human one second and then being quite a lot of birds and small animals and partly some dryads the next is that you can see what's going on from a lot more angles than you previously could. I could see Dionysus through many pairs of eyes, and hardly any two worked in the same way. Some saw him clear and sharp. Some saw him in colours I'd never known about, with kinds of light I'd never seen. And some things that knew he was there weren't seeing him at all, but they could build an idea from what they did know in the same way I built ideas from seeing. They knew his weight on the earth, and how fast he moved, and that the alchemy of him was different to the other things that looked like him. They were grateful for the blood soaking into the earth.

It was too much. I started to come apart. I'd thought I knew what I meant when I said *me*, but that was wrong; it was just so much sand in a bucket, and *me* was the bucket shape, but now I didn't have a bucket. Although I'd held the shape of it for a few seconds, the sea was pouring in now, and there wouldn't be any shape at all for much longer.

Through all those other eyes and other ways of seeing, I saw him buckle onto the ground next to what had been me a second ago. He didn't make a sound, because no one would help him even if he did. He tipped forward so that the ends of his hair coiled against my chest. He wanted to cry, but he was too wrung out, after too many centuries. He was so old, and so tired, and maybe it was now another time of turning; maybe there should be new gods again and the old ones should just be forgotten. What was the point?

"So you're not a god, then," the Queen said. She wasn't being cruel, or wasn't meaning to: she was just thinking aloud, and there was a kind of heavy curiosity to it more than anything else. "You would be able to bring him back if you were."

He could; he could, but there were the Deathless, and the Dying. For him, life was just a fact: he was always alive, and so in order to make sure one particular part of him—the one that looked like a human—remained so, all he had to do was rearrange other parts of himself.

For the Dying . . . it was different. To pull a human being away from the Unseen, there was a horrible cost, and it wouldn't be him who had to pay it.

It was so horrible that the Deathless largely agreed never to do it. The agreement had always been there, an unuttered contract to prevent the wars that had harrowed the beginning of the world, when they had all thought they should be entirely free, not realizing that if they tried to be that, then no one was free except the very strongest, and that if they were all a little less than free, then nobody was a slave. The King in the Thunder was assiduous. He let his own sons die on the field, even though each death was a hammer blow, and each one made him harder, more tempered, more frightening.

How many deaths had Dionysus allowed over the years? He didn't know. He was older than the thunder king.

There were the Deathless, and there were the Dying.

Of course, it was his choice in the end whether he *stayed* Deathless.

That jolted me into pushing back against that sea of other things. I *could* hold together the little thing that was me. It was an effort, but that didn't matter.

No. Fight.

I didn't mean to, and it startled me as much as anyone, but I'd made about forty people say it. Archers still on horseback, people who'd been thrown, the slaves behind.

The Queen looked around fast, looking disconcerted for the first time since I'd known her. Everything was still now. The birds, feeling confused, had gone back to the trees. The dryads had stopped growing.

Dionysus had his hand over mine. There was nothing there now, no pulse, but I could see him, with other eyes.

I couldn't touch him with my hands, but I could move ten other people around him. *Please. Don't die here.*

He wasn't interested. He knew I would scatter to nothing in a minute. He let his head rest against my chest, and he didn't seem to care that the Queen was raising her hand to tell the archers to aim.

All at once I was furious.

I wasn't good enough at any of it to make anyone drag the Queen and the hunters off their horses, or I would have. It felt too complicated to try to move so many different hands in so many different ways, like trying to do arithmetic in your third language under pressure, but I could make people do one thing all at once. That was simple enough. All I could think of was to make them sing. Even though I was sure I couldn't reach further than about fifty people—it was too many minds, too heavy, and they were all different—the song rippled around the mountain as other people sang it themselves.

Sing, sing to lord the of the dance,
Thunder-wrought and city-razing
King, king of the holy raging,
Rave and rise again.

Dionysus looked up like he was coming out of a trance. He was shaking, but all those voices had been enough to bring him back, more or less, to now. I could feel him starting to come away from shock into something more like what I felt, maybe because I felt it. Anger, slow, because he was one of those people who always took far too long to get angry, like anyone truly strong, but it was building.

Will you show me some magic?

"Yes," he said.

I'd understood more or less what he had meant, when he told me the story about the old goddess who had made him what he was. Dying and rising: he lived in a body that could be damaged and which could die, and did sometimes. I hadn't understood that he lived in the man I recognised in exactly the same way he moved around in owls or snakes. The man was no more *him* than the owl. He just borrowed it more often, because it could do more and he liked things that could speak, like humans and dolphins, and bees.

What he was, was everything. He was everywhere, in everything that was alive or had ever been alive, anything that had grown or could grow. It was why he would never die. He was part of those great deep-down minds, the trees, even the bedrock that had slow, strange memories of churning when the ground was made in fire. And when he wanted to, he could move it all as easily as he could move the tattooed hands of the man.

I didn't *see* what he did. It was different to seeing; there was more of it. There was a thing that was *three*, but you never saw it in itself, you just saw its shadow cast on things: three apples, three bees, three witches.

He took the Queen's mind, and he held it up to the light like a bronzesmith would study the mechanisms of a faulty marvel. Now that I had everyone else's to compare it to—I could see them all as clearly as I could see their faces—it wasn't quite how human minds usually were. There was hardly any . . . any human in it. It was glittering clockwork, exquisite, wonderful in its own way, but not . . . really . . . a person any more.

He stripped away the clockwork, carefully, like any good craftsman, and set it aside.

She realized what was happening while he did it, and with a cold moonrise of horror, she tried to argue. She tried to say that she had never chosen to be like this: it had been done to her. She hadn't wanted to be married, she had wanted to stay in the legion with Helios, but her mother had said, *No, you must do your duty, because duty is honour*, and she had bowed her head. After that, she had to be almost nothing but clockwork because she had no patience with madness or running away or walking into the sea, and it had been a kind of victory.

But it was your choice, he told her, very soft, in a way that was to language what he was to the man he sometimes moved around in. *I do not care why, or what drove you. I only care what you have done. What I will do now, will remind people not to choose like you did for a thousand years.*

THE HYMN TO DIONYSUS

Everyone on that mountain lost their minds. Or rather, he took them all, and kept them for later.

The Hidden forgot who they were hunting, and swung joyfully towards the trees to look for mountain lions and lynxes. Some of them stopped to make themselves ivy crowns from the vines that rioted up the trees. There was a triumphant howl not far away as someone found the trail of wolf. Deep under the earth, the dryads noticed and watched because this was strange. In the forest, the deer, who had learned to listen to the dryads too, heard the shift and ran.

Not far away, Pentheus was nocking an arrow. He wasn't mad. There wasn't enough of a person left in him to go mad: he couldn't any more than a marvel could.

He didn't know what was happening, or how the witch had done it, but the Queen looked glassy and strange, and whatever kind of trickery it was, he wasn't going to complain.

The Queen knew when she was being watched, and she slung to the side as the arrow sang past. But she didn't really know there had been an arrow. She wasn't seeing a boy with a bow any more.

She was seeing a young lion.

Dionysus watched quietly. Around him, everyone whirled: singing his song, dancing, trailing ivy and laughter. Somewhere under it, real but maybe more real than other things, the horn of the old Hunt called. There were drums from somewhere. Yes; other people were coming up the mountainside, ordinary people, families, with children. All of Thebes.

Some others saw the lion too and ran with the Queen. Much, much too late, Pentheus understood that they were faster and stronger than him.

Around us, around Dionysus, the drums rolled on, and the song was a tempest. A little girl set an ivy crown in his hair. He let her, and then directed her mind away, after some butterflies, so she wouldn't see what came next.

When the Queen and the others caught Pentheus, they tore him apart. It was like watching children with a straw doll: there was something innocent about it, even as the doll went to pieces, and they were all laughing, because it was incredible to have caught a lion without weapons, this was how people must have hunted in the long ago when bronze was still a dream and a spear was a bone spar from one of the giants that walked the great steppe in the north. She had never been this happy, the Queen: she had never just flung herself at anything with no thought for duty or honour or law, just laughed and moved as hard and fast as she could, unweighted by the crown.

Bring down a thing that wants to kill you with all your tribe and there is the foundation stone of what humans are, all the joy in being alive, and the drums, and the song, and instead of keeping it for yourself, you sacrifice it and sing it to the lord of the dance, the render of cities and men, the king of the holy raging, because he *is* this, all the joy and the wildness and humanness, distilled into one thing. Every now and then, in one searing precious instant, you can see him, in the way you can see three.

He let them sing, and dance, and light fires, and hunt for a while, into the dusk. He didn't move. I didn't either. It was difficult to keep holding myself together, but the leopard let me ride with her. We sat next to him, paws on his knees. Then, gradually, he let it lift. He had kept all their minds safe, and few by few he put them back, and though there was still a merry glow in the air, and singing, it wasn't the mad god's song any more, just folk rhymes, the first rounds of lullabies for the littlest children.

Very slowly, the Queen realized that what she was holding was not the head of a lion.

It was like watching someone wake up. She was still for a second, and then she threw it away, jolting onto her feet. For a long time, she just stared down at it; then at Dionysus. He stared back, unmoving, except for the wind pulling at his hair. Then she walked into the forest, and I don't think she ever came out again.

And I . . . wasn't there any more.

38

The shore was black, and so was the water. Mist hung in rags here and there, and from somewhere—in a way that sounded like everywhere—there were voices. Some of them were whispering, and some were singing, much too softly to make out. There were people too, but they were silent: facing the river, waiting for the Ferryman. None of them seemed to know that the others were there. It wasn't cold, or warm, only quiet, except for that whispering song that sounded, in tiny snatches, very familiar. The river flowed to my right, into a great cavern. There was light that way, silvery.

"Phaidros."

It wasn't exactly a voice, and it didn't exactly call. It was another strand of the singing-whispers; it sounded like whoever had said it had been saying it for a long time, not in a way that expected any immediate answer. It was more like a beacon lit on a difficult shore, and every time it repeated my name, it was another swing of the mirror to make the light flash.

I turned around twice, trying to track where it was coming from.

"Phaidros."

In an inlet was one last living thing. It was a white tree. The voice was coming from there.

I'd thought it was in full bloom, the tree, full of leaves and blossom, but as I came nearer to it in the dimness, I saw I was wrong. They weren't leaves: they were scraps of cloth, and ribbons, and silver and clay prayer tokens. Some were messages. I stared up—up and up, because it was taller than any tree I'd ever seen—and the way they flickered in the breeze was mesmerising. There were languages I recognised and languages I didn't, languages that didn't look like writing at all, and somewhere deep down, I knew there were languages here that had died a thousand years before we thought humanity had been created, and languages here that wouldn't be born for a thousand years after everything I knew was dust.

"Phaidros?"

The voice was different. A real voice, not that echo from before.

It was Helios.

And there he was, under the tree, sitting in the high roots, exactly like I remembered: he still had his armour, my armour now, and his shield. His spear was propped up next to him. I stared at him, and then crumpled onto my knees. Dust puffed up, and fell much too slowly, like we were underwater. Or—like there was no time, and each mote could do whatever it liked, without any urgency.

"You waited."

"I told you I would," he said, sounding puzzled. He smiled, the kind of smile that was all eyes, not teeth. "Has it been long?"

I was already seeing through a haze of tears. "Ten years."

His eyebrows flickered upwards, but like always, he was good at taking things for what they were, and not wasting energy exclaiming over what they ought to have been. He was looking at me with a smile still in the lines around his eyes. "You're grown up. You look . . ."

"Like you," I said, my throat tight. I could see it, it was right there. It always had been.

"Yeah," he said softly.

I swallowed, even though I could already feel that having a throat, never mind one that had gone dry, was more a habit of thought than a physical fact here. "When you left your ward behind at the temple," I said. "You never did go back, did you?"

He lifted his head, just slightly. On anyone else it would have been nothing, but he had always kept his mannerisms slight, always the perfect knight, almost unreadable in the face of bad things unless you knew him, and I knew this too. It was what he did when something had gone so far wrong there was no getting away from it without losing lives.

"Do you remember that game with three cups I used to play with you, when you were tiny? There's a ball hidden and you have to guess which cup . . . ?"

"Find the Lady?"

"Three children," he said. "Semele's baby. My ward. And another boy with a scar I bought at a slave market outside the Temple of Hermes."

I frowned. "Three."

"Before I say this—I know it's ridiculous. But I was fifteen, and the Hidden were coming, and I couldn't think of anything else."

"No, I . . . I understand," I said, but I stumbled over it because although I had known that of course he'd been fifteen, I'd always heard that through a child's mind when he told me the story. Fifteen had seemed unreachably grown-up then. Now—the idea of expecting any one of my little knights, even the most cunning, to find some way of hiding a baby caught in a royal blood feud was so far beyond ridiculous that it hurt to think of.

"I took Semele's baby to the Temple of Hermes. I was looking for witches. He was already the image of Semele, and the King, and the only thing I could think of that would keep him safe was growing up under the veil."

I sat back, and only realized once I did that I'd been pushing my fists into the ground. There was moss among the black stones, living, even here, although the stones were strange. They were all eroded perfectly smooth, not like normal shore-shale at all; as though all the tides there could ever be had already worn them down. They were stones for the end of time.

"Hermes has always allowed people to give children to the witches, but a prince turning up in the middle of the night while the Kadmeia was on fire with a stolen baby—I thought I'd have to give them my armour to take him." He frowned into the memory. "But as soon as we arrived— there were moths everywhere. Those huge ones that look like little ghosts. They were going to him like he was a lamp, and he was laughing. The witches all came to see, and the Holy Mother came out herself. She said I didn't know what I'd brought them. She said *he* had brought *me*. Gods save me but—I believe it."

"I don't . . . understand," I said, because that had to be Dionysus—but he had begun this story after I'd said I looked like him. I'd thought it was going to be an explanation about why.

He caught my eyes and nodded slightly to say he was getting to it. Commanders never apologise to their wards and nor should they, but this was the closest I'd seen him come to it, and I didn't like it at all. I'd thought I knew what he'd done, or at least suspected, and I'd been getting ready to be hurt and angry, but now I was off balance again, and I felt like there was a very deep drop on one side of us.

"Round and round she goes," he said, miming moving the cups, and I had a painful flash of being five and completely delighted that he could make things disappear. "Where she stops, nobody knows. When I left Hermes, I went to a slave trader and I bought a little boy, about four. With a scar. About your age. I took him to Apollo, told them he was called Phaidros. I left my dagger with him. I told the priests in not very cryptic terms that he was to find me if he ever had questions about where he came from."

"A decoy," I said, still struggling to catch up. Helios Polytropos, even now, even when I'd thought I knew all his tricks.

He nodded slightly. "And then, I took you back to the legion." He paused, like it was hurting him to talk about it. He closed his hand over one of those timeless pebbles, which creaked against the others, and a little stream of dust-without-time lifted in its eerie, leisurely way. Across the river on the other shore, something laughed. It didn't sound human. "I made sure that it looked strange. I took a year to get back, I told everyone I'd been shipwrecked. When I did rejoin a Theban unit, it wasn't my original. You were little for your age, because we had had some bad years before then; so I told them you were a year older than you were, but I made sure I was giving you the kinds of toys much littler children would have—you didn't care, you were happy with a rock—and so that made it sound like a lie: you *looked* three years too young. Word got round that I had a ward who was clearly younger than I was saying. I wrote messages back to the Temple of Apollo, knowing they'd be intercepted, asking after the boy there. That was all reported back to Agave. After that, I made sure we kept falling off the map. Trading runs to Tintagel, Scythia, even India once. To make it look like I was outrunning anyone who might be watching me."

"You made it look like you took Semele's baby with you," I said. "So . . . gods. So that no one would look for him with the witches."

"Yes." He looked miserable. "But there was a problem."

I waited. I don't think I've ever listened to anyone more closely.

He put his hand out and covered mine. He was warm. It was a shock. It seemed insane that he *could* touch me here, but he felt as solid as he always had, and though the light was strange, our hands looked like they always had. Mine darker, his lighter.

"You never looked like you could be Semele's," he said. "I got you in Egypt. You were a child of the river. When we sieged Tanis and it fell, the Nile filled with babies in reed baskets. You were one. If I'd put you in a turquoise collar everyone would have thought you were a son of the Pharaoh. It was obvious you were nothing to do with the House of Kadmus."

"But I do," I said. "Look like her. You. I look *really* like you."

I'd seen him look afraid once or twice before, but never of me. He did now. "The witches told me that it would be a problem. They . . ." His focus shifted to the side. "They told me something very strange. They told me to go to a bronzesmith, and have a new helmet made."

I didn't need to breathe any more, but I had been doing it until then. I stopped.

"They told me that the mask should be of me, not a god. And to let you play with it." He really looked as though he was ready for me to punch him. "So I did. You loved it, you were always stealing it. And— the more you wore it, the more you looked like me. I don't know what that magic was. They told me it would only work on you, you were— god-touched. By the time you were twenty . . . people were asking if you were my son. Nobody said nephew. But that was what they meant."

I was grinning like the Festival of Apollo had come around early, but he didn't see because he was still staring at the ground.

"It was a terrible thing to do. I put you in horrible danger. But you were fucking tough, Phaidros, even when you were tiny, and clever, and . . . I thought it wouldn't matter down the line if someone accused you of being the heir. You'd find a way of out of it. I'm so sorry. Semele's boy—he was blood kin. And you *loved* him. I couldn't leave him for the Hidden. I don't mean I didn't want to, I *couldn't*."

"Helios—that's fucking *genius*. I love it."

His eyes came up fast. "What?"

"Don't be silly, of course I love it."

He laughed, just a bit.

There was a creak behind us; there was a ferry, drawn on groaning ropes that would take it to the far shore. A shadow stood at the great wheel that wound the ropes in and out. Soon we would be two of those figures on the shore waiting to go. I wondered what it would be like. We'd board the ferry knowing each other, and then—how long did it take for the river to make you forget? Would we reach the far shore and still know, sort of, that the other one was important, or would it just be gone—would it be like standing with a stranger?

A wave of sadness rolled through me. I loved Helios, of course I did, but somewhere in another world, Dionysus was alone. This river might as well have been the ocean. There would be no crossing. I'd never be able to keep that vow I'd made to him so long ago on the sea. What a way to die, on a broken vow.

"Phaidros," Helios said quietly. "I think that man is waiting to talk to you."

Dionysus had been standing about twelve yards away all the while. He was holding a lamp, the kind miners have, the shade almost closed, but there was a crack of light inside. The light didn't look like it belonged here. My heart swooped with something that felt like hope and dread at the same time. I jolted upright and across to him, which slung dust and strange cold crystals into the air, where they hung and winked, not falling.

"Please don't say you let them hurt you—"

"No, I'm—alive, I'll always be alive. This place isn't mine. I can't cross."

On the river, the ferry was vanishing into silver fog, with its silent cargo of ghosts.

"This is my commander," I said. Helios had come after me more slowly, not cautious exactly, but considered. It was obvious Dionysus wasn't an ordinary person. I laughed for no reason except that it so strange and so fizzily wonderful to introduce them. "He saved you, once, when we were both very small."

Dionysus bowed, even though witches don't bow to anyone. "Then I owe you a debt, sir."

Helios looked up at him for a long time. "No debt. You're family."

"Don't . . . write off a debt from something like me so quickly—"

"You're still family," Helios cut him off, unmoved. He was watching him. "The river sings of you, I think."

"Yes." For the first time since I'd known him, Dionysus sounded nervous. I felt it too. I felt like I was introducing lightning to the sea, or something else with equal and opposite charge.

"Are you here to take him back?" Helios said, about me.

"I'm here to give him the choice," Dionysus said. He hesitated, and tilted slightly to me. "But if you come with me now, you can never come back here again. You'll be like me, forever. You can never cross the river; you can never forget. I think—there's a lot you'd like to forget." His eyes flickered to Helios, then the river.

I was paralysed. Helios had waited for ten years in this dark place. I couldn't leave him alone now. But Dionysus had been alone for twenty generations, and there was no way—I could see it very clearly in this dead silver light—that he would do it for much longer. In the silence, there was singing. It was like Helios had said; it was the river. On the far shore, things chittered. I heard the creak of a ferry rope again.

"Well?" Helios said to me. "Off you sod."

"What?" My voice cracked over it. "But—"

"You heard. I'm not taking you over this river."

"But you waited—"

"So?" He gave me the strangest, clear-eyed look. "You promised to protect this boy once, but you didn't. Do it now. Do not dishonour me, knight."

"Sir," Dionysus began, "if you think your duty—"

"Nobody asked you," Helios told him with exactly the same authority he'd always had, the one that spoke to your nerves without having to go through your mind first, even though he barely reached Dionysus's shoulder. It was glorious witchcraft: Dionysus flinched. "Now what have you done with my sister?"

Dionysus stood a little aside so that we could see past him.

Waiting among the shades at the shore, there was one so pale that she was barely there. She was just a shape sketched in the air, sometimes clear if the silver light fell right, sometimes almost gone. With her, there was a wisp that might just have been a boy, but only if I tipped my head just right. I didn't think they could see each other.

"Goodbye, little knight," Helios told me. He put his arms around us both, then gave us both a tiny push. "Look after each other." And then he turned and walked away, to his sister and the ghost that might have been Pentheus, and he did not look back.

"You can still go with them," Dionysus said to me. "He decided for you when you were a child. You need not let him decide now."

I locked my arms around him. He felt more—there—than other things. He was still in time. The hours were moving for him, somewhere. He hugged me too, his cheek pressed against my hair. He was warm, even here. "Don't be so bloody stupid."

"I have to ask you three times," he said, very soft. "There are laws, even here; especially here." He touched his head to mine. "My lord, may I take you above?"

"Yes, sir."

"You consent never to return here."

"I consent."

"This has to be your desire, not your duty," he said.

"Things can be desire *and* duty," I said.

He let his breath out, and his shoulders sank. He seemed smaller.

Helios was fading into the shades as they boarded the ferry. I couldn't tell if what he had just done for me was duty or desire or both. I'd thought maybe he would be more fathomable now we were the same age, but I'd never get an accurate count of those fathoms. He went all the way down, Helios.

"It's a fair way to walk," Dionysus said, and I realized at last that he had been waiting at the mouth of a cave. His lamp, the only light but the disembodied silver light of the shore, gleamed on a narrow stairway. "You can't look back."

"You know me," I said. "I could stand at the top for a thousand years and never look back."

He moved his shoulder in a sort of one-eighth shrug. "I know. It just feels—well, the story." He put me in front of him to make me go first, and gave me his lamp. "I never understood why Persephone ate the pomegranate. Death steals you and takes you here: even then, even if it's kidnapping, if you take something you owe something. Why would she?"

I smiled at the way ahead. It was rocky, but the stairs were sometimes a little lost, not often walked, but there. Soon the only light was his lamp. "Because he didn't steal her. She stole him. But . . . she knew her mother would be distraught if she just chose him, and so she took the pomegranate. And the old laws kicked in: she had taken something from him, and so she owed something. Her mother could think it was just a mistake and this was an irritating compromise, not that her daughter had *decided* to leave her behind. It's a diplomacy pomegranate."

He laughed, and it was a real laugh. It smoked up through the cave, and it was the best thing I'd ever heard. I put my hand back for him without looking back. He took it and didn't let go, his fingertip hooked over the red string around my wrist.

39

Dionysus was moving life—borrowing it—from the forest, and the things below. A tiny fraction from each tree and vine. The things that had shut down in me began to work again. Flickers of electricity, blood moving, damage knitting up, very fast. I was coming back too, the thing that was me, that had been on the shore before. Then I was back in my own mind, not everyone's, and it was like putting on armour I knew very, very well.

I sat up, and for a whole second, it was paralysingly strange to have hands.

"Was I just . . . somewhere else?" I felt sure I had been. I'd been under the earth, and in the trees, and then there had been a dark shore and a river and maybe Helios had been there, but I couldn't catch hold of any of it. The way my memory worked wasn't right for things like that. It was like trying to carry water in a basket.

"Can you tell me what your name is?" Dionysus asked. He had one hand on my back like he was worried I might not remember how spines worked.

I had to think about it. Something to do with brightness, and the sun. "Phaidros."

He looked into my eyes. Those had always been difficult, eyes, although why was floating just out of reach. Whyever it was, it was something little and silly.

"Where are we, can you remember?"

I could still feel the dryads underground. "This is the place where the great bulls first agreed to the ploughing, and where the witch made wine with honey."

He looked frightened and I realized that was right generally, but wrong for me, or, the shape I was now: that was an old answer.

"Thebes," I said. "This is Thebes."

"That's good, knight," he said, sounding strained. "Do you remember what my name is?"

I was getting the hang of it, the pathways in my own mind, the more he spoke. "Well, you *said* it was Dionysus but you made that up."

He sort of laughed. "Right. I—do you want to know my real name?"

I frowned. He wasn't supposed to. There was something about witches. "But I thought you couldn't say?"

"You've done a lot of things you weren't supposed to for me," he said. "It's Ivy. My name is Ivy."

That was familiar for some reason. I touched the ivy crown in his hair. "I know you from a long time ago, don't I? When we were younger."

"That's right."

"You turned the ship into a forest. It was lovely." I looked around properly. All around us, the campfires were cracking and sparking under the last of the bronze sunset, and lots of people were telling stories, or playing on bone whistles, or teaching the little girls a new kind of dance. Around them, the grass was growing lush and green, and nothing like the strawy beige scrub it had been this morning. The horses were grazing. It was the most peaceful thing I'd ever seen.

Dionysus was watching me, still looking worried I wasn't all there.

I was, though. It was just taking a little while for me to flow through into all my old tributaries and streams.

I paused. "And I remember something about you owing me dinner."

He hit my shoulder, and then he started to cry, or maybe he was laughing, or both. I pulled him sideways into my lap, and all around us, even though they didn't really know he was there, people sang his hymn.

40

A long time after, centuries and more, when Troy was just a story and our language was lost, and all the marvels were melted down for ploughshares and spears, people wondered what had happened. City after city fell: Pylos, Mykenai, Sparta, Hattusa, right from Achaea, to Syria, to Egypt. If you go to those places and walk around the ruins, you'll see something strange. They weren't destroyed by earthquakes, or by invading armies. You won't find arrowheads in the earth. In all those places, it's like people there just . . . went mad one day, and set fire to everything.

I've heard philosophers say that really this is just what happens to humans when it's very hot and there's no food. Kings make stupid decisions and end up hanged in their own palaces; people loot and then run for the hills, and never come back down again. Some of them like to say that there were invading armies, but they cleared up after everything, which no army in the history of anything has ever done.

Both of those ideas are wrong.

What happened was that one day, a queen tried to be too much like a marvel, and a god broke her and everyone else for a thousand miles around. The holy raging swept half my world. People stretched to breaking by the heat and by hunger snapped. Buildings burned, and kings hanged; in the places where men kept their wives like prisoners, the women tore them apart; on the galleys, the slaves exploded from the holds. The world turned upside down, for maybe six hours. No more.

After that, though, a lot of what there had been before was ash.

Now, they don't know we ever built marvels; they don't know we had calculating machines, or astronomers, or witches with great magic, because nothing is left but those scraps of tax records—just like Dionysus said, because even when he's joking you have to watch out for prophecy— noted down on clay that baked in those fires. Some people even think Troy never happened, and the memory of those futile, brave infantry legions, built of pairs of sworn knights, is fading into legend. For a long time, the world I used to know shrank. Knights became shepherds, and cities stood empty.

They came back, though. Slowly, few by few. There was new writing. New cities, new people. It was like watching bluebells push up across the forest floor after a fire. And then one day, after we had wandered far enough east to see the people who painted with fire in the sky, and far enough north to see where it rained feathers, we arrived in Athens, just as a festival was starting.

I was ready to be grumpy about it, but I had to work hard at that: it's difficult not to like a place where someone hands you a flower for no reason when you come down off the ship, and the fountains are running with wine.

"What is going on?" I said, because it wasn't just the festival. People looked—*happy*. Half the world was there. There were traders from Egypt and a caravan from Aleppo laden down with bronze; there were priestesses dancing in red on the steps of a temple, and even though it was Athens, there were women everywhere, even noblewomen, with parakeets on their shoulders and fleets of daughters and slaves laughing after them. Lots of families too, where everyone was playing a game—the slaves were in charge, well-dressed gentlemen hurrying to bring them drinks or food, or even borrowed cloaks in the autumn wind, which was established enough now to be getting its wisdom teeth.

There were puddles winking on the ground.

"Don't look at me," Dionysus said, much too innocently. "We should go and see where everyone's going, though. Who knows, maybe it's a horrifyingly violent boxing match—maybe they throw people they don't like to lions now, you'll like that."

"Can't we just find an inn—"

"No, no, no . . ." He steered me left to keep us with the crowd. Up ahead was a big building, circular, heaving with people, green flags flying, and children selling ivy crowns outside. Dionysus bought one with a scrap of silver and set it into my hair.

"What have you done?" I said slowly.

"*I* haven't done anything, *I* just arrived. You were there. You were cross with me about growing wisteria up the rigging—"

"How do you expect anyone to take in the sails if there's sodding *vines* growing up the—"

"It's pretty!"

"You're pretty," I growled.

"I am n—hang on," he said, and then he looked pleased.

I gave up on a proper answer. It was true I'd been there *today*. But seven hundred years was a long time. We had been apart for decades of that, sometimes because of storms and wars, sometimes on purpose. He still had the witching instinct to make sure nobody, including me, knew everything about him. He thought I wouldn't like him any more if I did, which I thought was funny and he thought I was *pretending* to think was funny, and round and round it went.

But anyway, he liked Athens. He kept coming here, lately, very much without me, on account of how I still had a powerful instinct to set it on fire that I was right now this second fending off heroically. They were doing some complicated thing with their government, he said, where they tried to give all the free men a vote in the Assembly. It seemed like a stupid idea to me—if you put a bunch of rich men together in a room alone without anyone who understands the real world to give them a shove in the right direction, what you'll get is mutually exclusive with any sort of sensible policy—but he thought they were onto something.

The little girl who'd sold the ivy crown gave me change for his silver. It was a coin. They were new inventions, stamped with images of gods or whoever the current archon was, and controlled tightly by something called the central mint, so that all of them were the same weight, standardised now across all Athens and its territories, like they did in proper countries in Africa and the Levant. I turned it over, feeling stupidly pleased that good inventions were making their way into our rubbishy, dusty corner of the world. I'd never really believed Dionysus when he said time was seasonal and I'd arrived in a long winter, and that I'd see things bloom soon—but here it was, the first blue of the new bluebells, and the turning of the world.

Stamped on the coin was a young man half hidden by grape vines.

"Is this *you*?"

"No. Why would it be me? Don't be silly, Phaidros." He was doing big eyes at me.

"I see," I said again, plotting revenge, depending on whatever terrible thing was waiting in the stadium. "But Dee?" I know: these days, everyone says *die-oh-neye-sus*, but it wasn't that, to begin with. It was *dee-oh*, like *theo*; it means "god." It was *deo-nusos*, the daughter of the god, because in the old days, witches were always *she*, like ships and kestrels.

"Hm?"

"This had better not involve poetry."

"You're a snob, Phaidros, you're an art snob. Oh, could people feel something about it? Boo, hit it with a rock."

"There are lot of things that would be much better if more people hit them with rocks," I said, watching another new invention while it declaimed about logic from on top of a box. They were called philosophers. This one was haranguing some poor man who was too polite to get a rock. As far as I could gather, the point of them was to try and reason out the truth of things—but only things you couldn't go out and check, because otherwise that was too much like hard work—and then yell about it a lot, to the eventual end of generating a following of attractive young men, ostensibly to teach, but in fact to stare at creepily.

"No there aren't," Dionysus said. "You know what would make things better? Universal suffrage and the study of art and philosophy. Why do you think people here are so happy? It—"

"Aha!" the philosopher shouted. "But if you *are* a father, than you're a father to *everything*! You're the father of this dog! You can't say you're not, or you're not a father, but you are, so riddle me that!"

"I really walked into this," Dionysus mumbled.

I looked around for a rock. There weren't any, but there was a geriatric turnip beside a vegetable stall.

"Oi dickhead," I said, and threw the turnip, not very hard. The philosopher squeaked and fell off his box.

It got a little cheer.

"Hey! How dare you! You, you, you *threw a turnip* at me!"

"No I didn't. Did I throw anything at you?" I said to the man who had suffered the harangue.

"No sir," he said, grinning.

"See? I didn't throw anything at him, so I didn't throw anything. So, now it's happening," I added to Dionysus, as the philosopher vanished behind a crowd of people who were catching on about the ontological impossibility of throwing vegetables, "I feel like I might be quite good at philosophy."

Dionysus only looked happy. "See? I told you you'd like Athens now."

Inside, the stadium wasn't quite like a stadium. Usually, the arena would be clear, or marked out for races, or wrestling. But this one was floored with wood. There were trapdoors in it, and to one end, there was a house-sized wooden building set up with all sorts of machinery and something like a crane, and things a little like marvels that looked like they were built to turn.

I hadn't been in a crowd like this for a long time; perhaps not even since the funeral games at Thebes. It was cooler than it had been then, though. The sun was just setting, and city-owned slaves all in the same uniform were lighting torches, and the first chill of the autumn was settled over the stone seats. Once we had sat down, Dionysus turned sideways and tilted me back against his chest, and wrapped his cloak around us both.

Down in the arena that wasn't an arena, there were people gathering—in strange clothes, very old now, and masks.

That gave me a little jolt of alarm.

"Nothing is going to happen," Dionysus said. "It's different here. They know how to use masks properly. They wear them for a living." He crossed his arms over my chest, one hand under my tunic so he could hold my shoulder. It put a little thrill of happiness all through me. I was waiting for him to lose interest, dreading it, knowing it had to come in the end, had been for a long time, but here he still was. "This is how they tell stories. They don't sing them to a lyre. They pretend to be the people in the stories."

That sounded strange, and intense. And with the masks—I could imagine it would be easy to forget who you were, when you weren't in the story. "Why?"

He took a breath and then held it, thinking. "Blue," he said.

It was called a stage, the new wooden arena, someone told me later. The people in the masks were actors. They were waiting for something. Slowly, the stadium quietened. Then all at once, the slaves snuffed out the lights—all but the ones around the stage—and down there on the boards, there was a primeval yell, fifty voices, and then drums, and a song that tried to fuse the pieces of my spine together. They were singing in their language, which was like ours but made new, clipped in some places, sprawling in others, but I knew the words anyway. The audience sang it too.

Only it felt different this time. There was no electric madness in the air. Nobody was about to lose their minds and turn on each other. The opposite. People were smiling. Along from us, a man was holding his baby daughter on his lap, holding her hands to help her clap in time with other people.

Dionysus squeezed my hand.

A woman bounded onto the stage, full of energy, and bowed. I didn't understand what she was doing until she spoke: she had one of those voices that could carry over battlefields. A herald, or something like.

"Good evening, my ladies and lords, slaves and citizens, all equal tonight in this, our twenty-fifth Dionysia!"

A roar of applause came from the crowd. A slave gave us some wine in pretty glazed cups. Dionysus touched his to mine, unusually shy. He thought I was going to growl at him about how this wasn't boxing.

"I just—thought it would be funny to show you. I didn't do anything, I didn't start . . ."

"I know," I said, starting to laugh, because even now, witches wore veils, and he did too, if he was working. It was hard to see how a man who spent half his life erasing his own face might think I'd imagine he'd do anything for the sake of vanity. "It's good."

"Really?"

I twisted back enough to kiss him, just. Because—I'd seen little festivals before, in isolated places where whoever was most downtrodden, whether it was the women or the slaves, worked themselves into a shadow of the holy raving, and turned it into a festival. That helped: that was a kind of shield wall against what had happened in Thebes. But I'd never seen a place where they had truly understood what he was, not on this scale, not everyone, all at once. He wasn't showing me because he was vain. He was showing me because what all this meant was that at least for now, Athens was safe: it didn't just have a shield wall but a great curtain wall. A festival like this—if it was what it looked like, and it did what I thought it might—would protect people all the year long. Armour: not anaesthetic.

The herald waited for enough quiet before she went on. "For these three nights, the Archon presents three great stories for you all to judge. As always, the victory laurels will go to the writer who best fulfils the demands of the god. Through the pens of our bards, may you find laughter, and tears . . ." People laughed, because she held up a happy mask, then a sad one. "And that holiest of things: catharsis."

Release. It meant release.

Blue.

"We don't have to stay," Dionysus said, close, because people were still cheering. "I know it isn't really your . . ."

"No, I want to see. I like stories."

He hugged me hard. I held his wrists so he couldn't let go.

The herald was laughing. "And so, people of Athens—and Sparta—and Thebes"—cheers from difference places in the crowd—"raise a cup: to the king of the holy raging, who, like the ivy, never dies."

AUTHOR'S NOTE

Very unusually for me, I didn't go on a gigantic research expedition for this book. I poked around Knossos for a bit and then I sat down and learned Greek from John Taylor's invaluable series of OCR textbooks. I did really well until I got to Plato, who I hate.

This book is based loosely on *The Bacchae*, by Euripides, Nonnus's *Dionysiaca*, and the original Homeric *Hymn to Dionysus*. There are lots of other resources that have been incredibly helpful, from Ted Hughes's gorgeous translation of *The Oresteia*, by Aeschylus, to Eric L. Cline's book *1177 B.C.: The Year Civilization Collapsed* and Elizabeth Vandiver's brilliant lecture series about Greek tragedy, Greek mythology, *The Iliad*, and *The Odyssey*, all available from The Great Courses. A big shoutout also to Emily Wilson's translation of *The Odyssey* (the best by far) and— for anyone who wants to listen to it like the original audience probably did—Claire Danes's performance of it.

I made up a lot of history here, because this period happened before the idea of writing down history was invented in the Mediterranean: the events of the novel take place about four hundred years before even *The Iliad* was first recorded. But among the things I didn't make up are: marvels, amazingly; the Krypteia, the unit of young knights who would murder slaves out after curfew (in Sparta, reckons Plutarch, who wasn't there); and the Theban battlefield unions between older and younger knights like Helios and Phaidros, which continued right up until the time of Alexander the Great. A lot of the dystopian details I've included— like the women who kill their sons for deserting the army, or the system wherein most people are slaves, including civil servants—are from real Greek records too.

Dionysus is a quicksilver figure who appears differently wherever you see him. Look in Aristophanes, he's a clown; look in Euripides, he's terrifying. He really is called *polyeidos*, "many-formed." Even his legacy is wildly varied. He probably made his way into Christian mythology, along with Osiris, as the source material for the god who dies and then comes back—and also for the devil figure with horns who stands for excess and revelry and upsetting the normal social order. I think many of his stories, though, come down to one fundamental idea: neglect catharsis, and you'll go mad.

ACKNOWLEDGEMENTS

Thank you as always to my brilliant brother, who read an early draft of this book and pointed out correctly that Phaidros was much too nice, which led to the bad-tempered swearing that went into the final edit. Thanks as well to my agent, Jenny Savill, who worked incredibly hard to find this book a home.

It takes teams of people to publish a book. My editors, Grace McNamee and Gillian Redfearn, one on either side of the Atlantic, have been fantastic. So have Bethan Morgan and Jenna Petts from Orion: they keep turning up at my events and pretending they haven't heard it all before. Thanks as well to all those people who worked on the cover designs, on proofreading, and typesetting.

And thank you, Dionysus. I think I'm a better human now that I half understand what you are.

A NOTE ON THE AUTHOR

NATASHA PULLEY is the internationally bestselling author of *The Watchmaker of Filigree Street*, *The Bedlam Stacks*, *The Lost Future of Pepperharrow*, *The Kingdoms*, *The Half Life of Valery K*, and *The Mars House*. She has won a Betty Trask Award, been shortlisted for the Authors' Club Best First Novel Award, the Royal Society of Literature's Encore Award, and the Wilbur Smith Adventure Writing Prize, and been longlisted for the Walter Scott Prize. She lives in Bristol, England.